CONJURING DESTINY

BRIDES OF PROPHECY BOOK 3

Brooklyn Ann

Acknowledgements

Thank you so much to my awesome critique partners and proofreaders: Bonnie R. Paulson, Shelley Martin, Layna Pimental, Rissa Watkins, and Shona Husk.

Grigoris Drakakis and Raven for much needed photos for my cover.

Thank you to Le Cygne for inadvertently inspiring me to add a certain kind of symbolism.

To Jeff Miller for helping me brainstorm a few things.

My newsletter readers: I love you!

Kent Butler, thanks for your never ending support.

My friends at Gus's Pub for your patience in waiting for this book.

Bad movie club for providing a wonderful haven to relax after a long writing day.

To all of my friends and family for believing in me.

Finally, thank you so much to my readers. I couldn't do it without you!

*Dedicated to my mom, Karen Ann who was the greatest
angel to ever walk the earth.
And to my own magic man, Kent Butler.*

Chapter One

Xochitl

Halloween. This was *my* night and nobody would fuck it up. Determination coursed through my veins for tonight's show to be our best damn performance ever. I owed it to my friends.

I opened the closet door and took out my costume, a wedding dress, dyed black. Sylvis, our guitarist and my best friend, chose this year's costume theme to be obscure horror movie characters. With an upside-down cross earring, tiara, and poofy 80's hair, I hoped some people would recognize me as Angela from *Night of The Demons*. If not, at least I'd still be seen as classically goth.

When I met Sylvis in the hall, I grinned at the sight of her blonde wig and pink baby-doll dress. The sloppy crimson lipstick lines drawn down her cheekbones and over her eyebrows in the shape of a heart were a dead giveaway. She'd also picked a character from *Night of the Demons*: Suzanne, who'd had an iconic scene with a tube of lipstick.

Neither of us told each other about our costume choices. The coincidence had to be a result of us being inseparable since the third grade.

Her blue eyes swept over my costume with an appreciative grin. "Great minds, Xochitl. Great minds."

She drew the syllables of my name out. *So-She*.

Aurora and Beau took forever to join us downstairs, both dressed as cenobites from the *Hellraiser* movies. The only reason I could tell them apart was because I'd never seen Pinhead with breasts before. Beau, our bassist, dressed up as the female cenobite... who's depressingly known just as "the female cenobite" in the film credits. Beau loved doing drag and Aurora seldom let him do it because she thought it was too "gimmicky."

Sylvis frowned at them. "I said the theme was obscure horror films, not famous classics!"

Beau waved her off with a hand worthy of a pageant queen. "We're not as creative as you two. Besides, we look fabulous."

I nodded, admiring them both. The vinyl outfits were custom, or tailored from expensive S&M store attire. Beau's sexy dress, complete with a realistic breastplate, was to be envied, but Aurora's makeup job with the meticulously placed "pins" blew my mind. So that's who'd been spray painting toothpicks.

"How did you get the pins to stick?"

Aurora grinned, her smile at odds with the creepy black contacts and white face paint. "Liquid latex. Beau has a lot of tricks."

"You didn't cut your hair did you?" I asked with alarm. She had gorgeous hair.

Beau shook his head. "Of course not! I let her use one of my bald caps. The rest of it is tucked under the high collar in back."

They'd out-Halloweened me, I realized with a twinge of envy. I'd always rocked this holiday... until this year, when I somehow forgot about it. What was wrong with me? The blow softened as they admired mine and Sylvis's costumes.

"You guys nailed *Night of the Demons.* I wish we'd thought of it." She pulled out her phone and glanced at the time. "We better hustle if we wanna make it in time for load-in."

When we formed our band, *Rage of Angels*, it became our tradition to do a concert every Halloween. Our first ones were at keggers in the backwoods of northern Idaho. Nowadays, the most exclusive venues would pay us a fortune to grace their hallowed grounds. But we still played the annual show at the club that gave us our start: The Mortuary in Bothell. Though in the middle of nowhere, the club remained a popular because it was near a reputed haunted cemetery.

"You look out of it," Aurora commented as we hauled our instruments out to the van. "Are you burnt out from the tour?"

I nodded, trying not to trip over Isis, my blue point Siamese cat, who wove around my ankles. "I think so. When I woke up this morning, I didn't even know where I was."

Sylvis carried her guitar case. "That's understandable, since we just got back from our tour. I think rock stars see more hotel rooms than hookers."

I laughed, then flinched as raindrops pattered on my head and shoulders. Isis growled and darted back in the house.

"I fucking *hate* rain." My voice came out harsher than I intended, due to lack of sleep.

Aurora raised a brow. "We're in Seattle. I figured you'd be used to it by now."

We packed our gear into Aurora's van and were off. As I watched misty raindrops hit the back window, a strange sense of foreboding washed over me.

My best friend leaned over to whisper in my ear. "You're having the dreams again, aren't you?"

I nodded, the back of my neck prickling. "Every night."

They'd started when I was seventeen, right after my mom died. Almost every night I walked in a garden of dying black roses. Two moons shone in an alien sky as a shadowed man in a black cloak beckoned me. His presence filled me with unfathomable longing, doing strange things to my insides. I always awoke before I reached him, covered with goose bumps and a need for something I couldn't identify.

The more I had the dream of the shadowy man and the world with two moons, the more disoriented I became.

I shook my head; the cross earring slapped my cheek. I tried to convince myself my imagination just ran wild... that I was only pissed because it was raining on my favorite holiday, but my foreboding refused to abate. I clutched my guitar as if it were my baby blanket.

Beau admonished Stlvis not head-bang too much and dislodge her wig, but I barely heard a word he said. However, when we arrived at The Mortuary and I saw everything decorated for Halloween, my spirits lifted.

Taffeta, velvet, plastic and other various materials rustled around us as we waded through the crowd, hefting our instruments. The breathtaking array of colors and textures made me giddy. On an average day, people who frequented The Mortuary dressed weird, but tonight, on Halloween, few even looked human. Faces under glowing masks and elaborate makeup gazed eerily at us under the red and black lights. Even now, the spooky ambiance of the holiday made me feel like a kid playing hide-and-seek with the boogey man.

Dominic, the club owner, greeted us while his house crew took our gear and readied the stage. While Aurora chatted with him over the night's set list, I scanned the crowd once more as if I expected to see the shadow man. His words in last night's dream echoed in my head.

I'm coming for you.

My stomach tightened. Had he said that before in the other dreams?

Irritation chased off the unfamiliar sensation. Determined not to let him distract me from my favorite gig, I straightened my spine. This night was mine, damn it.

***

Zareth

Zareth Amotken, high sorcerer of Aisthanesthai, wove through the crowd of jabbering mortals, his lip curled in scorn at their lack of magic. With such tepid fare, his hydra would starve if he remained too long in this desolate world. Already, his power dwindled. Disdain faded to unease at that prospect. Zareth quashed the debilitating emotion. He would secure Xochitl and be back in his own world tonight.

The mortals stepped warily to the side as he passed, either intimidated by his height or because they sensed that he was other. He wore a hooded cloak to conceal his luminescent hair, even though unnatural colored tresses swarmed his vision, he likely didn't need to worry about anything except for his hands, which he kept in his pockets.

Delgarias had been right. Locating Xochitl Leonine had been simple.

"She shines like a beacon," the Keeper of the Prophecy had told him. *"And she'll smell like a banquet to your hydra. Even if she didn't, she'd be easy to find."*

"Why is that?"

"She's the lead singer of a world famous heavy metal band. They call themselves Rage of Angels."

Zareth had gaped at the Faelin sorcerer in disbelief. "She's a troubadour? The bastard daughter of

Mephistopheles and the princess of Medicia, the one who will save our world, is naught but a minstrel?"

"*Think about it, Zareth. What else would she be given the words of the Prophecy?"*

"*'With her triumphant roar...'"His eyes widened at the implication. "You can't be serious."*

"*Has the prophecy ever lied?"*

Now, here he stood, in a raucous Earth realm tavern on the Spirit Feast —what the people here called Halloween— to at last lay eyes on the woman he'd been dream-summoning for the last four years.

As he wove through the costumed masses, he detected several non-human presences. One could be Xochitl, though it was doubtful as the stage remained empty. Strengthening his shields, Zareth surveyed the crowd.

His breath caught when he glimpsed two dark-haired men. They were Mephistopheles's fallen monsters.

Two millennia ago, the would-be god created some metaphysical mutation, which morphed humans into blood drinking monsters with unnatural strength. They'd acted as his foot soldiers until they'd displeased him, forever banished to Earth, punished to live in a world free of magic.

Zareth couldn't think of a worse punishment.

Eyeing the creatures, who the people here called vampires, he wondered if they had a connection with Xochitl. After all, she was Mephistopheles's daughter. Zareth prayed they were only here for the music. He had no wish to interact with those abominations.

The lights dimmed and all went still as a vampire appeared on the stage. His fangs gleamed in the stage lights. The humans grinned in admiration, assuming the teeth were part of his costume.

"Welcome to the annual Mortuary Halloween bash!" the vampire shouted. "As many of you know, tonight's honored guests got their start in my club. Some of you even saw them doing covers of *Megadeth*, *Iron Maiden*, and my personal favorite, *Metal Church*."

The creature owned this establishment. Zareth ground his teeth in disgust.

"Despite landing a major record deal and recording two platinum albums, they've never forgotten us. Every Halloween, they perform a concert and all the proceeds go to a charitable cause. This year your cover charge and drinks will help homeless veterans." The vampire spread his arms wide. "Without further ado, I present to you, *Rage of Angels!*"

Zareth felt her before she emerged. Once again, Delgarias had been correct in his assertions. Xochitl's radiant presence and effervescent power washed over him like a force that made his knuckles tighten.

He cursed her inwardly. *Foolish creature.* Hadn't her mother taught her to shield properly? His hydra, a bodiless demon that gave him immortality, roiled with hunger for her essence.

The audience erupted into a cacophony as *Rage of Angels* came into view. Zareth's breath caught at his first sight of the savior of his world. Delicate and ethereal, her fine-boned features and pearlescent skin made the humans around her seem coarse by comparison. Her black and purple waist-length hair gleamed under the stage lights. Unbidden, his gaze swept across her firm, lush breasts and exquisitely curved hips, drinking in the sight of her like a man starved.

Lust, hot and immediate, surged through him in a relentless wave. Zareth sucked in a breath. That wasn't what he was here for. She was an imperative means to a crucial end.

Still, the intensity of his unexpected desire caught him off guard. He'd been too busy with his studies to crave female companionship often. He shook his head. Maybe it had been too long since he'd shared pleasure with a woman?

So captivated with her beauty, he hadn't taken notice of her costume. The full-skirted black taffeta dress at first resembled a ball gown, but the lace veil on her head clarified its true purpose. Many of his people also wore such veils for the same occasion.

It was a wedding gown.

The realization gave him a twinge of unease. Could her garb be an omen? The foreboding dissolved into fury when she hugged the vampire. Zareth's fists clenched in effort not to charge forward and tear her from the monster's embrace.

A red haze obscured his vision even after the vampire left the stage and Xochitl addressed her audience. Outrage kept him from hearing her words. What did she think she was doing, consorting with those *things*? Protective rage coursed through him, making his shadow spell waver.

His hydra roared in protest. *No! She is mine!*

A memory froze him. He'd uttered those words in a dream-summoning mere years ago. Something had intruded upon Xochitl's dream. Had it been a vampire?

Every fiber of his being longed to incinerate every blood drinker in sight. Only the dangers of revealing himself stayed his hand.

The other vampires congregated at the base of the stage, scanning the crowd with narrowed, watchful eyes.

They'd positioned guards. *Have they sensed me?* Zareth held his breath, poised to fight if necessary. So they meant to protect Xochitl and the others. A slight measure of his hostility waned, though his distrust remained.

Music filled the air and banished all thoughts of the loathsome creatures.

Heavy metal was an explosion on the senses. The wailing guitars, throbbing bass, staccato drums, and the vocalist's enraged screams evoked a primal life force within its listeners. A force that had them thrashing and jumping with exhilaration... a force that stirred his hydra into a frenzy. It spread its invisible form outward, opened its mouths, and fed. Zareth closed his eyes in pleasure, rejuvenated from his exhausting effort of coming through the portal to this world.

Zareth had heard electric guitars before, but never heard the instruments distorted and played in such a blistering style. Leaning forward in fascination, he tried to decide whether or not he liked this music. Either way, it had power.

An impossibly fast drum beat pounded through his consciousness. Whipping his attention to the source of the sound, Zareth studied the drummer. This one held a glimmer of magic. Humans of that ilk were rare on Earth, descending from the time when mages, faelin and luminites dwelled here until they were persecuted by non-magical humans. However, he was unsurprised that Xochitl and this woman had become friends. They must have sensed their kinship, as Zareth could.

Guitars joined the rhythm and he shifted his scrutiny to the other minstrels. The bass player also held power... and so did the guitarist. They all did.

"How in the realms?" he whispered, staring in shock.

For two of them to meet was probable, but *four*?

His speculation broke off as Xochitl's voice permeated his consciousness. Rich and operatic, punctuated by bone chilling screams of rage, it was more than pleasing to his ears. Her voice was thick with power which imbued its listeners with pure, unadulterated emotion.

Zareth closed his eyes and pictured the people of Aisthanesthai hearing this voice, their passions renewed, their magic rejuvenated enough to bring forth the dawn of their salvation.

***

Xochitl

By the time Dominic mounted the stage and introduced us, I was ready to rock.

The audience roared as Sylvis and I picked up our guitars and waved. Beau slipped the strap of his bass over his shoulders and Aurora sat down before her drum kit.

"It's All Hallows' fucking eve!" I screamed into the microphone as the crowd cheered. "The night of tricks, treats, witches and Sabbats! So tonight we're going to have our own Sabbat. We're going to rage and have a hell of a night!"

Applause filled my ears, silenced as I struck the opening chords on my guitar and shrieked the first words of the song. The people in the mosh pit thrashed and jumped. The notes on Sylvis's guitar ripped the air. Aurora's drums pounded and Beau's bass reverberated through the floor as he roared the background lyrics.

The moshing masses below became a blur, fading from my awareness as the song progressed. I concentrated on nothing but the soaring notes of my voice and playing my guitar, going through the process of losing myself to the music once more.

Nothing else mattered. Nothing existed but the pulsing rhythm of the drums, the deep vibrations of the bass, the soul piercing melody of our guitars, and the resonance of my voice rising out of my being, lightening my spirit and celebrating everything.

My soul throbbed in intoxicated ecstasy. I felt alive, pure, at peace. But most of all, I wasn't lonely. I belonged.

Beau strummed the rhythm to the next song and my attention returned to the music. I straightened my spine and willed my mind and body into the power stance I used on stage and…if the situation merited, a potential fight. I watched the crowd's eyes widen and knew I looked bigger now. My cat taught me the trick.

As we finished the song, the audience held its breath in collective anticipation as Sylvis's guitar breathed its last vestige of passion. My best evil grin spread across my face. This was my favorite part. I clenched my fists and gathered the inhuman force within. It built in the center of my chest, shot down my arms and out of my hands. Twin purple fireballs raced over the heads of the crowd, curving upwards at the last second.

I basked in the applause of my "special effects," doing my best not to bust out with a *Beavis n' Butthead* laugh and shriek, "Fire! Fire!"

As the fireballs climbed toward the arena's high ceiling, their reflection flickered in the eyes of a man… black eyes, rimmed with silver. My heart stopped, my legs turned into pudding. A black hood obscured his features, but not enough to hide those eyes. It was *him*.

His eyes catapulted me back into the dream.

I walked through the garden of black roses. My hair lay like a heavy blanket over my back and shoulders, welcome warmth against the cool wind whispering through the thorny bushes. Goose bumps rose on my skin. It shouldn't have been cold enough to dispel my magic, but this place rendered me as powerless as the human I'd once believed myself to be.

I looked up at the sky, frowning at the two moons, one a silver crescent amongst the stars— not silver like poets say Earth's moon is, but true silver like the finest jewelry. The other was gold as Egyptian treasure.

A rustling sound pulled my attention back to my surroundings. All around me, roses withered and died. The petals shriveled until they resembled flattened prunes. They dried with a crackle and fell to the ground. Dead leaves rained upon the garden. Thorny branches curled in upon themselves like gnarled arthritic hands.

I pulled my robe tight across my breasts and shivered. I hated this part. Something pulled in my chest as I watched things die in fast-forward. Fog poured in with the speed of stage effects.

Shadows slithered through the air. Darkness flowed around and through my body to converge around a figure gliding toward me. He towered over me like a movie villain. Face obscured by the night and the cowl that covered his head, only his eyes were visible. They glowed in the moonlight like lightning-struck obsidian. His power thundered through my being, almost bringing me to my knees.

I resisted. No one would bring me down. I'd die on my feet, or stand triumphant.

I turned to run and the branches of the rose bushes reached out. Thorns caught my clothes, trapping me until I whirled back around to face the shadowy man. He opened his arms as if offering a safe haven in the velvet folds of his cloak.

"Come to me." His voice was deep, rich, decadent.

Unbidden, my lips parted and my belly tied itself in knots. My skin tingled, my heart pounded. Part of me longed for the warmth of his embrace, the feel of his lips on mine. The other part resisted the consuming power of my attraction, reluctant

16

to give up my sense of self. I'd never been so affected by another person before. Only he made me feel this way.

Unable to resist the compulsion, my feet waded through the fog that curled around him like something alive, bringing me closer.

Awareness returned as the audience murmured in confusion. How long had I been zoning out? Sylvis met my gaze, eyes full of concern. I looked back at the crowd.

The shadowy man remained in place.

He mouthed his command once more. "Come to me."

Either I was going crazy, or the man from my dreams was real.

***

Zareth

He stared at the twin bolts of bright purple fire that Xochitl shot over the audience. Such power, such control …such irresponsibility.

"The little fool," he muttered.

Oblivious to his scrutiny, Xochitl's lush lips curved in a blissful smile that filled him with heat, despite his chagrin. Then, her honey brown eyes met his and lit with recognition. Zareth sucked in a breath as electricity jolted between them. That sweet mouth opened and time froze for an indeterminable instant before she turned her attention back to the microphone and thanked the audience.

Zareth smiled in triumph. She recognized him. His dream magic *had* worked after all. The question was, how much of his communication had she understood? Did she know that his world was dying, that it was her destiny to save it? Or had her dreams of him been as indiscernible and fleeting as his?

He shrugged. It didn't matter anymore. Soon he would learn everything she knew.

As Xochitl sang along to a blistering guitar riff, he closed his eyes...and released his hydra again. He fed until sated. Magic coursed through his veins with more power than he'd had since the sun vanished from his world.

Power that would sustain him until it was time to take her to his world.

Chapter Two

Xochitl

"You okay?" Sylvis peered at me as we headed to the VIP section.

I took a deep breath and composed myself before anyone else noticed my shock. Sylvis was the only one who knew I was *different*. Okay, my friend Akasha knew too, but we had a "don't ask, don't tell" policy because she had some big secrets of her own.

"I'm fine." I giggled, but it sounded like something out of a sanitarium. "I'll tell ya later. We have autographs to sign and friends to see." My gaze roved the crowd, though I wasn't looking for fans. *Where did he go?*

She raised a skeptical brow. "Really."

We stared each other down like gunslingers in a spaghetti western. ...or maybe more like *Blazing Saddles*.

She pushed the blonde bangs of her wig off her sweaty forehead. "Okay."

The line of bouncers nodded to us and raised the velvet rope. Beau slowed his pace to drop behind them and check out their muscles.

A few fans crept my way, pens held in trembling hands, like slinking puppies expecting to get kicked.

They must have picked up on my tension, because they stayed just long enough for me to sign my name on pictures and stuff before hurrying over to the other members of the band. Most of the time, I could coax a bit of small talk, but not tonight. I sighed and sipped my hard cider. Now I was the one who felt like a kicked puppy.

Unbidden, the dark man's eyes flashed in my mind, sending tremors down my spine.

I used to believe the man from my dreams was my knight in black armor, some dark prince who would whisk me away to happily ever after. During my high school years, when it seemed every girl had dates to the prom, while the boys shrank away from me and called me a freak, I consoled myself with the conviction that soon the dark man would come and claim me.

Years passed and he never came. After awhile, I stopped believing the self-spun fairy tale. Partly because my dream of becoming of a rock star had come true, but mostly because I'd come to accept that he wasn't real. Further, more mature analysis of the dreams made me realize the dreams weren't that romantic anyway. After all, who would court a girl with dying roses?

I took a big swig of cider as I struggled to calm down. He couldn't have been real. It was just exhaustion from the tour. A hallucination.

Yet I couldn't stop looking for him as I sat on the bar stool, swiveling back and forth, sipping my drink and smoking my e-cigarette. Between the fucked up dreams and the dream-man-turned-real, I had no idea what to do. For years I'd wished for this encounter, rehearsed everything I would say to him. But every word vanished when I gave up on finding him. Now I just wanted to live my life and have fun like a normal person.

My eyes scanned the club, searching through the costumed masses for the black cloaked figure. He remained out of sight.

I shrugged and turned back to my friends. Maybe he'd given up and decided to leave me alone. I took a deep drag of my e-cig and blew out a cloud of blue vapor, wishing I had a real smoke.

No, I shook my head. He was *here*, I'd seen him. My stomach dipped again. Why hadn't he approached me yet? What did he want? And what would I say to him if we came face to face? Not for the first time, I wondered, *was he like me?* Longing seized my heart. I'd been alone for so long.

Too fidgety to sit still for long, I downed the rest of my drink. Fine. *I'd* seek *him* out.

The bouncers gave me a nod when I left the VIP area. The crowd parted as I crossed the dance floor, as if afraid to touch me. Would he experience the same aversion to me?

I barely completed the thought when I collided with him. Silently assessing each other, we froze in a moment I'd anticipated forever.

Well over six feet tall, he towered over me, dark eyes burning with an intensity that made me tremble. He'd lowered the hood of his cloak, and for the first time I saw his face. Its fine chiseled planes made his visage look both noble and ruthless. His eyes were a dark indigo, with silver lines through the irises. And his hair, wow, I'd never seen anything like it. The strands were translucent, but shot with alternating cores of black and silver.

He swept a courtly bow suited to his elegant black velvet robes.

"Dance with me," he said.

Shivers ran down my spine. He was dangerous. Not in the forbidden *oh-God-what-if-people-find-out* kinda way like dating a fellow musician. No, this was serious. This went beyond the risk of damaging my reputation or getting my feelings hurt. I knew if I touched him I'd lose something worse than a reputation. In his embrace I could lose my soul.

And yet, he drew me like a magnet.

"Dance with me," he repeated, eyes holding mine. His accent was one I'd never heard before, delectable as butter, yet full of dangerous spice.

"I can't dance," I mumbled, unable to hear my protest above the chaotic party and my raging emotions. After all these years, he asked for something that sounded so mundane— I'd never danced with a man before. Did he somehow know that? Was he mocking me?

His eyes flared as a sinister smile curled his lips, making my knees weak. "That wasn't a question."

With lightning grace, he seized my hands and pulled me to him. My body tingled like a livewire at the contact.

"Fine, but it'll be your feet that get bruised." Sylvis and I had earned our black belts in Kung-Fu, but I was a disaster on the dance floor. Hell, I had more coordination when I played with Aurora's drums. And I didn't want to dance, I wanted to talk.

The smirk widened on his chiseled lips. "I won't let that happen."

His confidence would make it even funnier when I tripped him. It would serve him right for subjecting me to all these odd feelings.

"Who are you, and why have you been following me?" I asked, not yet having the nerve to bring up the dreams.

"Don't you recognize me?" His head cocked to the side as he dipped me low.

"Well, yeah, but..." I trailed off as I looked down at my feet.

Something was wrong.

The dark man lifted me into his arms, holding me tantalizingly close before spinning me with a flick of his wrist. It was like one of those dance competition shows. I was moving in perfect tandem with him.

But I wasn't doing it.

I opened my mouth to say something, but then he released my hand and gripped the other harder before he spun me again. Against my will, I pirouetted around him like I'd been doing it for years.

I should be afraid. The thought roared in my mind.

If I was human, I'd be terrified. He had total control over my movements, as if I were a puppet. I jerked away, breaking his hold. Before I fell on my ass, he caught my hand. Relief flooded me that I could get away if I tried.

"Please, trust me." His voice was gentle and imploring.

The strange magic returned, coordinating our movements once more. I looked back down at my feet. I was *dancing.* Like in the movies! My chest tightened. Maybe my dreams *had* predicted romance after all.

I glanced over at my friends. They gaped at us like mental patients.

"Why are you here?" I finally asked.

His expression changed to something potent and indecipherable. "Before I can tell you, I need to verify that you're the one I seek." He dipped me again. "You're smaller than I expected."

"Oh, that's original." I hated when people said that, though at least his tone wasn't condescending.

"My apologies for my lack of cleverness." He inclined his head and twirled me. The skirts of my gown flared out like a bell. "It's just that my perspective is so different, with meeting you in person at last."

A bubble of laughter escaped my lips as I once more broke his magic hold. He was one to talk. Had he been this tall in my dreams? So imposing? So unearthly beautiful? I tamped down the dangerous line of thought and focused on the matter at hand. "Who are you?"

His answer was infuriatingly vague. "I am Zareth Amotken, High Sorcerer of Aisthanesthai."

Zareth. I had an urge to taste the name on my tongue. Was he really a sorcerer? He certainly looked the part. "And what do you need to verify?" My voice sounded breathless as he released me, breaking the tantalizing contact

The song ended and he extended his hand as if requesting another dance. "Come with me and I will show you."

I stared at his outstretched fingers in mute awe, realizing what was so striking about them. His fingers were longer than normal, not quite Nosferatu long, but still noticeably long. Yet I found them strangely beautiful.

Unbidden, my hand reached toward his.

A man stepped between us.

"Come with me," he said gently, as if coaxing a cowering animal out from under a bush. "I can keep you safe from him."

For a moment, I couldn't help but stare at him. With his sun-kissed skin and golden blond hair, he looked like a fairytale prince. His blue velvet doublet brought out the cornflower shade of his eyes. Not my type, but my, he was pretty. Was he a sorcerer too?

Zareth glared at the newcomer in fierce recognition. Then his gaze met mine, blazing with intensity, yet somehow pleading. His jaw clenched and he shook his head in firm negation. Clearly he didn't want me anywhere near this other guy.

I looked back at my alleged rescuer. "Who are you?"

"My name is Stefan Carcineris." He gave a bow identical to Zareth's. "People from my land call me the Winter Prince."

With his strange accent and the fact that my dream stalker seemed to know him, I was betting Stefan also came from that strange place in my dreams. Hell, even their accents were similar. "I don't know, Steve..."

Those angelic features turned brittle. "Don't call me Steve." His voice softened, banishing the former note of petulant irritation. "Please, my lady, we must hurry." He tugged on my arm.

I yanked myself from his grasp. Despite his offer of protection, something unnerved me about him. And in a completely different way than Zareth, who at least seemed to be honest, even if he was cryptic. Steve's saccharine attitude combined with a flash of coldness through the mask made me certain he wasn't the gallant he was pretending to be.

"I don't think I want to go anywhere with either of you." I needed time to think.

"Is there a problem?" Dominic Slade, the club owner approached. He glared at the men, baring a gleaming set of fangs. I blinked, impressed at his costume. Those things looked so real they could be movie quality.

Stefan blanched like he believed the club owner was a real vampire. Zareth gave Dominic a long stare rife with abject hatred, as if considering attacking him.

"No problem at all," I assured him, not wanting any more trouble. "I was just heading back to my table."

Dominic nodded curtly before turning back to the men. His face contorted with wrath I'd never witnessed from him before. "You both need to leave. This is a private party and I don't see your stamps."

Stefan gave the club owner another wary look before inclining his head and stalking off. On his way out the door, he glanced over his shoulder at me and smirked. Zareth watched Stefan's retreat, eyes narrowed into slits of fury. His gaze shifted back to me and the anger bled into something different, but no less potent.

"We will speak again soon," he said, and followed Stefan outside.

"What the hell was that all about?" Aurora demanded the moment I returned to our table.

"No fucking clue." I answered honestly. With a grateful nod, I seized the fresh new bottle of hard cider one of them ordered for me.

Beau laughed. "That blond guy was cute, but there's something about the tall one. I wanna know where he got that wig." Amusement faded from his features, replaced by scrutiny. "When did you learn how to dance like that, anyway?"

Shit. I couldn't think of an excuse for the miraculous deftness of my uncoordinated feet. Sylvis noticed my unease and gave me a subtle nod of understanding. She knew there was an unnatural explanation.

"Hey," she changed the subject. "At least you're finally getting some action."

I wished it was the kind of action she implied. "Must be the wedding dress."

"I knew you should have done the demon makeup," Beau teased.

My laughter rang hollow as confusion spun through my head. Now that I'd given up on the existence of my dream man, he'd appeared in the flesh... along with some other strange guy. And they both wanted me to go with them to God knew where.

Should I have left with Zareth when he'd asked? Or was he dangerous and I was wrong to turn down Stefan's offer of protection?

"You looked intense with the tall one," Aurora's speculative tone cut through my musings. "It seemed like you know him."

I took another swig of cider. "No, I don't know him." It wasn't a complete lie.

Beau waggled his brows. "Do you want to?"

I thought about it. If Stefan hadn't interrupted us, would Zareth have explained what the dreams meant? "Maybe."

My mind spun like a hamster in a wheel. God, I needed a cigarette, and not one of the fake vapor things. Grabbing my purse, I scooted off my bar stool. "I'm going out for a smoke."

"Aw, Xochitl." The disappointment in Sylvis's voice almost gave me pause. "But you'd been doing so well."

Beau waved his hand in a dismissive gesture. "After a dance like that, she needs one."

I nodded and hefted my bag over my shoulder. I headed to the front door and stopped. Stefan and Zareth had gone out that way. Instead I went out the back, gathering my magic just in case one of them lurked in wait. I shivered in the cold October air, flinching as raindrops pattered my hair and shoulders. That was one thing I hated about Seattle. It rained all the damned time.

To my relief, I didn't see either of the strange men. Even better, I wasn't alone in the little brick cordoned smoking area. A witch, a Ghostbuster, and Jason Voorhees huddled near the ashtray, or at least I think it was Jason. The guy pushed up his hockey mask so he could smoke.

"Angela!" the Ghostbuster said with a huge grin as he saw me.

I gave him a high five. About time someone else recognized my costume. Digging through my purse, I found my crumpled emergency pack and withdrew a smoke. The Ghostbuster lit it and I closed my eyes in bliss.

"*Night of the Demons* is one of my favorites," my smoking buddy said.

I nodded and let him ramble on, savoring my forbidden vice as calm seeped into my bones. Zareth had said we would speak again soon. Of that I had no doubt. And maybe then he wouldn't be so damn obscure.

Movement flickered from the corner of my eye. I looked to my right at the empty dark alley, dumpsters, and shadows. Dizziness swam through my head. I was getting a buzz from the cigarette. I looked to the left. The dizziness ebbed away. The witch and Jason put out their cigarettes and headed inside.

I frowned. Neither of them finished theirs and smokes were expensive these days.

The back of my neck prickled, and again I felt a sense of movement behind me. I turned back to the right and the dizziness returned. This time, I peered closer into the alley. The air rippled, as if the sight before me was a mirage.

The Ghostbuster crushed out his cigarette, again unfinished. "I'm going inside. Would you be up for talking more movies? I'll buy you a drink."

Feigning interest, I nodded. "Okay. See you in a few."

I took another drag of my cigarette, this time blowing the smoke at the ripple. Hell, it worked for ghosts. Slices of light and movement became visible in the blue haze. My neck tingled again as I heard voices coming from the seeming emptiness.

With careful steps, I walked further into the shadows, opening my senses like my cat had taught me. The air rippled like a heat wave, and then I saw them. Stefan and Zareth circled each other, faces twisted into masks of fiery hatred.

Stefan sneered at Zareth. "Give up, brother. No woman would ever consent to go willingly with the Lord of Storm and Shadow."

My jaw dropped. *Brother?* They looked so opposite I never would have guessed. However, Zareth did indeed look like a "Lord of Storm and Shadow" ... whatever that was.

Zareth's eyes flashed sparks. "I don't need her to be willing."

Before I could protest that sentiment, something whitish and translucent burst from Stefan's fingers, flying through the air like daggers. Zareth swept his hand in a wide arc, making the objects halt in midair before dropping to the ground and shattering. At first the glistening shards looked like glass. Then they melted, leaving puddles of water on the asphalt.

Ice. I gasped. That guy shot ice out of his fingers. My cigarette dropped from numb fingers.

Zareth gathered his power. I could feel it like static electricity nipping at my skin. Fine hairs rose on my arms.

Lightning shot out of his fingers, straight at his rival. Stefan threw out his arms and a shimmering bubble formed around him. The lightning flickered and bounced around the shield, reminding me of the time travel effects in the *Terminator* movies.

But then the shield wavered and a thin jagged line of electricity pierced through the metaphysical membrane. Stefan jerked like a puppet on a string. He looked so ridiculous that I covered my mouth to hold back laughter.

Guttural words spat from his mouth as his hands traced a rapid pattern in the air. Blue light flashed over Zareth, paralyzing him.

I must have made a sound, because Stefan jerked his head toward me and smiled. "Why hello, Princess. How convenient."

He moved toward me. I gathered my magic and flung a fireball at him. Before it could strike him, he gestured and engulfed my flame with ice. Droplets of steaming water exploded through the air.

Zareth recovered from his paralysis and charged. Stefan's arm snaked around my waist and his hand clamped over my mouth before I could scream. He ducked his head until his chin rested on my shoulder. The son of a bitch was using me as a shield. His hand moved from my waist and I struggled until cold sharp metal dug into my neck. When had he pulled out a knife?

I looked at Zareth, silently pleading for him to help me.

Stefan pressed the blade into my flesh. "One move, brother, and I will slit her throat."

Zareth's eyes narrowed. "Do that, and you'll destroy us all."

"Try me." The words made dread pool in my gut.

The dark man met my gaze as if trying to pass on some message. Then he vanished.

Tears suddenly prickled behind my eyes. How could he abandon me?

Stefan whispered in my ear. "I didn't want to do it this way, but you left me no choice." Horrid chanting echoed through my being.

Cold slammed into me like a semi-truck. The rain struck my skin, making me feel weak inside and somehow violated.

Like a candle deep inside had been snuffed out. Cold was my kryptonite, but it usually didn't weaken me this fast.

My heart thudded as I tried to call upon my powers to do something— anything. Another fireball, or perhaps beguiling him to letting me go. Yet there was nothing. I didn't feel the slightest spark of response within. He'd done something to me that took away my powers. Was it permanent?

The hand left my mouth and I felt him reach in the pockets of his doublet. I let out the loudest scream I could manage, hoping to either deter him or bring help.

"Scream all you want." He smirked. "It will not make any difference. You're mine now."

He raised a crystal above our heads. I had no idea what that would do, only that it wouldn't be good. I raised my knee and kicked back, slamming the heel of my boot into his balls. The knife nicked my throat before it clattered to the concrete.

Stefan fell to his knees, clutching his wounded manhood. If every instinct wasn't screaming at me to get away from him and the crystal, I would have laughed before beating the shit out of him. Instead, I ran like hell.

I glanced over my shoulder. Zareth was nowhere in sight. *Great.* Some help he turned out to be.

Stefan regained his feet. He blocked the way to the rear door of the club. There was no way I'd make it back inside.

I didn't know what else to do, so I took off down the road, hoping to lose him and maybe finding somewhere to hide.

Horns honked as I ran across busy streets, darting between cars like a cat. The rain poured harder, stinging my face and blurring my vision. I cursed myself for not bringing my coat. I ran through alleys and backyards, scaled fences, and thanked the powers that be that I'd almost quit smoking.

The skirts of my black wedding dress whipped in the wind, tangling around my legs as Stefan chased me. My feet froze in my low heeled shoes until I could hardly feel them.

I turned another corner and the footsteps faded. The cold air burned my lungs. My eyes watered, mixing with the rain on my face. The frigid air felt like a thousand needles pierced my flesh. Fatigue weighted my muscles. I wondered how much further I could go when I saw the gates of the Maltby cemetery.

It took almost all the strength I had left to heave myself up and over the high gate. When I landed, I stopped to take a breath. I was so exhausted I wanted to lie down on the wet grass and fall asleep. The thought was tempting. Maybe I lost him.

His footsteps clattered on the road nearby. Damn it. Why wasn't he tiring?

I pulled the tiara off my head, wincing as it tore my hair. As Stefan's shape came into view, I hurled it at him like an awkward boomerang. Luck was with me. The silvery crown struck him in the face. I hoped I drew blood and blinded the fucker, but I didn't wait to see.

My muscles protested as I resumed running. The rain poured, soaking my clothes and matting my hair. My sides ached and my breath came in short gasps, burning my lungs. Still, I kept the pace, frantically searching for a hiding place.

It grew harder to see the further I got into the cemetery, away from the streetlights. The cloud-obscured moon reflected dimly on the tombstones. I bashed my shin on a headstone and bit back a shriek. I was slowing down. He had to be getting closer.

My thoughts halted their race as I saw a copse of trees ahead that still had a lot of orange leaves left. If I made it, I could climb up and hide in the boughs. Despite the agonizing pain in my legs, I forced myself to go faster.

It took an eternity to reach the trees. Each muscle cried out with every movement. Despite the pain and exhaustion, a joyous sound escaped my burning throat when I made it.

Zareth stepped out from the shadows, looming over me more ominously than any of my dreams. His power thundered in my skull with a force that caught my breath.

My heart tripped and I tried to stop. My feet skidded on the wet grass and sent me sliding forward. I crashed into his arms. His hood fell back to reveal dark eyes reflecting the lightning. His sculpted lips twisted into a sinister smile. The scent of spices and dead roses emanated from the velvet of his robes. His body was hard and hot under the soft fabric.

Maybe it was the shock of running into him, or pure exhaustion. The last thing I heard was rumbling thunder and whispered chanting before I collapsed in his embrace in a dead faint.

Chapter Three

Xochitl

Cold. I was so cold.

Whimpering, I curled into a ball and reached for the covers. My hand touched frigid ground. The memory of being chased by Stefan… and then falling into Zareth's arms flashed through my consciousness. My eyes snapped open and I bolted upright. *Where the hell was I?*

I stood and wrung water out of my sodden skirt. My heart slammed in my chest when I saw two moons in the sky. The gold moon was waning, the silver at its first quarter. I was in the place from my dreams.

But I saw no garden of black roses, and I was still freezing my ass off, so I was betting I was here for real this time. Where *was* here? For that matter, where was the bastard who brought me?

"So the Lord of Storm and Shadow has delivered my prize." Stefan's voice echoed behind me.

I whirled around as the prince-charming-douche-bag stepped forward. My fists clenched in effort to gather my power, yet my body felt as empty as a cold furnace. Whatever he'd done with that crystal remained in effect.

Why had Zareth abandoned me to Stefan? From their hostility, I would have assumed this was the last thing he wanted to do. Betrayal weighted my heart like lead.

I hid my confusion. "The last time I saw you, you and Zareth were fighting over the privilege of dancing with me."

Stefan smirked in a way that made me want to kick him in the balls. Again. "Why else would he leave you here between me and his Nightmare Forest? None can pass through those woods without growing mad from terror." He stepped closer and my stomach churned in disgust. "Surely between me and the forest, I am the preferable alternative."

Ah. Things began to make sense. I smirked back, hoping my lips imitated his smarminess. "You mean this forest?"

His smile fractured, but he nodded. I studied him closer. The whites of his eyes showed a lot more than before and his posture became stiff and awkward.

He can't come any closer, I realized. *He's afraid. But I'm not.*

"And what's in this Nightmare Forest?" I asked mildly.

"Zareth's tower." Stefan spat his brother's name.

Come to me. Zareth's words flitted in my memory. Apparently he'd meant them literally.

Softening his tone, Stefan beckoned me closer. "If you come closer, you'll be able to see it from where I am. Dreadful, ugly thing that it is."

"I don't think so." Taking a deep breath I turned back to the forest. I glimpsed black spires thrusting above the trees in the heart of the dark, foggy woods.

"My tower is far more pleasant, I assure you. Come with me and I'll make you my queen."

I turned back to that angelic face, poisoned by malice. The face of a liar. "I'll take my chances with the forest."

"You can't!" He lunged forward and froze, like someone used his ice-magic on him. His face paled and his body wracked with tremors. He pointed at me as if to attack. His fingers trembled arthritically, and he dropped his hand impotently at his side.

Whether it was the effects of the forest or he'd used up his magic with his fight with Zareth, he was as powerless as I was. Served him right. Taking a deep breath, I turned my back and plunged into the shadowed woods.

Stefan's petulant voice echoed behind me. "You can't hide from me forever, Princess. Soon you will be mine."

I gave him the one finger salute and continued on, snatching the skirts of my dress from the grasping undergrowth.

Lightning flashed off in the distance, near the tower. Zareth's voice whispered through the trees, making leaves dance on gnarled branches. "Xochitl, come to me."

My fists clenched at my sides. Who the hell did he think he was? First he stalked me in my dreams, then he showed up and forced me to dance, *then* he brought me to a strange place and ditched me, and *now* he expected me to hike through the woods in my Halloween costume to find him.

Though I had to admit, the Nightmare Forest was pretty cool. If I wasn't so pissed at the so-called "Lord of Storm and Shadow," I would have taken more time to explore. There were some nifty ghost-looking things, which I would have believed if I hadn't seen real ghosts, and a few spots where I stepped that gave me a fun sensation of falling, like in an amusement park ride. The things that grabbed my ankles were kind of annoying, though. Brambles caught in my dress, tearing the fabric.

Lightning flashed again like a beacon, closer this time. The brush and trees gradually spread out to reveal a path. With a grateful sigh, I quickened my pace, ignoring the darting shadows and shrieking specters.

At last, I made it to the tower where Zareth waited, cloaked in his embroidered black robes and wielding a large wooden staff with a glowing orb on the top.

Would you believe the son of a bitch was clapping?

"Well done, Xochitl. You passed my test."

I gaped at him. "This was a fucking *test*?" Rage coiled in my belly like a venomous snake. After years of wanting him to rescue me, to be my dream lover, he'd turned out to be a jerk.

He nodded and stepped towards me, a mistake on his part. I caught him in the chest with a roundhouse kick. My foot throbbed at the impact. He looked at me and chuckled. I was going to kick his ass.

"This is the way you want it?" He set down his staff and went for me.

Zareth was too quick. He blocked every punch I threw and maneuvered out of the way every time I tried to kick him. Not only was I out of practice, but fighting in real life was different than fighting in class, and I had little experience with the former.

I was about to scream in frustration when I hit him with an uppercut to the jaw. My victory was short-lived, for he then chanted a spell in a soft silky voice and a transparent shield appeared around him. No matter how hard I hit, I couldn't hurt him. I beat on the shield until my fists went numb.

Damn him for not coming sooner. Damn him for abandoning me.

"You fight well, little luminite, but have you had enough yet?" he asked.

Luminite? What the hell was that? His laughter broke off the thought, his amusement fanning the flames of my irritation. If I could pass through his friggin' forest, I could leave, and maybe find my way back home.

When I turned to bolt, he grabbed me with the speed of a cobra. Squirming like a cat trapped in a trap, I kicked out until he swung me around and pinned me on the ground by lying on top of me. My fight continued until the fury that had seized me wore off and exhaustion set in. Even though the voice inside me screamed defiance, my struggling ceased and my body went limp beneath him.

Silence stretched the air as I waited for him to say or do something...anything.

I'd never had a man on top of me before. The heat of his body seeped through the velvet of his robes and past my wet clothes, bringing warmth to my chilled skin. His long hair swept down to brush against my cheek, making me shiver in a different way.

He raised a brow as he gazed down at me. The pull of his strange, beautiful eyes held me captivated.

"Xochitl." His voice rumbled against my body, breaking the silence so abruptly I jumped. He gave me a strange look before he loosened his grip on my wrists. "I won't hurt you. If I let you up, will you promise to not attempt to run away or fight me, at least until you hear what I have to tell you?"

What other choice did I have? Besides, how else would I learn why he haunted my dreams? I had been looking for answers. He offered them. Although anger continued to flare through me at his abduction and mind games, a tinge of shame trickled through me for attacking first and asking questions later. That wasn't my nature. And if he did have nefarious intentions, I would find a way to escape him.

Avoiding his gaze, I nodded.

His grip gentle on my shoulders, he pulled me up so we were sitting next to each other on the steps in front of the tower. It would have been cozy if the situation wasn't so screwed up.

I felt his warm fingers grasping my chin, raising my face to meet his gaze. "Xochitl, look at me."

I looked. The moonlight danced in his enigmatic eyes. I felt again as if I were losing my mind. His hypnotic voice caressed my entire body. "I am not going to hurt you, I promise. I wouldn't have even brought you here without your permission if the circumstances had not been dire."

He leaned closer until his lips were almost touching mine. "I need you."

His breath against my lips made me lightheaded. "For what?"

"You're shaking," he commented softly. "You must be freezing." He stood, pulling me up with him. The velvet of his robes was soft in my grip. "Let's go inside, and once you are warm and dry, I will explain everything."

Warm and dry... those magic words, along with the gentleness of his touch persuaded me to follow him. I allowed him to lead me to the rounded black marble steps before I looked up at the tower.

It rose from the earth like a leviathan, made of a gleaming black stone that looked like a cross between granite and obsidian. Silver and gold moonlight gleamed from its polished surface, extending to the bevels and turrets and balconies. The tower looked like someone carved it from one piece. And it seemed to go up forever. My neck craned in effort to see the top.

Zareth steadied me before I stumbled backward. "Careful," he laughed. "You will have the chance to see it better later."

His amused smile and the feel of his hand on the small of my back made my knees go weak. Before I could ponder that odd response, my attention diverted to the sight of the enormous double doors. At least ten feet tall, the arched doors were a dark, lacquered wood matching the stone walls, and inlaid with silver filigree that looked like lightning.

Awed by its beauty, I took a moment to figure out what was off about it. "Where's the doorknob?"

He chuckled and pointed his staff at the doors. I didn't remember seeing him retrieve it. With a muttered word, the doors swung open, quiet as a whisper.

"Whoa." I murmured. Despite all the insanity he'd put me through, I had to admit, this was all pretty awesome.

He smiled over his shoulder and led me inside.

Immediate warmth flowed over my cold skin, making me sigh in pleasure.

Phosphorescent globes hung from the high ceiling, illuminating a long corridor with stark black walls and a stone floor. Once we made it through the hall, stone gave way to plush carpet and ornate tapestries as we entered a cavernous chamber. Elegant furnishings graced the round room and curving staircases shot off in all directions.

Zareth beckoned for me to follow him up the third one on the right. I cast a wistful look at the chairs in the receiving room before following him up what felt like a hundred steps, though it was probably only ten. By the time we reached the next floor, my legs throbbed. At least I'd warmed up a bit.

When he opened another intricately carved door, I perked up with interest, hoping to see some nifty magical paraphernalia. My shoulders slumped in disappointment at the sight of what looked like a normal, albeit fancy, living room.

Without waiting for an invitation, I slumped on an overstuffed blue velvet couch. My aching muscles gave a cry of relief to be sitting down. I glanced up at Zareth. "You know, if you'd just brought me here instead of making me trudge through your spooky forest, I might not have gotten as pissed."

"I apologize for having to do that," he said. "But I needed to be certain you are Kerainne Leonine's daughter. None but a luminite can pass through my Nightmare Forest because they feel no fear."

I stared at him, incredulous. "You made me walk through the woods all the way to your freakin' tower, knowing perfectly well that I'm soaking wet and exhausted from being chased by your psycho brother, just to make sure I'm my mother's daughter? Why didn't you just fucking *ask* me?"

"This matter is too important for verbal assurances. Only complete proof will suffice."

Still annoyed, I rose from the couch and approached him. "I think common courtesy would have—" I halted and took a step back as another realization struck me to the core. "How did you know about my mom? And what's a luminite?"

Zareth's brows rose and he peered down at me like I was some new species... which, according to him, maybe I was. "She did not tell you?"

"She told me we were different from normal people."

He stared at me, stunned for a while before bursting into laughter. "Different?" he sputtered. "You're not even human."

"I know *that*, and I bet you're not either." My gaze swept over his hair, which held so many colors locked in translucent strands. I looked down before the urge came once more to touch it. My attention shifted to his hands. My belly flipped over at the memory of him touching me. "Are you...like me?"

He shook his head. "I'm not a luminite and unless your father was human or faelin, I'm afraid we share no common ancestry."

My mind swam with questions. "What's a faelin?"

"The second highest race of magical beings. I suppose you could compare us as a cross between your legends of elves and fairies, though we differ from those as well." Zareth shrugged. "Though I suppose I'm somewhat like you in that I'm also a half-breed." A small smile tugged his lips. "My father was human. I don't suppose your mother told you what yours is, did she?"

There it was again. "What" instead of "Who." The night had taken on a decidedly objective theme.

"When I was little, Mom said he was a very bad man. After that she refused to tell me anything else." The words slipped out automatically. A reflex whenever anyone brought up my father.

My mom hadn't been a comedienne, but Zareth seemed to think so. Though there was less mirth in his laughter this time. "A bad man. That is an understatement."

"Who was he?" My fists clenched with frustration. "And why the hell did you bring me here? Where is here?"

"It is a long story and you are wet and exhausted." His eyes roved over me with concern. "As I said, let's get you warm and dry and I will explain everything."

He procured a towel from nowhere. Eager to be dry again, I grabbed it and rubbed at my hair. I attempted to pat down my dress, but it was impossible. I felt a tap on my shoulder and turned to see Zareth handing me his robe.

He stood shirtless before me, and for a moment all I could do was stare.

His shoulders were broad and his chest was hairless and lithely muscled. The planes of his abs were toned from hard work, with one thin line of hair trailing from his belly button and disappearing down his pants. With his black and silver hair framing his face and body, he looked like a wet dream made flesh. I had an urge to lick down the line of his stomach. What was wrong with me?

If Zareth noticed me staring, he didn't let on. "Get out of those wet clothes. I'll turn around while you put this on."

For what I could swear was the zillionth time, my cheeks burned. "I'm not taking my clothes off."

"Circumstances are too dire for me to allow any possible harm to come to you, and your kind is weakened by cold. If you don't take those wet clothes off, I will."

"Isn't there a bathroom that I could change in?" The thought of being unclothed in his vicinity was disturbing as hell.

"You've been trying to escape me since I first laid eyes on you. Do you think I would give you another opportunity? Besides, there are things here that are dangerous to the untutored." He flung the robe at my feet and turned around. "You have thirty seconds."

"Only thirty?"

"You've tried my patience enough!" he growled. "Now hurry up, or I will lend my assistance whether you like it or not."

I tore off the dress as fast as possible, and with the black lace still puddled around my legs, donned the robe. It was huge. The sleeves hung to my knees and it dragged on the floor. The scent of dried rose petals, spices and his masculine scent teased my nostrils like forbidden perfume. Though I knew I looked ridiculous, I had to admit that the robe was more comfortable than my soggy wedding dress.

I'm done!" I snapped.

Zareth turned around and gave me a nod of approval, if not with an amused grin.

"I forget how tiny you are compared to me." He bent over to pick up my clothes. "I'll put these on the hearth to dry." With a flick of his wrist, the giant marble fireplace roared to life.

"If your stupid brother hadn't taken my magic, I could have done that," I grumbled. A shiver wracked my body at the memory of Stefan killing my magic. "Is it permanent?"

Zareth shook his head. "No, the effects of the spell should wear off within a day or two." His gaze turned sympathetic. "I am sorry he did that to you. I hadn't known he could work such evil magic."

The compassion in his voice put me somewhat at ease

A bowl of steaming soup materialized in his hand. "Now, you must eat."

My stomach growled, but I didn't reach for his offering. "You take a bite first."

He blinked. "You think I'd poison you?"

I crossed my arms over my chest. "You've used magic against me more than once. Just because I can't feel fear doesn't mean I'm not cautious."

"Very well." He lifted the spoon and sipped, humming in appreciation. "I hope you like it. I made it myself."

I took the bowl. "Thank you."

The warmth of the bowl made my hands tingle as the feeling returned to them. I hadn't realized how cold I was. I sat back down on the couch and pulled the robe around me, grateful for its soft warmth. The soup tasted kinda like Pho and was damn delicious. It didn't take long to polish it off.

Zareth watched me intently as if to make certain I ate every drop. His scrutiny made fresh shivers rush up my spine.

"That was delicious." The idea that he could cook made me smile despite myself.

He nodded and made the bowl vanish with a gesture. A bottle of wine and two glasses appeared on the table before us. I would kill to know how to do that. "Are you ready for me to explain why you're here?"

I nodded. *About fucking time.*

Instead of trailing off into a grand speech, he reached into his pants pocket, pulled out a folded up piece of paper and handed it to me.

"Read this," he commanded, pouring the wine.

I unfolded the paper and read.

"Raised in a land bereft of power, the Lioness of Light will return to banish the darkness.

On the night of the Spirit Feast, two scions hunt to claim her.

The lioness will prowl through a nightmare for knowledge.

A joining will birth new power.

When the twin moons are full in the sky, Storm and Shadow will clash with Winter's Ice.

And with the Lioness's triumphant roar, the people will free themselves from darkness and despair.

The Queen shall crown the King under the new dawn."

My brows drew together. "What does this mean?"

"Four years ago, my father, the king of this world died and the sun hasn't risen since. The Prophecy foretells that the Lioness of Light will bring back the dawn." His gaze swept over me. "You're the lioness."

I shook my head. "There must be a mistake. This can't be me."

"Well, it is." His voice blazed with authority.

My mind spun. I was a musician, not a savior. "How are you so sure?"

"The Prophecy is never wrong." His eyes blazed with confidence.

"What is the Prophecy?" Frustration laced my tone. Every other word he said opened a new mystery.

"It is a book compiled of soothsayer's divinations from around the world."

I raised a brow. "How do you know they're real?"

"For something to be documented in the Prophecy, there have to be at least four identical Recitations in opposite parts of the world," he explained. "The Conclave is responsible for collecting and analyzing them before submitting it to the Prophecy's Keeper."

"And why do you think I'm this lioness?" Though the term sounded cool, I couldn't fathom it applying to me, despite my last name.

He scooted closer and began to point out quotes on the page I had just read. I tried to ignore the awareness his nearness evoked in me.

"See here, the expression 'Lioness of Light?' The Leonine's family sigil is a mountain lion. And luminites are sometimes called 'light bringers.'"

"My last name is Leonine," I whispered. "And for the last time, what's a luminite?"

Zareth leaned back against the couch cushions. "Luminites are powerful humanoid beings with wings. People of the Earth realm know them as angels."

"Are you saying that my mother was an angel?" I recalled my dreams and visions of my mother with wings.

When I was little, I once drew a picture of my mom as an angel. She'd smiled and put it on the fridge, but later I caught her standing in the kitchen, looking at it and crying. I took the picture down and never drew another. If what Zareth said was true, it explained a lot.

Another thought occurred. "You mean there's a God?"

"I don't know, but there are angels." He shrugged. "As I was saying, it is in the luminite's nature to want to help and nurture others. When the Earth was young and still had magic, the luminites saw how uneducated and helpless its creatures were. Many of them flew down to the Earth realm to guide them. But humans, as per their nature, became greedy and violent.

"Luminites everywhere were imprisoned, murdered, and some say even raped, though that would be near impossible. People either mistrusted their powers, or wanted them for themselves. So the luminites left the Earth realm. Most went back to Luminista, but a few, still desiring to help, went to the newly discovered Aisthanesthai, where many beings fled from persecution in the Earth realm."

He continued, weaving a spell of fascination with every word. "By the time I was born, there was only one family of luminites left in Aisthanesthai. The Leonines, who ruled the land of Medicia. Their kingdom remained peaceful until about twenty years ago. An evil sorcerer named Mephistopheles set his greedy eyes on Medicia.

"With his great army of demonic minions, he attacked the Leonines. Afterward, there was nothing left, and I mean nothing. For when Mephistopheles conquers a land, he absorbs it and adds it to his own twisted realm he has been in the process of creating for thousands of years. That's what happened to Earth's legendary kingdom of Atlantis, in case you've ever wondered."

"Holy shit," I whispered. "What happened to the family?" *My family.*

He placed his hand on mine with a rueful frown. "The Leonines were destroyed defending their land, though it is told that they put up more of a fight than the evil sorcerer had ever encountered. It is said that he is still licking his wounds. But there was a rumor circulating that one of the princesses had survived. I had doubted it, for I knew the full extent of Mephistopheles's capacity for destruction. It wasn't until the high sorcerer, Delgarias confessed that he found the princess Kerainne alive and pregnant with Mephistopheles's child and spirited her away to the Earth realm."

I blinked at hearing my mother's name.

Zareth's gaze held mine as he continued. "That is how I know you are the Lioness of Light. You are the only child of Aisthanesthai that I know of who has been born in the Earth realm. But I wasn't sure it was you until I tested you. I knew that your mother was the last of the Leonine family; the one who survived the attack on Medicia. I now know why Kerainne was so desperate to conceal your existence and why you are so powerful. Not only are you the daughter of a luminite princess; you are also the daughter of the most powerful sorcerer ever known to have existed."

I stared at him in stunned silence.

"You're joking, right?" I found my voice at last, knowing deep down inside he wasn't. I reached for the bottle of wine and poured myself another glass. After alternating between sips and puffs on my e-cig, I laughed. "Well I'll be damned. I'm the daughter of an angel and an evil being trying to become a god. No wonder I'm so fucked up."

I remembered how out of place I felt among others throughout my life. Hell, this all could be true. I wanted to ask him about the dreams, since that was the only thing left so far that he hadn't explained, but I was too embarrassed. He would probably deem the subject insignificant.

Zareth took my hand. "Will you help me?"

"Help you do what?" Irritation laced my voice. "I don't know how the hell I'm supposed to bring back a sun."

"You only have to sing."

My brows rose in disbelief. "Sing?" That sounded too simple.

"Your voice holds great power. And on the Solstice, that power will be magnified."

"Okay," I said tentatively. "I'll sing or whatever, but you have to understand that I have obligations at home too." I fought the pulse of warmth at his touch. "My friends gotta be worried sick about me and I can't let them down, so I have to go back home."

"Too bad." He tightened his grip on my hand. "I cannot let you go. Stefan will stop at nothing to have you under his power in hopes that you'll crown him, and many others are also looking for you."

I fought the tendril of heat at his touch. "Why would I have the authority to decide who's king of this place?"

"As our savior, you will be worshipped."

I shrugged, not sure I liked the sound of that, but too tired to protest. "Fine, but I still need to get back to my friends."

His eyes narrowed. "It wouldn't be safe."

"I can take care of myself." I pulled my hand away. "You're going to have to take me prisoner if you expect me to just stay here and ditch my friends, because I won't do it."

Zareth stared at me in silence; his features were stony and unreadable. Was he mad?

I softened my tone. "I know that you need me and all, and I promise I'll try to help, but... well... you must understand..."

He sighed in resignation. "I'm sorry."

Relief flooded my being. He understood and respected my feelings. He was going to let me go.

"But I will have take you prisoner then," he finished with a sarcastic smile.

I gasped in outrage. "What? B-but I—"

"Shhh," he whispered.

Then with a simple gesture and a few chanted words, he put me to sleep.

Chapter Four

Zareth

Zareth studied Xochitl's slumbering form. Dwarfed in his robes, she looked so small and vulnerable that he still couldn't believe she'd mustered the strength to engage in combat with him and his brother. Luminites were powerful, even young ones, but for her to fight without magic impressed him. Rubbing his bruised chest, he wondered where she had learned that particular style of combat, which was similar to that of the Shyr warriors of Mei-Lu.

Still, her efforts took a toll on her. Her delicate features were lined with fatigue. Her lush lips pouted as if even sleep couldn't dispel her worries. Unbidden, he reached out and smoothed a lock of purple hair away from her forehead. A pang of remorse gnawed his gut for making her trek through his Nightmare Forest after Stefan's pursuit.

In truth, it had been agony to relinquish his hold on her shapely warm body and lay her down at the border of the forest. But it was necessary.

What a relief it had been when she passed his test. He also took irreverent pleasure in seeing her thwart Stefan, even though Zareth been cloaked in an invisibility spell, staff poised, ready to attack if Xochitl got too close to his brother.

Watching her taunt the Winter Prince just out of reach before dismissing him and walking into a place he could never enter nearly made Zareth laugh out loud and reveal himself.

His smile died at the thought of his half-brother. He hadn't expected Stefan to have made it to his territory so soon. Hell, he'd been somewhat surprised to encounter him at the club. Though Stefan had to be the other scion in the Prophecy, Zareth hadn't been certain he'd also know how to find the Lioness. How had he done it? It couldn't have been dream summoning because Xochitl didn't appear to recognize him, and Delgarias certainly wouldn't have given him any aid.

Though he wasn't sure he would be the best ruler, he knew his half-brother would be a disaster. Despite the courtly façade Stefan displayed to charm the people, Zareth knew what lay beneath was twisted and cold. And though he couldn't prove it, he suspected Stefan had a hand in the last king's death— their own father.

He glared out the window of his tower. The silver and gold moons in the starlit sky used to be a tranquil sight. Now they symbolized despair.

It had been four years since the sun had failed to rise and his world was cast in darkness. For the first three years, the people managed to keep the lights on and the crops alive with their magic, but now, as their powers faded, they'd had to rely on generators smuggled in from the earth realm.

Four years. In his eleven centuries of existence, they should have ticked away like seconds. Instead, they'd been the longest of his life.

Though the promise of a savior following the sun's disappearance had kept the world from total despair, Zareth had been disheartened with the seemingly impossible task of first discovering the Lioness's identity— which he never would have deduced if Delgarias didn't reveal that a Leonine princess had survived Mephistopheles's attack on Medicia, followed by the realm-shattering news that Kerainne Leonine had been pregnant with Mephistopheles's child.

The Conclave had erupted when he'd dropped that bit of news. Even Zareth wanted to throttle Delgarias for keeping such a momentous secret.

After the meeting, he'd headed to the nearest portal to the Earth realm and gathered that dismal world's essence in a bottle before returning to his laboratory. Taking a precious vial of luminite blood from his store of magical supplies, he began a locating spell. Utilizing the spell and his scrying pool, he detected two of them on Earth, but only one felt young enough to be the one he sought. So he moved on to dream summoning.

Communicating across dimensions was a tricky task. Impossible for all but the most powerful sorcerers. To further complicate matters, Xochitl was a slippery subject. Either she didn't sleep much, or her imagination was too frenetic for her to focus on one dream for long. He wondered if that was a trait of all luminites, or just this one's personal idiosyncrasy.

Worst of all, he'd never been certain the woman he dream summoned was indeed the prophesied savior.

Not until tonight.

Zareth turned back to Xochitl's diminutive form. He shook his head. A rock star was supposed to bring back the sun and save the people of Aisthanesthai. The disasters befalling his world were only increasing.

However, even asleep, the force of her presence buzzed across his skin. Everyone in the vicinity would sense her. He would have to teach her to shield, lest a mob of curiosity seekers would gather outside his gates within days. The thought filled him with fresh weariness, compounding his exhaustion from this night's work.

He needed rest to be able to face tomorrow's challenges. Rising from his seat, he lifted Xochitl from the couch. Pleasure curled in his belly at the warmth of her body. He fought to ignore it. Walking as softly as possible, he carried her up the stairs to the bedchamber next to his.

Laying her down on the bed he'd prepared for her, he again felt a stab of reluctance to relinquish his hold. Something on her ankle caught his eye. He looked closer and saw a tattoo of a sprig of lilacs. An interesting choice. Although Xochitl meant "flower" in Aztec, she didn't strike him as the sort of woman who liked flowers. Yet lilacs held powerful magic for those who were able to utilize it. He wondered if she knew that.

Unbidden, he reached out and traced the delicate purple blooms.

She squeaked and kicked out at him. He smiled. She was ticklish.

He pulled the downy covers over her, his fingertips lingering on her small shoulders. With a whispered command and gesture, the fireplace burst to life.

Still asleep, Xochitl breathed a small sigh of satisfaction as warmth spread through the room. Her lips curved in a smile as she burrowed deeper into the covers.

The sight filled him with a previously unknown tenderness.

He reached out to touch her again and snatched his hand back.

Before she could tempt him further, he left for his own bedchamber.

***

Xochitl

I flew above the world. The silver moon waxed while the gold waned. From the corner of my eye I could see my wings. Their feathers were black as a raven's, edged in silver.

Wait, I had wings?

My attention diverted from the wings as I flew lower and saw people. There were multitudes of human beings as far as I could see. They were in their homes, but it was like I had x-ray vision, for I could see through the roofs and walls of every dwelling. The people's clothing was more diverse in one area I'd ever seen. Some wore Victorian gowns, others, jeans and t-shirts, some in medieval garb. They had one thing in common. They were all crying.

Despair washed over me in sickening waves. Within the sea of grief I saw painters staring at empty canvases, musicians smashing their instruments, and writers tearing up paper. Entire families clutched their stomachs in hunger. The people's prayers all consisted of the same words: "Please, let the Lioness of Light bring the sun back as foretold...please, let her come!"

They all looked up at the same moment and saw me. Hundreds of pairs of eyes held me trapped as everyone ran outside and gathered below me. Against my will, my wings fluttered and I descended. The mob jumped and multitudes of arms reached for me.

"It's the Lioness!" they cried. "Save us, save us, bring back the sun. Please..."

Their pleas were a deafening roar in my ears. Fingertips grazed my body. Sadness and misery hung so thick I feared that I would drown in it.

"How?" I screamed at them, my voice broke with approaching tears. "What can I do? I'm nothing. I'm just a freak."

A great gust of wind, tangible as a phantom hand, swept under me, and I rose upward. The people below shrank. Up and up I rose, accelerating as I gained altitude. My head swam with dizziness. White light shot around me until I was engulfed.

At last my ascent ceased with such abruptness that my stomach leapt to my throat and I almost collapsed on the… ground? The white light dimmed enough for me to see that I stood on a solid white marble floor.

A magnificent throne, carved of the same marble, came into my vision. It was gold and adorned with white velvet cushions embroidered with gold thread. Very Louis-the-something. I looked around, expecting other furnishings to appear, but they didn't. Only the throne and the marble floor were visible. Like the "Nothing" in The Neverending Story *devoured everything else.*

I looked back at the throne. Someone sat upon the plush cushion. I gasped.

Bathed in golden light, Kerainne Silvara Leonine resembled a goddess of tranquility. She wore an unadorned shimmering white gown. Pale blonde hair framed a face of angelic beauty. Her wings folded gracefully behind her back. The feathers were a soft ivory. Each one was gilded with gold. Her peridot green eyes shone with serenity as she gazed down at me.

My eyes filled with tears at the sight of her. After four long years, my heart never stopped aching from losing her. Now here she sat before me. Was I dead? Part of me hoped so. That meant I could be with her again.

"Mommy?" My voice came out pitiful and broken.

"Xochitl." Kerainne said and held out her arms. "My darling daughter."

At the sound of my mother's warm nurturing voice and the sight of those soft lips curved in the age-old smile of maternal love, I ran into her embrace, clinging to her and sobbing into her shoulder like child.

She rocked me in her arms and stroked my hair. "Shhh…it's all right." I never thought to hear her soothing voice again. "Shhh. Don't cry."

When I finally calmed enough to raise my eyes to hers, she helped me to my feet and regarded me with a glowing smile. "Look at you, all grown up. I am so proud of you."

I had longed to hear those words from her, now that I had made it on my own and fulfilled my dreams with my music. Her praise made me choke on my sobs, but I held on, for Mom's face had grown serious.

"Now, listen to me very carefully, daughter." Her voice was stern. "Your people need you. You must fulfill the Prophecy, but remember, saving the world is only the beginning. Your next path is more perilous.

"But Mom," I protested, "I still don't know how I'm supposed to bring back their sun."

Mom laughed. The sound was like the pealing of silver bells. "Don't 'but Mom' me. You'll figure it out. I believe in you."

She faded away, her form dissolving into incandescent light.

"Wait, don't go, Mom! Please!"

I awoke with a whimper, tears streaming down my face. My hand reached out to pet Isis, but she wasn't there. I dug around under the covers for my baby blanket, and didn't find that either. Then I realized that the blankets were softer than my own. Sitting up in bed, my eyes adjusted to the darkness in the room.

Memories of the previous night flashed back. Dancing with the dark man of my dreams, the magic war between the brothers, being chased through the cemetery, waking in another world and trek through a Nightmare Forest...

Being told I was the foretold savior of this world.

"No way, it had to have been a dream." Every instinct denied my words as I climbed out of the comfy bed and walked across the thick carpet to the window. Throwing back the curtains, I stared at the two moons, silver and gold. They cast their light on the Nightmare Forest below.

"All real," I whispered.

Where was Zareth? My eyes darted through the shadowed room, as if expecting to find him looming in a dark corner. I remembered the last thing he said to me before putting me in an enchanted slumber. "I'm going to take you prisoner."

Fresh outrage coursed through my being at the thought of him keeping me locked up like a war hostage. Why couldn't he be the noble hero I'd imagined? Why did I still have the urge to seek reassurance from him? Why did he have to be so damn gorgeous?

"We'll see about that," I growled. Gathering my power, I summoned a ball of flame.

Chapter Five

Zareth

A high-pitched chiming awoke him, seemingly moments after he'd closed his eyes. The clock read that it was morning... or would be if there was a sun. Someone had activated the gate stone to petition for entry. With a grumbling protest, Zareth rose from his bed and quickly dressed in clean robes.

The chiming continued as he headed up to the scrying pool in his laboratory. He summoned the gate stone with a few chanted words.

The surface of the pool rippled and shimmered a moment before revealing a tall cloaked figure.

Zareth smiled at the image and willed his voice to reach the figure. "Delgarius, I've been expecting you."

The Keeper of The Prophecy smiled. "Then let's not waste any more time." His voice rang with implacable authority.

Zareth nodded and gathered his magic, opening a glowing portal beside the pool. As the faelin sorcerer stepped into the chamber, a wave of comfort swelled over Zareth at the sight of the man's long fingers and luminescent hair, so like his own.

The faelin had avoided Zareth ever since he'd achieved immortality by taking in a hydra. Most days, the power was worth the isolation.

Eyeing Delgarias, a thought struck him. The Keeper of the Prophecy was over two thousand years old, a millennium longer than a faelin's natural lifetime. But he had not taken a hydra. What sacrifice had he made to achieve his immortality?

Whispers had circulated, but nothing near a credible answer was presented. Instead, the people of Aisthanesthai regarded Delgarias as a permanent fixture in their world. A realm-wide ambassador and herald of the Prophecy.

Delgarias gave him a knowing smile as if guessing his thoughts. "You have her."

"I should have had her four years ago." Zareth couldn't keep the bitterness from his voice. Too many had perished and suffered with this waiting.

"She wasn't ready."

"The difference between seventeen and twenty-one is nothing. She's still immature and unschooled."

Delgarias snorted. "That is not an appealing way to speak of your bride to be."

Zareth growled at the reminder that the Prophecy had been interpreted by some to mean that he was to take the throne and make the Lioness his queen. "I don't need to wed her for her to save the world."

"Who says I'm speaking of saving this world?"

Zareth's eyes narrowed. "What do you mean? Is there another Prophecy?"

Delgarias shook his head. "Not yet, but I know another will be forthcoming. Either way, you know Stefan won't waste time wedding her if he has the chance."

"I can't." Zareth bit out the words.

He'd been married twice before. The first he'd lost when he'd taken his hydra and gained immortality. Power was more important to him. His wife had been heartbroken and left him, unwilling to watch him stay eternally young as she wasted away in old age. Fate punished him for his choice, because the next woman he'd fallen in love with had seemed a dream come true. Beautiful, ambitious, and powerful. But when they mated, neither their powers nor ambitions coalesced. Instead, his power had drained hers and she left him, cursing him over her shoulder.

She'd only wanted him for his magic. Zareth had been too heartbroken to feel pleasure in her downfall.

He couldn't risk endangering the life of another woman, much less his heart. And Xochitl was so young. Commitment among immortals was far more significant than for the humans of her world, something that took years to prepare for. And the likelihood of their magic being compatible was very low.

"Very well, I won't pester you about it for now," Delgarias dismissed the conversation with a wave. "May I see her?"

"She's still asleep." His voice came out harsher than he intended. "Last night was tiring for her."

"I can imagine," the sorcerer said, unable to mask his curiosity. "Tell me about it."

"Her band put on a concert that night. I heard her sing. Her voice is..." He shivered in memory of her singing permeating his senses. "It's powerful. I've never heard anything like it. I just don't understand how it will bring back the sun."

"Can't you guess?" Delgarias cocked his head to one side. "Why did the darkness come in the first place?"

"I don't know. One moment Father— ah, the King was dead, and the world collapsed into despair and political upheaval. Then night fell and never ended." The moment Zareth finished speaking, he understood. "It was the despair wasn't it? Because of how our world was made." He leaned back. "She needs to inspire them."

"Precisely. Just as her father has forged his world from destruction and pain, his daughter will save ours with creation and passion." The faelin sorcerer stared out the window a moment before returning his gaze to Zareth. "You were telling me about your initial encounter with Xochitl?"

Zareth struggled to absorb the enormity of the parallel Delgarias had pointed out. "Yes, but let's go down for some refreshments. I've been a terrible host."

With a flick of his wrist, he transported them down to the dining area and conjured pastries and tea from the kitchen. Delgarias nodded thanks and wrapped his hands around the steaming tea cup. "Eternal Praises to the creator of the ever-hot kettle. So, how did you like your first foray into a goth club?"

"There were vampires there." Zareth spat the words.

"Oh?" Delgarias said mildly. "I am not surprised, considering that her father created them. Naturally they would be drawn to her. Did they seem to be a threat?"

"No," he answered with a scowl. "They appeared to be protecting her."

"Then I wouldn't be too concerned. Leave them be unless they force you to do otherwise."

That sounded too much like a command for his comfort. Before he could protest, Delgarias continued. "How did you succeed in convincing Xochitl to come here?"

"I didn't. Stefan interrupted us and we were told to leave the club... by the vampire who owned the establishment." He scowled.

The sorcerer chuckled. "And then?"

Zareth told him about his fight with his brother, and how Xochitl interrupted it with a fireball. "Stefan had hold of her and almost took her, but she kicked him and ran. She gave him a merry chase before I intercepted her." He couldn't hold back his admiration at how she thwarted the bastard.

Delgarias stroked his chin. "So she was not charmed by the Winter Prince?"

He laughed. "Not at all." Suddenly, he felt Xochitl's presence amplify, as if someone had brightened the room.

"She is stirring."

***

Xochitl

Triumphant relief filled me as I beheld my purple fire, warm in my palm, but deadly to everyone else. At least Zareth told the truth about my powers returning.

Quenching the flame for the time being, I gathered up the dragging hem of Zareth's robes. The scent of him permeated my senses, making me dizzy and tightening things low in my body.

I shook off the disconcerting sensation and strode out the door, ready to do battle if necessary.

When I looked out the door and down a long, curving hall illuminated with wall sconces, Zareth wasn't in sight, so I headed down the stairs, too impatient to check the array of doors. The damn robe tripped me on the stairs, though I was grateful for its softness and warmth.

Voices below made me pause on the stairwell.

They spoke in another language. It sounded like a strange cross between Mandarin and Latin, both of which I could speak somewhat fluently. The moment I caught the similarity, I almost understood a word here and there.

Frustrated with the effort to understand the conversation, I continued around the staircase to see who Zareth was talking to. My captor's gaze turned to me and he inclined his head in my direction.

"Delgarias, may I present to you, Xochitl Goldmoon Leonine, daughter of Princess Kerainne Leonine and the Lioness of Light."

Zareth's guest stood as if I really were royalty. He bowed and gave me some sort of formal greeting, but I didn't hear a word he said.

I froze at the sight of his pointed ears, long fingers, and waist-length hair that resembled a starry night sky. He must be a faelin, like Zareth.

But it wasn't his appearance that shocked me. It was recognition.

"*Uncle Del!*" I shouted and rushed down the steps into his arms.

For now, I didn't care how he came to be here. Joy overcame to see a familiar and long-missed face.

He lifted me up and spun me around just like he had when I was little. "Xochitl! I'm so happy to finally see you again. And look how you've grown!"

"Uncle Del?" Zareth's voice rang with surprise and a tinge of outrage. "So you did *more* than send Kerainne to the Earth realm. But you have no relation to the Leonines."

"I was a friend to the family," Del said in a tone that implied he didn't want to elaborate.

When I was little I'd heard some kids refer to their mom's boyfriends' as "uncle." My elation ebbed. "Wait, you weren't boning my mom, were you?"

"Of course not," Del protested with enough sincerity that I believed him. "But I loved her sister. If things had turned out differently, I would have been your uncle by marriage."

My mom had a sister? I had an *aunt*. The concept of a family, a heritage, engulfed my mind, too great to swallow and leaving me breathless.

Zareth's surly expression remained. "If you were so close this whole time, why didn't you fetch her?"

"Because it wasn't my place. The Prophecy was clear that the task lay with one of the heirs to the throne."

Though the politics of this world piqued my interest, I had a different concern. "Why did you stop coming to visit?" My voiced quavered with betrayal.

Delgarias held out his long fingered hands, so similar to Zareth's. "Because you started to notice that I was other. I couldn't risk you speaking of me to your human peers."

"I had no peers," I protested bitterly. "All the other kids thought I was too weird to play with them. You and my cats were my only friends. Everyone else avoided me until I met Sylvis..." I trailed off as he nodded and I remembered. Uncle Del *had* quit coming around about the time I made my first friend. "Oh."

Remorse glimmered in his crystalline blue eyes. "I still kept watch over you from a distance. And after your mother... left... I appointed someone to guard you. And now I'll be able to make it up to you and spend more time with you."

I crossed my arms over my chest. *Too little, too late*. His abandonment still stung. I looked at Zareth, who continued to scowl, and I resented his presence for intruding on this long awaited moment of closure.

Then I had a thought. Maybe Del could make it up to me.

I raised my eyes to his, and gave him a pleading look. "Zareth took me prisoner. I need to go home and let my friends know I'm okay. Can you make him let me go?"

Zareth's gaze whipped to mine. The silver in his irises flashed like the lightning he wielded.

Del shook his head. "He must keep you safe until you fulfill the Prophecy."

Zareth's lips curved in a smug smile as if to say, *I told you so.*

"However," Delgarias turned to the sorcerer. "You can't keep her locked away in your tower until the Solstice. Your people are gathering outside your gates. And the Conclave will demand for her to be presented to them soon."

"Why should I care? They can't pass through my forest."

"Because Xochitl's safety isn't your only worry." Del's voice rang with authority. "You need to cement your claim on the throne. The people will not follow a man who hides in his castle."

Zareth's eyes narrowed. "I don't want the throne, I want the world saved."

"You are the firstborn heir." Uncle Del said plainly. "And do you really want Stefan in power? You have to face him on the Solstice. And Xochitl has to crown one of you."

Zareth spread his hands in defeat. "What do you propose I do?"

"Take her back to her Earth home to reassure her friends and visit. She still has duties there as well."

"Yes!" I latched on his suggestion. "We're working on our next album and—"

Uncle Del ignored me and continued on. "Between visits to her home, I would advise that you show her as much of our world as you can. She needs to see the people she's going to save… and you need to reacquaint yourself with them as well."

Zareth stroked his lower lip with his index finger. I stared at those lips, transfixed by their shape and texture before paying attention to what he was saying. "Your suggestion has merit. She has much to learn. And keeping in constant motion will thwart Stefan's interference."

"Not only that, but it will give you the opportunity to see to your kingdom and possibly address some of the conflicts that have been cropping up since the Great Darkness fell." His eyes blazed ominously.

Zareth frowned. "What happened now?"

"The Wurraks have invaded Laran and put the territory under martial law." Del's narrow lips curved in a mocking smile. "For their own protection, they claim."

Zareth sighed. "What a coincidence, given Laran is my ally and the Wurraks swore fealty to Stefan only last year." His fists clenched and his eyes darkened like thunderclouds. "This will not stand."

"I'd hoped you'd say that." Del's smile quirked from cynical to wicked. "There is word that they've turned their gazes to Tolonqua."

Zareth laughed at that. "They'll find a much fiercer foe in the tribes-people. If they're not careful, they'll return from their campaign to find their own lands raided and their children adopted by Dalaas, and Nakis."

"It would be good if you could cement an alliance with the tribes."

"The Acoya and Sikwe may be receptive, but the rest insist on neutrality."

I listened to the conversation with unadulterated fascination. All these people and their battles and struggles... it cemented the fact that this was a real place with real issues.

And I was fascinated with the way they spoke of these tribes-people. They sounded like Native Americans.

Before I could ask about them, Delgarias rose from his seat. "Now if you'll excuse me, I have other matters to attend to. There is a seeress I must check on."

"Yes, even when our world is cast in darkness and verging on civil war, you always have something more important to see to," Zareth said acerbically.

Del gave him a look that would have quelled lesser men. "The Prophecy does not only pertain to this world. There are other worlds, other players, and other events." With that ominous declaration, he kissed me on the top of my head like he had when I was a kid, then vanished like a spirit.

Once again, I was alone with Zareth. Without the heavy permeation of Del's presence, the intoxicating force of the sorcerer's proximity overwhelmed me. My belly wobbled. I shook off the unnerving sensation. "He talks like he's playing chess against the universe."

Zareth's lips curled up in a smile. "In a way, he is."

That smile made my stomach dip again. "So, we're going to be travelling back and forth between my world and yours?"

He frowned. "*This* is your world."

I rolled my eyes and shrugged. "Fine, I'll rephrase that. Will we be travelling between Earth and this world?"

"Yes."

Impatience rose at the vague answer. "When are we going back?"

He shrugged. "Right now, if you'd like."

Chapter Six

Xochitl

Now? For all of Zareth's ominous talk of holding me captive, he'd changed his tune quickly. Was he that beholden to Delgarias, or had he just been all talk?

The immediacy of going back home dampened my enthusiasm with a new worry. "Oh fuck, what am I going to tell my friends? I need to come up with a good excuse."

An excuse that would explain Zareth's presence at my side... and why I would be temporarily moving in with him. Only one thing would be remotely plausible.

My face burned as I looked up at him. "I'm going to have to say you're my boyfriend." My heart skipped at the words. I looked down before he saw me blush. "But they still might not buy it."

His head cocked to the side. "Why not?"

The awkwardness increased as I concentrated on my bare toes peeking out from the robe. "Because I've never had a boyfriend before... except for Beau, but that didn't count because he's gay." No guy had ever wanted me. Admitting it aloud sounded pathetic.

"A beauty like you?" Zareth asked with the same skeptical tone I'd heard a million times.

I couldn't hide my exasperation even as my chest tightened at him calling me a beauty. "They all say I'm beautiful, or at least they did once I became famous. Before that, guys would bark at me when I walked down the halls at school and call me a freak."

Except for the time a group of the football players attempted to rape me to "teach me a lesson." I didn't want to talk about that.

"I suppose that makes sense, given that they're humans... and powerless ones at that." His voice was a soothing balm of logic. "On some primitive level, they must know you're too powerful for them to be able to mate with you."

He gave me more comfort than anyone had ever been able. Before I was tempted to ask if he'd be powerful enough to "mate" with me, I changed the subject. "We can't go this second. I need my clothes back and you..." My gaze swept over his glittering hair, electric eyes, and long fingers. "Are you able to disguise yourself better? You know, so people don't, um... stare."

He chuckled, the sound like rough velvet. "Yes, I can use glamour to appear human."

"Why didn't you last night?" I wondered aloud.

"For one, I needed to see if you recognized me. For another, it was the Spirit Feast, when even Earth-folk wear costumes."

The words of the Prophecy rang in my mind. *On the night of the Spirit Feast...* Halloween.

There were more parallels between my world and his than he wanted to admit.

I returned to the current situation. "Where are my clothes?"

Zareth gestured for me to follow him. "Your bedchamber has an adjoining dressing room. I hung them up in the wardrobe." He led me back up the long winding stairs. "Meet me back down when you're ready to depart."

He left me and went into the room next to mine. I craned my neck and glimpsed an enormous bed before he closed the door. It shouldn't have surprised me that he kept me so close, but the realization had my pulse fluttering again.

I shook my head and went into my room. Zareth must have done some magic on our way up because the chamber was now illuminated by glass globes hanging from delicate chains from the ceiling. I spotted two doors on the left.

One opened to a lavish bathroom with modern plumbing that I vaguely remembered using sometime in the middle of the night. The other revealed the dressing room, which was as huge as the bedroom. A wardrobe that looked like something out of a fairytale dominated one corner, lighted perfectly with the same ornate fixtures. A mirror covered one wall like a rock star's dream.

I opened the wardrobe and found my black wedding dress looking pitifully lonesome in the cavernous space. It was dry and clean, but rumpled and torn from my dash through the graveyard and trek through the Nightmare Forest. Still, there was nothing else, so I put it on. My shoes were set out below and I put those on too.

My purse lay behind my shoes. I'd dropped it somewhere when Stefan chased me. When had Zareth found it?

I headed over to the mirror and immediately regretted it. In my tattered dress, gnarled hair, and mascara and eyeliner ringing my eyes, I looked like an extra from *Return of the Living Dead.*

My face reddened at the realization that Zareth saw me looking like this the whole time… not to mention Uncle Del.

Grabbing a hairbrush from the corner vanity, I wrestled my hair into submission before heading to the bathroom to wash off my makeup.

By the time I met Zareth downstairs, he was tapping his foot in impatience. He looked so odd in a black t-shirt, trench coat, and jeans that it took a moment to notice the rest of his disguise.

His hair was solid black, his eyes dark blue with no captivating glints of silver. His hands also looked normal.

He looked like a cover model from a romance novel... but in that moment I realized he was far more attractive in his true form. My heart ached at the sight of his muted hair.

"Are you ready?" He extended his hand.

Fingers entwining with his, I allowed him to pull me closer. Some part of me felt a twinge of reassurance that he at least smelled the same. He withdrew a crystal from his coat pocket and chanted in a soft, silken language. Everything in my sight blurred and twisted. I closed my eyes before I grew nauseated.

The traffic and noise of Seattle roared over us, overwhelming my senses. Zareth fared worse, flinching at the clamor. His nostrils pinched, as if he found the stench unbearable. He squinted and rubbed his eyes as if we weren't in a nook under a freeway overpass and our meager view of the sky was bright instead of overcast and gray. Then I remembered he hadn't seen the sun in years. I was a night owl, but I couldn't imagine what that was like.

Distracted by Zareth's reaction to the bustle of the city, it took a minute to figure out where we were. The smell of Puget Sound and the painted logo on the side of a nearby old red brick building confirmed our location. We were behind Big John's PFI, one of my favorite stores. You could get spices, meats, and cheeses from all around the world.... and apparently a portal to another world right around the corner.

It kinda fit.

Still, we were miles away from my house in Queen Anne.

"We're going to have to catch the bus." I pulled out my wallet, checking to make sure I had cash.

As if summoned by the dead presidents, a bus pulled up. I cringed at the reek of people packed in together like a can of anchovies. I don't know why the bus smelled so different than a crowded arena, but it did. Some people gave me odd looks at the sight of my tattered Halloween costume. The rest either ignored me or gave me a knowing smile, like I had a good time last night.

Zareth pressed tight against me on the seat for the entire ride, face pinched with revulsion at the stench. Despite all the crap he put me through, I felt bad for him. My hands twisted in the fabric of my dress, resisting the urge to reach out in comfort.

When we arrived at our stop in my neighborhood, he couldn't get off the bus fast enough. We still had a long walk ahead of us.

And we needed to come up with an excuse for me running off with a strange man for several days at a time.

"We'll tell them you're a travel journalist," I said suddenly.

"A what?"

"You know, one of those people who write articles about vacation destinations and touristy stuff for magazines and websites." I shrugged. "My friends will be too bored to ask for details, and it will explain why we're travelling."

"And just where will we allegedly be traveling to?" he asked.

I thought for a moment and came up with the perfect place. "A haunted hotel... No, *the* haunted hotel. They'd totally see me going there for a romantic vacation." My cheeks heated at the word "romantic." The thought of even pretending this gorgeous, enigmatic man was my boyfriend made me tingle. Even if I was still mad at him.

As we walked, I outlined our story. Guilt gnawed at my gut for the deception, but I couldn't tell anyone except Sylvis the truth.

At last we reached the house I shared with my band. A blue Victorian with a covered porch and curling gables, we'd chosen the place for the four-car garage, five bedrooms, and the pool.

My heart thudded as we made our way up the walkway. Zareth took my hand. Even though it was for the act, I took comfort in his touch.

The front door was unlocked, so at least I didn't have to ring the doorbell like a supplicant, since I'd left my keys on the counter last night.

When I opened the door, the pitter-patter of feline paws sounded on the carpet as Isis ran to me, somehow managing to simultaneously purr and meow at me.

Where were you? she demanded, *What is that strange scent? What is that male creature with you?*

I bent down to scratch her between the ears and rub under her chin. *I'll tell you later.*

Sylvis, Aurora, and Beau sat on the couch, watching *Buffy* reruns. Their heads swiveled to me and Zareth in unison, eyes wide in surprise... and relief.

Aurora was the first to react. "Where the fuck have you been?" She charged over to me, eyes scanning my disheveled state before swinging to Zareth. "And who the hell is this?"

Unconsciously, I leaned back against the sorcerer and braced myself for her wrath.

***

Zareth

Zareth fought to restrain himself as Xochitl's friends verbally lashed her. The urge to protect her roared in his veins. Taking advantage of their pretense, he pulled her against him, stroking her shoulder in soothing circles while her blasted cat yowled.

Now, surrounded by her friends, he came to an interesting discovery. Whatever bond Xochitl shared with her band mates acted as an amplifier on their powers. The three humans had only held a slight trace of power before they walked through the door. Now they shared a dim glow that could be found in any respectable apprentice mage in his kingdom.

He would have speculated further, but then the dusky one turned her scrutiny to him. Eyeing him like he was a brigand, she radiated suspicious disapproval.

Even though he had the power to vaporize her where she stood, he felt a strange urge to placate her. Instead of extending his hand to shoot a bolt of lightning, he offered it to shake. "I am Zareth Amotken."

With mistrustful eyes, she grasped his hand in a hold meant to hurt before dropping it like garbage. "Aurora Lee. And what do you do, Zareth?"

With her commanding posture and regal features, Aurora looked so much like the ruler of Kanuri that she could be the Chieftain's daughter. It took him a moment to remember the lie he and Xochitl fabricated. "I'm a travel journalist."

"Hmmm." Her frown deepened.

The others weren't as hostile. The male shook his hand and scanned his face and form with appreciation. "I saw you two dancing last night and just knew there was something there. I'm Beau. Bass player extraordinaire and self-appointed stylist of the greatest band in the world. Are you a fan of *Rage of Angels*?"

He nodded and answered with conviction. "Very much so."

The blue-haired female regarded him with a disconcerting combination of knowledge and curiosity, as if she knew there was more to the situation than they'd said, but was too polite to press for the truth. However, there was no hostility in her blue eyes and she greeted him courteously enough. "I'm Sylvis Jagwolfe, lead guitarist."

Introductions made, Aurora turned back to Xochitl. "So I was thinking we could go to the studio tonight and lay down a few roughs." She inclined her head in Zareth's direction. "I guess he can tag along as long as he doesn't interrupt our work."

"Um," Xochitl said softly, looking so uncomfortable and ashamed that Zareth wished he could offer comfort. "Zareth invited me to a trip to the Stanley Hotel in Colorado for a few days. You know, the one that inspired the Overlook in *The Shining*? I hear it's really haunted!"

Her friends gaped at her as if she'd sprouted a second head.

Aurora recovered first. "Don't you think you're moving a little fast?"

Zareth didn't have to feign remorse for causing such a disruption. "Yes, I normally wouldn't have done this so soon, but this is the only opportunity I have to visit the place before the snows come, and after last night, I don't want to share it with anyone but Xochitl."

Xochitl chimed in. "And I'll be back to start recording next week, I promise." She looked up at her friends, brown eyes large and imploring. "I'm so sorry to drop this on you, but I've been dying to visit the Stanley for forever."

She put her arm around Zareth and rested her cheek against his chest, reinforcing the act of new love. Warmth radiated through his body at her touch, causing an odd ache in his heart.

Unable to withstand her entreating plea, her friends visibly softened, even the implacable Aurora. Zareth concealed a smile of admiration. He'd read that luminites could endear themselves to even the hardest heart.

"All right," Aurora sighed. "I guess we can survive a couple days without you. We can work on the bass and drum tracks."

Her smile widened. "Great. I have to pack."

Not wanting to be left alone to be cross examined by her friends, Zareth followed her up the stairs. The cat trailed at her heels, meowing at the top of its lungs as if not satisfied with her explanation. He had little doubt it wasn't. There was no way to fool most animals with mere glamour. The feline could see and smell that he was not human.

Xochitl's bedchamber was an explosion of chaos. He couldn't discern the color of her floor for all the clothes and clutter. Posters of long-haired men with guitars competed on the walls with depictions of nightmarish characters from movies.

Somehow she found her way through the clutter and wrestled a large suitcase out of an overflowing closet. Clothes and miscellaneous items tumbled out. She pulled out two more bags before opening her dresser and filling them with various garments.

The bedroom door opened and Sylvis stepped in around the mess. "You may have fooled Aurora and Beau with that story, but I know there's more to it." She pointed at Zareth. "He's that guy from your dreams, isn't he?"

"Yup, that'd be him." Xochitl shoved more things into an already overstuffed bag.

Zareth raised a brow. She'd been so fixated on keeping the truth from her friends that such nonchalance caught him off guard.

She glanced over at him. "I tell Sylvis everything."

Sylvis turned to Zareth and glared at him with icy blue eyes that matched her pixie-cut hair. "If anything happens to her, I'll make you pay."

Though the woman had such a pitiful amount of magic that she wasn't even aware of it, he still felt the force of her determined vow. "I swear she will remain safe under my care."

She frowned, still unsatisfied. "What exactly is going on? Where are you taking her?"

"That is a very long tale, I'm afraid, and one we have little time for. I beg for you to allow us to explain everything at a later time."

For a minute it looked like she would argue. Then her lips compressed in a thin line and she nodded before grabbing two of Xochitl's bags. "You want me to load these in the car?"

Xochitl nodded and handed Zareth two more bags as Sylvis went out the door.

"You should take that too." He inclined his head at her guitar. "And the amplifier."

After she packed her guitar, Xochitl handed him the heavy amplifier. "I need to get cat food."

"Why?" he asked, though he suspected the dreaded answer.

She crossed her arms over her chest. "Isis is coming too."

"I do not think that's wise."

Her honey-brown eyes flashed red. "She goes with me, or I swear I will not 'triumphantly roar' or whatever it is that I'm supposed to do to save your world."

Zareth looked down at the cat, who also stared him down in blatant challenge. He sighed. "Very well. But if she runs off in our travels, you have yourself to blame."

Isis gave him a narrow-eyed look before turning back to Xochitl. Some sort of communication must have passed between the two, for she laughed and scratched the cat behind her ears.

As she hefted a backpack and the guitar case, Xochitl sighed. "I wish I could take Little Beast too."

"Who is Little Beast?" Was this another pet? A dog, a lizard, or the fates knew what?

"My car."

His shoulders relaxed. This was something he could handle. "We can take it."

She leaned toward him and whispered, "You mean we can drive through the portal?"

He chuckled at her incredulous tone. "No, but I can bring it with us all the same."

Beau and Aurora remained in the living room, passing a water pipe back and forth. The bassist eyed her multitude of bags. "Damn, girl. Are you sure you're not moving out?"

She giggled. "I'm a clothes-whore. You know that."

Zareth ground his teeth, not liking her to refer to herself in that manner. Eager to avoid their suspicious stares, he hefted the amplifier and followed her out to the garage. Isis darted ahead of him, on Xochitl's heels.

"Little Beast!" Xochitl ran to the vehicle like a long lost friend.

Zareth stared as she embraced the thing. He knew some Earth folk were sentimental about their automobiles, but he'd never seen anyone go so far as to hug one. He was shocked to feel a pang of envy for the car.

It wasn't an attractive piece of machinery, like the muscle cars from forty years ago he admired. Still, there was something unique about the light blue station wagon with flames painted on the sides and skull and crossbones hubcaps. The front end, with its large round headlights, massive bumper and the large "D" in the center of the grille, seemed like the car was looking at him.

After she lifted the hatch, they loaded her bags and music equipment in the spacious back compartment and got inside.

"I bet you've been sick of being cooped up in the garage," Xochitl chattered to the car as they buckled their seatbelts. "We're going on an adventure."

Zareth heard a faint hum as a blue-green glow lit the dash before she put the key in the ignition. It responded to her. "What have you done?" he whispered, unable to hide his shock.

Xochitl blinked at him. "What?"

"This car is sentient." He could feel its alien consciousness. "What did you do to it?"

"I didn't do anything," she replied as she pushed a button to open the garage. "I just talk to her a lot. Sylvis thinks she's possessed, though."

Zareth frowned. "There's no spirit inside of Sylvis, aside from her own."

"Not Sylvis," Xochitl countered impatiently. "Little Beast."

He blinked. "You think the car is possessed."

"If a house can be haunted, why not a car?" The engine roared to life, sounding smoother and more powerful than he would have expected from such an old and small car.

He shook his head, unable to argue with her reasoning, despite his dissatisfaction with it. Somehow she'd worked some influence on the car. "I'll examine it later. We must go."

"Where?"

"Back to the place where we emerged through the portal. Although we can open one anywhere in Aisthanesthai that isn't warded, the ones on Earth are stationary."

As she backed out of the garage, harsh heavy metal music blasted through the speakers. The style sounded similar to that of *Rage of Angels* with the rapid drums and squalling guitars, though the snarling vocals were jarringly rough compared to Xochitl's ethereal voice. As if prompted by his thoughts, she sang along. His knuckles tightened as his hydra awoke to the power of her voice.

Unable to stop himself, he allowed it to feed. A twinge of guilt gnawed at his gut. Zareth frowned. Why should he feel guilty? He wasn't hurting her. Taking in her boundless emotion was akin to filling a bucket from the sea. Furthermore, he needed sustenance to be able to gather the power to bring them back to Aisthanesthai. Yet the shame remained even as his hydra reveled in the taste of her potent essence.

Xochitl interrupted his tumultuous thoughts. "Here we are. The good 'ole PFI. I wish we had time to grab some cheese." Her brows drew together in a mournful frown. She guided the car into a narrow alley and turned off the ignition.

Zareth glanced out the rearview mirror for any sign of passersby. Seeing none, he nodded in satisfaction. "Take your cat and get out of the car."

Xochitl eyed him curiously as she unbuckled her seatbelt and pulled Isis from beneath the driver's seat. She winced at the sound of claws scratching the carpet. Cuddling the cat close to her chest, she murmured soothing sounds as she got out of the car. Isis refused to be placated. The cat's ears flattened against her head and her turquoise eyes remained fixed on Zareth, narrowed in suspicion and hostility.

"Stand in front of me," he commanded.

Once she was safely in place, Zareth gathered his magic and focused on the blue car, chanting to bring focus and will to his spell.

"Holy shit!" Xochitl breathed behind him as the car began to shrink.

Zareth's lips thinned in disapproval. A lower mage's concentration would have broken at such an interruption. Yet another sign of her dismal lack of proper training.

But when he placed the miniaturized incarnation of her car in the palm of her hand, he couldn't hold back a smile at her wide eyes and parted lips. The sight of her wonder compensated for his exhaustion at working magic Earth-side. He hoped he had enough power to get them back home.

"Wow," she said softly. "Will you be able to get her back to normal?"

Her breast pressed against his elbow, filling him with warmth where he'd long been cold. "Yes," his voice came out harsh with a blend of fatigue and lust. "I'll restore it...ah, *her*, to her previous proportions, along with the plethora of baggage you crammed in her hold."

She cradled the car in her palm like it was a priceless jewel. "That is so awesome."

Isis didn't share her awe. The cat sniffed at the toy-sized car and gave Zareth another disdainful stare. He resisted the urge to glare back. "Keep hold of your pet. If she bolts while I open the portal, I will not be held at fault."

Xochitl nodded and slipped her car in her pocket, adjusting her grip on Isis.

"No, he isn't," she said suddenly.

He frowned. "What?"

"Isis thinks you're going to hurt us." Xochitl gave him a slight smile. "She can feel your magic."

He nodded. So she *could* communicate with the cat.

Zareth tucked Xochitl under his shoulder. "Be silent this time. Distractions are dangerous when crossing." The cat's tail struck him hard in his side. He was grateful to be out of reach of her claws.

With his other hand, he reached into his pocket and withdrew a violet focus crystal. Closing his eyes, he prayed to the Fates that his indulgence wouldn't come at a heavy price.

Chapter Seven

Xochitl

The trip back to Zareth's world was jarring. Instead of traffic and the clamor of crowds, all was silent except for the wind whispering through the trees. And it was dark. I blinked and willed my eyes to adjust. Isis's claws dug into my shoulder and her tail puffed up like a bottle brush, tickling my neck. It was odd to go so abruptly from day to night.

The two moons in the sky shone on tall pine trees ringing a courtyard of some sort. For some reason he'd transported us outside of the tower instead of back to the room we'd left.

Zareth stumbled. His weight pressed against my side before he steadied himself. His glamour vanished. His glorious black and silver hair gleamed in the moonlight and his eyes once more looked like orbs holding captive storms. My admiration at his striking appearance faded as I noticed how pale he was. His face was strained with fatigue and his breath came in short pants.

"Holy crap, are you okay?" I felt like an idiot for saying it. Of course he wasn't. It had to take a ton of energy to travel between worlds and work all the magic he had to get my stuff here.

Isis seemed to understand. She spoke in my head in the language we shared. *He is weak. We can escape.* Her tail brushed my cheek. I shook my head and scratched between her ears.

"I'm only a little weary from the journey." Zareth's voice was hoarse as he pulled his staff out of his pocket like a street magician.

His vulnerability filled me with worry. I tucked myself under his shoulder and wrapped my arm around his waist to steady him as we made our way across the courtyard and up the stairs. By the time we reached the gargantuan door, he panted heavily. Still, he managed to get it open with his magic staff and usher us inside.

With one hand balancing my cat, and the other supporting the sorcerer, I led us over to the nearest seat in the cavernous receiving room. My heart ached to see him in this state.

Zareth slumped down and rubbed his eyes. "Thank you for your assistance."

"What can I do to help?" I wanted to do anything to make him feel better. "Where's the kitchen? Maybe I can get you something to eat or drink."

"Sing," he said softly.

"What?"

"Sing," he repeated. "Your voice has power. Please."

"Um, okay." He looked like it would take more than a lullaby to bring him back to health. I worked Isis's claws out of my coat and put her down. She crouched at my feet, nostrils flaring and ears flat as she took in her new surroundings.

My mind raced with indecision. What the hell would I sing? I specialized in loud, angry songs with pounding drums and shredding guitars. Most of which wouldn't sound good *A cappella*.

After wracking my brain I settled on "Memory" from *Cats*. A generic song, but I loved it all the same.

I stood to give my lungs all the air they needed, sang the first verse, and immediately fell in love with the acoustics of the place. Closing my eyes, I leveled my voice to the perfect resonance and succumbed to the pleasure of singing a favorite song.

When I finished, I opened my eyes to look at him, ready to insist that he let me do something more useful for him. But miraculously, he looked better. The lines of strain vanished, and color returned to his face.

"H-how?" I stuttered, awed at his transformation.

"I have a hydra." He met my gaze then looked at the floor. "It's a non-corporeal demon that feeds on emotions. In return, it gives me power and eternal life."

"A hydra?" I echoed. "Like the many-headed monster in Greek mythology? How does it have heads if it doesn't have a body?"

He chuckled. "The heads are symbolic for the plethora of emotions that sustain it."

My mind struggled to process such a crazy explanation. "So you ummm... fed on me just now?" I couldn't hide a note of accusation.

He nodded, every line of his body radiating discomfort. Was he ashamed of using me to heal himself?

"I don't feel any different." Hell, if anything I felt energized from singing like I always did.

"Emotion is infinite and impossible to deplete from a person." He sounded defensive, like he expected me to be outraged.

Though somewhat annoyed that he did whatever he did without my consent, honestly, I was more curious. He had a bodiless demon inside him that gave him superpowers?

Before I could ask more, he sat up straighter. "Now I am ready for sustenance." Bread, cheese, meat, and some vegetables appeared on the end table by his seat, almost knocking over a vase. "I promise our next meal will be more substantial."

My stomach growled. The trip made me hungry too. Isis circled the table, ears pricked with interest. I picked up a piece of what looked like salami and tore off a piece for her. She nipped the meat from my fingers. I put the rest in my mouth and closed my eyes in bliss at the salty, spiced flavor. In what felt like seconds, I'd devoured almost half the food on the tray. Zareth matched me bite for bite.

"Tell me about yourself, how you grew up," he said as he poured tea from a pot that again came from nowhere.

Even though I'd heard it a million times during interviews, the question caught me off guard. "I'd rather you tell me about your demon thing."

"Later, when your education begins." He leaned forward, watching me with an intensity that made my insides squirm. "For now, I want to learn about you."

In interviews I usually gave a generic answer, along the lines of "just a small town girl who was determined and fortunate enough to realize her dream." But Zareth's gaze compelled me to answer truthfully.

I took a bite of cheese and began. "My mom was a preschool teacher at a daycare center, so we didn't have a lot of money, but at least she was able to take me to work with her."

He nodded. "Yes, I'd heard that Kerainne drew children to her, so such a profession makes sense."

Hearing her name spoken by someone who really knew about her brought a lump to my throat. I nodded.

He frowned. "Delgarias had to have furnished her with Earth realm identification papers. I wonder why he didn't give her more money."

A memory of Uncle Del sometimes handing her envelopes came to mind. *Afterward we always went shopping or out to a nice dinner, or went to the movies.* "I think he did sometimes," I answered defensively. "But maybe she didn't want to be fully dependent on anyone. Besides, I had clothes to wear, toys, books, and enough to eat... most of the time." Mom *was* kinda bad with money. Now knowing that she used to be a princess, I understood why. She never had to worry about money before.

He arched a brow. "And what happened when you didn't?"

"We picked berries and I caught fish... then when I was older, I got us a deer almost every year."

Zareth's eyes widened. "You killed the deer yourself? How?"

"With a rifle." I resisted the urge to add a duh. "Sylvis's dad taught us. I wish I could have learned to shoot a bow."

He still stared at me, brows raised like he didn't believe me.

"What?" Did women not hunt in this world?

"Luminites aren't supposed to be able to destroy. They can only create. Did anything happen to you after you killed the deer?"

"Yeah, I usually got the flu, you know, all tired and achy, but I thought it was from being out in the cold too long." I shrugged as if it was no big deal even as I remembered how sick I really got every time I brought down fresh game... and how shocked my mom was when I brought home my first doe. "Besides, I *created* many delicious meals with those deer."

He leaned back in his chair and steepled his fingers. "Interesting. You inherited the luminite's creativity, bonding, and immunity to fear, yet you are capable of destruction to some degree, like your father." He fell silent for a moment before adding, "You could be very dangerous."

I grinned. "Thank you."

"That wasn't a compliment." His eyes narrowed in irritation. "For the daughter of a luminite princess, you are extremely ignorant. Did she teach you anything?"

Tongues of fire flicked from my clenched fists. Nobody talked shit about my mom. "She taught me to read and write when I was two. She taught me to speak and read Latin, Mandarin, and German. She taught me to make fire, make things float, and to call her from far away. And she taught me to keep my magic secret, except for Sylvis."

"Yet she didn't teach you to shield?" he countered.

I imitated his cynical eyebrow-raise. "If I was shielded, would you have found me?"

That shut him up. His eyes widened as he visibly assessed my point. "I wonder how much she knew."

"A lot more than you give her credit for. She even told me that I'd have a new teacher." I shot him a glare. "She must have meant you."

"I suppose she did." He inclined his head in acknowledgement of my words. "I apologize. You mentioned she died when you were sixteen. What happened after that?"

"The State put me in a group home. Then I got stuck in foster care with a couple of bible-thumping assholes." Memories of Bill and Susan's mental and sometimes physical abuse rushed through my brain, making me cringe. "I really don't want to talk about them."

His head cocked to the side. "Did they mistreat you?"

"I said I don't want to talk about it." Isis hissed at him to emphasize my point. I'd been bullied almost all my life. I didn't need to tell him all my sob stories.

Something that might have been sympathy flashed in his eyes before he nodded. "Very well. Tell me about your music career."

I smiled at the more pleasant topic. "I met Sylvis in the third grade. Before she moved to Hayden Lake, I had no friends. The thing about growing up in small towns is that your first day of kindergarten will be held against you for the rest of your public school life. In my case, I'd somehow managed to evoke such hostility from my classmates that they tried to hang me in second grade."

Zareth flinched and uttered what sounded like a curse.

The pain of that memory faded as I told him about one of the best days of my life. "I don't know what possessed me to approach the new kid on the playground, but I'm glad I did. I don't remember what we talked about, but I remember her kindness, her smile, and laughter. Laughter that began that day and never ended."

The story poured out of me. "In the midst of our weekly sleepovers, we discovered our love of music. When my mom took us to a garage sale, we found an acoustic guitar, and for some reason we just had to have it. We pooled our money together to buy it, despite Mom warning about not having any left to do any more shopping.

"We played with it as soon as we got home, and although our fingers couldn't make a tune, we still loved the sounds. Observing our fascination, our moms pooled their money to get us lessons. The following Christmas we each got new guitars of our own, though we still loved our first one.

"By the time we finished eighth grade, we were kicking ass with our guitars and determined to become badass rock stars like Dave Mustaine from *Megadeth* and Dimebag Darryl from *Pantera*. The problem was, we needed a bassist and a drummer to make a real band, but we were both pariahs. Every time we hung up a flier, it was either torn down or scribbled over with a Sharpie."

Zareth shook his head. "That's terrible."

I nodded, touched that he cared. "Then one day, destiny seemed to intervene. Shortly after we began high school, I started smoking to kill time waiting for the school bus, and like all the other poor suckers, I got addicted. The smoking spot was a miniscule forest around the corner from the high school. Sylvis never picked up the habit, but she was kind enough to accompany me to get my nicotine fix."

Zareth leaned forward with curiosity.

"That's where we met Aurora and Beau. Both were outcasts like us. Beau mostly because he was gay and Aurora... well, it wasn't so much that she's black, though there were a few Aryan jackasses that gave her and her older brother shit. But her brother was a Varsity All-Star, both in track and on the basketball team. While Jerome was celebrated, Aurora was shunned mostly because she was goth, and into metal, like us."

Zareth grinned while I went on.

"It turned out that Aurora played drums, and Beau played bass. Sylvis was stunned silent, so it was up to me to recover my voice to inform them that we both played guitar and I sang. Simultaneously we said, 'We should form a band!'"

I paused as the memory warmed me. Like Stephen King often said in his Dark Tower series, it was *Ka. Fate.* I still remembered shivering in the September sun as we made plans to meet after school to jam. From then on, things came together with a speed that was almost frightening. We went from a garage band practicing in an abandoned church in the backwoods to playing on stage before thousands.

And through it all, we'd remained the best of friends.

"But things really started happening when I met Akasha," I continued the tale. "She was at the group home too. Unlike me, she got an awesome guardian. She ended up marrying him, which sounds crazy, but if you were there, you'd understand. Anyway, we ended up practically living with Akasha and Silas. He has this huge castle and he let us use the basement for practice. They gave us new gear for Christmas, and Silas's business partner, Razvan gave us a lot of good tips on perfecting our music. He also introduced me to *Dio* and said I should emulate his style and it really worked. We ended up doing a cover of 'Stargazer'— that's from when he was in *Rainbow* with Ritchie Blackmore— and we rocked it so well that people started taking us seriously. Razvan got us an audition with the owner of The Mortuary— where you and I met— and he hired us to be his house band." I took a sip of tea, out of breath from rambling. "Anyway, the rest is history."

I expected Zareth to look bored or exasperated like most people did when I went into chatterbox-mode. Instead he looked even more interested than before. "Did Akasha or Razvan have magic too?" he asked.

I blinked. "What do you mean 'too'?"

"Your band mates have a glimmer of power of their own." He frowned. "Did you not know?"

Holy crap, really? I shook my head. "I don't think they do either. I wonder if that's why they became friends with me when most people treated me like I had the plague. Well, Aurora's grandma is a genuine voodoo priestess. She helped us out with a haunted church. Aurora and Sylvis come from normal white-bread families as far as I know." I took another sip of tea. "Akasha is a mutant from a military experiment, so she's super-strong."

Instead of giving any reaction to what I said, his eyes continued to burn into mine. "What about her husband and his business partner?"

I shrugged. "They're just eccentric rich guys from what I've observed. But they're really sweet."

"What was *eccentric* about them?" he asked sharply.

I spread my hands, not sure why he was so concerned. "I dunno, they worked really odd hours. Silas would be away all day, but then he'd also be running errands and meeting with clients late at night too."

"And this Razvan introduced you to the owner of that club?"

"Yeah." *Really, what was the big deal?* "We owe a lot to him."

"Hmmm." His look was as dark and inscrutable as his reply. "Let's unpack your things and then I'll teach you to shield."

"Um, okay." I wondered at his odd reaction to my descriptions of my friends and abrupt change of subject.

Chapter Eight

Zareth

As Zareth transformed Xochitl's car back to its original size, he marveled at how the power of her voice alone had rejuvenated him so well. Normally, when depleted as he'd been earlier, he would have had to feed off the emotions of multitudes. Her voice, dear Fates, it was potent as a drug. With such power, she alone might be able to sustain his hydra.

The cat perched on the hood of the car and washed her paw, watching them unload the car.

As they brought her bags upstairs, he pondered everything she'd told him.

First was the matter of Kerainne's mysterious death. When a luminite's physical body died, they transcended back to their realm of origin and returned in another. He understood why Xochitl's mother couldn't return from the dead on Earth, but she should have at least come back briefly to explain everything to her daughter. However, he wouldn't tell Xochitl because he didn't want to give her false hope.

Those eccentric, wealthy mentors of hers were doubtless vampires. There was no better explanation for her close association with the vampire who owned The Mortuary. As the daughter of Mephistopheles, his creations would be drawn to her like flies on honey. Yet she didn't seem to know about them at all. He wasn't about to enlighten her. With her inquisitive nature, she would likely welcome them with open arms.

He needed to teach her to shield her essence so the abominations would no longer be able to sense her.

The gate-stone chimed, repeating its ring before the first peal faded. Cursing under his breath, he went up the stairs and out to the third floor balcony to see who was there.

A mob gathered around the Nightmare Forest, composed of what looked to be almost every denizen of Raijin. Their faces were illuminated by torchlight.

Zareth sighed. Delgarias had warned him this would happen. Even from the distance of ten stories up and a quarter mile of forest, he recognized Rickard Malkin, his high seneschal, just before the man lifted a crier's horn to shout. "Lord Amotken! We understand that you have the savior of our world in your care. Please, let us lay eyes upon her."

"I'm afraid she's weary from the journey and needs her rest," he called back.

As grumbles and protests rained upon him, Xochitl darted onto the balcony. A roar went up as she held out her hands and made a gesture with her fingers that he'd seen her use on stage. As they knelt, she leaned toward him. "Are these your loyal subjects?"

"They're supposed to be," he said darkly. He'd issued a command that he was not to be disturbed this week. Even without the sun, they should have still been able to keep track of time.

"People of Raijin," she shouted down to them, "My name is Xochitl Leonine and I am happy to be here with you!"

Zareth quirked a brow. She'd been trying to avoid him since the moment they first met. "No, you're not."

"That's what you're always supposed to say to the audience." She grinned and waved at the masses.

The seneschal lifted a spyglass to peer at her. "Will you come down so we may get a closer look at you, my lady?"

Xochitl shoulders drooped, her enthusiasm diminished. "Zareth is right, I'm very tired."

He watched her curiously. As gregarious as she was on display, she seemed to be uncomfortable facing people up close. Like a rare tropical bird, she wanted to remain out of reach. He wondered if it was due to the uneasy way humans behaved around her.

Memories of her talking about her past flitted through his mind. He wanted to obliterate all those who'd been cruel to her.

Predictably, the crowd protested, pleading for her to come down to talk to them. More accusations of imprisonment were hurled up at him, along with a few shouts of "murderer!"

Unbidden, he flinched at the accusation. Xochitl turned her head and looked at him with an inscrutable look. Pity? Suspicion? He had yet to tell her what happened to his father.

"How do we know you're not keeping her against her will?" One man shouted.

Zareth clenched his teeth and held her gaze. He had told her he'd take her prisoner… but he hadn't really meant it.

Her musical laughter trilled over the treetops. "Of course he's not. I—"

"I will be taking her to the village tomorrow to purchase her robes and supplies for her lessons." Zareth announced before Xochitl was forced to lie. Gratitude filled him at her support. "You may see her then. Rickard, please summon your ten best village guards to ensure her safety. We will meet you at the gates at the seventh hour."

Many appeared placated at this news. The seneschal lifted his horn once more. "Perhaps we could have a feast in her honor."

Though he would rather dedicate that time to Xochitl's training, he couldn't think of a reasonable excuse to decline. "Of course, as long as we mind our rations. Now if you would excuse us, the Lioness must rest and regain her strength."

As they left the balcony, Xochitl grinned. "Cool, a party. I wonder what I should wear."

He blinked, surprised she took this so well. "Why don't you unpack and find something while I see to our supper?"

Still smiling, she scampered off.

Before heading down to the kitchen, he went up to his laboratory, where he worked most of his magic and summoned a seeking spirit to deliver a message to Delgarias. The spirit took on the form of a transparent crow. The entity bobbed its head like a real bird as Zareth infused it with energy and will before he sent it out the window to deliver the missive.

With all the chaos of this day, he'd forgotten to get something simmering, so he made a quick meal of sautéed carrots in a ginger glaze and fried some chicken breasts in butter and herbs. While the food cooked, he rummaged through his stores for some cakes for dessert. The sight of the dwindling supply made a stone drop in his heart. Though his people managed to keep many crops and livestock alive, the lack of the sun had still diminished food production significantly and they'd had to import food from Earth.

And his people wanted to have a feast. His lips curled in a derisive sneer. *Fools.*

Even if Xochitl... *when* Xochitl— he corrected himself— brought back the sun, it could take years for them to replenish their crops. Their powers were bound to dwindle until they'd be unable to make trips to Earth and back. They were all living on borrowed time.

When he brought their plates up to the dining room, the pitter-patter of Isis's paws and strident meow heralded the cat's approach. Xochitl followed closely behind. "That smells delicious."

A twinge of pleasure from her praise warmed him anew. "Thank you."

After polishing off her chicken, she froze with her fork in midair. "Hey, those people spoke English. How?"

"Our ancestors immigrated here from Earth."

Her eyes widened. "You hypocrite! All your scorn for my world and you're *from* there?"

"*I* wasn't. My ancestors were." He bit back a smile at her outburst. Truly she had a point, but he wasn't going to acknowledge it.

"Why did they bow to me and not to you?" Xochitl cut up her chicken. "And why were some of them so rude?"

"I used to encourage it. For one thing, I was left alone to my studies, and for another, my hydra fed off their fear... And of course, they think I killed my father, the king. Taranis was found in his throne room with his heart burned out of his chest, like it had been done with fire... or lightning. His crown was never found." He closed his eyes and waited for the inevitable, "*Did you?*"

Instead she said, "I bet it was Steve."

"Who?" Surprised pleasure curled in his belly that she didn't consider him to be a murderer.

She waved her fork in the air. "You know, your asshole brother, Stefan."

He nearly choked on his carrots. "Steve? Oh yes, I remember his reaction to that pedestrian moniker. He didn't care for it."

She nodded. "I'm going to keep calling him that."

"And why do you think ah, Steve killed our father?"

She took a bite of carrots and hummed appreciatively. "Because he's more interested in power than you are. He kept rambling on about the whole 'when I am king, yada yada.' You don't do that. Hell, you've even said you don't want to be king."

Despite her blithe attitude, she was perceptive. He leaned forward. "And why do you not suspect the frightening Lord of Storm and Shadow?"

She shrugged. "Because I'm unable to find you frightening."

Warmth suffused him. She was the first in centuries who didn't quell at the sight of him. The realization made his chest tight.

He took a large bite of raspberry-filled cake to quiet the sensation and changed the subject. "Would you like the tour now?"

Xochitl nodded and wiped cake crumbs from her mouth. He fought the urge to lick her lips. Taking a deep breath, he remembered to be a gentleman and extended his arm to escort her. As he showed her the spare rooms, the kitchen, and the larder, she exclaimed over every detail with an enthusiasm that astounded him.

As if sensing his observation, she cast him a sheepish glance. "Sorry, I grew up in a small house, so this is incredible to me."

"It's all right. Would you like to see the library or the ballroom next?"

She did a little hop and clapped her hands. "The library!" She paused. "Wait, you have a ballroom?"

He nodded. "My mother insisted. So far I've only used it for spells that need a lot of room to work. I was thinking of storing your car in there."

She giggled at that as he led her up the stairs to the library. By the time they reached the sixth level of the tower, she was out of breath. A measure of fatigue weighed on him as well. He would have teleported them, but he needed to conserve energy.

Xochitl recovered her own zest when he opened the door to the library.

"Oh my God," she breathed. "This is the most beautiful thing I've ever seen."

Zareth didn't expect her to be much of a reader. As he watched her walk through the room, hands behind her back in reverence, he saw he was wrong. Her lush lips parted as she stared rapt at the circular chamber. Four levels of bookcases rose to the ceiling, with staircases leading to balconies for each one. Bright globes lit the area and a double-sided fireplace in the center of the room kept the reader warm.

Xochitl dashed to a wheeled ladder and went sliding along the rails with a giddy squeal.

He'd spent the last centuries in practical solitude and rarely had guests. He'd preferred it that way, until now. Seeing Xochitl's joy in his tower and watching her peruse his books gave him a sense of pride.

She looked up from a book on the history of Aisthanesthai. "Are you going to show me your laboratory?"

He shook his head. "Tomorrow will be soon enough for that. I need to rest. You may stay here and read, if you like."

"Okay!" Xochitl hopped down from the ladder with the book in hand.

She plopped into his favorite overstuffed chair by the fire. Her cat curled up in her lap and blinked at him with turquoise eyes. They painted such a cozy picture, he felt a pang in his chest, wishing he could join her.

Shaking off the ludicrous thought, he decided to take a walk to clear his head. Going to bed would only lead his imagination to dangerous territory. Once outside, Zareth sucked in deep gulps of the cold night air. It did little to cool his heated thoughts.

Only the second night of having Xochitl under his roof, she already drove him mad. Her rapid turnabout from defying him and her destiny to glib acceptance had him dizzy. Her lack of discipline made his jaw ache from grinding his teeth.

Yet her rampant curiosity and enthusiasm about the smallest things touched a long forgotten part of him, recalling him back to his long lost youth. And her beauty and power made him—and his hydra— roil with lust.

He would have to teach her to shield tomorrow. Of course, that would do nothing to mute her beauty. He remembered the sadness in her eyes when she told him no one ever wanted her before. Even though he'd explained the reason, it was still hard to fathom.

She was the most desirable creature he'd ever encountered. Yet people avoided her, aside from her friends. How lonely she must have been before she found them.

He looked up at the starry sky, so devoid of clouds that the vast darkness resembled a gaping mouth on the verge of swallowing the world.

Walking the tower grounds, he focused on tomorrow's lesson plan. The best course would be to find out what she knew about magic first and build from there. As he pondered how to proceed, he sighed at how rusty his teaching skills had grown. It had been three hundred years since he'd taken an apprentice.

His boots struck a cobblestone, ceasing his musings. He paused and looked down the path to the garden his mother created for outdoor spells. He hadn't used the area for decades because it brought back the pain of losing her. Now he used the lilac grove by the herb garden.

Heading in that direction, he frowned at the pitiful state of his herbs. He'd kept about half of them alive with artificial light, but some plants were too delicate to thrive without real sunlight.

The lilac grove appeared even more dismal, but that was normal for this time of year. Though the small trees remained in bloom far longer than the ones on Earth, even they could not withstand the heat of summer or the cold of fall and winter.

Zareth was grateful they were still alive. He reached out to the largest tree, which stood twenty-four feet high and spread out just as wide. Wrapping his fingers around a long, nearly straight branch, he felt a faint thrum of life pulse through the wood. If Xochitl succeeded in bringing back the sun, the tree would burst with myriad blooms of tiny violet flowers just like the ones depicted on her ankle tattoo.

He caressed the rough bark, considering it thoughtfully before he reached into his bag of holding and withdrew a large knife.

Whispering words of apology and gratitude for the tree, he sawed off the branch.

Chapter Nine

Xochitl

After being with Zareth almost nonstop for the last twenty four hours, the room felt oddly empty with his absence. But it didn't take long for me to become engrossed in the book.

According to the history of Aisthanesthai, no one knew whether someone created the world, or if it was discovered through portals. Earth used to have magical beings, but many were wiped out when Mephistopheles attacked three of the most powerful regions. The few who remained became oppressed by non-magical humans. The remaining mages found the portals— or formed them, historians couldn't determine which— and they immigrated to Aisthanesthai.

I couldn't help but wonder who was there first.

The book directed me to an appendix at the end for their locations. I marveled at the amount; twenty in the United States, including Seattle and my home town of Coeur d' Alene. Now I knew why my mom chose to settle there.

Every continent held portals, with Africa and Asia having the most, estimated forty at least. There was even one in Antarctica. I wondered how they remained undiscovered so long.

I also checked out the various maps. But the measurements were unfamiliar to me, so I couldn't get a perspective on how big it was. All I knew was that there were only four continents and that the silver moon was bigger than the gold moon.

I flipped back to the descriptions of the beings who inhabited this world. Zareth told me about the faelin and luminites, but I was surprised to find out leprechauns and dragons also dwelled here.

High Sorcerers were also considered to be separate species. I looked for mention of the hydra Zareth had, but found nothing. I wondered if it was a forbidden secret or something.

The section on luminites said only one colony resided on Aisthanesthai up until year 5042— which I had no perspective of since their calendars didn't seem to match Earth's. A map and the introductory chapter listed the last known members of the royal family.

Queen Natalya, and her consort, King Kiernen and the Princesses Kerainne and Nikkita. Reading the names of my grandparents and aunt that I hadn't known existed made a lump form in my throat.

Not able to handle any more sadness, I read more about Zareth's father. Taranis the Fair had reigned for twelve hundred years. The praise about him went on for four pages before souring on the next two. Apparently when his wife, Queen Bellanatha died, he withdrew from the world.

The people's hopes returned when he wed his second wife, a human from Boreaus, who gave birth to Stefan, but Taranis only half-heartedly renewed interest in the realm. In the last three hundred years, he became a recluse.

Before he was murdered. I wondered if Zareth had been close to his father. He was born only a century after Taranis ascended the throne. I couldn't imagine losing someone after so long.

I stuck a piece of paper between the pages to mark my place and put the book down. My eyes watered with a combination of exhaustion and information overload as I shambled up the stairs to bed.

After hours of tossing, turning, and punching my pillow into a pulp, I rolled out of bed and gave in to my restless urge to meander. As I slipped on my boots and coat, Isis leapt up from the foot of the bed.

Where are you going?

"Exploring," I whispered.

It's about time. Isis followed me out of the room. I paused at Zareth's door, tempted to press my head against the wood and listen. Isis cocked one ear to the side. We crept through the darkened corridor and down the stairs. I wandered down multitudes of steps and through the maze of Zareth's tower before I encountered what appeared to be the back door. I bet he had some mystical secrets hiding in his backyard.

I opened the gilded door and stepped outside. A cobblestone path lined by shrubs and flower bushes beckoned me. I walked down the path, curious to know where it would lead. Isis trotted ahead of me. The sound of a trickling stream reached my ears.

I followed the winding path until I came upon a grove of pine trees that reminded me of home. A pang of longing stabbed my chest at the sight of them, making me wish I could go back to Coeur d'Alene. To be a kid again, driving my Datsun up in the mountains to a kegger, or to pick huckleberries, with no other responsibilities aside from meeting up with my friends for a horror movie marathon or jam session.

Now the fate of another world rested on my voice... and I also had to work in time to record another album on Earth.

A faint rustling noise interrupted my self-pity. Isis and I halted and turned toward the sound. Isis's ears flattened as I stood rooted to the spot for a while before I gave up, hearing nothing more. I let out my pent up breath, allowing my heart to slow its rapid beat. It was probably a squirrel.

I quickened my pace, anxiousness to find out what lay at the end of the path growing with every step.

The path thinned out. Many of the cobblestones I came upon were cracked, or missing. Weeds devoured their edges. I pushed my way through the brush, awash in anticipation and oblivious to the leaves clinging to my coat and dirt gathering on its hem.

Then I reached a tarnished gate that might have once been silver. I could barely see it for the weeds obscuring the bars. Sticking out between the bars of the gate and practically hidden in the shadows was a single fully bloomed black rose.

My heart pulsed at the sight of another thing from my dreams.

Grasping the bars of the gate, I tugged hard. The gate didn't budge. It wasn't that tall, though. I leapt up, grasped the top of the gate, found a foothold and threw myself over the rail.

When I landed on the other side, my breath caught as I stared in amazement at the sight before me.

I stood in a massive garden of black roses. Though overgrown and choked with weeds, for some reason, the sight of the place was so wildly beautiful that it touched a part of my soul that had been dormant. Just like in my dream.

Now a fire burned inside of me and my mind cleared of all debris.

I don't know how long I stood there, marveling at the incredible sensations and emotions coursing through my being before I noticed other things in the garden.

Various marble statues graced every turn. Most were so covered with roses and weeds that I could barely make them out even in the bright moonlight. I approached the most visible one, a detailed figure of a young woman. She wore a simple, yet elegant dress.

Each fold and crease perfectly carved and chiseled, it looked smooth as real silk. Her palms opened, arms outstretched in a gesture of peace, bounty and love. Her face was the true masterpiece. Luminous and tranquil, her full lips curved in a slight harmonious little smile. I had a sudden urge to kiss those lips. But I held back the impulse, not wanting to be sacrilegious. I laughed under my breath. Sacrilege had never before been an existing concept in my mind.

After communing with the statue, I noticed the sound of the trickling stream was closer. I pushed my way forward through the overgrown path until I found it. The stream in the garden held the clearest source of water that I had seen. The moonlight reflected off of its surface, turning the stream into a ribbon of glittering silver.

Impulsively, I reached into the water and grabbed a handful of stones from the bottom. I held them in my open palm, fascinated by their glistening colors. Smooth and round, the stones gleamed in hues of dark blues, greens and violets. I pocketed them and rose to explore the wondrous garden further. Soon, I found that the remains of the path split and led to various locations of the garden. The layout had probably been symmetrical at one point in time. I followed the path most likely to lead to the center of the garden.

When I found the center, I came upon an immense marble table encrusted with jewels. I smoothed off the dust and dried leaves covering the surface. The part I wiped clean reflected the moonlight so bright it hurt my eyes. What was it used for? A sacred place to practice magic? Or a sacrificial altar? Maybe I would ask Zareth sometime and risk him getting angry about me wandering without his permission.

As if conjured by the thought, Isis growled, tail bristling. *He's coming.*

Zareth stepped out of the shadows; his eyes locked on mine menacingly. To my irritation, my knees trembled.

"What are you doing here?" I struggled to sound calm.

"I was about to ask the same of you." His voice held a thread of steel.

"I...c-couldn't sleep," I stammered.

All my poise and confidence blew away like a leaf in the autumn wind. Why did he always make me feel this way, so awkward and exposed?

"You could have put yourself in a lot of danger, wandering outside like this," he growled. "And you disrupted my rest, which a sorcerer desperately needs."

"How did you find me?" I ignored a twinge of remorse for waking him up. He really had been exhausted from the day's events.

"This place is warded." His eyes narrowed as he realized he allowed me to stray from the original subject. "But that doesn't matter. You should have been inside the tower, safe in your bed."

I glowered at him, hands on my hips. "I thought since I was still within the border of Nightmare Forest, it wouldn't be such a big deal."

He crossed his arms over his chest and gave me another inscrutable look.

"Well?" My voice rose a few nervous octaves.

He remained silent, frowning as his gaze raked across my body. I shivered and looked down, realizing that my coat was unfastened and framed my black satin night gown, which revealed a lot of cleavage in the moonlight. To my embarrassment, my nipples poked through the thin fabric. It was cold out here, but my face flamed. Part of me wondered if he liked what he saw. A big part wanted him to.

I jerked my coat closed and looked up at him.

"Zareth...?" My voice lost its bravado.

He stalked toward me. "We'll have to do something about this."

"About what?" I stepped back.

"About your penchant for ignoring my orders and putting yourself in danger." He seized my shoulders and bent down until his face was level with mine. "I can't sleep worrying about where you are every night and wondering whether you wandered off again. And you will learn quickly just how important sleep is for a mage. I have no choice but remedy the situation."

"What are you going to do?" Something in his tone raised the hairs on the nape of my neck. Was he going to bust out the whips and chains?

His lips were inches from mine as he spoke. Instant longing for him to kiss me almost distracted me from his words.

"For me to know exactly where you are at night so I can rest peacefully, there is only one place where you can sleep."

I tried to sound flippant. "Where? The dungeon?"

"In my bed."

My jaw dropped and my heart skipped a beat. His dark eyes gleamed in the moonlight and I drowned in their depths. How could I handle sleeping next to him? Unbidden, I pictured his lean, muscled body beneath his robes. I imagined that body stretched out on the bed beside me, close enough to touch, close enough to hold. *Would he...?* I shivered.

Did I want him to? *Yes*, an inner voice answered.

"In your bed?" I repeated like a dumbass. Anger washed over me for letting him turn me into a simpering schoolgirl.

Zareth nodded slowly, his sculpted lips curved in a smile of amusement at my shock. It occurred to me that I had rarely seen him smile. More to my chagrin, I also noticed that he looked devastatingly handsome when he smiled. His chiseled features became more apparent and his eyes shone brighter. Self-loathing filled me. How could I be attracted to him in this situation?

"That's bullshit!" I argued, fighting my desire. "You have no right to take away what little privacy that I have just because I wanted to go outside. Because of the danger, you say. I'm capable of protecting myself. You said I'm powerful." I poked his chest and he released me and stepped back. "You can't make me sleep in your bed, so why don't you go play a game of hide and go fuck yourself!" I finished the retort with a favorite line of Sylvis's, tempted to stick my tongue out at him, but I held back. I stood with my hands balled up in tight fists at my sides and glared up at him, hoping that I looked threatening.

Apparently I didn't, because the garden echoed with his laughter.

"Fine." He stepped closer and I struggled to hold my ground. "Protect yourself from *this*."

He grabbed me with lightning speed and threw me over his shoulder. I gasped in outrage and tried to calm down enough to gather my power. But the only things I could do were fire and some sort of invisible force that could knock stuff over. I didn't want to burn him, and if I used the other trick, it would just take us both down.

He then proceeded to carry me like a sack of goddamned potatoes back to the tower. I was pissed. More for him proving me wrong than anything else, but I wasn't going to admit that.

"Damn you!" I beat on his back with my fists, but he'd put up another of those magical shield things, so it had no effect. "Put me down and take me like a man!" I wanted to kick him, but his arm was locked around the backs of my knees like a steel band. The ground swayed in my vision from his long strides.

"Be quiet. If you keep this up any longer, I will."

My heart stopped. That wasn't what I'd meant. *Fight like a man*, that's what I should have said. Yet now that he mentioned taking me, an inner voice said, *"Oh, please do!"*

Isis hissed and swiped at his ankles with her claws, reminding me that this wasn't intended to be a seductive moment.

When we got inside, he set me on my feet with surprising gentleness and held out his hand. Wordlessly, I took it.

Frustration roiled through me. Yet again he'd bested me, and yet again uncontrollable desire heated my veins even though he showed no interest in me in that way. I put my head down to hide my blushing cheeks as I followed him up the stairs.

He led me down the corridor and into his room. The bed looked larger and more intimidating than I remembered. Zareth drew back the covers before he sat down and untied his boots. He then took off his robe and pants and I couldn't repress a gasp at the sight of him wearing nothing but boxers. He was sleek and lean and toned like a powerful cat, not big and muscular to the point of being lumpy in the way most women liked, but repulsed me. My gaze travelled down his flat stomach, with just a hint of a six pack and a thin line of hair running from his belly button down to…his boxer briefs hid the rest from view, though I could see a bulge that made the place between my thighs quiver.

"Are you going to take off your boots and coat?" he asked impatiently.

I tore my gaze from his body. My face flushed in embarrassment.

"I— um…"

"This isn't the time for modesty, Xochitl."

I bent down and took off my boots and shrugged out of my coat, careful not to let it snag my nightgown and accidentally flash him. Not knowing what to do with the coat, I held it up and gave him a questioning look.

"Set it on the floor. We'll need to clean it tomorrow."

I followed his suggestion and got under the covers with lightning speed. Zareth extinguished the lights and climbed in next to me. This was it. I was in bed with him. Did he expect us to sleep? *Or did he want to…?*

I clutched the covers to my chin, waiting for him to make a move toward me. Principle demanded I should protest if he did, while my body trembled with anticipation.

But when he rolled over on his side with his back to me, it was clear he'd meant what he said about needing rest. As his breathing turned smooth and even in the rhythm of sleep, a heavy feeling settled in my stomach. Was I disappointed? The throb between my legs seemed to think so.

Slowly, my taut muscles relaxed and I turned my head to look at the shadowy outline of his form beside me. I'd never slept next to a guy before. Beau didn't count. It shouldn't have been any different than sleepovers with my friends, yet it was. Even in sleep, his presence was palpable, making my skin tingle. The silver streaks in his hair gleamed in the moonlight like captive stars, tempting me to run my fingers through the silken locks. His scent all over the pillows and blankets deepened the ache in my core.

Biting my lip, I rolled over to face away from him. Isis padded up from the foot of the bed to curl up against my chest. I took a deep breath and tried to slow my racing thoughts.

Tomorrow was going to be awkward as hell.

Chapter Ten

Xochitl

I awoke to Zareth tapping me on the shoulder. "Wake up. We have much to do today."

A drop of water struck my cheek, jolting me to full consciousness. My eyes snapped open and my breath caught at the sight of him wet and dripping, wearing nothing but a towel around his waist. Droplets from his damp hair rained down on the bed as he leaned over me.

Mouth dry at the sight of his sinuous form, I nodded and climbed out of his gargantuan bed and dashed out the door to my adjoining room.

Frowning at the sight of my snarled hair, I showered and dressed before meeting him in the dining room.

During breakfast, which was biscuits and gravy washed down with an ungodly delicious tea, Zareth outlined our plan for the day... or night, since it was still dark out. I might be nocturnal, but the lack of a few hours' daylight already messed with me. And Zareth's people hadn't seen the sun for four years. A pang of sorrow stabbed my heart. I couldn't imagine what that had been like.

He interrupted my thoughts. "Before we go to the feast, I think it is time to begin your lessons."

"Okay." I glanced up at him and my face grew hot as I remembered the feel of his strong arms around me as he carried me to his bed.

After that, how could he act like everything was all business?

I looked back down at my plate, my appetite fled with the fluttering of my stomach. Still, I forced the rest of the food down, not wanting what was surely becoming a rare commodity to go to waste.

Zareth cleared the table with a sweep of his hand and stood. "We had best begin. Follow me up to my laboratory." Before I could nod, he headed off.

I rushed to follow him, but as I rounded the corner, he was nowhere in sight. Only one staircase went this direction, and he hadn't shown it to me on the tour, so I headed up, hoping to catch up with him. The damn steps circled and wound upward for what seemed like an eternity. My legs throbbed before I could even see the top.

By the time I made it up to the door to the laboratory, Zareth sat on the landing, carving the bark off a long stick with a small knife. I was so exhausted from the agonizing climb up the stairs that I nearly collapsed at his feet. The fact that he looked so calm and his breathing didn't appear labored filled me with irritation.

"I bet you didn't even have to walk up these stairs," I growled.

"You're right, I didn't." His lips quirked in a half smile as he fingered a violet crystal around his neck. "And if you follow my lessons, neither will you."

He turned the stick in his hands and made it vanish with a flick of his wrist. Zareth put his hand over the doorknob and spoke a few words in a beautiful lilting language. His voice sent tremors through my body. There was an audible click when he opened the door.

He bowed and extended his arm in an introductory gesture. "My laboratory." Despite his curtness, a note of pride echoed in those two words.

I gazed in awe at the mammoth chamber. The ceiling was made of solid transparent crystal and the walls and floor were of shiny polished obsidian. Countless oak shelves lined the circular room and they contained array of objects, curious and strange. One shelf overflowed with bottles and vials of multicolored liquids, another contained jars of herbs. Each item was meticulously labeled. Another wall held cases and cases of books and scrolls.

Not far from the magical library lay a gigantic desk. Made of an exotic black wood, it gleamed with silver highlights. At the far end of the room I saw a glass door to a massive balcony that appeared to be twice the size of the chamber. The golden moon was waxing, bathing obsidian in a fiery light.

My eyes darted around, trying to take in every detail of the place. I knew I was gaping like a jackass, but I couldn't help it. Zareth put a hand on her shoulder and I jumped.

"What do you think?"

"It's... it's...." I stumbled, searching for the proper word to do this place justice. "Incredible."

"Thank you." He replied warmly.

Elation filled my being. My lame response pleased him.

Zareth spoke a few more soft words of magic and a large chair in a corner floated over to rest before the desk. He walked over to the desk and pulled out the chair behind it. He sat and gestured for me to take the other chair.

He looked regal and powerful with his midnight velvet robes, the cowl shadowing his face and his dangerous staff resting nearby. Moisture pooled between my thighs as attraction hummed through my body at the sight of him. *What the hell is wrong with me?*

I forced my rubbery legs to cooperate and made my way to the chair. Velvety and large, it seemed to swallow me when I sat. I appreciated the chance to rest after the climb up the stairs.

A decanter of ice water materialized before us and he poured two glasses.

We sipped our water in silence and though I appreciated the relief for my parched throat, anticipation built in my chest as I waited for him to speak.

At last, he began. "Before we start, I would like you to tell me what exactly you perceive magic to be."

I considered my words before replying. "Well, in my world— I mean, the Earth realm— they say people generally only use a percentage of their brains. So that leads me to believe magic is merely exercising parts of the remaining percent."

A few years back I'd told Sylvis my theory one drunken night. She thought it was pretty cool. "For example, I've always thought that gravity is just density of molecules, y'know like the molecular density is greater in water than in air and that's why you can float better on water than on air. So, I believe telekinesis is when one is able to emit an electromagnetic force from their brain to gather molecules around an object and bringing them closer together so the object can float, and stuff."

Zareth remained silent for a while. He sat and stared at me with the strangest look on his face. I squirmed under his scrutiny. Was he looking at me the same way that my grade-school classmates used to? Like I was a freak?

At last, he nodded. "I don't believe that I've ever before heard a more accurate assumption. Did you come up with all this theory on your own?"

"Um...yeah..." My finger traced the desk's smooth surface. "I had a science-geek phase in middle school and it kinda stuck with me."

Zareth chuckled. "You can discuss your theories with me anytime. I'm sure I'll find them quite interesting. This one is apt. Magic is merely molecular manipulation."

A smile crept to my lips. I felt like we shared a certain camaraderie. It had been so long since I'd been able to talk about magic with anyone. I wondered if my mom would have liked him.

Shaking off the ever-returning shadow of grief, I focused on the subject at hand. "But you wear amulets and say magic words. Where do amulets and chanting come in if my theory about magic is true?"

"Ah yes, that is a good point." He picked up a rock on the desk— tiger's eye, it looked like— and ran his thumb across its polished surface. "Chanting is a more straightforward way of meditation and channeling one's energy to produce magic. It is an important aid to concentration and in combat situations, it's useful to frighten and distract the enemy, much like a war cry."

"Wow. I never thought of it that way." I leaned forward, invigorated with new knowledge. "What about stones and crystals and amulets?"

His brow arched. "Can't you guess?"

He acted as if the answer was obvious, but it still took me a moment to come up with a guess. "Do they have anything to do with electricity or magnetism?"

"You are correct, Xochitl."

I shivered at the sound of him saying my name.

He didn't notice. "Just as copper and gold are efficient at conducting certain types of electricity, others are good at conducting electricity within the brain. Each kind of stone or crystal puts off a different frequency. Each one can aid in specific use. When you combine that frequency with your own, you can amplify it. We use such stones to make a spell come faster and easier or to enhance its effect. We can also use certain crystals to store magical energy for later use." Zareth scooted his chair back and stood. "Shall we begin?"

"Sure," I answered with more confidence than I felt. What if I screwed up and accidentally turned him into a frog or something? *Could* I turn someone into a frog?

"First, make a fireball," he instructed before I could go on a tangent of questions.

Confused as to why he was having me do something I already knew, I held out my palm and summoned my signature purple flame. I focused more of my will to shape it into a ball.

"You have to learn endurance. I want you to hold that flame as long as you can."

It proved to be more difficult than I expected, but with a little extra concentration, I held the flame in my palm for an entire five minutes.

"Well done."

I warmed at his approval. The lessons continued and he taught me the basics of meditation and herbs and gave me a brief tour of his library of spell books. I learned that the color of robes a mage wore determined the level of their power, like the belts in martial arts. Black robes were the most powerful and rare. He then taught me how to shield, which was easy to do, but hard to maintain.

"When shielding," Zareth lectured, "people often make the mistake of using their own internal energy to create the barrier, which drains them. The key is to use the energy around you to feed the shield."

It kinda tickled. By the time the lesson was over I was tired, but exhilarated and more than ready for the feast.

"You've done very well. Now shall we go purchase your robes and supplies?"

I perked up. "Shopping in another world? Hell yeah!"

A dozen guards waited at the gates. They wore dark blue robes with official-looking crests embroidered on their lapels and wielding short staffs like clubs.

In unison they bowed to Zareth and me before surrounding us in formation, flanking us from all sides as they led us down the path. None of them said anything. I wondered if they'd taken a vow of silence or something.

As we entered the village, everyone stared, which was fine because I was staring back. It wasn't exactly Daigon Alley from the *Harry Potter* books, but still impressive. A striking combination of modern and old world mingled before my eyes. People mixed jeans and tunics in an appealing combination. Electric lights illuminated shops with elaborately carved eaves and latticework.

Cats darted out from pavilions and alleys to purr and rub against my legs, garnering more attention from passersby. I grinned at the return of a constant in my life. *Friends!* Good thing Isis was used to me smelling like other cats and didn't get as jealous as she used to.

Zareth nudged me. "Your shield is wavering."

The people gave up all pretense of minding their own business and circled around us. "It's the Lord of Storm and Shadow!"

Zareth rubbed the bridge of his nose and looked uncomfortable. I felt sorry for him. Did he have issues with crowds? My friend Akasha hated crowds so badly she had trouble breathing.

Before the curiosity seekers got closer, he guided me into a shop.

I stared at the array of potions, stones, powders, books and bunches of dried herbs. Excitement fired my belly at the prospect of learning how to use this stuff.

Instead of a kindly old wizard, the shopkeeper was a middle-aged woman with a sloppy bun and major frown lines. Despite her disheveled appearance, she exuded an air of competence and control over her domain. I bet no one wanted to get on her bad side.

Zareth greeted her with a slight bow. "Hello, Mordaine."

She eyed him with an odd combination of wariness and greed. He must shop there a lot. "Ah, Lord Amotken, have you finally decided to take an apprentice?"

Zareth nodded, but didn't introduce me.

Mordaine's gaze flicked to me briefly. "What color of robes?"

"She hasn't been tested yet. She might be powerful enough for black, once she's been trained," he told her.

"I will be the judge of that." She beckoned me forward.

Zareth inclined his head in assent and I approached the counter, hiding a pleased smile that Zareth deemed me worthy of black robes.

"Hold out your hand," the shopkeeper ordered brusquely.

Eager to win her approval, I obeyed and she swept her palm over mine. "Your main element is fire. Let me see your flame."

I grinned and formed a fireball in my hand. It was so wonderful not to hide my magic.

She didn't look as impressed as I'd hoped. "Why is it purple?"

I shrugged. "I like purple."

"Hmmm..." Her lips pursed. "Now make that book float."

She ran me through a few other tests, making miscellaneous things float, and shrinking stuff, which I sucked at. I did okay for my first try and wondered why Mom didn't show me in the first place.

"It seems your favorite color was prophetic." Mordaine handed me a dark purple velvet robe. "You may give her the black when she has finished her training and can pass the Conclave examinations."

Directing me to a stool, she tossed the robe over my head. The thing was huge. The hood obscured my vision and when I threw it off, the hem pooled on the floor. The woman withdrew a wand from her voluminous robes and flicked it around me as she hummed a melodic tune. The robe shrank until it fit me perfectly.

I turned on the stool to look in the mirror, admiring my reflection. "I wish clothes shopping at home was this easy."

The woman made a small noise that might have been agreement. I turned to Zareth. "How do I look?"

His gaze swept over me and I thought I saw a flicker of heat.

"It shall do," he said curtly before turning back to the other wares in the store. He selected some herbs and crystals, a few books, and a small velvet bag with a drawstring.

"Do I get a nifty staff like yours?" I admired the staffs behind the counter.

"Not yet."

"Awww." I pouted. "Why not?"

He gave me a stern frown, unaffected by my puppy-dog eyes. "You will have one when you don't need one."

When the shopkeeper rang up the purchases on the oddest looking cash register I'd seen, Zareth handed her some coins and put everything in the tiny bag, which shouldn't have held more than a few crystals.

"Bad ass!" I whispered as he tied the bag around my waist. The feather light brush of his fingers and the heady scent of his nearness made me dizzy.

The corners of his mouth lifted as he pulled my guitar out of the bag on his belt and placed it in my new bag, along with the amp. I didn't know he'd grabbed them.

"They will want you to play at the feast," he said, and extended his arm to escort me out.

My fingers sank into his soft velvet sleeve and I peeked up at him from beneath my lashes. First he'd taken me shopping and now we were going to a feast. It was almost like a date.

The minute we exited the shop, a man charged toward Zareth, wielding what looked like a garden shovel.

"What have you done with my boy?" he roared.

Without thinking, I darted in front of Zareth.

Chapter Eleven

Xochitl

Zareth snaked his arm around my waist and thrust me behind him. With a muttered word and a gesture, the shovel flew from the attacker's arms.

I blinked through a haze of relief. *Oh yeah. I wasn't the only one with magic around here.* This would take getting used to.

Losing the weapon didn't faze the guy. He continued forward, pummeling Zareth's shield with calloused fists.

Zareth froze him in midair just as the head guard ran up. "I am sorry, my lord, I will arrest this ruffian at once."

"No, I want to hear what he has to say." He turned back to the frozen man. "Who is your boy and what have I supposedly done with him?"

"Terrance Miller, my only son." The man's voice strained through his stiff lips. "He was on his way to your tower to speak with you about the disappearances of others from the village and I haven't seen him since. Have you taken them all?"

Zareth's gaze darted to the guard. "Why wasn't I informed about these missing people?"

"I reported it to Rickard," he said, as if that cleared him of everything.

I shook my head. *Way to pass the buck, dude.*

Zareth growled and thrust him aside. He turned back to the first man and knelt, placing a hand over his heart. "I swear, on my father's crown, I had no hand in the disappearance of your son or any other citizen of my lands. I vow by the light of the moons to do everything in my power to find them." He then released the man. "You may go."

The guard protested as the man gave a hasty bow and picked up his shovel. "But he attacked a high sorcerer! And a royal at that! That's a capital offense."

"He didn't attack me. I stopped him before he was able."

"But he must be punished!"

Zareth seized the guard's shoulders, his teeth bared in a snarl. "Need I remind you that I am the lord of this kingdom and the firstborn heir to the throne of this entire realm? It is my decision to make and I say he may go." He stared the guard down, lightning flickering in his eyes, and didn't release him until an audible whimper broke through. "Now I must see my apprentice to the feast. Tell Rickard that I will speak with him afterward."

The guard gave a reluctant bow and slunk off like a dog with its tail between its legs. The other guards remained expressionless aside from their hands tightening on their ministaffs.

Zareth took my arm and led me down another road to a large pavilion in the village square. Glowing orbs lit the area almost bright as day. Aside from the lanterns, patio heaters warmed the place along with a few roaring fireplaces. Dozens of long tables awaited, loaded with platters and giant bowls of various dishes of food. My stomach growled at the delicious smells. Other tables were arranged with bowls, plates and napkins. Some were larger and more elaborate than others, like a medieval great hall seating people according to rank.

Over a hundred people sat at the tables. As we approached, they stood and shrank back from Zareth before they bowed.

Zareth ignored their trepidation and moved me forward with a gentle hand at the small of my back. "People of Raijin, I present to you: Xochitl Leonine, daughter of Kerainne Leonine."

"And Mephistopheles," someone muttered in the background.

The seneschal stepped in front of us. "She is the Lioness of Light." Though he'd been a distant blur last night, I recognized his booming voice.

The crowd rushed forward, peering at me with avid curiosity and asking so many questions that I couldn't make them out.

One woman broke out of the crowd and knelt before me, just out of the guards' reach. "Milady, will you do it? Will you bring back the sun?"

"I'll try," I stuttered, unused to this kind of adulation. Celebrity awe was one thing, but this was another.

She beamed like I'd promised to not only herald the dawn, but to conjure some rainbows as well. "You will. It is foretold."

"She doesn't look like a lioness." A kid eyed me skeptically. "She's just a short girl."

"She's the daughter of the last princess of the luminites," his mother told him. "Their sigil was a mountain lion, remember?"

Questions bombarded me in a torrent of desperation and curiosity. Zareth tried to pull me away, but I walked over to them, as close as the guards allowed. Delgarias was right. I needed to see who I was saving. Besides, I was just as curious about them as they were of me.

Earth fascinated them, especially the young ones. To my surprise, a few stores dealt exclusively in imports from my home planet. Everything from clothes, to music, books, and movies were sold. After answering questions about cars and video games, and assuring them that I was with The Lord of Storm and Shadow willingly, I tried to ask them about their world.

The guards pressed the people back as the seneschal cleared his throat. "Tonight we feast in honor of the Lioness of Light."

He guided Zareth and me to the most lavish table. The moment I sat, a trail of servants came to me, each holding a tray of delicious looking dishes. I accepted a little of everything until my plate was too full for more.

"I am so sorry we don't have more variety, my lady," Rickard said as he heaped his plate with what looked like ham. "With the rationing and dwindling seasonal fare, we were only able to manage a tenth deserving for a lady of your rank."

"This is more than enough," I assured him. "Everything smells delicious. I'll be lucky if I can taste it all. This didn't deplete the stores too much did it? And how do your store the food? I don't want the fresh stuff to go to waste."

"How caring you are. To answer your question, we have special containers that suspend the food in time." The woman at my left patted my hand. "I am Jeanette, Duchess of Kinsen. I am honored to meet our savior ...and to see Prince Amotken out of his tower. We're seldom graced with his presence." She glanced over him with a teasing smile.

The duchess chattered on about Zareth's kingdom and described the politics of his area and other nearby kingdoms, but I couldn't concentrate. My mind spun at the fact that they could freeze things in time. Would a hundred year old soufflé stay fresh and fluffy?

Eyeing the food with new appreciation, I dug in. Some of the fruits were familiar, like oranges and raspberries, but I tried a pale blue berry I'd never seen on Earth. Tear-drop shaped, the berry tasted like a cross between a huckleberry and a blackcap. They were called "sky tears" and I couldn't get enough of them. I also gorged myself on crab legs and some glorious fish swimming in butter and herbs.

"The Piscani on the coast keep us well supplied in sea fare." A man explained. "They are one of Zareth's prime allies since his power over storms gives them safe voyages." He frowned. "Though it is very unlikely for Stefan to attack by sea."

He was right. I pictured the map I'd studied on my second night here. Piscanos lay to the northwest, whereas Boreaus, Stefan's kingdom, was northeast, with Raijin and the country of Niji between them, where King Taranis had resided.

"Who else is allied with Zareth, I mean, Prince Amotken?" I addressed him by his rightful title like Jeanette had. I'd had little interest in government class in school, but now that I was thrown into the thick of otherworldly politics, I was fascinated.

"Not many. The Tolonquan tribes support him, Laran, and possibly, the faelin in Shellandria," Jeanette said. "But it's not as dismal as it sounds. Stefan only has the Wurraks, and a few others. The rest of the world is neutral. A conflict between two potential heirs has never happened before, so most hope the problem will solve itself when they duel and you bring back the sun and crown the king. However, some are eager for war..."

"Enough talk about war," Rickard cut in. "This is to be an evening of celebration." As if summoned, the servants returned to clear away the plates and silverware, leaving the glasses. "It is time for music and dancing."

"I hear you play an electric guitar," Jeanette said. "Will you play it for us and sing?"

"Yes," the others shouted. "Sing for us!"

I looked at Zareth. He nodded assent and gestured toward a raised dais. The people gathered around, staring in ravenous expectation. For the first time, except for choir class and karaoke, I was alone onstage.

I didn't like it.

I reached into my bottomless pouch and pulled out a jar of herbs. Laughter broke out at my amateur mistake, but it was good-natured. Cursing, I rummaged through the sack, concentrating on summoning my instrument. This time I withdrew my Dave Mustaine signature Jackson King V. Akasha and Silas gave it to me for Christmas during the height of my *Megadeth* obsession, along with custom gear for the rest of the band in our senior year of high school. Later I got an autograph from Dave himself.

It took a few more tries to get the amp out. I had hold of the handle, but the angle was wrong, so I set the bag on the floor and wrestled it out.

"That's where object summoning comes in handy." Zareth chuckled.

His nearness at the foot of the stage eased my tension.

The seneschal directed me to a Honda generator, which looked out of place in this magical world. The crowd ooohed and ahhed as I tuned the guitar. I hid a smile.

Taking a deep breath, I struck the first chords of "Retribution," our first song to hit the billboard charts. I put my usual mischievous attitude and moves into it, but without Beau's thrumming bass and Aurora's rapid-fire drums, the song seemed hollow and empty. And though I was able to alternate between my rhythm riffs and Sylvis's lead solos, it lacked the same impact without us playing together.

Despite my diminished performance, everyone clapped and cheered and begged for another. I couldn't refuse, but I couldn't bear to play another one of our songs all by my lonesome. Instead, I played one of my favorite *Megadeth* songs: "A Tout Le Monde."

That one went a little better. Still, once I struck the last chord, I declined to play another and stepped off the dais. The audience looked disappointed, but I couldn't bear to be up there alone anymore. Ignoring their frowns, I focused on getting my guitar and amp back in the bottomless pouch.

After the applause faded, someone hooked up a music player and low strains of some classical-sounding tune played. People coupled up and danced.

Zareth stood alone in a shadowy corner, watching me with an intensity that brought back that tingly sensation.

No one talked with him and the butler-guy didn't even offer him wine. He was the lord of this place. How long had people been treating him like a pariah? He had to be lonely. I wanted to hug him, but I didn't want to embarrass him.

However, I knew a way I could show everyone that I didn't think Zareth was a villain.

Even as my stomach rolled like I was on a rollercoaster, I approached and gave him the same words he'd given me the first night we met. "Dance with me."

He quirked an eyebrow at my command and my cheeks heated.

I stammered, "But, could you do that spell that makes me do it right?"

He was silent so long I thought he'd refuse. Then he inclined his head and took my hand.

Now that I was expecting it, the dance was exhilarating. I savored the feel of his touch, one hand on my waist, the other entwined with my fingers. The heat of his body emanated from his robes, tempting me to press closer. I'd been bereft of touch for so long that it was becoming a drug.

I like him. The realization roared in my head as we swayed and turned. Okay, I more than *liked* him. No longer could I hold onto my anger.

When the music ended, I closed my eyes and held onto him for just a moment longer, reluctant to break away and return to the world.

With aching slowness, Zareth released me. "Thank you," he whispered.

A few people knelt before us. Zareth's eyes narrowed, his features hardening. Was he upset that the others didn't bow?

Then a dreaded voice spoke behind me. "How kind of you, brother, to keep my princess entertained before I came to collect her."

I whirled around to see Stefan striding toward us, a smarmy grin on his Disney-perfect face.

Gasps sounded all around. "The Winter Prince!"

I rolled my eyes. "Steve, we've been over this. I'm not going anywhere with you."

I heard a few nervous titters and incredulous whispers. "Steve?" a woman echoed, sounding amused.

Stefan glared at me, eyes like chips of ice. "When you are my bride, you will pay for your insolence."

Gasps and a few loud whispers sounded at his words. Some people were smart enough to step back.

"That's it. I'm going to kick your ass." I lunged forward, but Zareth's arm snaked around my waist, pulling me against him.

"Get out, Stefan. You are forbidden from my lands." His voice held more commanding wrath than I'd heard before.

The Winter Prince sneered. "But you have something that is mine."

"I am *not* a *thing*," I shrieked as my back gave a twinge of pain. "And I don't belong to you, colostomy bag."

More exclamations and murmurs erupted from our audience. "She has chosen the Lord of Storm and Shadow," one woman whispered so loud she may have been shouting.

Before I could turn to her and explain that I was autonomous, Stefan pulled out his staff, which looked like some kind of Eighteenth century walking stick. A blaze of light catapulted at Zareth, knocking his staff out of his hands. Zareth shot a concentrated bolt of lightning from his fingers, taking care not to hurt the spectators. Stefan had no such care, and an agonized cry rent the air as a woman's arm was sliced by a shard of ice.

Zareth whirled around to his guards. "Get the people back!"

As everyone scrambled away, Stefan moved to attack Zareth from behind, but I intercepted his icy blast with such a hot gout of flame that scalding steam blasted his face. I took that moment to dart forward and kick him in the face. At least he was short enough to reach.

He lunged forward to grab me, but I jumped back and Zareth seized me. He thrust me behind him and pointed his staff at Stefan. He must have recovered it while I was beating up his brother. Muttering some incantation in his silken language, his staff glowed a soft blue. His eyes flickered with electric light, then he paused, one hand poised with heart-pounding stillness.

Stefan's fingers moved and ice crystals danced in the air around his fingertips. It would have looked pretty if not for his deadly intent.

My breath caught in my throat. *Do something!* I cried in silence.

Zareth's hand swept down and he thrust his staff forward. A blast of white light shot out and Stefan vanished.

I stared at the frozen spot as I recovered my breath. "What did you do to him?"

"I teleported him to the nearest pond."

"Damn, that was just in time. He was about to blast you with more ice!" My heart still pounded in dread that he'd be hurt.

His lips curved in a wicked smile. "That was the point."

I gasped as his strategy became clear. "You timed your spell so he'd freeze in the pond. Do you think it killed him?"

He shook his head and pointed. "No. His minions are on their way to get him out as we speak. Look over there."

My gaze followed the direction of his finger. Shadowed figures darted past the trees, growing smaller as they ran further away.

I laughed at the mental image of Stefan's minions chipping him out of the pond with ice picks. My amusement died as I realized I hadn't known they were there until Zareth pointed them out. How many had there been? What if they'd joined the fight?

Zareth seemed to be thinking the same because his smile faded and he turned to face his seneschal. "Who let Stefan and his entourage past the village walls?"

"I'm not certain, my lord." He looked down at his feet. "But I will look into the matter immediately."

"See that you do." His attention returned to the rest of the people. "Who was hurt?"

A woman stepped forward and bowed. "Only Vivian and Thomas, my lord. She has a cut on her arm and Thomas got a touch of frostbite. They were taken to the healer already."

Another woman approached with tremulous eyes. "I owe you an apology, milord... I thought you sinister and cruel. But it is the Winter Prince who is wicked. You kept us safe from him. You should be the true king."

She went to her knees and everyone else followed suit.

Zareth stared at them in silence. He looked flustered.

He inclined his head to his people. "Thank you for the wonderful feast. You have done Xochitl and me great honor." He took my hand. "Now we must retire."

As I waved goodbye and said my thanks, Zareth raised his staff in the air. I blinked and then we were in his tower.

"Damn, that was fun!" I couldn't sit down yet, still amped from the feast. "We totally kicked his ass!"

Zareth didn't respond. He stood by the fireplace, staring at the flames.

"What's wrong?"

He turned to face me, jaw tight in apparent anger. "You shouldn't have been involved in the fight."

My jaw dropped. "What? I saved your ass. He was going to attack you from behind."

"I was perfectly capable of deflecting him." He folded his arms across his chest. "And then you recklessly got close to him."

I matched his scowl. "He had it coming."

His long strides crossed the room to meet me. "And what if he'd dispelled your magic again, or teleported you away to his lands? That was his goal."

I shrugged. "Well he didn't because I was too busy kicking the crap out of him."

His lips twisted in a mirthless smirk. "And he was taking your blows to keep you distracted while he pulled a transport crystal from his pocket."

I froze. "He was?"

He nodded, brows drawn together. "Next time, stay back and let me deal with him. You are too young and inexperienced to engage a high sorcerer in combat."

His scornful tone made my chest tight in humiliation. "Will you quit griping at me because of my age? Just because you're God knows how old doesn't mean you know everything. I was handling him just fine."

He seized me so suddenly my heart stopped.

Wrapping those long fingers around both of my wrists, he lifted me off the ground until his mouth was inches from mine. "You may not be able to feel fear, but you should have some respect for my authority."

"Why?" I struggled not to lose myself in his electric eyes.

His grip tightened around my wrists, almost enough to hurt. "Because I am older, stronger, and far more powerful than you."

"But you can't kill me," I argued, my head swimming and stomach fluttering at the scent of rose petals and spices emanating from his robes. "And I'm sure you don't want to hurt me."

"Yes, but I can give or withhold knowledge, I can overpower you, or I can..." He trailed off, staring into my eyes until I was lost in his gaze.

His other hand splayed against my back, pulling me tight against his body. He released my wrists and threaded his fingers through my hair as his lips came down on mine. The utter savagery of the kiss startled me while at the same time made me dizzy with elation.

Yes. This is what I wanted.

I gripped his shoulders for support. I didn't understand where his passionate outburst came from, but I didn't care. A moan escaped my throat as I tangled my fingers in soft, silky hair and gave myself up to the ecstasy of his kiss.

His tongue slipped between my parted lips to caress mine. Tremors coursed through my body as I echoed his movements, reveling in the new sensations. I wrapped my legs around his waist with a harsh intake of breath as I felt his hard length pressing against my core through the fabric of our robes. A throbbing ache pulsed between my thighs. I ground my hips against his hardness, consumed with need for more of him.

Zareth's mouth parted from mine, making me whimper.

"No," he gasped raggedly as if he were having trouble breathing.

The word doused over me, leaving me cold and bereft.

With painful reluctance, my legs relaxed their grip around him and I allowed him to set me back on my feet. I swayed before catching my balance, my head swimming with dizziness.

"This never should have happened." His voice was quiet. *Final.*

"Why?" Frustration roiled within me. "Don't you want me?" It certainly felt like he did.

"I do, but sex is far more significant for my kind... as well as yours. The consequences are heavier." He looked like he would elaborate, but then he sighed and shook his head. "I need rest, and you must sleep in your own chamber from now on. It was a mistake to bring you to mine."

Before I could reply, he turned and walked away.

Chapter Twelve

Zareth

After tasting Xochitl's lips and feeling her in his arms, Zareth went mad with desire. His hydra fed on the lust, urging him in its own way to continue the insanity that possessed him to kiss her. He wished he could blame that impulse on the demon. It had taken every ounce of his centuries-built self-control not to tear open her robes and taste and touch every inch of her body.

Hoping a distraction would abate his rampant desire, he took the lilac branch he'd cut the other night and sanded the wood until his hands were raw and his eyes burned from exhaustion.

Yet she still haunted his dreams. The feel of her in his arms, the taste of her lips, his hardness pressed against her softness, so close yet provokingly out of reach...

His eyes snapped open in a fever and he returned to work on the branch.

When she met him downstairs for breakfast, the blush on her cheeks made him want to ravage her all over again. He didn't trust himself to speak, so he gave her a quick nod and served them porridge with honey.

They ate in silence, Zareth's flesh tingling every time he felt her gaze on him.

Xochitl finished her orange juice and looked up at him. "What is the lesson plan for today?"

"I have to meet with the seneschal about the missing people. You will remain here and study." There was no way he could handle an entire day in her presence. "I would like you to start with *Principles of Elemental Magic* and *Ground Spells*. They're both in English. I've placed them in the library for you.

"Okay." She gazed back down at the table, looking so vulnerable that he longed to pull her into his arm and kiss her. "Zareth? You're not mad at me, are you?"

He shook his head. "No. It was I who was in the wrong last eve."

Her wide, sorrowful eyes threatened to drown him. "But—"

"I must go." Before her beauty could torment him further, he teleported to the seneschal's manse.

The butler escorted him to the study, where Rickard awaited. "My lord, it is a pleasure to see you."

Zareth did not return the sentiment. "I want to thank you for organizing the feast."

Rickard smiled and shook his head. "No, that was mostly the Duchess's doing."

Zareth wasn't surprised. Of all his vassals, Jeanette always had her fingers in the thick of things. But he had to admire her efficiency and organization. He wished that she could be his high seneschal rather than the lackluster Rickard. His father, King Taranis, had appointed him twenty years ago, and he used to be very efficient, but ever since the king died, his dedication to his responsibilities seemed to have dwindled.

It was past time to begin looking for a replacement. Pity the Duchess had her own responsibilities.

He leaned back in his chair and set down his coffee cup. "Why was I not informed that my people have been disappearing?"

The seneschal shrugged. "I thought you had higher concerns."

Anger spiraled in his gut at the passive response. "What could be a higher concern than my people?"

Rickard opened his mouth and closed it.

Zareth sighed and ran a hand through his hair. "How many?"

"I'm uncertain as to the exact number, my lord, I think maybe a dozen?"

A dozen? Zareth's fists clenched in mounting rage. Why in the fates had no one told him? Memories of the man who'd tried to attack him flashed through his mind. The agony in the man's eyes as he'd accused Zareth of taking his son. His chest tightened. "And have you found any information regarding where they could have gone?"

The seneschal shook his head, still looking unconcerned. "No, my lord. I had assumed that most went to Earth to see the sun and perhaps a few were traitors who sided with your brother."

Lightning crackled from Zareth's fingertips. "I will not tolerate assumptions. I want facts. I want a detailed list of who has gone missing. I want their families interviewed. I want to know who saw them last and where. Can you do that for me? Or do I need to appoint a new seneschal?"

Rickard blanched. "No! That is, I will attend to this matter right away, my lord."

"See that you do." Unable to bear being in the same room with the simpering fool, he walked back to his tower to burn off his anger.

As he walked, Zareth scanned the village. Some of the people he passed on the main road bowed to him, others cringed and fled back into their shops and dwellings as they always had. Either way, their faces were drawn with tension, eyes reflecting fear in the lantern light.

One cottage caught his eye. Dead leaves covered the porch all the way up to the front door. Foreboding building in his chest, Zareth approached the window and peered inside.

He saw furniture and other miscellaneous belongings all in order, except for a tin ewer that had been knocked to the floor.

A dead dog lay next to the sofa, the outline of its protruding ribs visible even in the meager light coming in from the street lanterns.

"Maybe they fled to Earth to see the sun," Rickard had speculated.

"Why would they neglect to bring their belongings? Or at least let their dog out?" he muttered. Not to mention the fact that anyone separated from Aisthanesthai too long would die.

Someone had taken them. And his people suspected him. He used to prefer their fear of him. Yet now, remembering the wild eyes of the man who'd tried to attack him, and his resigned grief, he realized the cost was too high.

Zareth's shoulders straightened with resolve. Not only would he prove to his people that he was not responsible for the disappearances, he would find the bitch or bastard who was.

As he continued down the road, he noticed more leaf-covered porches. Far more than a dozen. His teeth ground. Rickard's obliviousness to the situation was even more severe than he'd assumed.

Still, it wouldn't hurt to be more vigilant when next they visited Earth and see if he could sense any magic of Aisthanesthai.

Once back in his tower he found Xochitl curled up in the library, studying one of the texts he assigned her.

"When will you teach me how to teleport?" She peeked at him over the pages. "Or to be able to read other languages?"

He bit back a smile at her enthusiasm. "We should work further on your shielding first." Before the radiance of her essence tempted him further.

She sighed. "Okay, but I suck at it."

He frowned at her self-doubt. "You'll get better. You just need to focus on bringing the magic through you before you work it around you."

They worked for an hour and she did improve. Once her first tremulous shield covered her from head to toe, a measure of his rampant awareness abated, though not enough to quench a lingering ache of desire.

"Very good. I want you to concentrate on maintaining that." He leaned on his staff. "How would you like to visit your friends today?"

She jumped and her shield flickered a moment before settling back in place. "I would! Aurora would be a lot less grumpy if I got some vocal tracks done."

And indeed she was. The band was already in the studio when Xochitl texted them after they emerged through the portal. After restoring her car to its natural size, they took a careening drive through the hilly streets to the studio. Zareth paused outside the doors and cast out his senses to the rainy air. Aside from Xochitl and her friends inside the building, he only detected one other being with magic... and he had a feeling who that was— or at least who had sent him.

The band greeted Xochitl with hugs and exclamations and offered Zareth tentative nods. Aurora then ushered her into a room and wouldn't let him follow. Instead she brought him into another room full of large tables covered in buttons and sliders. He gave the devices a curious glance before he saw Xochitl in the other room behind a large pane of glass.

Aurora handed him a set of headphones. "You can listen if you want, but don't talk or do anything distracting."

He nodded and put them on, marveling as Xochitl's potent voice filled his ears. Zareth opened his hydra and fed, remaining transfixed until she fell silent.

Aurora frowned and pressed the microphone button to talk to her. "That was okay, but it needs more anger. Let's do it again."

Xochitl bit her lip and nodded as she strode to the opposite end of the prison-like chamber and grabbed a water bottle.

"I thought she sounded wonderful," Zareth argued.

The drummer gave him a cross look. "You're not helping." Something in his expression made her soften. "Look, it may sound perfect to a regular listener, but those of us in the business know that she can do better, and our listeners deserve to hear the best from us."

"I understand." And he did. He had the urge to tell her about Xochitl's magic lessons and how she was a quick learner, but impulsive.

Aurora gave him her first genuine smile and flicked another button on the console. "Ready, Xoch'?"

Xochitl took her place before the microphone and gave them a thumbs-up. Aurora turned the music back on and Xochitl's ethereal voice filled Zareth's ears. Enraptured at the sound, his gaze studied the curve of her jaw, the shape of her lips, the intensity in her amber eyes as she sang. She opened her eyes and looked at him. For a moment, the world fell away and only she existed.

Her voice wavered and she cursed and yanked off her headphones. "I'm sorry, 'Ror. I fucked that one up. I don't know what's wrong with me today."

"I do." Aurora grinned and pointed her thumb at Zareth. "He's distracting you." She turned to him. "Why don't you go get us some coffee? There's a really good place around the corner."

He chuckled. "Trying to get rid of me?"

"I know that if I had a handsome man watching me drum in the studio, I'd be messing up all over the place." Her lips curved in a slight smile before her features composed back to her usual air of authority. She pulled out her wallet and counted out money. "I'll take plain black coffee with a lot of sugar, Sylvis and Beau will take Chai lattes and Xochitl will have a Red Bull. Just get her a twelve-ounce, though. Anything bigger, and she'll be up all night. And you can get whatever you want."

Zareth took the money and bit back a laugh. He, a high sorcerer and future king of an entire world had been relegated to running errands like a servant. Still, Aurora was right. If his presence was impeding Xochitl's work, he would do best to stay out of the way. Despite her wariness of him, he couldn't help but respect the drummer. Under her strict and abrasive exterior, she was adept at command while still nurturing.

He headed out of the studio and into the drizzle. As much as he disliked Earth, it was a relief to see the sun peeking through the gray clouds and to be away from all the politics and Stefan's scheming. He thought back on his talk with his seneschal.

Could it be true that the missing people had moved to Earth? Did they miss the sun so much that they'd give up their magic, and inevitably, their lives? And if so, who among them even had the power to pass through the portals?

As if summoned by the thought, he once more detected a magical presence. Shoving his hands in his pockets, he continued walking, allowing the mage to follow him. Stepping around the corner to the rear side of the building, he waited until a shadow fell across the pavement. Zareth reached out and grabbed his pursuer by the throat and slammed him against the wall.

A mage struggled in Zareth's grasp, likely a blue robe from the power his hydra detected. "Stefan sent you to spy on me, I presume?"

The mage nodded. Zareth wasn't surprised. After all, that was how he'd found Xochitl in the first place. His brother was one to have others do all the work for him.

"Well you can tell him he needn't bother. Xochitl is mine. And if he keeps sending spies, I will make him regret it."

"Begging your pardon, m'lord, I'd rather you kill me." He looked up at him with wide fearful eyes. "If the Winter Prince is displeased with my report, he'd do much worse."

Zareth knew Stefan was cruel and selfish, but something about the absolute terror in the man's eyes gave him pause. "What would he do?"

The spy shook his head, his lips twisted in a parody of a smile. "I'll not be aiding you that far. Now you had best end me quick. We don't want to attract the attention of the plebeians."

Zareth regarded the little man who stood with his eyes squeezed shut, ready for his execution. He knew he should kill him. Leaving any of Stefan's people alive would be a poor decision. Glancing around for passersby, he withdrew his staff from his pocket and pointed it at the mage.

He vanished on the spot... a thousand miles from any portal back to Aisthanesthai.

Zareth pocketed his staff and headed back around the building back to the sidewalk and to the coffee shop. After ordering the band's requested beverages, he got himself a coffee that was mostly chocolate and bought muffins for everyone.

Sylvis and Beau visibly warmed to him as they accepted their victuals. Aurora took her coffee, gave him a brisk nod, and marched over to talk to the sound technicians.

A wicked smile curved Xochitl's lips as he bent down to hand her the Red Bull. Before he could react, she tangled her fingers in his hair and pulled his head down for a kiss. Electric heat crackled through his body, stealing his breath.

Her mouth trailed to his ear and she whispered, "When undercover cops are trying to bust a drug deal, they might have to smoke a little weed."

"Hmmm," was all he could manage.

What did police or "weed" have to do with the hot feel of her mouth on his? Desire spiraled through him until he gathered himself and interpreted her words. She had been making an analogy to their deception for her friends.

But did she truly need to go so far as to kiss him? She was playing with fire.

As Xochitl went back into the isolation room, it was torture to see her singing without being able to hear her. A sound technician gave him a disparaging look and gestured for him to step back.

He sat next to Beau, who seemed less wary around him. "How long have you known Xochitl?"

The bassist smiled. "Since freshman year in high school. She was my beard."

He coughed on his drink. "Your *what?*"

Beau grinned. "Being a gay in Northern Idaho was hard. She posed as my girlfriend until I was ready to come out." His expression sobered. "She and her mom took me in when my stepdad beat the shit out of me and kicked me out." Taking a deep breath, he continued, eyes wistful. "Her mom was an angel. She bandaged me up and comforted me like I was her own kid. I wish she could have adopted me, but instead she had a talk with my mom. I still don't know what she said to her, but shortly afterward, she left my stepfather. Things were better after that."

Silence hovered over them as Zareth pondered the young man's painful memories. "Yes, she told me about her mother. It was good of her to help you. I gather that her loss affected many."

Beau's jaw clenched as he looked at him. "Xochitl means the world to me. If you hurt her, I'll hurt you." His hazel eyes were hard as stone before softening. "Sorry to break out the testosterone, but it's just that you're the first boyfriend she's ever had. I don't count."

Zareth patted his shoulder intrigued by the flare of power that emanated from the young man at his declaration. "I understand."

Xochitl stepped out of the booth, a satisfied smile on her lips as she spoke with Aurora about her session. Then she and Sylvis went into another room with their guitars and the drummer joined him and Beau.

"Do you smoke weed?" she asked without preamble.

He thought of Xochitl's unexpected kiss and chuckled. "Not today."

Aurora shrugged and headed outside, Beau at her heels. He moved on to the room where Xochitl and Sylvis were playing. He couldn't hear them, but he could see them through the glass. Their fluid synchronicity was a wonder to behold. Even through the barrier of the soundproof walls, he could feel their joined magic undulating.

After they finished, Xochitl skipped out of the room to join him. "I hope Aurora wasn't too bitchy." She wrapped her arm around his waist. "She gets kinda militant when we're recording."

"She was fine." Unbidden, he caressed the ends of her hair. "I spent most of the time with Beau. He told me about how your mom helped him when his stepfather..." he trailed off, unwilling to voice such cruelty.

Her eyes grew distant and misty. "Yeah, she helped my friends whenever she could. I remember when mom brought a guy home back when she decided to try dating. Aurora was sleeping over and we were jamming in the living room. The guy freaked out on us. He thought all goth kids were Satan worshippers or something. But his biggest beef was with Aurora. He turned out to be a racist prick and he called her names even I won't repeat. He thought Aurora was Mom's daughter too. Instead of denying it, Mom bitch-slapped him and kicked him out. Then she held Aurora as she cried and said she would have been proud to have her as a daughter too."

Seeing her closeness with her friends and how protective they were of her, Zareth felt a pang of guilt for disrupting Xochitl's life. He'd only seen her as the key to saving his world. A crucial endeavor, but a means to an end nonetheless.

That realization left him in a ponderous silence for the rest of the afternoon. Even when they finished their work and headed to a nearby restaurant, he had little appetite despite the plethora of food that was now unavailable in his world.

Watching her devour crab legs and teriyaki clams like a woman starved deepened his remorse. She worked hard today, and doubtless labored just as much at all times with her musical career. And the moment he took her to his world he'd burdened her with a slew of new duties and obligations.

But there was nothing to be done about that. She had to save Aisthanesthai and she needed to be trained.

As they paid the bill and rose from the table, Zareth extended his hand to Xochitl. "Shall we go now?"

"Go?" Aurora cut in, dark eyes darting between them. "But you've been gone for two days! Aren't you coming back home?"

Xochitl gave him a nervous glance and shifted on her feet. "Well, ummm."

"We can stay at your house tonight, dearling." He was surprised at the words coming out of his mouth.

She gave him a grateful look. "Okay, but we should head back to your place early. I don't want Isis to run out of food."

They headed back to the house she shared with her friends, following Aurora's van. Once there, they dug into the fridge, which was full of beer and hard cider. Zareth asked to try one of the ciders. Aurora and Beau stared when Xochitl handed him one.

"Xochitl *never* shares her cider," Beau whispered in awe.

A warm feeling engulfed him at that news. They then sprawled out on the massive couches in the living room as Beau and Aurora passed a pipe around loaded with marijuana. It was called "sugar bud" in his world. Zareth sampled it and determined that better could be found in Shellandria.

When the pipe came to Xochitl, she passed it back to Aurora.

"You don't smoke?" Zareth asked.

She shook her head. "I used to once in awhile, but after I had a bad trip on a pot brownie in Amsterdam, I haven't touched it since."

The others nodded and soon Xochitl and her friends lapsed into a discussion on their day's progress and their plans for the next session.

Beau passed him the pipe again. "So, what did you think of seeing how we work in the studio?"

"Your music is incredible," he told them all. "Do you have a favorite song?"

"Not a favorite song so much as an important one," Sylvis said shyly. "It was a cover song, but if it weren't for us mastering it, we never would have gotten our big break. It literally changed our lives."

"What song was that?"

"'Stargazer' by *Rainbow*." They answered in unison.

Xochitl picked up the story. "We originally intended to play it for the school talent show. Even before that, the song had a big impact on us. We were practicing it in the school auditorium and the football coach heard us and made his team sit down and listen." She shook her head and smiled. "The football players were some of our biggest bullies, but the coach loved that song so much that he told his boys that if they messed with us again, they were off the team."

Her expression darkened before she looked down to avoid everyone's gazes. Zareth wondered if the team betrayed their word.

Sylvis took over the story. "Then we blew everyone out of the water during the talent show. We won, and later recorded 'Stargazer' on our demo."

Aurora took a sip of beer and tossed her braid over her shoulder. "As much as I think we did great on our original tracks, I'm pretty sure it was that song that got us our record deal. And it was definitely what put us at the top of the charts."

The gleam in their eyes when speaking of the song made him indelibly curious. "I'd like to hear it sometime."

All four nodded. They spent the next few hours lounging on the couch watching a movie that he assumed was supposed to be frightening, but instead was ludicrous. Xochitl and her friends transformed the idiocy into hilarity with their mocking remarks.

His hydra fed on their laughter... and his own. To his surprise, he enjoyed himself. However, once they retired to Xochitl's room, the torture began. After all, they couldn't betray their lie by having him sleep in a guest room.

"Won't your powers fade being away from your world so long?" she asked worriedly as he lay down beside her on the bed, which was narrower than his.

"Your mother lasted in this world for seventeen years. I hardly think a night will make me perish." Zareth's hands balled at his sides to resist touching her. "Besides, you replenish me." *Even as your closeness is driving me mad*, his mind added.

Chapter Thirteen

Xochitl

I awoke to a delicious smell of spices and masculinity and a throbbing pulse of longing between my thighs. Moaning, I nuzzled against the solid warmth pressed against my body.

My eyes snapped open. I was snuggled up against Zareth, my arm draped around his waist. God, he felt so good. Warm and solid. Memories of his hypnotic kiss the other night washed over me, making me bite my lip to keep from moaning. *Why did he have to stop?*

Damn him, I wanted *more*. And he'd told me he wanted me.

"But sex is more significant for my kind and yours," he'd said.

What did that mean? If it was some old-fashioned, moralistic thing, I was determined to change his mind.

But could I handle another rejection?

Careful as possible, I extricated myself from the embrace before he woke up and pushed me away again. Immediately, my body cried out at the deprivation.

Zareth sat up and rubbed his eyes, looking adorably sleepy instead of his usual forbidding demeanor.

"I suppose we better grab some cat food and get going," I whispered.

He nodded and rose from the bed.

Another pang of guilt caught in my throat as we crept out of the house without saying goodbye.

As we got in Little Beast and buckled out seatbelts, I took a deep breath and asked the question that had kept me up for most of the night. "If my whole destiny is to save the world, what if my music career was pointless? My friendships, all our hard work to form a band and get a record deal... Did it have no meaning?"

Zareth was silent a moment, considering my words. "At first I might have said yes, but after seeing you together on that stage and getting to know you all, I know that it means everything. Your music inspires thousands around the Earth. You cannot deny the meaning of that."

I loved him then. And yet... "But what will come afterward?"

"I don't know."

My shoulders slumped. At least he was being honest. We gassed up the car and swung by a drive-thru before crossing through the portal back to Aisthanesthai. Isis greeted us with an outraged yowl the moment we entered the tower.

Where were you? she demanded, rubbing her sides against my legs to mark me with her scent. Her tiny nostrils flared before she answered her own question. *You were with my other humans. And you had crab and clams!* She stood up on her hind legs and dug her claws into my thigh. *Did you bring me any?*

Zareth frowned down at the cat as he leafed through a stack of letters. "What is wrong with her?"

"She smells the shellfish I had for dinner and is mad at me for not bringing her any."

His lips curved in a smile. "Well, the Piscani have invited us to feast of the Arch-Captain's ship, and their sea fare is far superior to what we dined on at that restaurant."

My interest piqued. I loved seafood. "Is that why you didn't eat much?"

"No. I merely had a lot on my mind."

About what? I couldn't help wondering. Was he thinking about our kiss? I know I couldn't stop thinking about it.

Before I made things worse by asking, I explained the upcoming feast to Isis. *But you'll have to wear your leash*, I added.

Her ears laid back. *I loathe that thing.*

"I can't have you wandering off and getting lost. You know how you are when you smell something new," I said aloud.

Zareth looked at us both and shook his head. "I'm going to shower and take a nap. I didn't rest as well as I needed."

I felt a wicked twinge of pleasure at that. If he'd been unaffected by our kiss, he would have slept fine. Even more wickedly, I pondered ways to get him to do it again.

My thoughts stopped me cold. I *wanted* him. I wanted him to make love to me, to introduce me to the mystery of desire that so many others took for granted. And I wanted him with a ferocity that shocked me to the core.

I shook my head. I had more important things to do here than fantasize about him.

As Zareth slept, I resisted the urge to go up and cuddle beside him and instead returned to the library. I curled up with another book, losing myself in the lore of dragons until Zareth announced that it was time to get ready for the feast. If we were going aboard a ship, there was no way I was wearing a dress. Instead I chose black leather pants and a matching corset over a lacy blouse. Kinda piratical. I liked it.... I hoped Zareth did too.

Isis had to be reminded of all the impending seafood treats before I could persuade her to let me put her in the leash and harness. But she refused to walk in it, so I carried her down the stairs. She could be such a butthead sometimes.

Zareth waited in the great room. His lips twitched at the sight of the leashed cat in my arms.

"I noticed that the ruins of Medicia aren't very far from here," I said as we loaded up in the car. "Could we go see it after the feast?"

His expression darkened. "I don't think that's the best idea."

I gave him my best pitiful look. "Please?"

"Very well," he sighed.

We drove northwest for about an hour on rugged dirt roads before I saw bonfires in the distance and golden moonlight reflecting on distant waves. As we drew closer I saw the ocean. It roared and foamed along the sandy beach. What looked like an old-school pirate ship was anchored aside a large dock, with a ramp leading down.

Isis squirmed until I let her down. She trotted happily along the sand until she realized we were approaching the dock, which was too close to the water for her comfort. I scooped her back up, stroking her soft fur as she shivered with dread at being splattered with the ocean spray.

She perked up when she smelled the fish.

The Piscani looked more like Gypsies than pirates, with their dark curly hair, bronzed skin, and black eyes. The captain was unmistakable with a thick beard braided with gold and trinkets, and an air of command.

He bowed before Zareth and held out a fat leather bag. He spoke in a language that was close to German and Latin. I was able to pick out a few words like "Storm Lord," "safe ships," "thank you," and "feast."

Zareth wasn't kidding. The food was incredible. Lobster tail broiled in butter and herbs, steamed mussels in a garlic-wine sauce, octopus, stuffed fish, and a chowder that made my toes curl in pleasure. Everything was so good that I struggled to pay attention to the conversations around me, not that I could understand more than snippets.

At least they seemed to be pleased with my appetite. And they adored Isis, fighting over the chance to feed her scraps. The captain tapped my shoulder and pointed at my cat before holding out a handful of gold.

Oh, hell no.

I shook my head. "She is my best friend and companion."

Zareth translated for me and the Captain nodded and scratched Isis between her ears.

After the feast, everyone departed the ship and headed back to the beach. The bonfires were fed and casks of what smelled like rum were opened.

But I wasn't in the mood for any more partying. Something had nagged in my mind since I opened my first book on this new world. If I didn't get it off my chest, I'd go crazy.

"Can we skip the party?" I asked Zareth. "I want to see Medicia."

Everyone fell silent and stared. They understood that word.

"Well," I stammered, "It was nice meeting you and thank you so much for your wonderful food. I've never had better chowder."

After Zareth translated, the Captain doffed his hat and bowed. A single tear trickled down his cheek. His visible grief made me even more curious to see the ruins of my mother's home.

Isis yanked the leash from my grasp and dashed across the beach to the car. Shaking sand from her fur, she crawled under the driver's seat.

"Are you certain you want to do this?" Zareth asked again. I nodded. "Yes. I need to see it."

He heaved a sigh, and dread filled his features. "Very well. Drive south as long as the road allows."

I put Little Beast in gear and pulled out, noting the sorrowful faces of the Piscani in the rearview mirror. Everyone's reaction to me going to Medicia indicated that it was a bad idea, but I couldn't stop. I had to lay eyes on my mother's home, or what was left of it.

Zareth remained silent as I drove. I wanted to put on some music, but for some reason that felt wrong for this journey. At first we passed through a town and then past a few sparsely lit villages. After passing the last and smallest village, the road grew bumpier and the darkness pressed around like a tangible thing. I turned on my high beams and slowed the car to a creep. Branches and twigs struck the car at random intervals, jolting in the silence.

Little Beast's engine sputtered, making her shake. She didn't seem to want to shift. But Akasha had done a full inspection and tune up on her, so nothing could be wrong. I sensed she didn't want to come here.

I patted her dashboard and eased off more on the accelerator. "It's okay, Beast. You can do this."

The engine evened out grudgingly. Zareth gave me a sharp look and I shook my head. I didn't feel like getting into my bond with my car right now. I had a mission.

The solemn quiet pressed on me and made me so drowsy that I had to slam on the brakes to avoid a fallen log blocking the road. Isis yowled under the seat.

"Fuck, I'm sorry," I said to everyone before turning off the ignition, leaving the lights on.

Zareth rubbed his chest beneath the shoulder strap of the seat belt. "We would have had to stop soon anyway."

We got out of the car and the crystal on the top of Zareth's staff illuminated the road almost as well as Little Beast's headlights. Isis elected to stay in the car and nap.

"Stay close to me," he said in a hushed voice.

As we walked around the fallen tree, I paused.

In the meager moonlight, the log resembled a pallid corpse, frozen in twisted death throes. The living trees bordering the path didn't look too good either. With the light of Zareth's staff, I saw the branches gnarled at unnatural angles and blighted spots on the leaves. Something was very wrong around here. The trees were sickly, the ground mostly barren, and the whole place was dead quiet, with no sound of wildlife.

"How close are we?" I found myself whispering.

"Only about a quarter mile." Zareth's eyes scanned the area, staff poised as if he expected a threat.

The decrepit trees gave way to scraggly bushes and shattered stones. The ground was mostly dirt with a few clumps of gray grass. Despite the lack of vegetation, shadows still engulfed the area. Though the sky was clear and full of stars, the light from the moons couldn't penetrate the darkness. The further we walked, the more the sense of utter desolation pressed on me. I shivered and pressed closer to Zareth, taking comfort from the velvet brush of his robes against mine.

A faint noise came from far off in front of us. It almost sounded like a woman's piteous wail. Zareth frowned but he didn't seem alarmed, so I didn't say anything.

Once we crested a hill, Zareth seized my arm. "Stop here. I don't know how steady the ground is further on."

"I can't see anything," I protested, standing on my tiptoes, my eyes straining in the darkness. I saw a few vague shapes, but mostly it looked pitch black in front of us.

"That's because there *isn't* anything." His voice was bleak. The light of his staff grew brighter and he pointed it down the hill.

Twenty feet from where we stood, the ground gave way in a sharp drop to what looked like a bottomless chasm. It was so large I couldn't see the other side. *Was* there another side, or had the maps lied? Did it go on forever?

The blackness was like a living thing, but empty of all feeling and instinct, except hunger.

It looked like it wanted to eat us.

The sight of the vast emptiness made my stomach hurt, but I forced myself to keep looking. This was once my mother's home for more years than I'd been alive. She had been a happy princess with gilded wings, full of magic and joy until my father came and killed everyone she knew before he raped her and turned her kingdom into an endless abyss.

That keening wail sounded again, closer this time. For a second I glimpsed a foggy wisp in the shape of a woman, her face and body contorted in agony.

"It's haunted," I said, hugging my arms close to my chest. Were the ghosts of my family trapped in there?

"In a way. Those aren't real spirits. Only echoes," he explained. "When a cataclysmic event happens, it will leave remnants, a sort of stain that we can see and hear."

I relaxed somewhat, relieved that the souls of my ancestors weren't trapped in this pit of agony. "How deep is it?"

"Bottomless, as far as we can tell. Or worse, it might open into *Qua'al-fán*, the world Mephistopheles has built from slaughter and suffering."

"Oh shit, that would be bad." Dread filled me at the thought of the man who did this being able to come back through, or some hapless being falling into his world. "What if it does?"

"The Conclave of high sorcerers meets every year to seal it with a protective barrier just in case." He bent down, picked up a pebble and threw it into the blackness.

A faint light undulated in the chasm, like ripples on the surface of a pond.

I stared into the blackness and listened to the shrieking echoes of violation and suffering. My body shook with a chill that my coat could never warm.

He put a hand on my shoulder and bent down to face me. "Kerainne got away from this place. Just remember that."

His comforting words and touch warmed me. "How did she escape?"

"Delgarias found her and took her away before Mephistopheles absorbed the land. And to ensure that Mephistopheles never found out, he told no one and hid you and your mother in the sole world without magic."

My throat was too tight to form a response. I'd thought that seeing the site of my mother's home would give me more clarity on her past, or maybe some sort of closure. It didn't.

Instead, seeing the place of her history only made it more apparent that there was so much I didn't know about her.

And it hurt.

More than ever, I wanted to pull her out through the veil of death and demand she tell me why she left me in the dark all my life. And why she had to leave me.

The abyss filled my vision like poison. Echoes of screams and sobs tormented my ears. Unable to bear the sight of the place, I turned away. "Can we go back home? I mean to your tower?"

Zareth nodded. His lips thinned in a grim line. "Of course."

I started walking back to the car, but stopped when I realized he wasn't following me.

Turning around, I watched him step to the edge of the crater. He knelt and worked a large stone out of the crumbling soil and slipped it into one of his robe pockets.

I wanted to ask him what he intended to do with that, but something about his furtive movement and forbidding expression kept me quiet. Maybe I didn't want to know.

The car ride back to Zareth's tower was solemn. My heart constricted in my chest. I'd expected the ruins of my mother's home to be a tragic sight, but I hadn't expected it to be a still-bleeding wound.

When we returned, Zareth headed up to his laboratory, rolling the rough black stone he'd taken from the ruins between his palms. I went to the library and continued my self-torture, pulling a book on the Leonine dynasty of Medicia from the shelf and taking it to my room.

To my disappointment, the words were in a language I couldn't understand, but at least there were pictures so colorful and realistic that they might be photographs. Vivid green grass covered rolling hills and flowered trees like hawthorns, lilacs and wisteria lined flagstone pathways.

They'd also had lakes and rivers and pine trees like in Coeur d'Alene. Was that why mom had chosen that town to raise me in, despite its sometimes harsh winters?

My breath caught as I turned another page and came upon photos of the royal family. My grandparents looked stately and angelic, while my aunt's golden eyes and quirked lips radiated mischief. Yet they were strangers to me. Dead strangers.

All I cared about was the luminite princess with the golden hair, emerald eyes, and nurturing smile.

As I looked at the picture of my mom, memories of losing her overtook my mind as if it were happening in front of me again. A pitiful mewl escaped my throat and I let the book slide from my lap onto the bedspread.

Closing my eyes made it worse. I remembered the day the light in her eyes dimmed and her laughter became forced. Mom grew pale and tired. Her exhaustion worsened until she collapsed on the couch as soon as she got home from work. Overcome with helplessness, I'd cover her in a blanket and make dinner and then we'd cuddle and watch movies.

Instead of getting better, she ate less and less and became more fatigued, until she quit going to work. My terror had magnified.

I begged for her to go see a doctor, but she refused. "It's not something they can help."

"How do you know?" I'd demanded as I stirred a pot of chicken and star soup, one of the few things she was still willing to eat. She wouldn't even touch Doritos or tacos anymore and those were her favorites. Impotent fury filled me that she wouldn't let me try to get help.

"Just listen to your mother on this. No doctors, and that is final. It would be dangerous." Her eyes were large and pleading as I brought her the soup in a mug. She hated spoons for some reason. "But you can stay home with me. I'll call the school."

Somewhat mollified, I dropped the subject. At least I could be there to take care of her. I fought to ignore the pulses of unease at her weak tone and stubborn insistence against doctors. "So, what do you want to watch? Horror, or chick flicks?"

Three days later, I awoke in the middle of the night to hear her calling me. I rolled off the couch and went to her bedroom, my stomach churning in dread.

"Xochitl." Her voice came out in a pitiful gasp. "It's time for me to go."

Heart in my throat, I turned on the lamp. Her eyes were glazed and she'd lost so much weight that the covers barely made a hump over her thin body. *No*, I'd screamed inside. *She can't leave me.*

"Mom?" I took her bony hand, too afraid to squeeze. "Let me call 911."

"No, it won't do any good. I want to be here with you. Until..."

I took her other hand. Tears blurred my vision. *No. This was wrong.* "I won't let you die."

"I tried to make it until you were eighteen," she said in a fragile whisper. "I really did."

"You mean you knew you were going to—" My words broke off in a strangled sob. "You can't leave me!"

"My will is on the dresser." Her voice was firm, despite her rattled breathing. "I requested that you be emancipated, but I don't know if the courts will allow it. I left you some money..."

Throat tight, I argued as if I could halt the inevitable. "But how am I going to live without you? You're the only one who's like me. You're the only one who understands..." The tears came in earnest.

"I'll be watching over you. Just stay close to your friends and keep making your music. Don't give up on the band, and don't let them give up on you." Her eyes held mine, no longer emerald green; now the color of wilted leaves. But they were no less commanding. "Promise me."

"I promise." I said through my tears. "But what about my magic? How am I going to learn how to control it?"

"You will find a teacher." Her lips turned up in a knowing smile. "Or rather, one will find you. Always remember, I love you and I believe in you."

And then she was gone, leaving me helpless to the state's bureaucratic heartlessness.

To greedy, abusive foster parents.

Tears burned in my eyes as I forced away the memories. I couldn't let Zareth see me like this.

I rolled out of bed, threw on my coat, and ran down the stairs and out the door. Little Beast was parked in the front courtyard. The silver moonlight reflected on her headlights, making her look like she was waiting for me. Biting my lip, I opened her driver's door and got inside. I pressed my head against the steering wheel and burst out in wracking sobs.

Whenever the memories got too bad, I cried in my car. At first it was because I didn't want my foster parents to see me cry. Now it was just habit. Something about being enclosed and the smell of old car made me feel safe enough to let go.

Isis jumped up on the hood of the car and watched me with concern. For some reason that made me cry harder.

The passenger door opened and Zareth slid into the seat beside me. His hand covered my shoulder, deliciously warm. "What's wrong?"

"I miss my mom," I whimpered through hitching sobs.

He didn't reply. Instead, he twisted in the seat and pulled me in his arms. All self-consciousness forgotten, I cried until my tears soaked the front of his robe.

After some time, my grief melted in the warmth of his embrace. I remembered his stormy kiss, the way his mouth devoured mine, and the hunger he awoke in me. That hunger returned, an inferno of longing. I pulled him tighter, needing more of him against me. Unbidden, a low moan built in my throat and I tilted my head back to regard his face. My lips parted as I gazed at him, wanting more than anything in the world for him to kiss me again.

He leaned forward, his mouth angled toward mine— and then he grunted in pain as the gearshift poked him in the gut.

Zareth drew back with a curse. Lightning flickered in his eyes for an instant before he shook his head like a dreamer awakening from sleep. His eyes turned cool and black and his head gave a minute shake.

The rejection was subtle, but it stung.

He gave me a chaste pat on the shoulder. "Your car is small."

"That's why I named her Little Beast," I whispered weakly, resisting the urge to punch her dashboard.

It wasn't her fault, but *damn it*.

We got out of the car and he walked me back to the tower, his hand reassuring across my shoulder blades. "We should get some rest before tomorrow."

"I don't want to rest, I want to..." *Rip off your clothes and find out what sorcerer skin tastes like.*

I blushed at the thought of saying that to him. But I could feel the tingling wetness between my legs, and a throbbing ache for him to fill me. What was happening to me? *Did luminites go into heat like cats?* I didn't dare ask him.

If Mom was around, she would know. Fresh anguish stabbed my heart. It wasn't fair.

"I want to break something," I finished.

He gave me a long, inscrutable look. "Well, you could use some practice with your levitation ...and I do have some dead trees."

"How will levitation break stuff?"

He raised a brow. "Don't you want to learn how throw rocks at targets with your magic? It's a very useful skill."

I knew what he was doing. His first priority was to train me, and he was determined to steer me back in that direction. However, flinging rocks at things sounded like a great way to vent, so I wouldn't argue.

Sure enough, smashing dead wood with magically launched stone projectiles was an excellent outlet for my frustrations. Afterward, I had my first good night's sleep since coming to Zareth's world.

Chapter Fourteen

Zareth

Zareth sanded the blackish-purple garnet he'd taken from Medicia as he observed Xochitl practicing her shields. She was improving with a speed that astounded him. Perhaps he'd been too harsh in judging her mother.

Isis hopped on his lap, sniffed the garnet, and lay down with a purr. He glanced down at her in bemusement. The feline had been hostile to him until now. What had changed?

Setting down the garnet, he stroked the cat, his tumultuous thoughts somewhat soothed by her rumbling purr.

The politics in his world were growing tedious. He'd made no progress finding his missing people. Rickard's reports were scant, and all the leads he'd followed interviewing the villagers had been unhelpful. For the time being, he commanded his people not to venture anywhere alone.

The Conclave's demands to for him to present Xochitl to them were growing more insistent, and the Wurraks had ignored his command for them to withdraw from Laran.

Rising from his seat, he told Xochitl to cease her practice on water magic. "Shall we go back to Earth for your work?"

With an eager nod, she raced upstairs to change clothes. He did the same, donning a pair of jeans and a black t-shirt before casting glamour to look human.

With the conflict of his world, their visits with Xochitl's friend were a welcome reprieve. To his surprise he'd grown fond of them.

After the day's recording concluded, Aurora gave them a sideways glance. "We've been working hard this week. We should go out and do something fun tonight."

Sylvis's blue eyes gleamed with mischief. "We haven't done undercover Karaoke in awhile."

"Oooh!" Beau and Xochitl exclaimed in unison.

"What is that?" Zareth asked.

Aurora smiled. "Sometimes we get tired of doing music for work and just want to have fun. And we all want a turn to sing. So we disguise ourselves and go out for Karaoke."

Xochitl nodded. "Yeah, and I get to sing girly songs for a change."

"I get to be girly too." Beau grinned.

"Do you sing?" Sylvis asked.

He shook his head. "No, but I'll be content to watch." And oh, how he loved to watch Xochitl. Her voice was a banquet to his hydra and a balm on his soul.

He still wasn't sure what Karaoke was, but as long as it featured Xochitl's singing, it would be enjoyable.

They stopped by the house and Sylvis disguised her blue hair with a blonde wig and cast off her usual jeans and tee shirt for a blue dress.

Beau remained true to his word and made himself into a convincing woman with a red wig and a sequined silver gown.

Aurora unbraided her hair and brushed it out until it formed a fluffy dark cloud.

Xochitl hid her purple streaks and curled her hair into tiny ringlets and donned a red dress that made his cock twitch in his pants.

They followed Aurora's van to a bar that smelled of stale smoke and spilled beer. Hardwood floors and old license plates adorned the place.

Zareth learned that karaoke was a tradition where music played while people drank and sang along to words on a screen. Aisthanesthai had something similar, except that there were no printed lyrics to guide the singer. The challenge was who could drink the most and still recall the verses.

He settled back into a booth with a pint of ale and watched with fascination. Some of the singers stumbled on the words, especially the drunk ones. Others had terrible voices that made him want to cover his ears. Many sounded pleasant and had him tapping his foot. All enjoyed themselves with an enthusiasm that was infectious. Even Aurora abandoned her brisk demeanor as she sang with a rich, throaty voice that pleased his hydra.

Zareth had always been scornful of Earth folk. How could they possibly be happy without magic? Now, seeing everyone's joy in singing made him wonder if perhaps music was a kind of magic.

Could *this* be the reason Xochitl was destined to save his world?

The first song she sang was jaunty and ribald and had the crowd clapping and singing along. Caught up in the charm, Zareth couldn't keep from laughing at the words.

As the bar patrons applauded, Xochitl sketched a little bow and passed the microphone to the next singer... who sounded like a braying mule.

"Are you having fun?" she asked, joining him at the table.

He nodded. "This is certainly different than I am accustomed to, but my hydra seems to enjoy it." Indeed it was.

The demon within fed on the revelry almost as much as it absorbed fear and lust. He hadn't expected that.

As Xochitl talked with her friends, he withdrew the garnet from his pocket and resumed polishing it with a rough cloth.

"What are you doing?" Beau asked him.

"Polishing a rock," he told him, taking a break to have another swig of beer. "I don't like my hands to be idle."

All thoughts ceased as Xochitl took the microphone again. A primal melody played as her hips undulated to the beat of the music, the hem of the red skirt swishing around her thighs.

Pure, unadulterated lust poured from her voice like drugged honey. Zareth gripped the edge of the booth to keep from going to her. Did she know what she was doing?

Then she danced in a hypnotic, provocative manner that put to mind the mating dances of the Kwani tribe. Her voice beckoned him like a siren's song.

"Holy shit," Beau whispered.

All chatter in the bar ceased as the patrons watched her with mouths gaping in desire. Zareth's hydra roiled in hunger even as it fed on the lust. His cock hardened in agony.

By the time the song finished, he was mad from desire.

Zareth barely heard the applause of the audience as he seized Xochitl's arm. "I need to speak with you," he said through gritted teeth.

"But—" Her words broke off as he led her out the back door into the alley.

When he raised his crystal above their heads, she attempted to tug free. "I need to tell my friends goodbye!"

"I am unable to wait." His blood boiled in his veins as his hardness strained against his pants.

Fury welled up in him as they got into her car. He wondered how she could make him lose control like this, even as his anger drowned beneath his torrid desire.

Even though he knew the consequences if he gave into temptation, he no longer cared.

Chapter Fifteen

Xochitl

My belly churned as Zareth transported us back to his tower. I had to jog beside him to keep up. His glamour vanished the moment we crossed over and the lightning in his eyes flickered dangerously.

"What the hell is your problem?" I asked, impatient with his ominous silence.

He released me in the living room, and paced around the couch in long, agitated strides. His long coat flapped like the wings of a crow. "I might ask you the same. What were you thinking, singing and dancing like that?"

I blinked. "Like what?"

"Don't feign ignorance, little luminite." His voice was savage. "You used your voice to call up lust."

My jaw dropped. Could I really do something like that? "I didn't know about that. I just wanted to be… sexy." It sounded so lame aloud.

His head cocked to the side. "Why?"

"I—" My explanation broke off as soon as it begun.

I couldn't tell him that when Beau looked at us and smiled, happy that I finally had a boyfriend, I felt more than guilt for lying to my friends.

I couldn't tell him I wished the lie was true. Remembering all the romance novels I devoured on the sly, of all the chick flicks I'd watched and the lump in my throat I got when the couple kissed and went on to their happily ever after.

I couldn't tell him I wanted that, ached for the warmth of an embrace, the taste of a kiss, the blissful passion of two bodies joined as one.

That I longed for all of that from him.

I threw up my hands and faked a casual tone. "You just don't know how to have any fun."

"Fun?" His incredulous tone made me flinch. "You call the torment you've put me through *fun?*"

"I didn't mean to torment you." Damn, I'd fucked up more than I intended. "I just, I don't know... I wanted you to like me."

"I *do* like you." His voice was so quiet I almost didn't hear him. "You are the savior of my world."

"Is *that* all that I am to you?" To my humiliation, my voice cracked in a broken sob. "The savior of your world? Can't I be anything else to you? I want you and—"

"It's not about that!" He jolted up from his seat so fast I jumped. "You cannot want me." He loomed over me, the lightning flickering in his eyes.

"But—"

"No, Xochitl," As he spoke, dark thunderclouds rose up and around him until the whole room was shrouded in darkness. A violent wind came at his bidding to swirl around him, making his coat flare out chaotically around him. He seemed to grow larger and more menacing by every harsh word he uttered.

"I could hurt you with one snap of my fingers." Lightning crackled from his fingertips. "You should be cautious around me, Xochitl. I have walked this world for too many centuries.

I have known anger and bitterness that mere mortals would go mad by just imagining."

He's trying to frighten me, I realized with shock.

Outrage welled within my being. What made me angrier was that it was almost working, if the quivering in my belly was any indicator. *How dare he*? All I had needed was a simple rejection, a mere *"No, I don't want you,"* but he had the balls to try frightening me? *Me*, who had no fear? The presumptuous bastard.

Despite his imposing display, I approached him, raising my chin as I focused my will to bring the storm he had summoned under my control. Its sheer force tore the bobby pins out of my hair. Black and purple ringlets whipped around my face. The wind tore at my dress, but I stood my ground until I was in the eye of the tempest. I tried not to get caught up in the ecstasy of the magic as I formed two violet fireballs to rest in my fists.

I glared up at Zareth, hoping that I looked as intimidating as he did.

"You don't scare me, Zareth and it insults me that you dare to try. I am no mere mortal. You were the first to say so." I spoke with a deadly calm, so there would be no doubt I was seething. "All you had to do was tell me that you don't want me. I would have accepted that. No one has *ever* wanted me. I would have accepted that the dreams I had after all these years were just that: fanciful girlish dreams."

A lump formed in my throat at voicing those words, but I swallowed it and continued. "I never asked for this, damn it. I didn't want to be a savior. I just wanted to be... me. And for a while I thought you liked me... for me. I thought you wanted me."

I didn't see him move.

His arms wrapped around me in a split second. Holding me tight in vice-like grip, he bent down to look me in the eyes.

"I want you," he whispered roughly.

He ran his fingers through my hair before his mouth devoured mine in another mind-blowing kiss.

I closed my eyes as I rose up on my toes to grasp his shoulders and pulled him closer. Electric heat filled my mouth as his tongue danced with mine. I never imagined that a simple kiss could be so intense. It made me wonder if I'd survive if things went further. My musings ceased as I became aware that his hands were no longer gripping me possessively, as if he feared I'd run away. They now caressed my entire body, molding me into liquid desire.

"I want you," he whispered again. A thrill ran through me at the sound of his words.

My knees wobbled at the pleasure of his touch. Zareth lifted me in his arms, and with a muttered word, we were in his bedroom.

He lowered me to my feet and shrugged out of his trench coat. I tugged on the hem of his shirt but I was too short to take it off. Zareth chuckled and removed his shirt. Rapt with his gorgeous muscled chest and stomach, I ran my fingers along the silken ridged expanse of flesh. I'd never touched a man's bare chest before and the experience was tantalizing. He jumped as I trailed my tongue down the line of his belly.

"That tickled."

The thought that an all-powerful, ancient sorcerer could be ticklish delighted me. I leaned forward to lick him again, but he pulled me into his arms and bent down to kiss my neck. As his teeth nibbled on that sensitive place, electric ecstasy zinged from my neck all the way to my toes.

A high sound that was half cry, half gasp, tore from my throat. Zareth's long fingers caressed my back, and crept up to unzip my dress. My hands plunged into his silken hair, silently pleading for him not to stop.

My dress pooled at my feet. The blazing sensation of his bare skin against mine made me suck in a breath. The tender place between my thighs pulsed with heat.

I wanted more.

He unfastened my bra and drew back. I whimpered in unfulfilled longing, but he remained still in hungry silence. His eyes devoured me as I stood before him in nothing but my red panties and high heels.

For the first time in my life, I felt desirable.

"You are so beautiful," he whispered.

And, for the first time, I believed it.

"So are you." Staring at him as he towered above me, his shimmering black and silver hair, and his lean, muscled body, I was enraptured with his otherworldly beauty.

My gaze strayed down to the large, long bulge in his pants. I reached for him again, eager to explore that thick ridge, but he took my hands and placed a kiss on each palm.

"You're a virgin," he said, between kisses.

I frowned. Was he thinking of stopping? "So?"

"I want to make certain it is a pleasurable experience for you." His words heated me further.

"Touching you *is* pleasurable." I argued, impatient to know what he would feel like in my grip.

His shoulders shook in a husky laugh. "If you touch me too much, I may not last long enough."

"Oh."

His hands encircled my waist as he lifted me up and set me on the bed. The sheets were cool against my bare skin. The muscles in his back rippled as he bent to remove his boots. As his pants slid down his narrow hips to reveal the erection straining through his boxers, my eyes widened at the size of him beneath the silk. Part of me wondered if it would hurt. The rest of me was curious to see what he looked like.

Zareth climbed onto the bed. His thighs straddled mine as he bent down and kissed me again. At first feather-light, then with seductive languor, his tongue danced with mine. He lowered his body so his bare chest pressed against my breasts. Thunder rumbled as I felt his hardness pressing against the aching source of my need.

I trembled from the delicious weight of him. Brushing my hair aside, he kissed and sucked on the other side of my neck. I wiggled my hips, needing more of him.

Lightning flashed from the window, echoing the electricity coursing through me.

When his weight lifted from my body, I cried out at the break in contact. But then his hands and mouth were on my breasts, teasing, caressing, and sucking. The myriad of new sensations made me gasp and squirm. When I couldn't take it anymore, he moved lower, trailing kisses down my belly and then to my hips.

Slowly, he pulled down my panties. At first I thought he would go down on me, but then he went lower still, kissing and stroking my thighs, my knees, my calves, even my toes. My clit throbbed at being ignored.

Then he worked his way back up. His lips and tongue laved my inner thighs while his fingers lightly caressed. His breath blew across my most sensitive place, but he didn't kiss me there yet.

When his finger grazed my labia, I nearly jumped out of my skin, the pleasure almost unbearable.

Zareth knelt between my legs, his fingers working incomprehensible magic. One of those long fingers slid inside me, feeling even more incredible than I'd fantasized. My face flushed at his wicked smile as he touched and teased my most intimate flesh. Instead of being embarrassed, I thrashed and moaned beneath him, hips arching up to meet his touch.

The thunder rumbled closer.

That sinister smile deepened as he once more lowered his head. A bright bolt of lightning lit up the room just as his tongue flicked across my clit. I tangled my hands in his hair as his lips and tongue explored everywhere his fingers had touched me.

Thunder drowned out my cry when his mouth closed over my labia, sucking lightly. The orgasm came hard and jolting in time with the flickers of lightning. Wind howled outside as I bucked and moaned, overcome with wracking shudders.

By the time he lifted his head, I couldn't stop trembling. Rapt with awe, I watched him slide off his boxers, taking in the captivating sight of his naked boy and his rigid length. He moved up further, covering me with his body once more. His cock pressed against my slick, hot core, making my clit pulse and tingle. My hypersensitive flesh surged at the contact. Zareth compounded the sweet torture by returning to my neck.

The aching need between my thighs intensified as I moved beneath him, seeking more of his hardness. At last I maneuvered enough that the tip of him pressed against my entrance.

Zareth propped himself up on his elbows above me. His turbulent eyes seemed to stare into my soul. "Are you certain you want this?"

"Yes," came my ragged gasp. I arched my hips, bringing him a millimeter further.

The thunder rumbled louder.

His fingers caressed my cheeks, whisper soft, as if he feared I would break. "I'll be as gentle as I can. Stop me if it hurts."

The words brought a wisp of clarity into my haze of mad desire. "Okay."

With torturous slowness, his shaft slid deeper inside me. I was so wet I felt like I could have taken him all in one thrust, but Zareth held back, entering me carefully. When his cock moved in another inch, a sense of pressure and tightness made me grip his shoulders.

I didn't tell him to stop.

Maintaining his gentle pace, he withdrew. Every nerve trembled at the feel of him. My hands caressed his back as he moved back in another inch. With exquisite gentleness, he worked himself in and out, penetrating a little deeper each time. The tight pressure became an ache of longing.

Wind outside whistled through cracks in the window. Flashes of light and sounds of thunder increased in frequency and volume. The storm heightened the sensuous suspense of the moment.

At last, he entered me fully in one smooth, slow thrust in tandem with a crack of thunder. The lightning blinded me as Zareth swallowed my gasp with a kiss. For a tantalizing eternity, he lay still, kissing me with ravenous hunger while allowing me time to get used to the feel of him.

I tasted my arousal on his tongue, the flavor heightening my desire. My hips moved beneath him, finding a hypnotic rhythm that touched all the right places. Zareth rocked with me, his breath hissing through his teeth in restraint. His fingers stroked my face and hair. My shoulders covered my flesh with goose bumps, despite the heat.

When he nibbled my neck, I moaned and bucked underneath him. The sharper thrust almost hurt in its intensity, yet I wanted more. Another crack of thunder sounded as Zareth quickened the rhythm.

Flashes of lightning punctuated his thrusts. My moans echoed the howling wind. I felt like I was being taken by the storm. As my pleasure reached another plateau, it was like we were the storm. Higher and higher, my body climbed, building my magic and ecstatic sensation in the ascent.

Lightning blazed white-hot before my eyes as my climax took me. Thunder boomed so loud it shook the tower just as Zareth's cock shook my core. My voice became the wind, and my clit pulsed with electricity as my center reverberated with thunder.

I felt Zareth's magic flow from within him. It emanated through his pores as it joined with mine. His cock jerked within me, an intoxicating pulse. He threw back his head with a roar. His eyes went white, flashing brighter than the lightning outside.

My orgasm multiplied with his. Our magic mixed together just as our bodies joined and pulsed. The storm raged outside.

Just as I thought I would die from the insane pleasure, Zareth collapsed on top of me, panting in sated exhaustion. Every bone in my body seemed to melt.

We lay there for an eternity, melded in magic and body. We trembled with the lightning; our hearts pounded together in a staccato beat in tune with the vibrating thunder.

Zareth lifted his head from my shoulder and brushed a lock of hair from my face. "Are you all right?"

I nodded, unable to speak. To reassure him, and because I didn't want to let him go, I pulled him down for a kiss. With my kiss, I tried to convey all he'd made me feel.

Earth shattering. Miraculous. Magical.

When I broke the kiss, Zareth rolled off of me with palpable reluctance.

I found my voice. "I heard that after sex, most guys roll over and go to sleep."

His lips curved in an amused smile. "Oh?"

"Please don't do that." I hated the begging tone, but couldn't help it. "Hold me."

"Of course." He pulled me into his arms, and I rested my head on his chest.

In the end, it was me who fell asleep.

Chapter Sixteen

Zareth

Every cell of his being crying out in reluctance, Zareth disengaged himself from Xochitl's embrace and rose from the bed. Thunder continued to rumble from the storm their mating had wrought. Wind buffeted the tower as lightning flashed through the windows.

His doubts and fears about mating her had been unfounded. Her powers hadn't rejected his. Nor had his neutralized hers. In fact, the opposite had come to pass.

Their magic had coalesced. And it had done so with a potency he'd never imagined. An intensity that made him lose control and unleash a raging storm.

From the way the lightning centered on his tower, there was no way his people wouldn't know where the tempest had originated. They all had to have seen it.

Fear prickled the back of his neck. How much damage had been done?

Dressing in his robes, he transported himself outside the Nightmare Forest. Before he entered the village, he cast an invisibility spell. A high-level mage would be able to detect him, but otherwise he would be concealed.

He marveled at how fast the spell worked. Mating Xochitl had done more than rejuvenate his powers. It had multiplied them.

The village was a mess of destruction, though not as bad as it could have been. He counted four downed trees, and breathed a silent prayer of thanks that only one had fallen on a house. Some homes had ragged holes in the roofs where whole sections of shingling had been torn away by the wind.

The villagers themselves were gathered beneath the stone pavilion, huddled around hearths and braziers, but safe from leaking roofs and fallen trees. Relief washed over him that at least someone had been wise enough to bring them to safety. If he hadn't been the one causing the storm, that would have been his responsibility.

Babies cried as mothers and fathers tried to soothe them. Some children exclaimed over the lightning while others hid under tables and blankets, frightened by the thunder.

The rest of the adults clustered together drinking wine and smoking while conversing in hushed tones.

"The storm came from His Lordship's tower," one man said to another, his pipe a glowing ember in the night. "Only a fool wouldn't be able to see that."

"But why would he do us harm?" Another rubbed his arms with a doubtful frown. "Perhaps it was the Winter Prince."

The first man uttered a laugh laced with scorn. "Do you see any ice or snow? If it was him, we would have faced a blizzard." He flicked the ashes from his pipe. "Lord Amotken is not known as the Lord of Storm and Shadow merely because it rolls off the tongue."

Other voices joined the speculation. "Could it have been an accident?"

"Perhaps."

"I'm more curious as to how he generated so much power," the captain of the guard said. "Has he not been dwindling like the rest of us?"

"I think he mated the Lioness of Light and their powers joined," someone else answered.

"But she manifests fire."

"Look at the lightning." Another pointed. "It's as violet as her flame."

"But they're not married."

Zareth no longer cared to eavesdrop. The shadows concealing him fell away. His people stepped back with startled gasps as he sank to his knees. "People of Raijin, I kneel before you in abject apology for causing this storm. I will do everything I can for recompense. I will repair your homes and assist you in moving the felled trees. But first, has anyone been injured?"

An old woman stepped forward. "Jarmen's leg broke when the tree felled his home. We managed to get him out from under it. He lost consciousness from the pain. The healer is tending him over there." She pointed.

Guilt contorted his chest as he rose to his feet. He'd prayed no one had been injured. "My remorse knows no bounds. I will see to him first."

The man who'd attacked him in the village emerged from the throng. "Begging your pardon, m'lord, but do you truly have the power to put this all to rights?"

He nodded. "The storm has returned my strength." He only wished he had the power to locate the man's missing son.

Rickard broke from the throng and charged over to him. "You bedded the luminite princess." His eyes blazed with so much fury that Zareth stepped back.

He met the seneschal's stare. "I did."

Gasps and mutters erupted from the pavilion. Their eyes went cool and accusatory.

"Without wedding her first?" Rickard thrust his finger toward Zareth's chest, stopping short of touching him. "You've soiled her, besmirched her honor."

Shame flicked through him before he straightened his shoulders. "You overstep yourself, Seneschal."

Mordaine, the owner of the mage shop nudged Rickard out of the way. "Your magic *Conjoined* with hers."

"Yes." The implications of *that* roared over him.

Fates help him, he wanted her again already.

Her head cocked to the side as she studied him. "The Conclave should be pleased to hear so."

A bitter smirk curved his lips. "Don't be so certain." He'd staved off presenting Xochitl to them, saying he wanted to train her first. Now they'd think he fabricated the excuse for him to seduce her.

"Are you going to do the honorable thing with Princess Leonine?" Mordaine crossed her arms over her chest, eyes stern and maternal.

"That depends on what she has to say about it," he answered truthfully. "Things are different in the Earth realm."

Doubt coiled within his stomach. What would Xochitl have to say? Would she recoil in horror when he told her what must be done?

Mordaine made a clucking sound with her tongue. "Earth realm or not, she is a luminite of Aisthanesthai. This is her home and she must abide by its rules. *Especially* where magic is concerned."

He sighed and ran a hand through his hair. Xochitl would might not agree with that sentiment. How would she react to the consequences of their lovemaking? One night of pleasure was one thing, but was it worth eternity?

The question tightened his chest. In this short time, he'd grown to care for her much. *Could she feel the same?*

Avoiding the subject, he turned to the villagers. "Where is Jarmen? I'll see to him first."

After healing the man's leg, he repaired the damaged homes. The magic coursed through him with more strength than it had in years. With Zareth's recompense, most of his people appeared to forgive him for unleashing the storm.

After Zareth told them he intended to do the honorable thing where the Lioness of Light was concerned, there were further placated.

Mags, the owner of the cook shop, even gave him a bowl of crab soup to warm him after his hard work. "Thank you for helping us," she said.

Bitterness coursed through him. "Don't thank me. This was all my fault." The crab meat was warm and buttery on his tongue. Xochitl would love it just as had she had enjoyed the feast the Piscani had provided them.

A dreadful thought struck him. "How far did the storm spread?"

"Ten miles, at the least."

He borrowed from Xochitl's vocabulary. "Fuck."

Scraping his bowl clean, he handed it back to Mags. "I need to look in on the Piscani."

Things were more dire for the sea-faring folk. One ship was sinking with its hull smashed against a rock. Another had a broken mast. Four others had torn sails.

Worst of all, one man had drowned.

The betrayal in their eyes was a spear thrust between his ribs. Just the other night they had thanked him for keeping them safe. Now he was responsible for damaging their home.

Even after he apologized, repaired their ships, and promised to attend the memorial feast for the drowned sailor, Zareth remained coated in guilt.

"Is there aught else I can do to atone for my folly?" he asked.

Captain Tyrone eyed him speculatively. "I understand that you did not intend to create this storm. You have my forgiveness, aye, even joy for your successful union with the Lioness of Light." He twirled his beard around callused fingers. "Nothing can truly compensate for the loss of Waltyn's life, but a bit of gold would help his widow and children, and some casks of ale could bring cheer to our bereaved hearts."

"Done." Zareth extended his hand and shook the Captain's. "I will also supply you with four new light globes for your ships to better ensure safe voyages."

A measure of his conscience eased, he returned to his tower.

Exhaustion weighed his muscles and burned his eyes as he climbed back into his bed.

Xochitl murmured in her sleep, a blissful smile curving her lips as she snuggled closer to him. Zareth pulled her into his arms and kissed her forehead.

Tomorrow they would have to face the consequences of their joining. But tomorrow could wait.

For now he would savor the feel of her in his arms.

Chapter Seventeen

Xochitl

"We have to get married." Zareth's words crashed over me like a tidal wave.

Dizziness turned my legs to water. "What? Why?"

I stared at him as if in a trance. *All of him.* Those sharply curved lips that felt so soft and sensual on mine, those long fingers which wrought inconceivable pleasure on my body. Luminescent hair like silk in my hands. Those intense, lightning-struck eyes that devoured every inch of me. The tender place between my thighs throbbed with renewed desire.

How could he bring up such a serious subject when I hadn't processed the magic of what happened last night? I'd just rolled out of bed and gotten dressed.

"Because our powers meshed so well that we created a storm." He jerked me back to the present.

My jaw dropped. "That was *us*?"

"Yes." His long fingers rubbed the bridge of his nose. "Now everyone knows I bedded you. I cannot besmirch your honor or my own."

"My honor?" I repeated with a dumb stare. Although the thought of marriage felt like a blow between the eyes with a sledgehammer, I couldn't fight a pang of hurt that Zareth wanted to marry me for the sake of morals, not for how he felt about me.

Unease trickled down my spine. How *did* he feel about me now?

Did he think I'd trapped him?

Something in my expression must have revealed my alarm. Zareth bent down and his hands cupped my face, one long thumb caressing my cheek. "I told you that lovemaking means more to my kind, but you wouldn't listen and I... I couldn't stop." Sorrow and some other indiscernible emotion reflected in his eyes. "I'm sorry, but it must be done."

"Okay." Uncertainty rang from my voice. *Marriage.* This was too much, too fast. Another thing he said gave me pause. "How is it besmirching your honor, much less mine?"

He sighed and released me. "I am the heir to the throne. If I do not wed you after our magic coalesced before so many witnesses, all will assume I'm the villain and despoiler of innocents the rumors make me out to be. They'll be eager to take you away from me and deliver you to Stefan, who will waste no time in wedding you."

Revulsion curdled my gut. "I will never marry that enema-nozzle."

Zareth smiled. "I can't deny that I'm comforted to hear that."

Unwilling to even contemplate Stefan, I returned to the topic at hand. "Why is it always the guy who's assumed to be the one to initiate sex, and the woman the one who's 'despoiled?'" My fists clenched at my sides in impotent frustration. "It's not fair. I'm the one who wanted you to make love to me. Hell, I begged you. I don't feel despoiled at all. In fact, I feel—"

"Our genders are irrelevant." He broke off my tirade. "It is because I am older and more powerful. Therefore I am the one who will be held responsible."

"So I have to marry you, or risk your brother being king?" I resumed my rant. "Don't my feelings matter in any of this? What about my job on Earth? I'm not about to give up music and become a housewife, or castle-wife, or whatever."

He placed his hand on my shoulder. "It won't be like that, I promise. On Earth, our marriage would not be valid. You don't even have to tell your friends and colleagues, if you don't want to." His words came out fast, like he was nervous. Releasing me, he pulled that black stone from his pocket again along with a cloth and polished the rock with frenetic swipes. "And you may divorce me later, after you've fulfilled your destiny, though an amicable separation would be more politically acceptable."

Something in his tone made my chest tight. He didn't want to marry me any more than I wanted to marry him.

Or *did* I want to marry him? Memories of his lovemaking intruded once more. I thought of my girlish dreams of him rescuing me from my abusive foster parents and high school bullies to live in a world of magic and love. The fates seemed to mock me, turning my most secret wishes into a sham.

My eyes prickled with tears, but I forced myself to seem calm. "All right. That sounds reasonable." My lips struggled to form a smile. "Does this mean I'll be the queen?"

His lips curved in a half smile. "I should have known you'd be ambitious."

I shook my head. "Wait, you don't think I did this as a power play, do you?" I raced to explain. "Although the idea of being queen of an entire world makes me want to say 'ha-ha' at all the people who treated me like shit, I don't think I'd make a good ruler." I shrugged. "My issues with authority, you know."

Zareth laughed. "Yes, but this time *you* will have the authority... in a way. We typically allow the people to govern themselves. The king is most often a figurehead unless a dire situation forces him to intercede. And I know it wasn't a power play. I was jesting. Besides, the Prophecy already implies you'd be queen."

The concept intrigued me, and at any other time I would have asked more questions. But the current situation encompassed my focus.

"So, when do we do this?" I asked with confidence I didn't feel.

"As soon as possible." His tone forbade argument.

Visions of my wedding dress, a bouquet of lilacs, and my smiling friends surrounding me as I walked down the aisle to join my happy groom washed through my mind. Taunting me.

I'd ruined everything.

"Will we have a cake?" My voice came out meek, clinging desperately for some familiar sense of tradition.

He gave me an incredulous look before his lips curved up in a gentle smile. He reached forward and brushed his knuckles across my cheek. "Yes, we may have a cake."

"Good. I love cake." Unable to help it, I threw my arms around his narrow waist and pressed my cheek to his chest, inhaling his unique scent of dried flowers, spices, and enigmatic masculinity.

Now there was something else. The scent of our lovemaking emanated from his body, making my breath catch and accelerating my pulse with renewed longing. Even after my lustful actions had such drastic consequences, I still wanted him.

Guilt gnawed in my gut. I'd ruined things for him as well.

"Are you mad at me?" I asked timidly.

"I should be furious," he said, though he stroked my hair. "I'd never intended to marry again."

My face jerked up to meet his gaze. "*Again?*" He'd had another wife? Or more than one? Jealousy stabbed my gut and I couldn't keep the glare off my face.

He chuckled and kissed me on the top of my head. "It was centuries ago. You are what matters now."

His words and kindness cheered me somewhat. Maybe there was hope that we could have a real relationship.

He held out his arm. "Well, shall we go pay the piper?"

"Now?" Even knowing that circumstances were forcing us to do this, part of me cried out for the missing romance and courtship.

He nodded. "Yes. We'll have a brief ceremony in the village, and another, more formal one with my mother's people." His mouth twisted in a sudden frown. "That is, after the memorial feast."

"Your mother's people...the faelin?" This was getting more real every moment. *In-laws?* Then I processed the rest of his words. "What memorial feast?"

He avoided her gaze. "One of the Piscani sailors drowned in the storm."

"Wait. You're saying someone *died* last night?" My stomach roiled with queasiness. "Let me get this straight. Our sex was so powerful that it actually *killed* someone? And now you want to get *married*?" The joy of last night's incredible lovemaking turned to ashes in my mouth. My hopes for a real relationship plummeted. "We can't do that again. I don't want to kill people."

He stepped closer to me and grasped my shoulders. "We won't. It was my fault that it happened. I didn't channel the power in time, or give you any focus." His hands moved from my shoulders to cup my face again. "Our lovemaking *also* gave me the power to repair damaged homes and ships, and to heal a man's broken leg. Next time we'll channel our magic properly and use it for good."

Next time. Despite the dire news I'd just received, my thighs quivered at his use of the word, "lovemaking." Did he feel the same about what we'd shared last night? My hopes bubbled back to the surface, though I didn't dare voice them. "Are you sure? I mean, a hundred percent?"

"Yes." Though he released me and went back to polishing the stone, he held my gaze. "The first time is always chaotic, because our magic was new to each other. I just underestimated how far the effects of the joining would spread." His features contorted in grief and abject shame. "It was a fatal mistake that won't happen again."

A fatal mistake. Guilt overwhelmed me. It was my fault. Zareth had warned me that lovemaking among mages was more complex, but I didn't listen to him. If I hadn't seduced Zareth, that sailor would still be alive. And yet, I still ached to touch him.

"How can I face the Piscani after what I did?" Tears choked my voice.

Pocketing the stone, he pulled me into his arms. "They do not bear you any ill will. They held me responsible. I restored their damaged ships and I'm providing the man's widow with enough gold to last her a lifetime. And wine," he added as an afterthought. "They will be far more upset if you don't attend the feast and pay your respects."

I clung to him, savoring his warmth and inhaling his scent before I dried my tears on his velvet robes. A croaking sound escaped my throat. "So we're having a wedding and a funeral."

His bitter laugh echoed my own even as he squeezed me tighter. "It appears to be so."

"Can Isis come to the wedding?" I asked when he released me. "I need someone to be my maid of honor. She's the only woman I know here." My only friend.

"If you can find her." He pulled out the stone again. "The storm frightened her."

As if to contradict him, my cat bounded into the room, regarding Zareth with feline scorn. *I was not afraid. I was giving you privacy when you took off your clothes as you prefer.*

I bent down and scooped her up in my arms. "Of course you weren't. Would you like to be my maid of honor at my wedding?"

She nuzzled my cheek and gave me a puzzled look. *What is a wedding?*

"It's a ceremony that will join me to Zareth." Even as I spoke, I still couldn't process the reality.

Her turquoise eyes squinted. *But you already mated with him. I can smell it.*

I struggled to explain it in a way she could understand. "Yes, but now we must declare that fact to others. Their sense of smell is inferior to yours."

Her ears pricked with comprehension as she preened her paw. *Ah, so they must see that you are mated. I am not certain I want to watch that. Your kind look, smell, and sound odd engaged in the act.*

Zareth raised a brow when I burst out laughing. "What is so funny?"

"She thinks we're going to have sex in front of everyone." I looked down at Isis. "No, we're just going to tell them that we're mated and have a feast."

Her ears lifted. *Food? I will be happy to be this maid of honor, then.*

With a wave of his staff, Zareth transported us to the village. My jaw dropped as I saw Delgarias leaning against a pillar as if he'd been expecting us.

"Uncle Del?"

Delgarias embraced me and met Zareth's gaze. "I see you've come to your senses."

A verse of the prophecy flitted through my mind. *A joining will birth new power.* Had it been about our mating? Had our lovemaking and impending wedding been foretold?

"Preparations for the feast are under way," Delgarias said. "And the Duchess of Kinsen is on her way to assist with selecting Xochitl's gown."

My wedding gown. My wedding feast. This was really happening. Most women had months, and sometimes years, to plan. I had mere seconds. But at least I was getting a dress and cake. And Del was here. He'd been like family to me. Maybe this wouldn't be so dismal. "Will you give me away, Uncle Del?"

"No. That is a barbaric Earth realm custom that I do not endorse. You are *not* property." His harsh tone startled me before expression softened. "I will, however, officiate the ceremony."

"Oh." I digested his words, pleased that marriages here did not see women as objects. "That does sound better."

The Duchess of Kinsen rushed over to us. "I wish we had more time. Such a prestigious union deserves more fanfare, celebration, and certainly more adornment."

I couldn't help nodding in agreement. If I had it my way, I would have outdone all the bridal magazines I sneaked peeks at when my friends weren't looking.

If I had it my way, I'd have zero doubt that my groom loved me.

I forced myself to be optimistic. He liked me at least. He wanted me. And his touch made me melt.

Zareth spread his hands in a helpless gesture. "I am sorry. There's nothing I can do about that."

Jeanette sighed and took my arm. "Very well, I suppose we'll just have to do the best we can."

In moments we were at Aisthanesthai's equivalent of a bridal shop. Wedding dresses were generally not white, I learned. Instead of purity, a bride's gown symbolized her power. Like in Karate, white represented the lowest level, the most inferior.

I didn't look good in white anyway.

The purple selection wasn't very large, so it didn't take long to check them out and try them on. The fourth one was a royal purple satin sleeveless ball gown with an overskirt of silver netting interwoven with amethysts. It was something I'd dream of wearing if I won a Grammy, or perhaps for the high school proms I'd missed.

Jeanette tsked as I twirled around before the mirror. "You should have a forty yard train, a furred cloak..."

"I love it." There was no way in hell I was taking it off to try on another dress.

At another shop we selected some accessories and I was swept up in the excitement of preparing for my wedding.

Jeanette dulled my enthusiasm when she coached me on what to wear for the memorial feast. Just as white had nothing to do with purity here, black had no association with mourning. I selected a shimmering blue-green dress with a skirt of aquamarine beads to pay homage to the sea the departed sailor loved.

Garb secured, she rushed me to a salon. My hair was washed, yanked, teased and twisted into submission. My hands and feet were rubbed with lotion, my nails filed and painted. The makeup woman was damn near as vicious as the hairdresser.

By the time they were done, I looked damn good.

Isis yowled and asked for the food I'd promised. We returned to the village square where everyone lined the main street, holding candles. Zareth met me before the line. He wore black velvet robes similar to those I'd first seen him in when we'd met, though with silver embroidery on the sleeves and hem. His cowl was down, revealing his magnificent hair. I stood rooted to the ground, breathless at the sight of his otherworldly beauty. I couldn't believe that in moments, I would be bound to this magical man.

Handing me a bouquet of black roses, he bent down and whispered. "Traditionally, brides don't carry flowers, but I want you to feel at home."

My heart fluttered at his kind gesture. He'd sheared off the thorns and tied the bundle together with black and purple ribbons. Memories of my dreams swam through my mind as I inhaled the roses, captivated by their exotic scent. "Thank you."

I pulled one rose from the bundle and beckoned Isis. She let me weave the stem around her collar in exchange for a promise of extra treats.

"She looks almost as exquisite as you." Zareth took my free hand. "Now we approach Delgarias and ask him to announce our union."

I squeezed his hand, gratified when he clenched mine back.

Instead of being delivered to my groom like chattel, he walked beside me, like we were equals.

There was no music, no bridesmaids, and no flower girl. But Isis marched before me, tail high in the air and ears pricked forward in pride. She was a beautiful cat and she knew it. Her complaints forgotten, she basked in the admiring glances of the villagers.

Though he was no match for Zareth, Delgarias looked imposing in black robes shot with silver embroidery. He wore what looked like a thimble on his right index finger... until I noticed the sharp spike on the tip. I noticed that he was an inch taller than Zareth.

Solemn diamond-blue eyes regarded us. "Who comes before me?" His voice boomed loud enough for everyone to hear.

Zareth spoke first. "Zareth Raiden Amotken, Lord of Raijin, High Sorcerer, son of King Taranis of Niji and Princess Bellanatha of Shellandria."

Delgarias looked at me expectantly. Throat parched, I announced myself. "Xochitl Goldmoon Leonine, lead singer and rhythm guitarist of *Rage of Angels*, daughter of Kerainne Silvara Leonine." I didn't rule over any lands, but my position in my band was important. I also didn't mention my father. He didn't count in my universe.

Uncle Del gave me a look of approval before he spoke. "And why do you come before me?"

"We wish to wed," Zareth's voice reverberated with authority.

Did we? I lifted my chin, feigning confidence.

"Does anyone object to this union?"

My heart seized as I heard a few mutters behind us. Tense seconds passed, but the voices didn't grow any louder.

To my surprise, relief flooded my being. I guess part of me did want this.

Delgarias launched into what sounded like a typical wedding ceremony, except that the themes were partnership rather than obedience, and building power rather than home and hearth. I couldn't help but prefer this version. Then everything became different.

Uncle Del tilted my chin up with his thumb. His long index finger moved forward, the sharp needle he wore pricked my lower lip. It stung a little, but I didn't make a sound.

"Don't lick it," he whispered before moving to Zareth and doing the same.

"With the five elements, Zareth Amotken and Xochitl Leonine are bound together," Del declared. "Let them seal their bond with a kiss of blood and magic."

The crowd cheered as Zareth pulled me in my arms and kissed me. My lip stung a little from the puncture, but his kiss washed over me in a wave of dreamlike bliss. The taste of blood flavored the evocative taste of his lips. Pain and pleasure intermingled in a dark harmony. My magic welled up and poured into him. His poured into me until our power felt like one force circling around us.

Thunder rumbled and wind whipped my skirts. I drew back, not wanting to cause another storm. Zareth licked the blood from his lips. The sight made my body stir with lust even as it increased the humming magic within me.

"Don't worry," he whispered. "We can control it now. You also made the candles flare."

I didn't want to discuss the ramifications of our joined power in front of everyone.

Instead I asked, "Can we go eat cake now?"

My stomach rumbled. We hadn't even had breakfast. The villagers were just as enthusiastic about the meal. Between accepting congratulations and well-wishes, Zareth, Isis, and I dined on what tasted like chicken in a rich, creamy sauce, crisp salad greens, various fruits, and of course, the cake. Isis only had eyes for the chicken and cake.

Afterward, there were hours of dancing and presentation of gifts. We were given spices, bolts of cloth, bread, wine, crocks of butter, wheels of cheese, and countless magical items.

By the time the festivities were over, I was tired and hungry again. I would have gone for more cake, but Zareth reminded me that we had the memorial feast to attend.

Jeanette and another woman helped me out of the purple gown and into the aquamarine one. The beads swished around my legs. I had more freedom of movement in this one. Which would have made me happier if it weren't for the fact that it was for a funeral.

Little Beast waited in the square to take us to the Piscani.

To my surprise, the villagers had followed an Earth realm custom. The Datsun was painted with strange letters and symbols.

"Does that mean, 'just married'?" I asked Zareth.

He shook his head. "They're protection runes for our travels."

"That was kind of them."

Isis gave me an inquisitive look as she climbed under the seat. *Where are we going?*

"Back to the Piscani for another feast." I was too tired to explain funeral customs to her.

The fish people? Excellent.

Bonfires blazed on the beach when we pulled up before the sand. Instead of accusatory glares, Zareth and I were hailed with joyful greetings and congratulations on our union. Before the feast began, Zareth insisted on us speaking with the widow in private.

On leaden legs I followed, feeling sick to face the woman whose husband I killed, newlywed and dressed in such finery. She met us in a cottage on the rocks, high from the tide and shielded from the winds.

A baby slept in a cradle by the fire and a young girl of around ten with a purple bruise on her cheek sat in a chair mending a fishing net.

Instead of cursing our names, the woman fell to her knees before us. "My lord, my lady, you have answered my prayers. Waltyn was wild and angry when he drank. I feared for my daughter.

When she looked up at us, I noticed her black eye and felt marginally better that at least the man I'd killed was an abusive prick. But what if he had been a good man instead?

"I cannot accept thanks for what had been an accident," Zareth told her. "But I can accept your forgiveness and ensure that you and your children will want for nothing."

Her eyes widened as he presented her with a chest of gold. "Thank you, my lord, and my lady! Bless you until the end of your days!"

"Hide at least half of it. Tell no one of the real amount, not even the Captain," he admonished before we escorted her and her children to the feast.

Another portion of my guilt eased as the sailors told us more about Waltyn's death. The man was falling down drunk on rum before the storm even started. When the lightning flashed, he'd refused all urges to take shelter and instead danced on the dock, howling at the wind until one of the ships smashed into the dock, knocking him unconscious and into the water.

For the moment I cast off my what-ifs and ate and drank and danced with Zareth while Isis begged morsels of seafood from all and sundry.

Hours later, as Zareth announced our farewells, and I stumbled at his side, drunk off my ass, there was something I could not forget.

We were married.

But instead of being carried over the threshold for a romantic honeymoon, I passed out in the car. Another blight on tradition.

Chapter Eighteen

Zareth

"Are you feeling better?" Zareth asked Xochitl after he directed her to pull over at the border of Shellandria.

"Oh, yes!" She beamed and unbuckled her seat belt. "That tea is miraculous. I wish I'd had that stuff when I was touring. There's nothing worse than playing a gig with a hangover. Though, I suppose meeting my in-laws in that state would be worse."

Between their wedding and the memorial feast with the Piscani last night, Xochitl had gotten so drunk that she passed out the moment they returned to his tower. Although a reasonable consequence of the festivities, he couldn't help but worry that she'd intentionally avoided their wedding night.

His thoughts were dashed away at the sound of hoof beats thundering towards them.

The faelin didn't ride animals.

"Get back in the car!" he yelled, and pulled out his staff.

For once, she listened and hopped back into her vehicle. She rolled down the window and leaned out. "You too!"

Before he could respond, an army crested the hill. One glimpse of their bronze armor over fur tunics and pennants displaying Stefan's snowflake banner and he cursed. *Boreans.* Sent by Stefan to capture Xochitl.

Gathering his power, he sent a wide arc of lightning from his staff at the vanguard. Horses screamed and toppled over, dumping their convulsing riders on the ground. Yet more soldiers circled around him, using Zareth's distraction to get closer.

The car's engine started with a roar, making the horses rear back and sending men toppling. As Zareth gathered his power for another spell, Xochitl revved her Datsun and drove right at the army, making the horses panic. Purple fireballs flew like missiles through the driver's window, chasing off more horses as men rolled in the grass to put out the blaze.

But even more came. One warrior charged Zareth, sword raised over his head with a battle cry.

A bolt of lightning felled the attacker, but another approached too quickly for Zareth to cast another spell. Seizing the sword from the dead man's grasp, he pocketed his staff and gripped the two-handed blade to meet his new foe.

The swords clashed with a sharp ring. As Zareth thrust and parried against the man's skilled blows, he wished he'd practiced swordplay at least half as often as magic. Zareth didn't dare look away from his enemy, though at least he was relieved to still hear Xochitl's car driving around the battleground, chasing off horses and riders.

The warrior met his sword with another clang, and slipped on the damp grass. Zareth thrust the blade through his throat, grimacing in distaste as blood gurgled from the fatal wound.

Before he could raise his blade, another warrior charged. Just as the enemy's sword swooped down for a fatal blow, an arrow suddenly pierced the man's eye.

Then the air filled with arrows, raining down on the Boreans in a deadly volley. Men and horses fell dead by the dozens before they called a retreat.

Xochitl pulled up beside him and got out of the car. Zareth grabbed her and conjured a shield around them to protect them from stray arrows.

She grinned up at him. "That was fun! I don't think those guys are used to cars. But man, Akasha's gonna kill me when she sees Little Beast. She's all scratched up and someone broke the side window with a sword!"

"Shhhh." He pulled out his staff and lit the crystal, searching for the archers who'd rescued them. "Thank you for your assistance," he called out. "Please, show yourselves so I can express my gratitude."

A voice rang out in Faelin. "Indentify yourselves, or you will be fired upon as well."

Zareth bowed. "I am Zareth Amotken, Lord of Raijin," he said in Faelin. "I have come to trade spells and artifacts as well as to introduce you to my bride, the Lioness of Light, who stands here beside me."

A flurry of excited whispers echoed around them, but hushed when the commanding voice replied. "Very well, Lord Amotken. You and the Lioness are welcome in Shellandria."

While Zareth translated, ivy covered bushes parted to reveal a glittering path that was almost as fine as sand.

Holding tight to Xochitl's hand, he led her forward. When they entered the grove of trees and stepped on to the path, they were joined by a party of faelin archers. He smiled as Xochitl visibly struggled not to stare at their smooth skin, luminous hair, and multicolored eyes. Unlike him, their ears were pointed.

These ones wore brown leather pants, green shirts, and wooden armor. They also wore wooden helms with leaves protruding out of them for camouflage. They stared back at

Xochitl with unreadable expressions on their beautiful features.

"I'm sorry for staring," she said. "It's just that I'm from the Earth realm and I've never seen full-blooded faelin before, except for Delgarias."

Even before translating, the faelin warriors drew back at the name. Equal parts of reverence and fear reflected from their faces. Zareth knew Delgarias had been cast out of Shellandria, yet he never knew why.

One of the faelin recovered himself. "My lady, let us apologize for staring." Zareth recognized the voice as the one who issued the orders. "We were not expecting to have the Lioness in our presence this night."

"Or Lord Amotken," another chimed in.

"Allow us to introduce ourselves." The first said. He was almost as tall as Zareth. "I am Levitian, commander of the royal guard of Shellandria." He bowed.

Zareth translated while the others followed suit in their introductions.

"I am Sanyit."

"I am Tilanta."

"I am Niko."

Zareth and Xochitl bowed. "It is a pleasure to meet you all."

Levitian then sent a cadre of troops down from the trees to dispose of the dead and heal the surviving horses. "I will escort you to the Queen."

Though the faelin considered him double-tainted due to his human blood and his taking a hydra, Zareth felt a sense of pride at the prospect of showing Xochitl the land where his mother grew up.

As they walked, it grew lighter outside. The path became easier to see and the trees were illuminated with lightning bugs.

They crested another hill and Xochitl's eyes widened as she saw a huge bright globe, suspended over the forest up ahead.

"They made their own sun?" she asked.

"In a matter of speaking. Their light globe is similar to what I constructed for the Piscani, though much larger. Unfortunately it doesn't do as well with warmth and crops as the real thing." He wished he could show her his mother's kingdom in real daylight, with the trees flourishing and flowers in bloom. "They also have a strict schedule in its activation. Eight hours are all that's allowed now."

The path widened as they neared the center of the faelin city. Zareth couldn't help but take joy the way the light, though artificial, illuminated the land. Gardens and orchards lined the path, with people working in soft soil, humming a cheery tune. They seemed almost resentful of the interruption of him and Xochitl passing by, despite their respect and curiosity of apparent high-ranking mages.

"Where are the houses?" Xochitl peered around curiously.

His lips tugged in a smile. "Look up."

She gasped in delighted wonder. "I'd always wanted a tree house. These are more like tree mansions!"

When they reached the palace, she froze in awe. Spanning across several giant trees, its walls blended seamlessly between the branches. The palace was rounded, with fluted columns that appeared far too delicate to support it. The building appeared to be made from pearls, though that would be impossible.

Her head cocked to the side as she studied a massive tree trunk. "How do we get up?"

"We climb. Only the old or infirm may use a lift." He guided her to a tree with handholds from centuries of use worn into the gargantuan trunk. After boosting her up, he couldn't help looking up her dress, admiring her muscled thighs and rounded backside.

The Queensguard waited in the antechamber when they emerged. "Queen Nicharana is waiting," the leader said.

They followed the guard to the throne room in the heart of the trees. The queen awaited on her throne of living ash, green tendrils and blossoms curling around the silver wood.

"Zareth Amotken, son of Princess Bellanatha, and Xochitl Leonine, daughter of Kerainne Leonine and Lioness of Light," the herald boomed.

The queen inclined her head. "Zareth, cousin, come closer. It has been so long since you've come to see us."

"I would think you would be grateful for that."

Her lips pursed in an angry frown. "Do not assume I share the opinions of some regarding your blood. I was close with your mother, my aunt, and when I look upon you, I see her more than that human she married. And though I disapprove of some of your choices, it seems the fates knew better."

The queen took his hand. As her long fingers entwined with his, Zareth felt a pang of sorrow. It had been long since he'd thought of his mother, yet now the pain of losing her returned like a fresh wound. Nicharana had Bellanatha's eyes and her same glittering silver hair.

"Queen Nicharana," Zareth replied with a bow. "It is indeed a pleasure to see you once more. You are looking well."

"Ha!" the matriarch scoffed. "You are a flatterer. I've just had my seven-hundredth birthday."

"Beautiful look you," Xochitl said in broken Faelin and a horrible accent after Zareth translated the queen's words.

He blinked at her. Her mother must have attempted to teach her the language. How much had Xochitl understood when he spoke with Delgarias?

Nicharana's eyes shifted to Xochitl, "Come here, bride of Zareth and daughter of Kerainne." Her long fingers reached out to grasp a tendril of Xochitl's hair. "You look just like your mother, though you are dark where she was fair and your eyes look like the gold moon while hers were emeralds. I am told your voice surpasses hers in power."

Xochitl asked Zareth to translate, then shook her head. "No person sang as beautiful as my mom."

"I spoke of power, not attractiveness." The queen waved a dismissive hand. "I will hear your voice later. But first we will trade and feast to celebrate your wedding." Her glittering gaze shifted to Zareth.

Xochitl perked up, missing the news about a second wedding. "Will there be any sky tears?"

Nicarana beamed. "Those were Kerainne's favorites too." Clapping her hands, she summoned the royal steward. "Summon the Priestess and order a feast prepared. We have a wedding to officiate."

When Zareth translated, Xochitl stepped back. "*Another* wedding?"

"Yes. The faelin won't recognize our union sealed among humans even though Delgarias officiated."

The queen's brows rose to her hairline. "*Delgarias* officiated?"

"Yes. He considers himself her honorary uncle from when he was friends with Xochitl's mother... and sister."

"I'd heard tales that he'd been in love with a luminite. A dangerous path, though I also heard he abandoned her for one far more treacherous." With another snap of her fingers, Nicharana summoned her maids and ordered them to prepare Xochitl for the ceremony. "Garb her in mine own marriage gown."

With obvious reluctance, Xochitl allowed them to lead her off.

Once alone, the queen regarded him plainly. "I assume you're also here to seek alliance."

Zareth nodded, Nicharana's providing Xochitl with her own gown not lost on him.

"If it comes to war, we will ally with you," Nicharana said. "Though our might is much depleted, we'll do what we can. Your mother would have wanted it that way."

"And you'd never ally with a full-blooded human, like Stefan."

Her laughter tinkled like bells. "Yes, that as well."

Zareth took advantage of Xochitl's absence to trade with the faelin. Their magical artifacts were superior to any in the world. They also had craftsmanship he lacked, but desperately needed for Xochitl's bride gift.

By the time everyone gathered in the courtyard for the procession, everything was in order. He wore a silver tunic of *mythra*, a faelin cloth made from the fibers of a root that was softer than cotton. His vest was embroidered in jet.

The people hardly noticed him as they gaped at the sight of Xochitl in a faelin royal's gown of *lei* silk. The pale violet creation floated around her with magic sewn in the crystal beads.

The queen herself bound their hands together with a gossamer cord of preserved spider-silk and said the words that bound them together in the eyes of his mother's people. He paid little attention to the royal decree as he was overcome with wonder that the unfathomably beautiful woman before him was his bride.

According to the faelin tradition, rather than exchanging a kiss, they were to make a small spell with their joined hands.

After they levitated ten feet above the crowd and did an artful twirl, Zareth kissed her anyway.

The faelin begged Xochitl to sing for them. When she finished, some of them wept, but all thanked her with abject gratitude and the queen kissed her on the cheek.

They then gathered at one of the large trestle tables and received gifts from the faelin. Xochitl exclaimed in wonder at the jewels, fabrics, spell books, and herbs she received. A lump formed in Zareth's throat at his gifts of rare herbs, a jeweled dagger, and a large clear crystal that would soon come in handy.

Perhaps his mother's people did not scorn him as much as the late queen had led him to believe.

Before they feasted, Zareth gave Xochitl her gift.

She gripped the staff of lilac wood he'd carved from his own grove, topped by a garnet of Medicia, which was set in elaborate and enchanted faelin silver.

"This was what you were working on this whole time!" Her eyes were large with wonder. "That wood you were sanding, that stone you were polishing."

He nodded, drowning in her liquid gaze.

"But where'd you get a star garnet? They can only be found in Northern Idaho and some place in India."

"And Medicia. I took it from the ruins," he explained, smiling as her comprehension dawned. "Your staff's magic will work better for you if your stone is from your homeland."

She set it on the table and threw her arms around him. "Thank you so much! It's beautiful. My own gift pales before this." Xochitl motioned for Levitian, who had something hidden under his cloak. "I don't know what I can give to an all powerful sorcerer. You seem to have everything you need."

"You're going to save my world and make me a king." His heart ached that she cared enough about him to want to give him a gift. "What else could I ask for?"

"Yeah, but that's not today at our wedding... our second one, that is. I still need to give you a present." She turned her back as Levitian handed her something. Then she turned back again to face him and placed something warm and soft in his hands. "I thought an ancient sorcerer would be lonely."

The tiny ball of gray fur gave a pitiful mewl. Zareth looked down at the kitten and his heart gave another tug.

Xochitl spoke with patent shyness. "Isis and I found him and his litter outside of the village. Their mother was dead. I'm going to give the rest to the Piscani because they wanted more cats for their ships. If you don't like him, I can give him to them too."

The kitten looked up at him with wide blue eyes and gave another mewl before nuzzling his finger. Xochitl must have used a sleeping spell to keep it hidden from him. "I would love to keep him. It has been decades since I've had a familiar." Their life spans were so short that he'd been through the pain of losing them too many times, but he missed having a furry companion.

Xochitl's eyes glimmered with relief. "Isis and I will train him, then."

Still stroking the kitten, he looked down at his bride with wonder. How could she possibly fear that he'd reject any gift from her? Especially one so adorable?

The presence of his new pet gave them a much needed excuse to cut their visit short. Aside from Xochit's need to return to Earth for her music work, this constant travel and socializing made him weary.

They bade their farewells after the feast and returned to his kingdom. After fetching accoutrements for his kitten and the others to be delivered to the Piscani, Zareth and Xochitl brought his new familiar to the tower. A letter from the Conclave waited for him, demanding Xochitl's presence. He ignored it and spent a pleasant evening with his bride playing with the tiny felines.

As they went upstairs to bed, exhaustion settled over him like a leaden cloak. The cataclysmic events of the past few nights had drained him.

Although the Prophecy had implied that he would be joined with Xochitl, he'd refused to believe it. Even now that he was bonded with her through blood, magic, sex, and two ceremonies, it was difficult to fathom that she was his.

He'd been alone so long that companionship was alien to him. Yet with Xochitl, it had come so naturally.

But how did she feel? He'd recalled her initial objection to their marriage, which stung even though it was expected.

Yet they hadn't had their wedding night. After their first ceremony, she'd been too drunk... had it been because she wanted to avoid it? He remembered her stricken face when she'd learned of the damage their storm wrought.

Though he'd reassured her such wouldn't happen again, did she believe him? Or worse, did she not want him again?

With his fatigue and all of the stress from the past few nights, Zareth found himself unable to bear her rejection.

Though his body stirred with desire as he watched her undress, after they climbed into bed, he merely held her.

He prayed tomorrow would be different.

Chapter Nineteen

Xochitl

"Where the hell have you been?" Aurora demanded when we arrived at the studio. "You had us totally fucked the other day!"

Shame filled me that I'd forgotten Monday's session. But I couldn't tell them I'd gotten married.

"I- I'm sorry, I was sick." I looked at Aurora with pleading eyes to not question me further.

"Why didn't you call, then?"

Drowning in guilt, I didn't know what else to say. How could have I forgotten my friends?

Zareth defended me. "Forgive her, Aurora, she's had a tough time these last few days."

"Well," Aurora's tone softened. "Try to let us know beforehand if anything happens again."

"I will." I choked on the promise. With war about to break out and Stefan and the Conclave after me, who knew what else would interrupt my recording schedule?

"We missed you, hon'." Beau gave me a big hug, but shot Zareth a look of veiled disapproval.

So they think it's his fault, do they?

I pushed the thought away and went to find Sylvis, who had hung back in the break room. Zareth remained behind to talk to Aurora and Beau to smooth over their anger. He could be very charismatic when he wanted to be.

Sylvis flung her arms around me. "I was so worried about you."

"Don't be," I reassured her before exclaiming, "Oh my God, I've got so much to tell you."

We sat at the lunch table and I launched off with my epic tale. After describing the Piscani and the faelin and my weddings, she interrupted me. "Wait, you got married?"

I nodded. "But it happened due to magic and political reasons." For some reason, saying it aloud made me feel sad. "I'll explain all that when I have more time."

I pulled my wedding gifts out of my bottomless pouch. "Here, this is for you." I presented her with a bracelet wrought of silver that resembled ivy leaves dancing across the vine.

"Wow. A souvenir from another world." Sylvis held the bracelet with awe.

"I hope you like it. I know you don't usually wear jewelry, but it was either that or a dress made of a material that's unknown here." I remembered my second wedding gown. It had been the most beautiful thing I'd ever worn. Had Zareth liked it? He never said. I bit back a sigh.

Sylvis's laughter brought me back to the present. "The bracelet is wonderful, but…" Her blue eyes flickered. "You don't think I can come with you to see this place sometime, do you?"

My heart clenched. Sylvis was my best friend. We'd gone everywhere together… until now. "After this whole Prophecy thing is done and over with, I'll demand it. Just think; we could have a whole concert tour over there!"

We would have speculated further, but Aurora and Beau came in to start the session. For a while I forgot the insanity of the past few days and concentrated on doing the best I could to make the next album great.

But when we were done and finished dinner at our favorite Chinese place, all my troubles came back in a wave.

"What do you mean, you're leaving already?" Aurora asked sharply when Zareth announced our departure.

"Zareth got a new kitten. We don't want to leave him alone too long." How long could I avoid telling them the truth? Did the promise I made to my mom still apply? Would they even believe me without Zareth having to bring them through the portal, and thus put them in danger?

When we returned to Zareth's tower, I was heartened to see at least that I'd been telling the truth about the kitten.

Mine, mine, mine, he squealed while running to the sorcerer. His siblings ambled in behind him.

Isis was already teaching them to talk. My husband scooped up the tiny ball of gray and white fur and nuzzled the top of his head with his chin.

My husband. The thought hit me like a two by four. We'd had two weddings, yet no wedding night.

The first time was my fault. Between the wedding feast in Zareth's kingdom and the memorial feast with the Piscani, I'd gotten so drunk I passed out the second we got back to his tower.

But after we left the faelin last night, he still didn't broach the subject of sex. After we played with the kittens and went to bed, I'd lain beside him with my fists clenched in effort not to touch him.

My mind raced. *What if he doesn't want me? Had I disappointed him when we'd first made love? Or what if he's just tired from all the traveling and it would be rude to approach him?*

Still petting the kitten, Zareth looked up at me and frowned. "Is something amiss?"

"Do you still want me?" I blurted.

His lids lowered and his lips curved in a wicked smile before he laughed, low and dangerous. "Shall we go upstairs so I may show you?"

That smile made the sensitive flesh between my thighs pulse. Licking my lips, I nodded. He fed the cats and scooped me up in his arms.

Licking my earlobe, he whispered, "I believe it is Earth realm tradition for me to carry you."

It's a good thing he did, because my knees went weak at his touch. I melted further as his grip tightened on my thighs and he paused every few steps to give me drugging kisses. By the time we reached his bedchamber, moisture pooled between my thighs. Magic swirled around us, pulsing through the air in a building tempo.

When he set me on my feet, I swayed. Zareth pulled me into his arms and, for a long moment, just held me. In his warm embrace I felt cherished and content. Then he lowered his head and covered my lips with his, his tongue teasing the corners of my mouth until I opened for him, allowing him to deepen the kiss.

As he slipped my shirt over my head, I paused. "What if we make another storm?"

"We won't. Now that we're bonded, we can channel the power we raise." He pulled a clear crystal from his pocket that was one of our wedding gifts from the faelin, and set it on the nightstand. "When the magic comes forth, pour it into me. If it becomes too much, will it into the crystal."

I prayed I'd remember those instructions once caught in the throes of passion. "Will we have to do that every time?"

He shook his head and ran his fingers through my hair, making me shiver. "Soon we'll be able to contain the power and be able to channel it back into each other."

I laughed and shook my head. "You weren't kidding about mage sex. There are a lot of complications." I stopped cold, remembering a different sort of complication that every non-asexual creature encountered. I slapped my forehead.

"Um, Zareth?"

His eyes were heavy-lidded with desire as his hands slid from my hair to my shoulders. "Yes?"

"Don't we need protection? And what if I got pregnant the first time?" Panic welled up in me. I wasn't ready for a baby. How could I have been so stupid? Oh shit, and what about STDs? My mind contorted in effort to find the words to ask about that. A small insecure voice in my head wondered if such subjects would turn him off. I recoiled in revulsion at such a dangerous and ridiculous thought. No, he'd just have to deal with it.

Zareth hugged me tight. "There's nothing to worry about. We're not human. A faelin takes time to produce viable seed. A mage only gives his when he wills it, and luminite females are usually fertile every fifty years, though you may have quicker intervals, being only half." Bending down, he cupped my face in his hands. "Either way, mages can sense when a woman is fertile, or if she has a disease. Luminites have clear signs and symptoms when ready to breed."

My tensed spine relaxed, though my anxiety dissolved into curiosity. "How?"

His eyes glittered as he gave me a sexy smile. "You will go into a state of uncontrollable lust."

I gasped. "You mean I'll go into heat?"

He chuckled. "In a manner of speaking." His hands slid down to cup my ass. "I confess, I'm looking forward to it."

I leaned into him and worked my fingers under his shirt. My fingers explored the smooth muscles of his back. Satisfaction welled up when he made a small groan of pleasure. "I think it's your turn to take your shirt off," I murmured.

To my delight, he complied. For a moment all I could do was stare at his chiseled chest and abs with blatant appreciation. He was all mine.

When he reached for me I shook my head. "No, this time I want the chance to touch you."

Tentatively at first, my fingertips ran across his firm, silken flesh. Captivated by the hot feel and his intake of breath, I deepened my explorations, caressing his stomach with one hand while playing with his hard nipples. I marveled at the feel of him.

Emboldened by his response, I kissed him everywhere I'd touched, stroking his back with every kiss. Oh, but how did he taste? Zareth sucked in another breath when my tongue flicked across his nipple. He tasted of magic and exotic spices. I licked across his belly before tasting the spot that intrigued me most, the indents of muscle above his hip bones.

But that still wasn't enough.

"I want to see you," I whispered, unzipping his jeans.

Pulling down the denim, I saw that his boxers bulged with his erection. Gripping the waistband of the shorts, I slipped those down as well. My center pulsed with heat at the sight of his rigid length.

Slowly, my fingers grazed the tip, captivated with its velvety texture. My explorations continued along his shaft, taking in the heat of him, the curves and ridges. Grasping his length, I was awed at how something could feel so hard and silky all at once.

As Zareth stepped out of his jeans and underwear, I sank to my knees.

"Xochitl," he whispered raggedly.

"I want to taste you," I said, wrapping my lips around the swollen head of his cock.

At first I was embroiled in new discovery, trailing my tongue around the edges of his tip and across the ridges along his shaft. But as his groans of pleasure filled my ears and I looked up to see his head thrown back, mouth parted in bliss, my explorations turned into experiments.

Although only two days ago I was a virgin who'd never had the slightest intimate contact with a man, I now felt like a sex goddess. My hands and mouth wrought magic, invoking gasps and deep moans of masculine ecstasy.

His hands grasped my upper arms and he pulled me up, capturing my mouth in a deep and thorough kiss.

"It's my turn," he whispered against my lips as his hands unfastened my bra.

He was so tall that when he knelt, his face pressed between my breasts. Taking them in his hands, he licked and sucked their sensitive tips. A moan escaped my throat as I tangled my hands in his hair.

By the time he finished his ministrations on my breasts my legs had turned to jelly. His lips curved in another wicked smile before he bent to remove my boots and pulled down my pants, taking my panties with them.

He lifted me once more and laid me on the bed. His welcome weight settled on top of me as he kissed and nibbled my neck, making me quiver once more. As I arched my hips in silent pleading to feel him inside me, Zareth rolled over, pulling me on top of him.

Straddling him, I worked his hard length inside me, slow and careful, still growing accustomed to the powerful new sensations. From this angle he felt deeper, more intense, and I was able to see Zareth's pleasure expressed on his face.

Hands splayed against his chest, I rode him slowly at first, undulating my hips in different ways to find out what felt best. We were able to touch each other in this position and took full advantage of that. His hands cupped my breasts as I teased his nipples with every gentle rise and fall of my hips.

His calves shifted under and over mine, coming around to pin my ankles. The action spread my legs wider and worked him deeper. I gasped as I felt the tip of him press against a sensitive spot deep inside. Just when I thought that was too much, his hand slid down my hip and between my legs. His fingers toyed with my clit, making me squirm. The movement heightened my awareness of him inside me.

Grasping my hip with his other hand, Zareth coaxed me to move faster, deeper, harder. Enslaved to the powerful sensations of his cock pulsing inside me and his fingers stroking my clit, I was helpless to do anything but obey.

Finding a savage rhythm, the pleasure built and fed upon itself. And so did the magic. Remembering what happened before, I willed the magic into Zareth. His throaty growl and tightening grip made me wonder if he received my pleasure as well.

My thoughts vanished as the climax tore through me. Too intense to be bearable, I tried to withdraw. Zareth was merciless, gripping me tight, his hips moving beneath mine, thrusting deeper and harder. I cried out and matched his rhythm, gyrating against his hand as the orgasm rippled through me with eternal electricity.

His magic entangled with mine, growing and pulsing until I threw it into the crystal. Plenty remained, passing back and forth through our bodies, heightening my climax and bringing forth his own.

Thunder rumbled from the distance as I collapsed on top of him.

The brief flash of lightning made my heart stop. "Did we make another storm?"

"No, but some thunder is inevitable," he untangled his legs from mine and pulled me close, pointing at the end table. "Look at the crystal. There is our magic."

The thing lit up like a beacon, pulsating with a rainbow of colored light. I stared, rapt. "What will we do with it now?"

"Later we can draw the power for almost anything we like, and even more when the sun is restored."

I gasped at the implication. "Like a battery?"

He grinned. "Precisely."

"Cool." I nuzzled my cheek against his chest.

So far, being married wasn't so bad. I hoped it would stay this pleasant. Even more, I prayed he'd come to love me.

Chapter Twenty

Zareth

Zareth cursed as the ghostly bird dropped the envelope in his lap.

"Lord Amotken

You are hereby commanded to deliver the alleged Lioness of Light, Xochitl Leonine, to Varshek tower before the gold moon is full.

If you fail to do so, we shall interpret your refusal as a declaration of war.

Regards,

Shin Zen Li,

Archmage of the Conclave of High Sorcerers."

Zareth's upper lip curled in bitter amusement. This summons was certainly more curt than the other three.

The phantom bird even pecked at his arm and paced across his desk, waiting for a reply. Resisting the urge to dissipate it with his magic, he instead gave it a few choice words while fetching a pen and paper.

He decided to rival them in being even more terse.

Very well, was all he wrote.

After the bird flew off, he went to the library where he found Xochitl studying a book on the Tolonquan languages. He kissed her on the forehead before delivering the news. "I'm afraid we have to do more traveling."

"But we've only been home for a week." She pouted.

Unable to resist those lush lips, he bent and kissed them. "The Conclave has given up requesting your presence and has now resorted to demands and veiled threats. We should pay them a visit." He gave her a wry smile. "Though we will make a few stops on the way. I see no reason to rush overmuch."

She laughed. "Oh, can we visit the leprechauns?"

"They're not on our way, but since I intended to delay, of course we can." He glanced down at her book. "And then we'll visit the Tolonquan tribes."

Xochitl gave him a sharp look. "That's near Wurrakia and Laran."

Pride filled him that she'd studied the maps of his world so thoroughly. "Yes, I mean to do something about the Wurraks' unsanctioned occupation of my ally's territory." He smiled as he watched Xochitl scoop up her cat. "How are you and Isis progressing with the kittens' training?"

"They took to the litter box right away and they've been eating solid food for two days." As if hearing her praise, the four kittens pranced into the room, tails high in the air.

"Do you think they're ready to go to the Piscani?"

"If they have someone on hand to give them extra care and love," Xochitl said with a stern frown. "And it will be some time before they're big enough to catch rats."

He nodded. "Good. I was thinking of having the Piscani sail us to Verdan and then to the coast of Tolonqua. That way, Stefan's people are less likely to intercept us. We can deliver the kittens and my other gift to them."

"Oh!" Xochitl set the book aside and leapt up. "I've always wanted to sail on a ship!"

Her enthusiasm made him smile. There were so many experiences he wanted to share with her. They'd spent the past week working on Xochitl's training, then going to Earth to work on her recording before making love and talking until they fell asleep.

After packing for their journey, they gathered the kittens. Zareth named his "Chaos" after the little scamp made a mess in his laboratory. Xochitl's cat yowled excitedly.

"She's happy to revisit the fish people and telling Chaos about them," his bride explained.

***

The Piscani were pleased with their new light globes for the ships, as well as the gold he paid for their passage to Verdan. But to his surprise, they seemed most pleased with the kittens. Fights broke out regarding whose ships would get a kitten until Xochitl promised to bring them more. For the time being, the three kittens would reside on the Arch-Captains ship until they were sea-trained.

Zareth and Xochitl, along with their cats, boarded *Tamara's Fury*, a sleek galley captained by Amadeo, a rangy Piscani man with a gold tooth and wild curly black hair. Thorak, the Sea Sorcerer, would also accompany them, as he had a seat on the Conclave.

"I am very glad to be sailing again. I've been at port for too long," he told them. "I hope there will be good trading in Verdan this time."

"What do they trade?" Xochitl asked.

Both Zareth and Captain Amadeo laughed. "You'll see."

When the ship set sail, Isis and Chaos spent the first few hours in their cabin, frightened of the bobbing sensation of the ship. Xochitl felt no such trepidation and instead remained on deck, staring out in wonder at the cresting waves, illuminated by the light globes.

The sailors adored her at once, teaching her to climb the rigging, helping her with their language, and providing her with a sealskin coat lined with bear fur, and gloves, which she'd objected to until she learned that unlike on Earth, seals were almost overpopulated here.

Her glee was uncontainable when one of the sailors gave her a fishing rod, rigged with bait and a large hook. She caught four fish before Zareth managed to tear her away for dinner with the Captain.

Later in their cabin, they made love in rhythm with the waves.

By the time they reached Verdan, Xochitl was frowning at the black sea. "I love the night, but I wish I could see this in the daylight. Why can't I bring back the sun now?"

Thorak, the Sea Sorcerer, patted her shoulder. "There are many factors that must be in place for your magic to work. Have patience, little Lioness, the Solstice is little more than a silver-moon's cycle away."

Chastened, she answered back in heavily accented Piscani, "I'm sorry. I'd forgotten everyone else has gone without the sun for four years. I must sound so childish." Her brows drew together. "If it's been four years, why isn't it colder? After so long without a sun, everything should be frozen."

Thorak and Zareth exchanged glances before the Sea Sorcerer turned back to Xochitl.

"Very few people question such things," Thorak told her. "You are as wise as you are beautiful. Lord Amotken is a lucky man. The reason we haven't frozen to death is because the sun isn't truly gone. It is merely obscured. Heat and other particles still pass through the barrier."

She frowned. "Like a cloud of despair?"

"An apt term." Thorak nodded in approval. "Your boat is ready to bring you ashore. Here is where I must say goodbye for now. I am off to Varshek tower. I'll see you there."

"You're not staying to trade?"

He shook his head. "I need a few days alone at sea to draw more power. The Captain is lowering my skiff right now."

The leprechauns awaited them on the beach with glowing lanterns to light their way.

"Wow," Xochitl whispered, staring at the rainbows of colors and flashes of jewels on the little folk. "They look different than I'd expected."

"What had you expected?"

She shrugged. "You know, green suits, red hair, top hats, shoes and belts with big buckles."

Zareth raised a brow. "That sounds even stranger than their usual garb." Leprechauns didn't have a formal style of dress. They'd wear anything they came across. They preferred brightly colored and ornamented garments and were in eternal competition with each other on who could look the most garish.

"Lord Amotken!" Prince Carrick called out. Dressed in a bright yellow surcoat embroidered with gold thread, an ungodly pink cloak trimmed with blue fur and lime green trousers studded with silver buttons, he was almost painful to look upon. "I was but a wee lad when last I saw ye!"

Indeed, it had been over a century since he'd visited Verdan to trade with Carrick's father, who was certain to be dead by now. Leprechauns only lived about two hundred years.

Zareth bowed. "Carrick, well met. I've come to trade and introduce you to my bride."

A swarm of leprechauns had already surrounded Xochitl, fascinated with her purple-streaked hair. It took a moment to spot her as she stood just a few inches taller than them.

Carrick's leaf green eyes widened. "You've wed at last?"

Zareth smiled. "Twice over, first by Delgarias, then by Queen Nicharana of the faelin."

"Then it would only do for us to wed you too," Carrick crossed his arms and gave him a look that refuted all protests. "But first we trade."

Carrick's people nodded. "Yes, trade!" Many darted off to their homes to gather their wares.

Zareth nodded. "Of course." Wading through the remaining leprechauns, he took Xochitl's arm. "Now you'll see why I asked you to pack some miscellaneous items."

Carrick led them over to a door set in a large hill. Zareth had to duck to pass through, but Xochitl didn't. He chuckled.

The gathering mound hadn't changed much since Zareth was here last. Rows of tables stood on one side near the adjoining kitchen, with a great open area. Streamers, tapestries and multicolored glass lights hung on the walls.

Everyone gathered in a carpeted section by the fire and sat in a circle. Those who wished to trade spilled their items out on the carpet and extolled the virtues of their "treasures."

Unlike the myths on Earth, leprechauns didn't hoard pots of gold. They liked anything shiny or bright. Zareth grinned as he saw buttons, ribbons, and even balls of tinfoil from Earth. Come to think of it, that would be a useful item in this world, for outdoor cooking. But he knew its owner would be horrified at the prospect of the foil being anything but ornamental.

As Xochitl dumped out her loot, everyone crowded around her and exclaimed over her mismatched hair clips, broken necklace chains, guitar picks, and other miscellaneous Earth realm items. Her treasures would be the most coveted.

Sure enough, few came up to observe his collection of crystals, glass vials, candleholders, and feathers. Still, he made satisfactory barters, coming away with a steel ladle and a salt shaker that he'd later trade to the Tolonqua, as well as a vial of rose oil and a sapphire that would be beneficial for his spells.

Many frowned upon trading with leprechauns, often scorning the majority of useless things to be had, but Xochitl embraced the negotiations, cheerfully haggling for a pewter figurine of a cat and a feather quill pen. Her unabashed delight in the custom made him look on the experience with new eyes.

"This reminds me of going to yard sales, but even better!" she exclaimed.

"What is a yard sale?" her new friends asked until Carrick held up a hand. "Let's save it for the time of tales."

All nodded solemnly and resumed trading, which took another two hours. The leprechauns laughed and played with Isis and Chaos. By then the feast was almost ready and Carrik declared it was time for the wedding. Zareth stood, joints creaking from remaining cross-legged on the floor so long.

A leprechaun wedding custom was simpler than most. There was no dressing up and little ceremonial gestures. They vowed to share their treasures, laughter, and adventures as long as they lived.

Then they were bade to jump over broomsticks and break plates. Zareth didn't understand the symbolism behind this part, but Xochitl's laughter and infectious glee made him not care.

After they feasted on racks of lamb and braised potatoes, everyone returned to the circle with mugs of honey-wine and exchanged tales, happy and sad. All were intrigued by Xochitl's description of yard sales on Earth, and delighted at Zareth's tales of their previous weddings.

But when a leprechaun named Donnalen spoke of his missing brother and another chimed in about their missing cousins, Zareth frowned. *More missing people?*

"I've had people disappear from my lands as well," Zareth told them. "Since then I've learned that all but the faelin have experienced this troubling calamity."

Carrick nodded. "Yes, we've grown worried upon learning that this is also happening to the tall folk." His gaze was wide and solemn. "'Tis a crying shame, with all the other troubles our world is suffering."

"Yes, in the face of this turmoil, it is good for us to band together. I propose an alliance between my people and yours." He bowed at the leprechaun king.

Carrick grasped his hand and pumped it with a surprising vigor for such a small man. "Oh yes, you have been friends to my people for centuries. 'Tis only fitting."

Though the leprechaun spoke as if he were approached for alliances all the time, Zareth noted the pleased gleam in his gaze. Most people scorned leprechauns for their size and odd customs. However, Zareth knew they were useful. With their small statures, constant travel, gift for languages, and most importantly, the fact that they were not highly regarded gave them the ability to acquire information no one else picked up. He couldn't hope for better eyes and ears.

Zareth bowed again. "You honor me."

After the festivities, he and Xochitl slept on several pallets put together in the royal mound, for none of the beds were big enough for him. Lovemaking was a little awkward at first, but they made it work.

In the morning he was surprised to find himself reluctant to depart such amiable company, but it could not be helped. He needed to speak to the Tolonqua and deal with Laran.

The Piscani met them along the coast where they'd been fishing for halibut and digging mussels in exchange for trading fishing lures and abalone shells to the leprechauns.

The voyage was quick, thanks to a wind he and Xochitl summoned.

A group of Tolonquan warriors awaited them near the shore as they banked. Mounted on large elk, they were a formidable people.

Zareth bowed and announced his intentions to them in their language. Xochitl even managed to greet them in their tongue, which gained her their immediate regard. Pride rang through him at her rapid learning.

The leader of the warrior band assisted them atop his own elk while he rode double with another. They were brought to Chief Runningwolf, who, after hearing Zareth's news, insisted on a Tolonquan wedding ceremony.

When he translated that to Xochitl, she laughed. Zareth was less amused, for according to tradition, he had to build her a tipi. Trading everything he'd received from the leprechauns as well as casks of salted fish from the Piscani, he was able to acquire good hides. A forage party then took him out to the woods to cut lodge poles and, taking mercy on him, they helped him select and cut them.

While he slaved over the tipi, Xochitl was taken to the river and scrubbed before garbed in a doeskin dress and presented with a cloak made from a mountain lion's fur, a gift from the chief. She refused to wear it until she learned the animal was killed in self-defense.

They were then brought before the Chief to negotiate each other's gifts. Runningwolf acknowledged that Zareth's gift of a staff was impressive and he was amused with the kitten Xochitl gave him, but he then ordered them to present each other with elks and sage, and hematite before two turns of the silver moon, lest they incur bad luck. Zareth smiled wryly at the realization most of these things could be acquired solely through the Tolonqua.

With the Chief's blessing, they were then escorted to the Shaman's tent to be painted with sacred symbols in henna and purified with smoke. Only then were they pronounced worthy to go before the people and announce their union.

This was Zareth's favorite part.

Scooping Xochitl up in his arms, he carried her into the tent he'd built for her. The tribespeople whooped at the rumbles of thunder and flashes of lightning.

The next morning— discernible due to the proliferation of torches and lanterns— was dedicated to the feasts. Zareth wanted to approach the Chief regarding alliance and then head off to deal with the Wurraks, but he knew better than to disrespect the tribe by interrupting the formalities.

Besides, it was a delight to see her sitting with the tribespeople, helping with the meal preparations as they coached her in their language. She would make a magnificent queen, with the way she was able to interact with other cultures and learn and respect their traditions.

After a sumptuous meal of roast venison, corn cakes, fry bread, and some delicious berry concoction, they sang and danced with the tribe until they were ready to collapse in exhaustion. After that, the Chief accepted his terms of alliance and promised to guard Xochitl while he dealt with Laran. The discussion went easy, likely because the Tolonqua and Wurraks were sworn enemies.

With a Tonlonquan war party at his back, he left for Laran.

He was disturbed to learn that the Tolonquans were also plagued with disappearances.

How many were the Laranese missing?

Chapter Twenty-one

Xochitl

Trying to keep my eyes on the road, I couldn't keep from glancing at Zareth. He'd been quiet ever since he returned from Laran and we departed for the Conclave. A cut healed on his brow and his eyes appeared shadowed and haunted.

"Are you okay?" I asked again.

He reached over and put his hand on my lap and squeezed my thigh. "The Wurraks refused to vacate Laran without a fight. I can still smell their flesh cooking in their armor from my lightning." His shoulders slumped in the passenger seat. "Now I have no hope of turning them from their alliance with Stefan."

I grabbed his hand and held it tight. "You did what you had to do to free your people. Don't feel guilty because they wouldn't go peacefully."

As I parked before Varashek tower and we got out, it was my turn for unease.

"Don't worry my Lioness, you will do just fine." Zareth gripped my hand as I took in the sight of the dark gray tower looming over us.

This was the place where the Conclave met. And today their meeting was about me. I clenched Zareth's hand tighter and looked down in disgust at my other hand that was shaking.

*Chill out, Xochitl. Think of it as a concert or an interview on
TV. You used to be nervous about them and did fine.*
I drew a deep breath in preparation of the encounter to
come. "Okay, let's go."
Zareth bent his head and covered my lips with his in a
sensual, teasing kiss. When he drew away, my knees felt like
water.
He led me to the entrance of the tower. The arched
doorway reminded me of a cathedral, but I didn't have much
time to admire it, for soon we were approached by a very old
wizard in black robes like Zareth's and a long beard that
nearly reached the floor.
"Lord Amotken, how good of you to grace us with your
august presence at last." The scathing disrespect in the old
man's voice made me step back.
Who the hell did he think he was?
Zareth remained composed under the vitriol. "I'd
dispatched more than one message stating that I would bring
The Lioness when we were ready."
"But it is up to us to verify whether or not she is indeed
the Lioness." the man countered. "You have cost us precious
time, for if she is the wrong one, you have doomed us all."
"Delgarias himself verified her even before I found her
through dream summoning." Zareth crossed his arms over his
chest. "I am accustomed to you refuting my word, Shin Zen
Li, but do you presume to doubt the most ancient sorcerer in
the world?"
Shin Zen Li spluttered and ran a nervous hand through his
beard. "The Revered One has been absent as of late." A
worried look flashed across his worn features before he
straightened his stooped shoulders. "Either, way it is protocol
for the Conclave to be present and share observations before

convening on important matters. Now that you've delivered the alleged Lioness, I will bring her before them. You may wait in the antechamber before we call you for your testimony."

He moved to take my arm but Zareth thrust his staff between us. "I will remain with my bride."

"You *wed* her?" Shin Zen Li's eyes bugged out so much that I was afraid they'd rupture.

"It was necessary."

Before Zareth could tell his version of the tale, I interjected, "*I* seduced him." For good measure, I brought forth small tendrils of fire from own staff. "Allow me to introduce myself. I am Xochitl Goldmoon Leonine, daughter of Kerainne Silvara Leonine, princess of Medicia."

Titles impressed these people, and maybe if this guy heard mine, he'd quit talking over me like I wasn't there.

Shin Zen Li changed his tune, bowing before me and even reaching to kiss my hand before I snatched it back. "It is a pleasure to meet you, dearest Lady, and welcome to the Conclave of the High Sorcerers. Of course your consort may accompany you."

We were led through a great hall adorned with torches and embroidered tapestries and then into a massive bowl-like room that looked much like an old college lecture hall. Shin Zen Li escorted us to the bottom of the bowl to stand near the podium. I looked up at about a hundred inquisitive faces staring down at us and tried to suppress my nervousness.

Zareth squeezed my hand and bent to whisper in my ear. "Don't worry, dearling. They shall likely find you more intimidating. Drop your shields"

I managed a weak smile, but did not let go of his hand as I obeyed. Admittedly, I was pleased with the collective gasp that ensued.

My pounding heart slowed when I saw a few familiar faces. Thorak, the Piscani Sea Sorcerer, Jeanette, the duchess of Kinsen, and Queen Nicharana of the faelin all had seats in the Conclave. My relief fled in a wisp as I saw another familiar face. Stefan Carcineris met my gaze with a look that reminded me of a wolf cornering a rabbit. His allies sat beside him, glaring at Zareth.

"Mages of the Conclave of Aisthanesthai," Shin Zen Li announced, "It is my pleasure to present the Lioness of Light to you. Lord Amotken has found her and they have recently wed."

I looked back up to see many other mages bowing to me in respect or peering at me curiously— except one. A thin man in black robes with raven hair streaked with silver, though not like Zareth's. He looked more human than faelin, except for his golden eyes, which peered at me as if he were reading my soul. His thin, arched lips then curved into a ghost of a smile, though I detected much cynicism in it.

Everyone wouldn't revere me, it seemed. I didn't know whether to be relieved or disappointed.

Stefan's eyes narrowed in icy fury at the news. Frost crept over his clenched fists. I cuddled against my husband and gave him a smug grin. No more disgusting overtures from the Winter Prince.

One woman's voice cried out in dismay. "Then it is the Dark Lord who will have dominion over us after all!"

Zareth's fists clenched at his sides, pain slashing across his face. I grabbed his hand and squeezed it. My heart ached to see him hurt.

Exclamations echoed through the hall at the woman's declaration. Stefan steepled his fingers and smirked. His allies exchanged smarmy grins.

"Lady De Jinn!" Nicharana hissed in outrage. "You will compose yourself at once. How dare you speak of Lord Amotken with such disrespect! He will likely be your king soon. You haven't even had a conversation with the man and you already judge him as evil? What a pitiful example of the human race you are."

"Aye!" Thorak pounded his ale mug on the table. "Lord Amotken is a good man and will make a worthy king."

The woman's eyes grew as wide as saucers as she realized that she had spoken out against one who wasn't as feared and reviled as she had thought. Chastened, she lowered her head and became engrossed in the whorls on the surface of the wooden table. I grinned at the faelin queen.

Zareth looked amused, but under it all I saw surprised awe at his defense.

Stefan visibly seethed. I half expected to see steam coming out of his ears.

There was a lot of shouting and arguing amongst themselves about our marriage, but Zareth's expression remained disinterested. I was not so composed. I vacillated between embarrassment and even a bit of anger washed over me. This argument centered around *my* relationship.

Oblivious to the conflict, Isis and Chaos chased each other around the chamber, drawing reluctant smiles from a few.

Stefan rose from his seat. "The marriage cannot be valid. Weddings amongst royalty and the most powerful mages must be sanctioned by the Conclave." He regarded everyone with such fury that they drew back. "The union must be dissolved."

A chill covered me like a shroud at the thought of our marriage ending. My heart constricted as I realized I *wanted* to stay wed to Zareth.

Lightning flickered in Zareth's eyes. "There will be no dissolution. We are wed... four times over."

The golden eyed mage appeared beside me. Zareth raised his staff in warning.

Rasping laughter met the gesture. "Four times? That *is* impressive." He glanced back at the Conclave. "Though just because she wed him does not mean she will crown him."

"Rayven Niltsiar." False cheer dripped from Zareth's voice. "It is surprising to see you here. What brings you away from your tower and your studies? Don't tell me you missed all of your friends here."

The way he said it made me realize that Rayven probably wasn't very popular in the Conclave of the High Mages. It was no wonder, if he was so scornful and sarcastic all the time. Thanks to Zareth's lessons, I also sensed great power in him, more than in most of the others in the tower.

Rayven smirked. "Of course not. The mage's council of Desmana were curious to look upon the Lioness. I was the chosen envoy. I confess I'm not as disappointed with her as I thought I would be." He inclined his head. "May I see your staff?"

I glanced at Zareth and handed my new treasure over at his nod.

Rayven ran his finger along the varnished wood and the top of the stone with genuine reverence. "Fresh carved lilac wood, a garnet of Medicia set in faelin silver..." Handing the staff back to me, he once more addressed Zareth. "Excellent craftsmanship. It must have taken you some time."

Heated whispers surrounded us. With a slight incline of his head, Rayven vanished to reappear in his seat.

"*You* made it?" An older sorceress exclaimed in outrage. "So you began courting her from the start without giving the Winter Prince a fair opportunity!"

My eyes widened. If the staff was part of a courtship ritual and Zareth had been working on it long before our abrupt wedding... did he mean to be with me in the first place? Since I'd jumped the gun and seduced him, maybe I'd never know.

Stefan latched on the sorceress's words. "Yes! How can this be a valid union when I had no chance to press my own suit!"

As the Conclave erupted anew, Delgarias appeared at the podium. "Cease this foolishness at once! Zareth and Xochitl wed of their own free will. Their joining was foretold. I wed them myself and they shared the kiss of blood and magic."

"Revered One!" the mages gasped in unison.

I grinned at the trick and wondered if Zareth would teach me how to poof in and out of places.

"I will hear no more questioning on this marriage. Our concern is the Solstice and the Lioness's fulfillment of the Prophecy."

Stefan leaned forward, knuckles white on his seat. "How do we know she is indeed the Lioness? If she's the daughter of the luminite princess, where are her wings?"

The cronies surrounding him nodded.

"Yes, where are her wings?" a man said in a voice laced with skepticism as his eyes roved over me. "She's quite small. Are you sure that she is capable of performing such a big task?"

"Joseph, you are a fool." Jeanette hissed. "Maybe someday you will learn that in many cases size doesn't matter.

Perhaps you have a subconscious insecurity that you need to deal with."

Joseph's face turned a furious purple at the innuendo. Coughs and a few muted snickers echoed in the chamber.

I giggled and silently congratulated Jeanette for her cleverness. The duchess saluted me with a wineglass.

"Enough!" Shin Zen Li pounded his staff on the floor. His gaze narrowed on me. "Can you bring out your wings?"

I shook my head. "As far as I know, I don't have them, or at least not yet."

A memory flitted through my mind. Something horrible had happened to me after school one day that overwrought me with pain and rage. I hazily recalled making it to Akasha's house, my back contorting with pain while she cleaned and treated cuts and scrapes. My friend's sharp intake of breath as my bones shifted beneath my skin. *What the fuck?* she'd said. *Are you a shapeshifter or something?*

When I'd calmed, the pain subsided. Had those been my wings trying to come out?

Before I could tell that story, Stefan's smarmy voice intruded. "You see? My brother has the wrong female."

"Then we are all doomed!" someone cried.

"Nonsense," Zareth's voice rose. "There is other proof. First off, luminites are incapable of fear. Xochitl passed through my Nightmare Forest on the Spirit Feast. Stefan himself witnessed that feat." The outbursts ceased as he continued. "Secondly, her voice holds the magic of inspiration that is required to banish the despair. When I went to the Earth realm to find her, I saw her on a stage in a tavern singing as she played haunting music on an electric guitar. Her voice touched my heart and awakened my soul. It gave me chills even as it burned me. I vow that it possesses a power unlike any that has ever existed before. Others have heard her power and can attest to it."

Jeanette and Queen Nicharana nodded in agreement. "Prince Amotken speaks true," Nicharana said, "We'd expected nothing less from the daughter of Kerainne Leonine."

Shin Zen Li crossed his arms and frowned. "Let's hear her sing now so that we may judge for ourselves whether her voice has power or not."

"Aye! Let's hear the bonny lass's song!" A high melodious voice called out.

I looked to see King Carrick at the end of the table. Funny, I hadn't noticed him before.

"Ah, Carrick, I see you've decided to join us." Delgarias said with amusement.

"The leprechauns rarely come to the meetings." Zareth explained. "They find them boring and consisting of too many 'tall folk.'"

"I don't blame them," I whispered back.

"Xochitl, would you please sing for us?" Shin Zen Li implored.

Biting back a sigh, I pulled out my acoustic guitar and played a song I wrote after my mom died.

As I sang, a few orange and red stone necklaces and rings glowed. The sight almost made me forget the next verse as my audience gaped in wonder. A few mages pulled paper and pens from their pockets and wrote frantically.

My voice stumbled, but I recovered under Zareth's tender gaze. I sang the rest to him to avoid further distraction.

When the final notes died away, the Conclave sat frozen. Their stares were so strange I was afraid I'd angered them. Then I noticed tears rolling down their cheeks.

I was about to apologize when Jeanette clapped and everyone else followed suit. "That was amazing my dear. Your voice is getting stronger."

"I agree." The faelin queen dabbed her eyes with a handkerchief. "I will have my minstrels write sad songs, to mourn the deaths of all living things."

"Her voice *is* magical!" Thorak declared, mopping away his tears with his long red beard. "Already I feel inspiration coursing through me again. I will carve a figurehead of the angel that was your mother and name a ship after her. You must describe her to me so that when I go to the afterlife I may recognize her and congratulate her for having such an incredible daughter."

Rayven's sardonic demeanor softened, gold eyes large. "The sun and fire stones glowed. For the first time in years!"

Delagarias surveyed them all with a smug smile. "Is the matter settled?"

The majority nodded.

"But if she sings now, what difference will it make on the Solstice?" Joseph pulled everyone back to reality.

I couldn't help but nod. Good question. Maybe the man did have a brain cell or two.

"I am certain it relates to the alignment of the moons," a Tolonquan shaman stated. "The Prophecy says that both of the moons will be full in the sky on the night of the Winter Solstice. We all know how rare of an occurrence that is. And every time the moons have been full on the same eve, something phenomenal happened."

"She is also the daughter of Mephistopheles." One of Stefan's cronies gave me a dark look. "How do we know she won't take after him?"

Queen Nicharana raised a brow. "The fact that she's prophesied to save us, rather than destroy us, is a good indicator of whose blood she follows."

There were a few more questions about me and the Prophecy and inquiries about Zareth's latest activities and congratulations on our marriage before Delgarias silenced everyone with a gesture. "Now that Xochitl is verified as the Lioness, where shall we gather on the Solstice to witness the fulfillment of the Prophecy?"

"Boreaus," Stefan said.

"Raijin," Zareth countered. "It's fitting for her to be presented at our home."

"Luminites cannot abide the cold," Delgarias told Stefan. "We don't want to risk mitigating her magic."

Zareth grinned until Delgarias continued. "And Raijin has no gathering area sufficient for the crowds who will amass to witness the miracle." He pointed at a great map that hung on the wall behind us. "I suggest the palace courtyard in Niji, before your father's old castle."

"That sounds fair enough." Zareth said. "I will have her there on the Solstice."

Stefan nodded. "Very well, I suppose that is a suitable location."

Although the jerk was being agreeable for once, I didn't like his odd half smile. He'd sent an army after us just a few weeks ago. I doubted he'd given up.

Shin Zen Li returned to the podium. "Now shall we address other business?"

Zareth stood. "Many of my people have vanished from my lands. During my travels with my new bride, I've learned that the Piscani, the Tolonqua, the Laran and even the Leprechauns also have missing people. What of the rest of you?"

All but the faelin raised their hands in confirmation. Even Stefan.

As they discussed the disappearances, it turned out that Stefan had the most.

"Perhaps Zareth is responsible," Stefan said with an accusing glare at my husband. "After all, he hates me."

I glared at him. "Or maybe they all left you because they hate *you*."

Shouts and mutters echoed around me until Shin Zen Li silenced them. Ignoring the accusations, he instead demanded everyone testify what they knew. No one accomplished anything in solving the mystery.

Other business and grievances were addressed, but my attention wandered as Stefan's presence infuriated me further. I couldn't wait to get away from him.

Thankfully when the session came to a close, he didn't pursue Zareth and me on our way out.

Chapter Twenty-two

Zareth

Xochitl laughed as they drove away from the Conclave's tower. "That went well."

"Well?" Zareth raised a brow. "Did you not see the dissent my brother sowed?"

"Yes, but since you worked so hard to gain so many alliances during our travels, I knew Stefan's scheme wouldn't work." She grinned at him before turning back to face the road. "How many feasts do you think he's been attending?"

"Probably very few, but that doesn't matter as much as we'd like to think." He sighed. "For as many who stood with me for having broken bread with them, others stood against me for slighting them by not paying them a visit."

Her eyes flashed in anger. "That's ridiculous. Aside from pissing off the Conclave with more delays, there's no way we could have visited everyone before the Solstice."

"Egos are never logical." He covered his mouth, yawning. "Either way, I'm relieved to be heading home soon." It was past time for him to have some peace and quiet with his new bride.

They were halfway home before Xochitl's Datsun sputtered out. The dash lights flickered as if in frustration before it made a noise that sounded unnervingly alive.

"Damn it," Xochitl groaned. "We're out of gas."

Zareth ground his teeth. Were the fates conspiring against him? After they exited the car, he shrank it down so it could be carried. "As soon as the sun is restored, we'll have to do some adjustments on this car so it won't need gas."

"We can do that?" she asked, pocketing her car and lifting Isis onto her shoulder.

Chaos curled up in his pocket, asleep. "Not exactly. We'll hire a metal mage. They're experts in blending the mechanical with magic. And maybe he or she will be able to see what you did to this car in the first place. For now, let us walk to the nearest village and see if we can get a ride closer to home. I do not have the energy to teleport this whole way. The absence of the sun weakens me every turn of the moons."

Xochitl's worried glance pierced his heart. Her lush lips parted and a soothing song flowed through him, giving him much-needed energy as they walked down a forest path.

Zareth halted when he spotted a familiar cave. An old acquaintance resided there. Xochitl would be delighted to meet him, though just in case his friend was still hibernating, he kept his intention secret.

He pointed out a cluster of purple wildflowers growing around the mouth of the cave. Purple was Xochitl's favorite color.

"Would you like me to pick some for you?" he asked her.

"Sure!" Her pretty blush gratified him.

Just when he bent down and reached for a stem, a deafening roar resounded from the cave's entrance, rooting them to the spot.

"Who dares to disturb my rest!" A loud voice growled.

Chaos squirmed in his robe, so he put the kitten back to sleep with a muttered word. Without being told, Xochitl did the same with Isis.

A pair of huge glowing yellow eyes peered at them before a dragon with glittering turquoise scales stepped out of the cave. Its reptilian gaze shifted to them and Zareth felt a twinge of unease. What if the dragon didn't remember him?

The dragon's snout edged closer, sniffing them.

"Lord Amotken!" he boomed. "I'm surprised to see you! It has been a long time since you've paid me a visit."

Xochitl blinked dumbfounded at the dragon's cheerful tone, though she couldn't understand what it said.

Zareth sighed in relief. His plan hadn't backfired. "Xandizion! You are looking well. I came to introduce you to my new bride." He gestured to her. "May I present to you, Xochitl Goldmoon Leonine, the Lioness of Light. She is the daughter of Kerainne Leonine, princess of the luminites."

"The Lioness of Light?" Xandizion raised a scaly brow. "She is the one to bring the sun back?"

Zareth nodded and translated their conversation to Xochitl.

The dragon snaked his head forward to examine her. Despite the dragon's daunting size, she stood her ground and smiled politely. "It is nice to meet you."

The dragon seemed to smile his approval when Zareth translated.

They spent the next hour describing their trip and Zareth explained the current political situations in the world from the last few years, for Xandizion had been asleep for an entire decade. And though he somehow knew everything the Prophecy had depicted in that time, he had no clue what else had happened during his nap.

When Xochitl was nearly asleep on her feet, the dragon offered to give them a ride to the border of Zareth's tower.

Zareth bowed in gratitude. One never asked to mount a dragon. Only the dragon could volunteer such a gift.

The flight on the dragon's back was more than a little unnerving. His stomach dipped queasily with the ascent. Xochitl, on the other hand, was delighted. She clung to Zareth's waist and cried out in glee as Xandizion swooped up and down through the sky. The kingdom below looked so tiny and insignificant from the grand and omniscient height.

Zareth closed his eyes against the dizzying view and focused on Xochitl's joyous squeals. Her voice coupled with the warmth of her body pressed against him made the flight more bearable.

Xandizion landed on the edge of the Nightmare Forest.

"This is as far as I can take you," the dragon said.

"I thank you for bringing us this far." Zareth extended his hand to Xochitl to help her dismount. They made it to the ground on wobbly feet.

"Farewell, Lord Amotken." The dragon then bowed his serpentine head at Xochitl. "Lioness, it was an honor to make your acquaintance. My kin and I will see you again on the Solstice."

After the dragon flew off, the kitten stirred in the folds of Zareth's robes. He transported them to the tower grounds before his little Chaos would sense the Nightmare Forest and bolt away. He was just in time, for the kitten wriggled free and darted away to explore the grounds. Isis followed suit.

Not seeming to be in any hurry, Xochitl walked through the courtyard, watching the cats frolic. Tenderness filled him as he looked at her. She was so ungodly beautiful, with silver moonlight reflecting on smooth skin and hair, gold gleaming in her eyes. What had he done to deserve her?

"I love you," he couldn't stop the words.

His heart thudded in the heavy silence as he feared she'd reject his declaration.

Then she threw her arms around him. "Oh, Zareth, I love you too."

When she withdrew from his embrace, he saw tears trickling down her cheeks. Grasping her face, he swept the tears away with his thumbs. "What's wrong?"

She reached up and stroked his cheek. "I'm just overwhelmed. It's not so much about me being the Lioness or my introduction to Aisthanesthai and its diverse people, or even my bizarre parentage. Actually, all that stuff explained a lot of previously unanswered questions I'd mulled over for years. What I'm still having trouble believing is that you, the man from my dreams, is real and that you love me. It almost seems too good to be true." Her expression grew wary. "If I wake up and it's all been a dream…" she trailed off.

Zareth embraced her and bent to nibble her neck, reveling in the way he made her shiver. "Now I'm going to show you how much I love you."

An impish grin curved her lips. "You'll have to catch me first!"

She darted away before he could reach for her.

Xochitl was far into the rear grounds when suddenly Zareth pounced on her, knocking her to the ground. She shrieked with laughter and tried to tickle him. They rolled around on the grass until she struck her shoulder on something cold and hard.

"Ow! What the fuck?" She pushed her hair away from her eyes and looked up to see that they were lying next to the silver fence that enclosed the garden of black roses. "Ooh, can we go walk through the garden?"

"I don't know," he replied with reluctance, but Xochitl was undeterred.

"I have to feel the peace of this place again. And maybe you can tell me how it came to be here and why you let it fall into disrepair." She gave him a winsome smile and crooned, "Pleeeeease?"

He regarded the fence, reaching out to caress the petals of a midnight rose between the bars. Unbidden, a sad, half smile crossed his lips. "I suppose we could do that."

He helped her to her feet and they walked over to the gate that was so overgrown with rose bushes that it was barely discernible. Zareth reached into one of the pouches at his waist and pulled out a tarnished silver key. Resolutely, he put the key into the lock he found from memory, and turned it. A loud groan echoed off the tower walls as the gate swung open. They winced at the agonizing noise and sighed with relief when it ended; though they could still hear the echo in the air and would continue to hear it in their minds for a long time.

"I think I'll just leave it open for now," Zareth said with a wry smile. "I have no desire to hear that sound again anytime soon."

"What if somebody gets in?" she asked with concern.

"That is highly unlikely. Aside from the Nightmare Forest, I have so many warding spells on this garden that it would be nearly impossible for anyone to violate its sanctity. Though somehow you managed to get past them." He wagged a scolding finger.

"I didn't know there were spells on it." She sounded defensive. "I just hopped over the fence with no trouble at all."

Zareth frowned. "It was locked for a reason, you know."

"I couldn't help it. I was curious. Besides, you're the one who pointed out that I have no respect for authority."

His memory flew back to that night, when he came upon her in the garden. How her transparent nightgown had revealed her curves, how he'd struggled to maintain discipline and scold her in the face of his mad desire.

Xochitl put a hand over her mouth, stifling a giggle.

"What are you thinking about?" Zareth inquired.

She shrugged her shoulders. "I just realized you're probably grateful I broke into your garden."

Zareth crossed his arms and raised a brow. "Oh? And why is that?"

Her breasts pressed against him as she whispered, "It gave you an excuse to get me in your bed."

He gave her a sideways look. "Perhaps. What about you? Were you really as outraged as you acted?"

"Wouldn't you like to know?" Despite the saucy reply, her cheeks were bright pink.

They entered the garden and walked in silence. Xochitl looked around in unmasked wonder at her surroundings. Everything shone with the light of the full golden moon, gleaming on the petals of the roses and on the exquisite statues even as it reflected off of the stream, turning it into a narrow ribbon of molten gold.

"I dreamed about this garden for years," she said, trailing her fingers across a rose.

"You did?" He looked at her sharply. How was that possible?

She nodded. "I'd thought this is where you'd been dream summoning me. I'd see you on the path and then the roses started dying, the petals shriveling and falling off. And you'd come toward me, commanding me to come to you."

"But I never summoned you from here." Zareth couldn't hide his shock. "I was either in my laboratory or the lilac grove."

Xochitl's head cocked to the side. "Where did you see me in your dreams?"

"It varied," Zareth spoke past his racing thoughts. Why did she see him here? "Sometimes you were in a forest, other times you were on a beach by what looked like a lake."

"And I was really in bed asleep every time," she said. "It's interesting that we saw each other in different places. I know the forests and lakes in Coeur d'Alene were important to me, so this garden must be important to you." She looked up at him, brows drawn together in a perplexed frown. "Why haven't you been here for so long, Zareth? Why did you let the garden get so neglected?"

He sighed. "I'm sure that you will not leave me alone until you hear the story."

She fixed him with a relentless stare. "Damn straight."

"Very well." They continued walking as he began. "Long ago, when I was still mortal, my mother gave me this garden as a quiet place for me to practice my magic. I had long admired it for its midnight roses and beautiful statues. They were carved by artisans of the Leonine family and given to her as a gift. For all I know, your mother may have even created one of them."

She reached out and caressed a statue's sculpted hair. "Wow. No wonder they're so perfect," she breathed in awe."

"I created many spells here, alone and with my first— and last— coven. They were my best friends until my father gave me the hydra. Immediately they demanded I tell them how to summon their own so we could be immortals together. But I couldn't, because it's forbidden without the king's and

Conclave's approval." His shoulders slumped as the old helplessness washed over him anew. "They accused me of hoarding the secret to myself and said I was no true friend of theirs for not sharing it with them. All cursed me on their deathbeds, except for Rayven, my last apprentice. He cursed me and found a hydra of his own. So instead of losing a friend to death, I lost one to a bitter misunderstanding."

Xochitl's eyes widened. "Rayven? Was that the sorcerer at the Conclave?"

"Yes." He still didn't know what had triggered the mage's outburst. Zareth had tried to renew their friendship four centuries ago, but the mage had thrown his offer back in his teeth.

"But he stuck up for us," she said. "Maybe he doesn't hate you anymore."

"Perhaps, one can never tell what Rayven's motives are. It might be that he hates the Conclave more." He hoped her interest would switch back to the Conclave, but it was not to be.

Xochitl touched his arm. "You avoid the garden because it reminds you of lost friends?"

"Partly, but more because it makes me think of my mother." A lump formed in his throat. "As my mother grew older and weakened, she came to live with me. She liked to sit out here with the sun at her back and commune with nature, for faelin do their best magic outdoors." He plucked another rose petal, awash in painful memories. "Still, she grew more frail. I offered her the hydra, but she refused, as the faelin consider it an abomination. A few months later, she died here." A tear fell on his wrist. He blinked the rest away. "After that, I never set foot in the garden again; at least until that night you found your way into it. I guess in a way, the garden represents the curse of my immortality."

They had come to the garden's center. The marble table's inscriptions glowed with an eerie gold luminosity in the moonlight.

Xochitl hugged him. "I'm sorry for bringing up memories that cause you pain."

"It's all right." Zareth cupped her face in his hands. Xochitl had lost her mother too. And she was a half-breed like him, not fully belonging anywhere. He took comfort in confiding with someone who understood such pain. "For the past few centuries I was indeed cursed. But you have broken the curse of my perpetual darkness and loneliness."

He bent down and his mouth captured hers in a kiss that was as sacred and pure as this place. His hands roamed down to caress her sides and her back. She was so warm, so soft, and her curves fit against his body like he was made for her.

Deeper and deeper he kissed her until he was caught up in a whirlwind of passion. Her hands crept up to tangle in his hair as she pulled him closer.

A small cry escaped her lips as Zareth lifted her and set her on the table. For centuries he only used it for spellcraft, but now he had other ideas. His lips trailed down her neck to the tops of her breasts, covering every inch of exposed skin with kisses. She tasted of summer and fire.

With reverent care, he lowered her until her back rested on the table's gleaming surface. Xochitl pulled him down with her, caressing him fervently. Her hands ventured into his robes. Her fingers felt hot and teasing against his bare skin.

Zareth groaned in her ear as he resumed kissing and nibbling her neck. He knew how much she liked that.

"Don't stop. Please don't stop," she begged, shuddering beneath him.

He did like to hear her beg.

Just then, Zareth became aware that the table was giving off a strange vibration that intensified as the level of their passion rose. *It's magical energy,* he realized, *and we are fueling it with our actions.* For some reason, knowing this heightened his desire.

Xochitl tugged on Zareth's robes with an urgency that inflamed him further. Pulling off his robes, he divested her of her clothing, arranging her robe beneath her on the table so she wouldn't get dirty. A chilly breeze made goose bumps rise on her arms, so he drew from the energy they were generating to conjure a circle of warmth around them.

For a moment he stood and drank in the sight of her naked body kissed by moonlight. He was feverish with the need to touch and taste her everywhere. Pulling her into his arms, he kissed the column of her throat.

Xochitl gasped when he covered her entire body with kisses. Zareth chuckled against her belly. He hadn't even gotten started. Reaching between her legs, his fingers delved into her wetness. Shivers of pleasure wracked his body as she moaned against his throat.

When he drew away to unfasten his pants he almost ached from the separation. But when he returned, an extreme sense of fulfillment engulfed him at the heat of his body against hers once more.

"Make love to me, Zareth. Please," she whimpered.

With a growl of assent he thrust deep inside her. He felt the thrum of magical energy beneath her. They were encompassed by a hurricane from within and without while he made tender and fierce love to her. Soon the energy was absorbed by their bodies, channeling to build up in one single place.

Thunder rumbled as he thrust into her, the power built until it erupted with Xochitl's climax. Zareth groaned as he felt her clench around his cock. She clung to him tight and cried out his name. His own orgasm came, earth shattering and blinding. Lightning cracked nearby. His release reignited her pleasure. His tongue ravaged hers in imitation of the pulsing rhythm.

When it was finished they collapsed in one another's embrace, gasping for air.

Xochitl twirled a lock of his hair around her finger. "I think you might have to carry me home, 'cuz I'm not sure I'll be able to walk."

Zareth chuckled and lifted her into his arms. "Very well, dearling. Though I warn you, I'm not finished with you yet."

Chapter Twenty-three

Xochitl

I knew it was going to be bad as soon as I saw the look on Aurora's face.

"So, you've finally decided that we are worthy of being graced with your presence."

"Aurora..." I groped for an explanation they would accept.

"Can he leave for a moment?" She glared at Zareth. "We need to talk. *Alone.*"

I looked up at Zareth and silently begged him to acquiesce. For a moment it looked as if he would refuse, but with a curt nod he turned and walked off, leaving me to face the inevitable backlash.

Like a prisoner approaching the gallows to be executed, I walked into the house I shared with my band mates. My legs were rubbery, so I sat in the recliner, my favorite place to read. Aurora gave me a cold look before she went down the hall to get Beau and Sylvis. I wiped my sweaty palms on my jeans, dreading the talk more and more every second that passed. Finally, Aurora returned with the others.

I studied their faces and saw that Beau looked just as cold and scornful as Aurora, and even Sylvis looked disappointed. My friends sat on the couch across from me and Aurora and Beau each lit a cigarette. A shiver ran down my spine. Aurora had quit. This didn't bode well.

A long awkward silence stretched the air before Aurora spoke. "You hurt us badly, Xochitl. You're our best friend and we've been through a lot together. And now you abandoned us and our dream, our vow, for a man!" Her voice rose as she blew out smoke. "I always thought that you would be the least likely of us to pull something like this."

"Yeah. I thought *I* was the most likely," Beau added with an impish smile.

Aurora shot him a dirty look and he fell silent and the dour expression returned to his face so fast it seemed that it had never left.

"What the hell is going on with you?" she demanded in a voice that pierced my heart.

Sylvis just stared at the carpet. Her shoe tapping with anxiety.

"I- I'm sorry," I said lamely. "It's just that... I'm in love... and..." My gaze traveled across their faces, willing them to have mercy. "There are things going on right now in my life that are very important and very.... Well... complicated."

"Like what?" Aurora pleaded. She crushed out her cigarette and fidgeted with her braid. "Is he forcing you to be with him? 'Cuz that's what it's starting to look like."

"No! He's not!" I protested in outrage. My cheeks flushed as I remembered Zareth had done exactly that, though not in the way Aurora implied.

Her lips compressed in a frown of disbelief. "Then what is going on with you two?"

"I can't tell you." My eyes begged Sylvis to be silent.

The last thing that she needed was for Aurora to think I was crazy as well as intentionally ditching them. And Sylvis didn't deserve to be dragged into this.

"If you can't trust us enough to talk to us, what kind of a friend are you supposed to be?" Aurora demanded in a voice that was verging on tears.

I swallowed a lump in my throat, feeling more torn and more shitty than I ever imagined possible. Unable to take the stress, I grabbed a cigarette from the pack on the coffee table and lit it, wishing I could just vanish into thin air.

"It's not that I don't trust you..." I stumbled over my words. The cigarette made me lightheaded... or maybe it was the stress.

"Don't trust us?" Aurora's voice rose to a fevered pitch as she paced in front of me. "The foundation of our friendship, and our career, depends on trust. And you not telling us exactly what's going on really seems like you don't trust us." She threw up her hands in exasperation. "Look, you are totally fucking us over!"

"I can give you money to make up for the sessions I missed," The feeble offer left me feeling lower than scum.

"It's not about the *money*!" Aurora shrieked, pounding her fist on the arm of the couch. "It's about the music." Her voice softened. "It's about our dream."

"I know," I replied, overwhelmed with helplessness. The cigarette tasted terrible, but I couldn't stop smoking it. "Just give me a month, okay? Then I can—"

"No!" She held up a hand. "No more false promises, Xochitl. We can't take anymore."

"Yeah." Beau leaned against the couch, his gaze severe. "It's us, or him."

"You have until tomorrow to decide." Aurora's eyes were merciless. "'Cuz if you're not with us in the studio tomorrow, and back home with us at least until the album's finished, we need to find a replacement. This band is going to make it. With or without you."

The words poured over me like acid, eating and tearing painful holes through my entire being. Tears burned my eyes and the back of my throat.

"O-okay," I choked, crushing out the cigarette and rising from the chair. "I-I'll b-be back tomorrow."

It was all I could do not to run out the door.

Zareth met me outside. The naked branches of the hawthorn tree he stood under didn't offer him much shelter from the freezing December rain. The sight of my husband soaked and shivering, coupled with the betrayed looks in my friends' eyes, tore my heart in two.

His eyes met mine, full of tenderness. "How did it go?"

I shook my head, nowhere near ready to begin the inevitable argument. "Let's just get back to your tower and get you warmed up."

After we crossed the portal and returned to the tower, I scooped Isis up in my arms and buried my face in her warm fur. While Zareth changed into dry robes, I mulled over what I was going to say.

I couldn't abandon my friends. I couldn't even contemplate not being part of the band. We'd worked so long and so hard to make *Rage of Angels* a reality.

But, I also couldn't abandon Zareth, and even more importantly, the people of Aisthanesthai. The Solstice was only two weeks away.

Why couldn't the blow up with the band have waited until after that?

Was there a way to satisfy both of my obligations?

Zareth joined me in the living room and handed me a cup of tea. He eyed me over the rim of his cup. "What did your friends have to say?"

I frowned into my mug. "They said I need to be back at the studio and back at home with them tomorrow or I'm out of the band."

"Though I am weakening, I can bring you back to the studio if you rejuvenate me." His brows drew together as he set down his cup. "However, you can't return to your home on Earth. It's too dangerous. Stefan has not given up."

"But I have to. I can't throw away everything we've worked for, all we'd been through. I can't give up on our music." I looked up at him, pleading. "Can't we just stay on Earth until the album's finished?"

He shook his head. "Being away from my world that long would drain my powers so much that not even your singing could rejuvenate me. As it is, between the constant traveling, the trips to Earth, and the sun being gone, my magic is dwindling. Not to mention the fact that Stefan has spies crawling everywhere Earth-side."

Shame washed over me. I remembered how pale and weak he'd been when we'd returned from our first trip to Earth for a recording session. Although our lovemaking and my singing rejuvenated him, there was no way he could keep up his strength for a week or two.

"Maybe I can go alone and you could come by and check on me occasionally?" As I said it, the idea became more attractive. My friends' dislike and suspicion of Zareth had heightened until having them in the same room was unbearable. If he wasn't around, the recording would go smoother and maybe I could patch things up with Aurora.

Hope rising, I continued. "And after the album's finished I could come back to Aisthanesthai and—"

"No." The cold finality of the word made me draw back.

"Why not?"

"It's not safe."

"I can protect myself. Between what you've taught me and my increased powers from—" I blushed and stumbled on the words— "making love with you, I can take care of myself."

"No, you can't. You have no concept of what power is. I've been building mine for eleven centuries, Stefan's been amassing his for two centuries." He pointed a long finger at me. "You've only been around for little more than two decades."

The scorn in his voice made me flinch. That same scorn and belittling had been heaped on me for years. On the elementary school playground, in the halls in middle school and high school, under the roof of my cruel foster parents' home.

Zareth's scorn hurt worse than everything else.

But I'd proved them all wrong on that stage. And I'd prove him wrong too.

"I am going back." I lifted my chin and stood. "And I'm going to tell my friends the truth. I'm sick of lying to them."

Lightning flickered in his eyes as he rose from his seat. "Firstly, it is forbidden for Earth folk to know about the existence of Aisthanesthai." His lips curved in an ugly smirk. "And second, you can go back... if you can create and cross a portal yourself."

He looked so smug and triumphant. He didn't think I could do it. Anger washed over me, purple flames flickering from my clenched fists at my sides.

"Fine. I'll go now." I turned and left the room.

His laughter followed me through the hall and out the door, but not his footsteps.

That stung even more. Did he really think I couldn't handle this on my own? I slammed the door and stomped across the cobblestones, taking strange satisfaction at the clacking noise. When I reached the edge of the Nightmare Forest, I heard Zareth call out.

"Xochitl, come back." There was a light chuckle in his voice, like he was indulging a child having a temper.

I glared back at him before I entered the forest.

"Xochitl!" His voice lost all traces of amusement.

He couldn't pass through the forest.

But I could.

I quickened my pace, batting at howling ghosts in irritation. Zareth's voice faded as the trees and shadows engulfed me. A sinking feeling plummeted in the pit of my stomach. I couldn't tell if it was the effects of the forest, or my fight with Zareth.

Tears blurred in my eyes as I darted around the trees, ignoring the alternating chills and falling sensations. I would not let him see me cry. I would not let him see me fail.

Wiping my eyes with my coat sleeve, I paused next to a gnarled oak with a sinister face. It was too damn dark in here. Leaning against the trunk, I kicked aside a corpse-like hand that tried to grab my ankle and dug in my coat pocket for my bottomless pouch and my staff.

Zareth had just begun teaching me how to wield it. I could at least make it light up.

Then I remembered that I'd left everything in my robes when I'd changed to Earth clothes to visit my friends.

"Damn it," I whispered under my breath. That meant I didn't have my car either.

But there was no way I'd go back and face the embarrassment of Zareth's inevitable smugness. At least the moonlight broke through between the trees.

Zareth would try to intercept me when I came out of the forest. Willing my shields into place, I wove around the trees in a diagonal path, hoping to emerge well away from him.

My efforts paid off. I came out of the forest on the borders of the village, with no one in sight.

A rustling sound made me jerk. He could come upon me any moment. Quietly, I crept away from the forest, keeping to the west. Although Stefan's lands were hundreds of miles away, I didn't want to risk being anywhere near his direction.

Not wanting to remain out in the open for long, I jogged to the village wall and crept along its edges, making sure I stayed in the shadows.

Just when my legs began to cramp, I reached a small lake. Slumping down on a log near the shore, I tried to think of what to do next.

How the hell was I going to make a portal? Zareth used some sort of crystal to do it and I didn't think I had that kind. Would Mordaine's shop have them? That would be my best bet. Maybe she'd even have a book with a spell or instructions on how to accomplish my mission.

My optimism broke under a flood of despair. Even if Zareth didn't catch me at the shop, Mordaine would refuse to help me escape.

The realization of what I was doing brought fresh tears to my eyes.

I was running from Zareth. The man who'd solved the mysteries of my past and taught me about my future. The man I loved. But he'd refused to help me rejoin my friends. He talked down to me like I was a child. He'd laughed at me when I said I could take care of myself.

Burying my face in my hands, I let the tears flow. Biting my lips to hold back a sob, agonizing pain pierced my heart. How could we have gone from being so happy and in love to this? Why did he have to hurt me?

A hand touched my shoulder. I leapt to my feet, twin fireballs forming in my hands, ready to attack.

Rickard, the high seneschal, jumped back and spread his hands to show he was unarmed. "I am sorry to startle you, my lady. I only wanted to see if you're all right."

I extinguished my flames. "I'm fine. Zareth and I had a quarrel. I need to go back to the Earth realm to fulfill an obligation." As his eyes widened, I clarified, "I'll be back in time to fulfill the Prophecy, don't worry."

"I see." Rickard fumbled with his beard. "So you need to visit your old home and Lord Amotken won't let you?"

"Not exactly." If I agreed with his wording, he'd deliver me back to Zareth. "He told me that if I can find my own way through the portal, I could go."

"Ah, but that is as good as a refusal since very few mages have the ability to pass between worlds." He gave me a sympathetic look. "But you're determined to try anyway. I can't help but admire your bravery, and although I should deliver you back to Zareth, I do have a soft spot for a lady in need. I will help you cross the portal." At my grin, he raised a finger and gave me a stern look. "However, Lord Amotken is guaranteed to follow you and bring you back, so all you'll accomplish is to teach him a lesson."

My shoulders slumped. That was true. On Earth I wouldn't be able to evade him for long. However, if I could just get back long enough to tell my friends the truth about what was going on, they had to understand. Maybe we could work something out. And maybe Zareth and I could make up from this fight.

"All right, if teaching Zareth a lesson on his arrogance is the best I can do, I'll take it." I threaded my arm through his. "Lead the way."

"There is a stationary portal nearby that Mordaine uses," he said. "But we'll have to take a discreet route so as not to be discovered. Now you must promise not to tell Zareth I helped you."

"Of course. That would defeat the purpose of proving to him that I can figure it out myself." I wondered why he was willing to help me. But then I remembered Rickard's earlier hostility to Zareth. And come to think of it, Zareth didn't seem to like him much either. His aiding me was probably just a way to stick it to the man.

Guilt gnawed at my gut for encouraging Zareth's seneschal to betray him. I tamped it down as best I could. I needed to get back to Seattle. If I could at least work things out with the band, everything would be all right.

"Just a little further, my lady," Rickard said as we neared a grove of pines near the village gates.

When we reached them, I was panting. Between my dash through the forest and my trek across the village, I was exhausted. Closing my eyes, I yawned.

I opened my eyes to see Stefan standing in front of me. His staff flashed with light and my legs cemented to the ground, immobile.

Before I could cry out, Rickard's hand clamped over my mouth. I sank my teeth into his palm, but though he cursed, he maintained his hold. Stefan raised his crystal over my head and muttered in his guttural language.

Again came that sense of violation followed by the feel of my magic ebbing away. I struggled, kicked and bit, but my blows weakened every second. Stefan's spell continued to drain me, bleeding away my power until my knees buckled.

Rickard jolted behind me and cried out. His grip slackened and I turned to see him collapse on the cold grass. An icicle impaled his heart.

My vision faded to oblivion.

Chapter Twenty-four

Xochitl

I awoke with a pounding headache. Reaching to rub a stiff spot on my neck, I frowned as I heard the sound of metal clanking and heavy weights dangled from my wrists. My eyes snapped open and I gasped with the terrifying realization that I was chained up. Stomach queasy, my gaze darted around, taking in the sight of barred windows and stone walls. Greasy, foul smelling torches cast dim light on the dusty stone floor.

Thick manacles encircled my ankles, cold against my skin. I struggled to stand and walked less than two feet before the chains pulled taut. With a groan of despair, I slumped back against the wall, skin prickling with unease.

What the hell was I doing here?

The memories came in a painful torrent. I cried out, the sound echoed off the stone walls like a wailing phantom.

My band's ultimatum.

My quarrel with Zareth.

Fleeing the tower.

Rickard's offer of help.

Being delivered to Stefan.

Now I was Stefan's prisoner.

The question was, what was he going to do to me? I had a feeling I didn't want to find out. When my gaze landed on a table with a display of torture devices upon it, my feeling was confirmed. Bile rose in my throat.

"Greetings, my petite beauty. It is good to see you awake." The door opened and light poured into the dungeon, framing Stefan's form.

He waltzed down the stone steps to stand before me, a cocky grin on his loathsome face. "I knew this day would come... the day that you are finally on your knees, humbled before me."

"Fuck you, asshole," I growled.

He slapped me so hard across the face that I fell back, slamming my head against the wall. Blood trickled from the corner of my mouth where one of his jeweled rings cut my lip.

"You will address me as *my Prince*, or you will be silent."

My Prince? Is he fucking kidding? I gagged and chose the latter option. My day was already bad enough without me having to put up with his shit. Making Stefan burst into flame from the inside out seemed appetizing. But nothing happened. I couldn't even feel the slightest shimmer of power within my being.

Stefan must have seen my distress. "What's the matter, dear? Can't you work up the energy to kill me?" His eyes hardened to slivers of blue ice. "Do you really think I would be stupid enough to let you keep your power? I think not. Though I am considering letting you have a guitar, for I do so want to hear you sing."

I licked the blood from my split lip and hissed, "When Zareth gets here, he's going to make you regret that you laid a hand on me."

It was a pathetic, "damsel in distress" thing to say, but for now it was the only threat I had.

Stefan burst into maniacal laughter. "The sooner he gets here, the better. Then my amusements can begin."

That's the shittiest villainous laugh I've ever heard. Aloud I asked, "What are you going to do?" I was unable to hide my anxiety. What if he hurt Zareth?

He gave me a triumphant grin. "I can't tell you. It would ruin the surprise. But let's just say that when my brother arrives, he will offer himself up to me as a willing slave before I kill him."

"And why would he do that?" Doubt laced my voice.

Stefan drew closer and tilted my chin up with his thumb to meet his eyes. I shivered in revulsion at his touch and my stomach churned as I smelled the some sort of liquor on his breath.

"He will submit to me because he doesn't want to see me hurt the love of his life." He whispered and drew closer. "And he especially doesn't want to see me violate her....again."

Before I could reply, his mouth came down on mine in a brutal, intruding kiss. I gagged and bit his lips. He slapped me and slid his tongue along my neck. I tried to struggle away, but the chains held me immobile just as his arms restrained me. His hand squeezed my breast so hard it hurt.

I screamed and he hit me again. The air around me seemed to change, to become slimy. Then I sensed Stefan's power building. His hydra was feeding, I realized with disgust. Feeding on my pain.

My thoughts ceased as he bent down and bit me. I shrieked again, and he laughed.

"Oh, I am enjoying this," he said before resuming his torture. "Soon I'll be ready."

Over and over again, he slapped and bit and punched me. Tears rose to my eyes, but I refused to cry in front of him. My back throbbed in agony as my anger mounted.

Through my haze of pain I felt something hard pushing against my thigh. *Oh, shit.* But he was human. He couldn't— He ripped my shirt open. "Now you will be mine!"

Stefan tore the rest of my clothes off, biting my nipples until they were raw and sore. When he kissed me again and forced his tongue into my mouth, I bit down, drawing blood. He hit me in the face again, so hard that I saw stars, but at least he didn't try to kiss me anymore.

He pulled down his pants. My stomach lurched as he wrenched my legs apart.

Closing my eyes, I prayed that this would go the same way it did when some stupid jocks tried to gang rape me back in high school. Flaccid flesh had pressed against me as I'd been tied up, just as I was now. When they couldn't get it up, they'd cursed and spit on me until flames burst from my palms and I'd screamed with an inhuman rage that I was never able to repeat again on stage.

That same scream tore from my throat as I felt his repulsive flesh push at my entrance. Tears cascading down my cheeks, I braced myself for the pain.

Then Stefan's flesh softened. Guttural curses exploded from him as he pushed his disgusting worm of a dick against me, trying to penetrate.

Just when I thought my mind would shatter, he withdrew and tucked his limp manhood back in his pants.

A broken laugh escaped my split lips and I spat blood at his feet. "I've heard of one minute wonders, but this was more of a millisecond-miracle."

He slapped me again and I forced another laugh. "You can beat me, but you can't take me, bastard."

"Silence, you blasted cunt!" he roared.

His fist crashed into my face once more. My head slammed into the stone wall and I blacked out.

When I regained consciousness, I glared at Stefan's back as he stormed out of my cell, slamming the door behind him.

All I could do was slump in my chains, relieved that it was over.

When his footsteps faded away, I allowed the tears that burned behind my eyes to pour forth and grant me what little release was plausible.

I'd made a grave mistake, I realized far too late. I hadn't taken Stefan all that seriously. Yes, I'd seen him as a villain, but just a weak and petty one, something to be laughed at. Shaking violently from sickness and horror, I looked down at my naked, bloody and bruised body.

There was nothing at all laughable about Stefan Carcinerus.

Worst of all, this was all my fault. If I hadn't been hell bent on proving Zareth wrong and trying to go back to Earth by myself, I wouldn't be here. He'd told me Stefan was still after me, but I didn't listen.

Shame dispersed my anger, subsiding my backache, but doing nothing for the stabbing pain between my thighs.

"Zareth," my voice choked with sobs. "I'm so sorry for leaving you. Please come for me. Please, please come for me!"

Over and over again, I repeated my plea to whoever was listening. Rocking back and forth, I clutched my chains like a rosary until I fell into an exhausted, dreamlike sleep.

Hours later, I awoke to the sound of the door opening. Nausea welled up in my stomach.

Was Stefan coming to try to rape me again?

Relief eased my taut muscles as a blue-robed mage approached me, carrying a plate of food, some water, and what looked like clothing.

His eyes widened in shock at my swollen, bruised face, but then his long mahogany hair fell to cover his face as he bowed before me. "I have brought you food and drink, Holy Lioness of Light."

I laughed, a bitter croak. "I doubt that I look all that holy right now."

The mage eyed my naked, manacled body covered with bite marks and scratches. He coughed uncomfortably.

"No, I don't suppose you do," he stammered, blushing.

I felt a touch of cynical pleasure at the man's obvious discomfort.

When he was done staring at the floor, he met my gaze once more. "My name is Artavian and I am Stefan's apprentice. I've been given the honor of guarding and feeding you."

"Hello Artavian, I am Xochitl, it is nice to meet you," I replied with sarcastic formality. "Are you here to try to rape me too?"

He wrung his hands awkwardly. Something resembling pity slashed across his pretty features. "No, my Lady. I would never even consider such sacrilege. I have brought you some clothing. I would heal your wounds as well, but Stefan forbade it this night. Would it be permitted for me to assist you in getting dressed?"

I considered it for a moment, reluctant to have another man's hands upon me again. Though at least it would be better than staying naked.

I nodded and Artavian gingerly tied a wrap-around skirt around my waist, and buttoned a sleeveless top that bared my belly but at least covered my breasts. He winced every time he touched me, as if he were committing a mortal sin when his fingers grazed my skin. I almost felt sorry for him, he was that uncomfortable.

When he finished helping me into the outfit, and draped a thin blanket over my shoulders, he was blushing worse than I was.

"I had best go," he said to the floor.

"Wait," I rattled my chains to get his attention. "Taste the food first."

With an understanding nod, Artavian waved his hand over the plate, eyes closed. He must have been trying to detect spells on the food. Satisfied, he sampled the courses and even drank from the tin cup of water.

"Thank you," I whispered past the lump in my throat.

He nodded, still flustered. He turned to leave, but then he turned back and knelt down to face me. He raised a trembling hand to touch my bruised cheek.

"My lady..." A pained look burned in his eyes.

"Yes?"

"I'm sorry."

Before I could reply, he turned and left without a backward glance.

Once again, I was alone and fighting back new tears.

In need of distraction, I turned to the plate, which held a piece of bread and a portion of greasy unidentifiable meat. Next to the plate was the water. I drank half of it down before I thought to conserve it, then turned back to the food. I was tempted to throw it across my cell. Then I reasoned that I needed to keep my strength up.

I was determined to get the hell out of here...or die trying.

Chapter Twenty-five

Zareth

Glamour in place, Zareth walked up the driveway to the house Xochitl shared with her friends. He'd decided to allow her two days to sort out her affairs on Earth before he brought her back home. He still couldn't believe that she'd managed to find a way through a portal. Now he prayed it was enough, that she'd go without another painful quarrel.

He raised his fist to knock, then paused.

Perhaps he should check the weather of matters first. Glancing back to ascertain there were no passersby, he dissolved into shadow and passed through the door. The living room was empty, but he heard music downstairs. Following the melody, he halted when he heard an unfamiliar voice singing along to *Rage of Angels'* music.

A click sounded as someone turned off the stereo. He moved further down until the music room came into view.

"No, I'm sorry. You aren't what we're looking for," Beau said to a pink-haired girl Zareth had never seen as she stepped away from the microphone.

"Okay," the girl said with a dejected pout before fleeing past him up the stairs.

Who was this? Xochitl was supposed to be singing. Unease nearly brought his molecules back together.

He focused just in time, for Aurora passed right through him. He'd never be accustomed to that disturbing sensation.

"How'd the audition go?" Aurora asked Beau.

"She sucked." A cynical smile tugged at his lips. "You know we'll never find anyone to replace Xochitl. Her voice was special. It had more passion and feeling than anyone I've ever heard. *She* was special."

Aurora sighed, her brown eyes red-rimmed. "I know, but we can't give our talents and our career up because she's gone."

Dread pooled in Zareth's gut as he rematerialized. *Xochitl hadn't come back?*

"But Sylvis hasn't touched her guitar since Xochitl left!" Beau snapped at Aurora, not noticing Zareth. "But you're right. I don't want any of us to go to waste. And who knows, maybe she'll come back." Beau crushed his cigarette out and opened a beer, continuing his tirade. "It seems I'm the only half-sane person left in this house. And I'm sick of it. I want to break down too. And most of all, I don't want to do these stupid auditions anymore. They're pointless. We have plenty of money and there will never be anyone with a voice half as good as Xochitl's, and nobody with the passion to measure up to hers. Hell, we were even able to finish the album by mixing in her earlier scratch vocals on the last three songs. I think the real reason you're insisting on this farce is more for the sake of punishing Xochitl for leaving. I still think she's coming back," he insisted. "Something else has to be going on. She couldn't be so cold as to abandon us forever."

Zareth heard enough. "Something *is* going on."

Beau and Aurora whipped around to stare at him.

"What the hell are you doing here?" Aurora demanded. "Is Xochitl with you?"

"I was going to ask you the same thing," he said, sweat dripping from his forehead. He was such a fool. "She left me two nights ago to return to you. Have you seen her since we were last here?"

Aurora shook her head, dashing his meager hope. "What do you think happened to her?"

Before he could answer, Sylvis came charging at Zareth like a raging bull, pounding at him with her fists. "You promised that you wouldn't let anything bad happen to her! You *promised*, you bastard!"

Heart aching with intense sorrow and regret, he did nothing to block her blows.

Beau and Aurora met one another's eyes in shock and confusion before they both pulled her off of Zareth. They each received a few punches from the guitarist before they restrained her.

"Calm down, Sylvis," Beau pleaded.

"Yeah." Aurora folded her arms across her chest and gave him a stern glare. "You better start talking, Zareth. What the fuck is going on?"

His shoulders slumped even lower but he met their perplexed gazes. "The night after we were here last, Xochitl and I had an argument. She left me to go back to you, to finish the album." He took a deep breath and exhaled slowly. "Obviously she didn't make it back here, so that means that my half-brother has kidnapped her."

"What?" Beau and Aurora exclaimed together.

"That creep, Stefan, has her?" Sylvis asked in a frightened voice. "Does that mean that he's going to rule Aisthanesthai?"

"Whoa, wait a minute." Aurora interjected. "What the hell are you talking about, Sylvis? Who is Stefan? And what does this have to do with Xochitl?"

Sylvis gave Zareth an imploring look. "Can I tell them?"

Zareth nodded reluctantly. "I suppose I have no choice."

"Tell us what?" Beau asked, sounding more confused by the minute. "I get the feeling you're not a travel journalist like you said."

Aurora was more irate than confused. She whirled on Sylvis. "You *knew* what's been going on with Xochitl this whole time and you've kept it from us? I knew there was something else, I fucking knew it!"

Sylvis nodded.

"Well? Aren't you gonna finally tell us?" Beau paced in front of her.

The lead guitarist of *Rage of Angels* raked a nervous hand through her blue spiked hair, and took a deep breath. "Xochitl made me promise a long time ago not to tell anyone about her, but now she's in trouble, so I guess it's all our business now. Maybe even our fault."

Aurora squirmed in impatience. "What's been going on?"

"Ever since we were kids, I knew that Xochitl had magical powers...so did her mom." Sylvis's blue eyes darted around, never settling for long on one person. "Up until recently I didn't know that it was more than that, and neither did she."

"Xochitl has magic powers?" Aurora radiated doubt. "I mean, I know she's a little different, but..." she trailed off, considering. "Wait. The fireballs. She'd never tell us how she did that trick. Are those real and not just special effects?"

Sylvis bit her lip and nodded. "Yeah. And ever since her mom died, she had dreams about a tall dark man. That man turned out to be Zareth. On Halloween, he came to claim her."

Aurora and Beau's disbelieving gazes flew to him. Zareth inclined his head in acknowledgement of the truth. "Claim her for what?" they both asked.

Sylvis met Zareth's gaze. "I think you better explain the rest."

Zareth explained to them about the Prophecy and Xochitl being the savior of his world. He told them of her parentage. He related Stefan's aim to gain control of Xochitl in hopes to rule the world. He even informed them of their marriage.

"You guys got *married*?" Aurora interrupted.

He nodded. "Now Stefan has her and the Prophecy will soon be fulfilled. Unless I can save her, the world is doomed if she crowns Stefan. I shouldn't have let her go alone." He hung his head in shame. "I'm so sorry."

Sylvis remained silent, ignoring his apology. Zareth couldn't blame her.

There was a long moment of silence as the other two band members stared at him.

"Are you for real?" Beau gaped at him. "Xochitl's supposed to save this other world? This world that you're from?"

"I don't believe you," Aurora countered. "I think you're insane."

"That's exactly why Xochitl didn't want to tell you guys!" Sylvis fired back.

"I want proof." The drummer demanded. "Prove to me that you're an all-powerful sorcerer from a different world."

Zareth sighed in resignation. Earth humans had become unreasonably skeptical these days. While that was often beneficial, now it was a nuisance. "Very well."

He removed his glamour.

All three drew back at the sight of his faelin eyes and hair, and inhumanly long fingers. "What *are* you?"

Zareth wasn't finished. Reaching into his pocket, he pulled out his staff, eliciting more gasps. Pointing the top of the staff at the couch, he chanted in a silky exotic language unlike any they'd ever imagined. With a shudder, the couch rose up in the air, revealing dust, cigarette butts, and pennies on the carpet

"Proof enough?" he asked with a lifted brow.

Beau's eyes bulged. "Un-fucking-believable!"

"Okay, maybe you're not insane." Aurora whispered.

"Told you so." Sylvis crossed her arms over her chest.

Aurora frowned. "Does Xochitl know you...um, look like that?"

He turned away before she could see how her comment hurt. "Yes." The pain dissolved with the word. Xochitl thought he was beautiful, and that was all that mattered.

"And here I thought it was just a badass Halloween costume when I first saw you." Beau stroked his chin and turned back to the subject at hand. "I knew she was acting strange the last time we saw her. She even said, 'There are things going on in my life right now, important, fucked up things.' I think that this fits the description."

Aurora nodded grudgingly. "But still, even if Zareth is telling the truth, and Xochitl's missing, and possibly being held prisoner in another world by an evil sorcerer who's going to use her to take over the world, what the hell are we going to be able to do about it?"

What indeed? Zareth thought with despair. Aloud he answered, "For the time being, you will all come to Aisthanesthai with me. If Stefan is seeking her, one of the first things he'll do is go after those she loves. Since you three have very little magic, that makes you vulnerable."

"Wait, *we* have magic?" Beau gaped at him.

Zareth sighed. "I'll explain that later. Come, we have little time. And maybe if we're lucky, Xochitl only got lost and may have returned to my tower."

Sylvis held up a hand. "I'm going to leave her a note, in case she does come here."

"That's an excellent idea." Though he was doubtful they would be that fortunate. He had another thought. "Actually, you had better pack your necessities. I do not know when I'll be able to bring you back."

With Xochitl's absence, his power was already diminishing.

Sylvis and Beau looked to Aurora. For a moment it looked like she would argue, then she nodded. "Okay. And we'll bring our gear too."

"What?" Sylvis stared at her, incredulous. "How will our guitars and drums help rescue Xochitl?"

"They won't." Aurora sighed. "But he said it could take awhile to bring us home. So if we're stuck in his world after we get Xochitl back, and we *will* get her back, we might as well get some work done." She turned back to Zareth. "Is there electricity in this world?"

Zareth froze at her words. When she'd mentioned their instruments, Aurora's voice had reverberated with a pulse of power. Shaking his head, he recovered himself. "Yes, there are generators and such."

Once the band loaded up their instruments and baggage into Aurora's van, Zareth directed them to the alley behind the PFI where the portal lay. Xochitl's friends were equally impressed when he shrunk the vehicle.

"Gather as close to me as you can," he told them, praying he had enough power left to transport all three of them through the portal.

At first they were reluctant to touch him, but at his urgent gaze they complied, pressing against his robes. Zareth was just as uncomfortable as he retrieved his crystal and put his arms around them. Such closeness was alien to him.

Gathering what strength he could from their meager magic, Zareth said a silent prayer before raising his crystal and chanting the spell.

Fortune was with them, for when he opened his eyes, all three of the musicians remained with him, though fatigue weighed his body.

"Ho-ly fuckballs," Sylvis breathed, staring up at the two moons.

Beau stood frozen, staring at the tower.

Wide-eyed, Aurora wandered around the tower grounds, nearing the forest. Before Zareth could tell her to get away, she screamed. "What the hell is that?"

"My Nightmare Forest. No one who is able to feel fear can pass through it, so we should be safe here."

Comprehension dawned in her dark eyes. "*That's* how she left you. Xochitl's not afraid of anything."

His head ached as he nodded. "Ironically I used the forest to test her when I first brought her here." If he hadn't, would she still be with him? Guilt roiled in his gut. "It is cold out, let us head inside and see if Xochitl has returned."

The moment he led them into the tower, he felt the emptiness in the air. She wasn't here. Exhaustion weighed down on him like his muscles were encased in lead. He swayed and Sylvis grasped his arm, steadying him.

"Are you okay?" she asked.

"I will be soon. I am drained from taking you all through the portal." He allowed her to lead him to the sitting room where he slumped on the couch.

Xochitl's friends milled around, tense and unsettled. A pattering sound made them whip around and smile as they saw

Isis bounding toward them with a strident meow. The cat purred and meowed and rubbed her body around their ankles like she desperately wanted to communicate something.

As if reading his mind, Sylvis's eyes filled with sadness. "If Xochitl was here, she'd know what she's saying."

Chaos hesitantly approached, sniffing at Beau's outstretched hand when he crouched. Then the kitten turned away and bounded to the couch, leaping on Zareth's lap. The gentle purr rejuvenated him enough to be able to stand again.

Leaning on his staff and cradling the kitten, he gestured for Xochitl's friends to follow him up the stairs.

By the time he reached his laboratory, they were all panting. But once Zareth reached the faelin crystal and drew some of the stored energy from it, he was somewhat restored. Sylvis, Aurora and Beau stared at his assortment of magical paraphernalia.

"Don't touch anything," he admonished.

Something tapped at the window, making them all jump. A chill ran down Zareth's spine as he saw the phantom pixie spreading patterns of frost on the glass.

"What the hell is that?" Beau whispered.

He held up a hand for quiet as he crossed the room and opened the window. The apparition of the pixie was elegant and fanciful with its wings sculpted with ice and body glittering with frost.

But the pure malevolence on the creature's face ruined its illusion of benevolence. The thing hissed and deposited an envelope on the windowsill before flying away, leaving a falling trail of snowflakes in its wake.

An icy blast of wind stung his face, but it didn't leave him as cold as the sight of Stefan's seal on the letter.

Chapter Twenty-six

Xochitl

Shivering in my cold cell, I rubbed my aching back. My captor didn't even have the decency to give me a pillow. A bitter laugh trickled from my dry throat. To think I'd been outraged when Zareth had threatened to imprison me. Right after bundling me in a warm robe, feeding me hot soup, and tucking me into a soft bed. My laugh turned into a choking sob.

I missed my sorcerer husband so much that it stung worse than the bitter cold. Every time I slept, I dreamed of him and those were now the only times that I knew something akin to joy. My heart throbbed for his smiles and laughter. My skin ached for his touch.

I missed my friends, too. It cut me deep knowing they thought I abandoned them and had stopped caring, giving up on our dream. I would give anything to be in Zareth's arms, or to be on stage with *Rage of Angels*, shopping with Beau, goofing off with Sylvis, or having a debate with Aurora.

Sighing, I slumped in my shackles. If only they knew what was really going on.

A scrabbling noise made me lift my head. An orange cat peeked through my glassless window and mewed before speaking in the language only I understood. *Friend?*

My chest tightened with longing, tinged with joy. *Friend, come.* I held out my hand as far as my chains would allow. The cat leapt down from the sill and scampered over to me, rubbing against me and purring.

Nothing sounded sweeter.

Why are you chained, friend? he asked with large, green eyes. *You are no dog.*

I cuddled him against my chest, savoring the feel of warm fur. Whenever I was alone and sad, the cats would come to me. I wondered how many more were near and if they could help me.

An evil one holds me from my mate, I explained in the simplest terms. Cats preferred to be succinct most of the time. *And from my Kin-Cat,* I added.

That was the term I'd worked out to explain Isis to other cats. I couldn't call her my cat because they don't recognize themselves as property and our relationship was too close for me to be considered as her property either.

The cat sniffed my skin, then opened his mouth and curled up his tongue to take in my scent deeper. *She smells mighty, but unknown. Would you like me to find her for you?*

Oh, that tempted me more than anything. To hold Isis again...

Reluctantly, I shook my head. *She is very far away and if she comes, the evil one may kill her. You must run when he comes.* I couldn't bear it if he was hurt because of me.

My new friend gave me a slow blink in assent. *I and my kin will help our friend any way we can. Would you like me to bring you a bird?*

If I'd had my magic so I could summon fire to cook it, I would have been tempted. Stefan hadn't sent Artavian up to feed me since I last slept.

No, thank you. Just stay with me and keep me warm. I'd read that cold weakens a luminite's power. Steve was likely keeping the temperature down on purpose.

My friend settled on my lap, soothing me with his purrs and infusing me with warmth. The bliss was snatched away when he leapt off my lap, his ears laid back and tail puffed up. *The evil one is coming,* he told me, *but I will return with my kin.*

"Thank you," I whispered as he disappeared out the window in an orange flash. A few seconds later, I heard distant footsteps.

Dread coiled in my belly. With every ounce of my will, I focused on summoning my magic. Just one fireball... I concentrated. I could blast him in the face when he entered.

A spark flared within. I willed it to come forth.

The door opened. I pointed and focused.

And Stefan doused my meager spark with a whispered word. I closed my eyes and shuddered. Terrible cold and emptiness washed over me once more.

"Hello Princess," his voice slithered over me like an army of slugs. "Aren't you going to greet your prince?"

"Hello, Steve," I mumbled.

His fist crashed into the side of my head, making my left ear ring. "I told you not to call me that!" He seized my chin. "Do you have to spoil everything? Look at me!"

Shuddering in revulsion, I opened my eyes. His face was only inches from mine. The cleft in his chin was more pronounced with his clenched jaw. Many women liked those, but I didn't. It looked like a butt crack. They also liked blue eyes, but these ones were merciless chips of ice.

I knew I'd get nowhere begging for the slightest scrap of merciful treatment, much less information on Zareth. I met his steely gaze with abject scorn. "Just get it over with."

"Get what over with?" his voice was laden with mock confusion.

I spread my hands, making my chains rattle. "Oh, for fuck's sake, just stop with the stupid games. You're here to assault me again." *If you can get it up.* I didn't voice the last thought because I didn't care to be hit again.

To my surprise, he backed away. A multitude of expressions —including defeat— flitted across his snobbish features before his lips curved in a forced smile. "No need to be melodramatic. It was hardly assault. I didn't even have a chance to start. My brother's binding and your freakish species makes you undesirable for my body."

So because you didn't penetrate, it didn't count? Pig. Still, that was the best news I'd heard all day... until he continued.

"But to not worry, my eager pet. When I kill my brother and take you for my bride, I'll be able to claim your body."

I gagged. Did he have Zareth? I didn't dare ask aloud. "Then what are you doing here?"

"Since you can't yet service me with your body, you may service me with your voice." He pulled a guitar from the pouch at his waist. "I've even decided to be generous and let you have this."

The sight of a Fender Stratocaster in his hands looked so wrong, even though it wasn't my Jackson V. I resisted the urge to reach for it in case this was a game.

"It won't work without an amp... and preferably pedals. And those require electricity," I said in the most mournful tone I could muster. "Is this another way to torment me?"

His brows drew together in annoyance. "No, I am trying to do you a kindness. Are you too half-witted to see that? A generator will be brought up."

I nodded warily and took the guitar as he summoned his servants. Playing it with the chains would be difficult, but at least possible. I doubt he'd be willing to unchain me for a mere song. Especially the songs I planned to sing.

As the servants brought up a generator, Stefan told me to instruct them on how to hook up my gear. They followed my directions, but never once looked at me. The way they cringed and ducked left no doubt that he abused them. One of them looked Tolonquan.

When everything was ready, Stefan crossed his arms over his chest and gave me an imperious look. "Now sing. Let me hear this power that will save the world."

My fingers tightened on the fret board. He'd already heard me sing. First on Halloween, then at the Conclave. What he really wanted was to feed on my power. But I could make sure he didn't like the taste.

I sang every heavy metal song about vengeance I knew. "Taste Revenge" by *Sanctuary*, "Screaming for Vengeance" by *Judas Priest*, and of course "Menocide," by *Otep*, a staple for feminine wrath.

Stefan yanked my guitar cord from the amp mid-chorus on the last and pried my guitar from my fingers. His face was pale as he strode out of my cell, taking my gear with him. Hopefully, I shook him up enough to be rid of him for the rest of the day. I'd rather be alone than in his presence. At least I wouldn't be alone, for my new friend would be back soon.

Artavian entered my cell with another tray. I breathed a sigh of relief. I'd thought Stefan would refuse to feed me.

The blue-robed mage set down the tray and bowed. "When I passed the prince on my way here, he looked infuriated and frightened. What did you do?"

I blinked up at him in mock innocence. "He asked me to sing him a song, so I did."

"That must have been quite the song." He lifted the lid of the tray to reveal mashed potatoes, some kind of meat, and green beans. "Did he touch you again?"

I shook my head, not wanting to talk about it. I took a bite of the potatoes, and debated on my next words. Fuck it, I needed to know. "Has Zareth come here?"

"No, my lady." The mage looked grim. "But Stefan is certain he'll come."

I cut the meat with my fork. "I wonder how long it will take him to Boreaus."

"We're not in Stefan's lands. We're in Niji, in his father's castle." This time, his look of disgust was unmistakable. "He's been building his new tower for the past three years."

I couldn't hide my shocked stare. So his arguing at the Conclave to have me in Boreaus had been a bait and switch. "He's been setting himself up to be king this whole time. It was more than arranging alliances."

A strange look flitted across Artavian's face at the mention of alliances. "And for a time, Lord Amotken had done nothing about it, until you came."

Thousands of questions swirled in my head. For now I asked the simplest. "Why is Stefan so sure that I'll crown him?"

"He will threaten to kill Lord Amotken if you don't. Though the Prophecy implies that it may come down to defeating him in combat. Which is the main reason he wants to imprison the Lord of Storm and Shadow." His shoulders slumped. "He wants him broken and too weak to fight." A cat appeared in the window as the mage spoke.

Hiding my joy, I frowned at Artavian. "You don't sound pleased with the prospect of your master's victory."

"I'm not." The mage's lips twisted in scorn. "At least you seem to have already begun defeating him."

I looked over his shoulder and met the cat's eyes. *Friend, is this one lying?*

No. He smells of truth and hate for the evil one. The cat ducked out of sight but I could still feel his presence.

Turning my attention back to the mage, I asked, "What do you mean? I've been chained like a dog for the last, I don't know how long."

"It's something the servants have been saying."

I chewed another bite of meat. "What have they been saying?"

Atravian smiled. "It is whispered that the Winter Prince has been plagued by horrible nightmares ever since you've been brought here. The maids say they hear bloodcurdling screams coming from his room every night."

His words brought me more pleasure than I'd expected. "I'd love to take the credit, but I'm not sure I have anything to do with that. He took away my magic."

Artavian's mouth opened to respond, then he froze. "I have to go. He's summoning me."

I didn't have to ask who *he* was. Before he left, Artavian did some sort of spell on my chains to make them a little longer. I wanted to hug him for that. Instead, I nodded thanks and finished my meal.

Not long after he left, the unmistakable sound of a cat meowing came from the small grated window. I stood and walked as far as the chains would allow. Three blissful steps.

Sure enough, I met the glinting golden eyes of a silver tabby. More meows echoed from the distance as more cats approached.

I smiled as they came inside and covered me with their warmth and soothing purrs.

I know how you can help me, I told them.

Chapter Twenty-seven

Zareth

Pacing through the laboratory, Zareth cursed as he read the letter to Xochitl's friends.

"Hello Brother,

"If you haven't yet discovered what happened to your wayward bride, I will save you the time. She is safe with me at Castle Taranis in Niji. I am collecting my long overdue birthright, and I will be very displeased if you intervene.

"Therefore, as your soon to be King, I command you to deliver yourself to me.

"If you do not, I will violate your luminite princess so savagely that she will barely be able to walk when she crowns me."

Zareth's heart constricted in agony for his love. "Fates be cursed. He does have Xochitl." And she was bound to be suffering under Stefan's care. He shook his head at another detail in the horrible missive. "I can't believe he's taken my father's castle. The cretin wasted no time usurping that which is not his right."

Though outrage tightened his chest at the thought of Stefan desecrating his father's home, his main concern was Xochitl. It took every vestige of his will not to charge to Niji and attack Stefan directly, which was exactly what his brother was trying to goad him to do.

"At least he's bluffing about raping her," he said at last.

Sylvis narrowed her eyes. "What do you mean?"

"Stefan is human. Humans can't mate with luminites." It was the only optimistic thought he could hold onto, for his half-brother would find other ways to hurt her.

All three relaxed in apparent relief.

"So that explains why no guy wanted to date her." Beau sighed. "I never understood. I mean she's so beautiful. But it looks like that saved her in the end."

"Either way, you can't deliver yourself to him," Aurora said. "He'll just kill you. Can't you just poof into the castle and rescue her?"

He shook his head. "The castle is certain to be warded. And even if I did manage to take her out of there, it would drain my powers. The Prophecy dictates that Stefan and I are to face each other on the Solstice. If I am weakened, he will kill me." His fists clenched in impotent frustration. "But if I surrender to him, I don't think he will kill me. For one thing, Stefan is the type to want to draw out his victims' suffering, and for another, he doesn't want to risk interfering with the Prophecy by eliminating me prematurely."

Beau nodded. "Yeah, I can see Xochitl refusing to sing if you're dead."

"Among other things." Though he was astounded that someone could love him enough that they'd doom the world in their grief, he hoped it wouldn't come to that. Yet if their positions were reversed he very well might do the same.

A high-pitched chiming interrupted the conversation. Grinding his teeth at the interruption, he headed over to his scrying pool and summoned the gate stone. As Delgarias's image was revealed in the pool, Zareth's vexation dissolved into relief.

He opened the entry portal beside the pool. As the faelin sorcerer stepped into the chamber, Aurora, Sylvis and Beau gasped.

Delgarias grinned at them. "Oh good, you're here. I've waited so long to greet you in person."

Sylvis raised a brow. "You must be Uncle Del."

"Xochitl has an uncle?" Aurora and Beau chorused.

"Not really," Zareth told them, impatient to focus on the present.

"Actually," Delgarias interrupted, "I am her uncle now, after your marriage."

He blinked in confusion. "My mother didn't have a brother."

"Your grandmother did, though I was disowned and cast out of Shellandria long before you were born, I'm sure you never heard." Grief consumed his diamond-like eyes.

"You're my great uncle?" Zareth reverberated in shock. "Why did you never tell me? And why were you disowned? Did it have something to do with your love for the luminite princess?"

Delgarias shook his head sadly. "Although the Leonines were outraged with my suit, I am far from the first faelin to have dared reach above my station." The ancient sorcerer sighed, looking as old as his two millennia. "No, the sin I committed was far more grievous. And my path of atonement will never end."

Zareth's eyes widened at the shame and grief in the sorcerer's voice. "What did you do?"

"Someday I will tell you the whole shameful tale. For now, suffice to say that it involved the darkest of blood magic." His voice thickened with urgency. "I only told you of our kinship to assure that you will trust me in the nights to come."

Blood magic was frowned upon among the faelin, even the human sorcerer's custom of the blood kiss at a wedding. Zareth used blood magic himself to summon his hydra, two things his mother's people found repugnant, so he was not in a position to judge the Keeper of the Prophecy. Still, Delgarias's words gave him a chill. "What makes you think I will mistrust you?"

"Possibly nothing. It is difficult to foretell as the time of the Prophecy races near." His eyes glowed with intensity as he spoke. "But I must ensure, at all costs, that Xochitl is able to bring back the sun, no matter what you or Stefan are doing when the time comes."

Though his tone was dire, Zareth understood the gravity of the situation. "Of course." He handed Delgarias the letter from Stefan. "And what do you advise we'll do about this?"

The faelin sorcerer skimmed the letter. "Clearly he wants you at every disadvantage."

"That's what I gathered," Zareth said. "At least he can't carry out his threat to rape her."

Delgarias shook his head. "I wouldn't be so certain about that."

"But he's human," he protested as thousands of nightmares threatened to drown him.

"So are these three." He pointed at Aurora, Sylvis, and Beau. "Yet luminite blood runs through their veins as well, though they could have ancestry from other magical beings, or perhaps faelin half-breeds, like yourself."

Zareth stepped back, staring at them. Of course they'd have to be. No wonder Xochitl and they were all so drawn to each other. But if that meant that humans could on occasion mate with luminites...

"Oh fates! I must go to her." Mind overcome with visions of his love suffering, he charged forward, intent on reaching her.

Delgarias placed a hand on his chest, holding him back with barely a touch. "Don't go rushing blind into what is certain to be a trap. Stefan is trying to goad you into it, surely you can see that. He has his owns plans laid out. We need to formulate our own." His gaze flickered over Xochitl's band. "Primarily, what is to be done with these three."

Zareth nodded. "I do have a few ideas."

Chapter Twenty-eight

Xochitl

The door to my prison opened with a screech, scattering the few cats that had been too deeply asleep to sense Stefan's approach. The cold of their absence hit me like an icy draft. I curled up in a ball and wished I was dreaming.

"Get up," he ordered, yanking me to my feet when I didn't comply fast enough to suit him.

I grumbled. "What now?"

To my shock, he unfastened my wrist shackles. "I think my queen could use some fresh air."

My spine crawled with suspicion. Although I longed to get out of this cell, nothing good could come of it. Still, I couldn't help rubbing the chafed skin on my wrists in blissful relief to be free from the cuffs. "Where are you taking me?"

"To see my new tower. It will be the tallest in the world. But first..." He yanked off my clothes, despite my struggles. To my relief, instead of attacking me again, he tossed me what looked like a sack cloth. "Put this on."

The fabric was rough, but at least it was warmer than what Artavian brought me and had sleeves. Stefan also tossed down a pair of moccasins that were a little big until he shrunk them to fit. The care he took made me nervous.

As we walked through maze-like corridors and outside, I hoped one of my new friends was following my scent so maybe I'd have a path out if a chance to escape arose. The night air was indeed cold, but not as frigid as Stefan's lands were known to be. I should have known in the first place that he was holding me elsewhere.

But how had he hidden his activities here from the rest of the world? Everywhere Zareth and I travelled people had talked of Stefan's raising armies and courting alliances, but there wasn't even a whisper of him constructing a new tower on his father's lands.

After a short ride in a horse-drawn carriage, I discovered the secret. Stefan used the same trick he'd done to hide his fight with Zareth on Earth.

A great fog stretched for a mile, impossible to see through. It left an oily residue on my skin as we passed through it.

My jaw dropped as I saw the construction site. Wood scaffolding surrounded a tower that already had to be two hundred feet high. Winches hauled up square cut stones that were brought in by men with wheelbarrows. Thousands of emaciated workers labored under the eyes of cruel-eyed men with whips. How long had this been going on?

Stefan pulled me out of the carriage with a tight grip on my upper arm and dragged me to one of the overseers. "This one has been insolent," he told him. "She needs to be humbled."

The man crossed his arms over his barrel chest and looked me up and down like I was a side of beef. "She looks healthy enough. Can she climb?"

I looked up at the tiny figures at the top of the structure. Normally I loved to climb... but falling from that height sounded unpleasant.

"No!" Stefan snapped. "I do not want any permanent damage." He turned to leave. "I will come collect her at the end of the shift."

"Very well, I'll give her a barrow." The overseer stroked the handle on the whip on his belt. "And if this insolence continues?"

He didn't know who I was, I realized. Stefan had drained my magic to the point that he probably even thought I was human.

"Don't damage her face or limbs. I'd like her to still be pretty when she serves me next." Stefan looked back over his shoulder. "If she gets to be too much of a handful, return her to me."

"As you wish. Though the mortar needs replenished soon."

The Winter Prince stopped at the carriage and turned around with a smile that made me want to knock his teeth out. "After the Solstice, you'll have more mortar than you'll know what to do with."

He climbed into the vehicle and the driver flicked the reins and they were off. Leaving me alone with the overseer. To be "humbled." I found myself missing my cell and hated myself for it.

The overseer leered at me. "Come," he said, and withdrew his whip. My back already ached, so I obeyed.

He led me to a group of people in tattered rags and gestured to one to bring me a wheelbarrow. The others kept their eyes averted as we progressed to a quarry where others were loading them up with stones for the tower.

I halted, frozen at the sight of such abject misery. Until the whip cracked and blinding pain engulfed my back. My lungs seized as the air was forced out with my startled yelp. My legs turned to jelly as I struggled to breathe.

"Get to work!" the overseer roared.

A multitude of Bruce Campbell one-liners from the *Evil Dead* movies swept through my mind. I had the urge to tell him who I was, but I knew Stefan would anticipate that. To my shame, I kept my mouth shut and scrabbled forward and grabbed a chunk of rock one of the others passed to me and placed it in the wheelbarrow.

"You have to be careful not to upset Hraka," a stooped man whispered as he passed me another stone. His gaze swept over me, a glimmer of curiosity amidst his apathy. "Where were you taken from?"

His words echoed in my skull. *Where were you taken from?*

My jaw dropped as the implication became clear. *This* was what happened to the missing people. Bile rose in my throat and my back throbbed as I answered his question.

"I was taken from Raijin." From Zareth. God, why couldn't I have listened to him and remained with him? If I hadn't been so stupid, I would be in his arms right now.

My coworker nodded as he bent for another rock. "Land of the Lord of Storm and Shadow. The Winter Prince delights in swiping his people from beneath his nose."

"His own seneschal led me to Stefan." And probably countless others. Bitterness dripped from my voice. "Where were you taken from?"

"Laran." His eyes were far away as we loaded more rocks. "The Wurraks delivered me and my kinsmen here."

I opened my mouth to tell him about his country's liberation, but then I saw another overseer glaring at me and reaching for his whip.

I bent back to my task.

When the wheelbarrow was full, we rolled it to the construction site. More guards with whips watched us with steely eyes and clenched fists. While we unloaded the stones, another worker passed by, carrying a ceramic jug full of what looked like red cement. He trembled as he carried the jug, holding it out from his body as if afraid it would spill on him.

The lash struck my shoulder making me stumble and almost drop a stone on my foot. The Laranese man gave me a sympathetic look and gestured for me to hurry.

I couldn't help turning back to look back at the tower. The stones were sealed together by veins of reddish-brown that resembled blood. A sinister, choking aura emanated from the structure. Hraka's words came back to me.

The mortar needs to be replenished soon.

Dread speared my heart so sharp that I barely felt the next lash.

***

Stefan

While Xochitl labored on his tower's construction, Stefan sat in his father's throne, rubbing a crick in his neck. For some reason, he couldn't get comfortable. The sooner his tower was completed, the better. Then he could have this castle leveled and build a bigger one in its place. The king of the world deserved better.

Surely then, the nightmares would end. No longer would he envision his father standing over his bed, the blackened hole in his chest still smoking as he glared down at him with accusing, dead eyes.

"It didn't have to be this way," he'd pleaded to the vision. "If you would have merely stepped down and named me your successor, I would have left you in peace. My patience had run out."

All his childhood he'd grown up hearing tales of King Taranis the Great and his brave and noble deeds. Yet his father seemed to have nothing in common with that exalted personage.

True, Stefan did recall a point in time where Taranis held court somewhat regularly and even accompanied him on diplomatic trips to other lands, but it wasn't long before Father stopped doing even that. Mostly all Stefan remembered was a broken man shut up in his castle with his books and mourning his first wife, who'd defected to Zareth's tower in the last years before her death. Taranis's second wife, Stefan's mother, never merited that attention when she died, much less than when she was alive.

As Taranis lost his care to rule and Zareth never showed any interest in it in the first place, Stefan had grown up assuming Taranis had married his mother and sired him to take his place. Especially after he'd shown him the way to summon a hydra.

Though it was frustrating to see the coffers taking in far less than they could and lands becoming less dependent on the crown, Stefan willed himself to be patient even as he studied and grew in power, preparing himself to rule. He established his lands and castle and gained the fealty of his people while his brother alienated his.

When seers all over the world foretold that the sun would vanish and a great despair would cripple the people, Stefan once more pleaded with his father to turn over the crown to him.

Taranis had shaken his head. "No, Stefan. You do not have the right temperament to rule. With shaking hands he fumbled for a pen. "I must speak with your brother…"

Mute with rage, Stefan watched him scratch out a missive to Zareth, looking feeble and dimwitted on his throne. This wouldn't do.

He'd wanted to encase him in ice and make him shatter, but then the crime would point to him. If only he could wield lightning like Zareth. He'd settled for the next best thing. Gathering his power, he'd built a ball of flame in his fist.

He still remembered his father's last words. "Stop that, my boy, the light hurts my eyes."

And then Stefan had torn out his heart. The room had filled with the odor of burnt flesh. As the king collapsed, his crown tumbled to the bloodstained marble floor and rolled to Stefan's feet. He tossed aside the charred lump of flesh that had been his father's heart, picked up the crown, and left.

Summoning fire took more energy than his ice, so he slept for a full day before he recovered. But when he awoke, it was still dark.

The people waited in vain for a dawn that never came. When the king's body was discovered, chaos ensued. Taranis had not left a will.

Many assumed that Zareth as the eldest son would take reign, but instead the sorcerer remained in his tower, studying his moldy books. Whispers echoed throughout the realm that perhaps the Lord of Storm and Shadow had slain his sire. Stefan was pleased. At least his efforts to direct suspicion to his half-brother had borne fruit.

He would have crowned himself right away, if not for the discord that erupted in the world. Wars broke out as people from some lands sought resources from others. Stefan and Zareth found themselves inadvertently working together as they broke up the squabbles and established plans for rationing and growing crops. However, Stefan made certain to secure as many alliances as possible.

And then the Prophecy had surfaced. Not only would they have a savior who would bring back the dawn, but she would also crown the king.

Stefan had been elated. He would secure the Leonine princess, she'd bring back the sun, he'd defeat Zareth and she would place the crown on his head. He would be king, with a beautiful queen at his side. He'd long heard tales of a luminite's beauty.

While waiting for the time to fetch his princess, he started the construction of his new tower. His father's wouldn't do. For one thing, Taranis was a Storm Mage, so the energy didn't mesh with Stefan's Winter magic. For another, something about the place didn't feel right. As the second son, he'd never felt welcome.

After surrounding his chosen site with an obscuring fog, he utilized captives he'd taken in the wars to mine stone from his father's quarry and begin construction. With significant bribes he'd then recruited mages who'd been exiled for working blood magic to create the binding mortar. His hydra fed best on the pain of others, so when his slaves were worked to capacity, they were turned over to the mages for the mortar.

When he ran out of captives, he sent his people out on abducting missions. With so much despair in the world, they were hardly missed.

He went to Earth expecting to bring home his queen, but she had to ruin his plans by rejecting him. Despite his power and with all his beauty and charm, she dared to flee from him.

Everything had progressed so well— until the night of the Spirit Feast. He followed Zareth to Earth with no problems and the luminite princess was indeed indescribably beautiful.

Her power made him salivate, yet his body did not respond to her. That didn't matter for the time being. He'd have an opportunity to recapture her and claim what should be his.

And then the unthinkable happened. She *mated* his monstrous half-brother.

Women across the world had been terrified of the Lord of Storm and Shadow, but Xochitl had actually allowed those freakish long fingers to touch her. Stefan's enraged shriek had echoed throughout the castle walls.

It had taken hours to calm himself enough to formulate a plan as to how to deal with that unfortunate development. To Stefan's fortune, Zareth's seneschal, Rickard, proved to be a useful spy and ally.

At last Xochitl was in his grasp. But the failure of his attempt to mate her curdled his belly. He would try once more after Zareth was dead. If it didn't work, he would kill her too.

After all, it was the crown he wanted most.

The sound of footsteps approaching the throne room pulled him from his reverie.

"My Lord, you wished to see me?" Artavian said as he opened the door.

Stefan eyed his apprentice. The lad had been nothing but obedient, yet lately Stefan thought he detected a glimmer of insolence in the blue robed mage's eyes. "I want you to deliver a message to the Duchess of Egina. I am requesting that she honor our alliance and send for armies to come to my defense in case Zareth is foolish enough to make a last minute move."

"Yes, my lord." Artavian bowed. As he turned to leave, he froze and gaped. "There's a dragon flying around the castle!"

"Yes, yes. I'm well aware of that," Stefan said with a dismissive wave of his hand. "It is the great Xandizion of

Abinitio. He can't do anything to me. The Prophecy dictates that only Zareth can face me, and he will not risk a confrontation if it jeopardizes the safety of his true love."

Suddenly Artavian gasped in shock. "Look!" He pointed.

Stefan joined his apprentice at the window. The sky was filled with dragons. Their scales of various hues glittered in the moonlight. Then a high pitched sound from below reached his ears and he peered down to see that several cats were gathered at the base of the castle, yowling and clawing the walls. Thousands of people approached as well.

"Yes, the time is close at hand. Representatives from all over the world are coming to bear witness to the miracle."

As if to herald the beginning of his reign, snowflakes began falling from the sky.

A movement from below caught their eyes. They peered down to see a black cloaked figure approaching the castle. Stefan burst into triumphant laughter.

"Ah, here comes my brother now."

With renewed enthusiasm he rushed downstairs to greet his newest prisoner. By the time he reached the castle entrance, Stefan's guards had seized his brother.

A broad grin spread across Stefan's face to see the Lord of Storm and Shadow so defeated. The loss of his bride had taken all the fight from him.

"Ah, Zareth. What a pleasure." He swelled with triumph. "I thought I would never see the day that you are completely at my mercy. That is why you're here, isn't it? To surrender to me?"

Zareth sighed in resignation, shoulders drooping. "Yes Stefan. It seems you've won."

Oh such sweet words. But Stefan wanted more. "Then say it! I want to hear it from your lips."

"I surrender to you, Stefan." Hate threaded through the abject misery of Zareth's voice. "However, you should know that my armies surround the castle and if harm comes to me, they will attack."

"You fool. They won't risk doing anything to risk harming the Lioness." The Winter Prince chuckled gleefully before summoning more guards. "I want him in chains."

They exchanged reluctant looks at first, recognizing their prisoner as Aisthanesthai's most powerful and feared High Sorcerer. But with a sharp glare from Stefan, they obeyed, restraining Zareth.

One held a knife to his throat while the others bound him with spell-forged chains and stripped him of all belongings.

Stefan raised his crystal over his brother's head. "If he moves or makes a sound, cut his throat."

Once he cast the spell that neutralized Zareth's magic, he felt better, though he wished he could take that magic for his own. "Lock him in the cell I most recently emptied," he instructed his guards. "His presumptuousness to me in the past will be punished." He regarded his prisoner with a smirk. "Remember this, my hated sibling, any move from you and Xochitl will pay for the mistake."

Zareth spit in his face. "Someday, brother, you will pay for the mistake you've made in taking Xochitl prisoner."

Stefan's fist cracked hard against Zareth's jaw. "I've always wanted to do that."

Wiping the saliva from his cheek, Stefan grinned at the sublime sight of his half-brother being hauled off in chains. It was worth missing the sight of Xochitl slaving away on his tower.

He wished he could make her labor until the Solstice, but it was too risky. For one thing, he could not risk her being harmed so severely she would be unable to fulfill the prophecy. For another, according to reports, the other slaves had been affected by her. It was as if they could sense that she was to be a queen. The last thing he needed was for her to incite rebellion.

Chapter Twenty-nine

Xochitl

Back and forth we went, filling the wheelbarrow with stones, unloading them at the tower. Rinse and repeat. Every muscle in my body screamed and blisters formed on my hands and feet.

After many long hours we were called to a pavilion and served bowls of what looked like Malt-O-Meal. I bit back whimpers as I took my portion. A Charlie horse shrieked in my left calf as I gingerly sat next to a sullen group near a fire.

The food was bland, but I didn't give a shit. I shoveled it up in greedy bites. A flash of gray darted in the corner of my eye. I glanced over and saw a cat dashing away from one of the overseers who tried to kick it. Great. I was putting my friends in danger.

Then I saw something worse. A woman shambled to the pavilion and fell in the mud. She tried to crawl the rest of the way, but then she was seized by guards. My fellow captives and I watched in horror as they dragged her off to a stone building near the construction site.

A sickly green light flashed from the windows, followed by an inhuman shriek of agony. Porridge stuck to the roof of my mouth as the other prisoners looked down, faces etched in sorrow.

"The mortar," I whispered, trying not to gag.

A Tolonquan captive nodded and spat. "Evil blood magic."

"Anna was so strong," one of the Piscani said. "I'd thought she'd make it to the Solstice."

Another laughed. "You think the Lioness will care about us when she crowns the Prince?"

"She will," I growled, wishing I could tell them who I was. Wishing they'd believe me. "And she won't crown that dickhole, Steve."

"Steve?" they chorused. A few even managed to crack weak smiles.

A woman glared at me. "So she'll crown the Lord of Storm and Shadow? And why would he care about us? He didn't seem to notice when we went missing."

"Yes he did. He questioned the villagers relentlessly," I argued. "And during his travels with his bride, he inquired about those missing from other lands. And he freed Laran from the Wurraks."

The Laranese man who'd been loading rocks with me looked up sharply. "I hadn't heard the last. Is it true?"

I nodded. "Steve threw the biggest tantrum in front of the Conclave."

A wistful smile strained his lips. But before I could say more, the overseers came and seized our bowls, ordering us back to work.

By then it had begun to rain. Between exhaustion and misery from the icy sheets of water pouring all over us, we didn't talk much more.

Two others were killed by the evil mages while the hours dragged in a relentless nightmare. I nearly sobbed in relief when the overseer's called a halt.

My coworkers were led to a fenced area with wooden shacks while I was loaded into a wagon bound for the castle.

"I hope the Prince brings you back tomorrow," Hraka told me. "You're a good worker for such a little thing."

Shivering in the rain, I bowed my head, refusing to dignify him with an answer. As the wagon wheels slogged through the mud, my mind replayed all the horrific things I'd seen and learned. For the past four years Stefan had been abducting people all around the world and enslaving them.

But he wasn't just enslaving them. He was sacrificing them with some fucked up kind of blood magic and binding their flesh and blood to his tower. What did that do with their souls? My stomach heaved. I didn't want to know.

Artavian waited at the castle doors. As he helped me out of the wagon, I sagged in his grip in relief. I didn't know if I could have handled facing Stefan. That dying woman's screams continued to echo in my soul.

"The Prince has decided to move you to another, more… ah, comfortable cell," he said in an odd tone.

I glanced up at him, prodding him to elaborate. Instead his gaze darted to the sides and over his shoulder.

I took the hint. Someone might be listening.

"You will have a bed," he continued. "And you'll be able to see out the window."

My brow rose. "What prompted such benevolence from our *Führer*?"

"*Führer*?" he repeated, sounding puzzled.

I sighed. "If you can get a book on Earth realm history, look up Adolph Hitler."

Comprehension dawned and a broken laugh cracked from his throat before his features smoothed into his previous mask of indifference. "Ah. I have heard of that person."

As he escorted me up a winding staircase, his shoulders shook with repressed mirth. Despite my weariness, I managed a smile.

True to his word, my new prison was far nicer than my last. The floor was carpeted, there was a privacy screen in front of the chamber pot, and even a small cot for a bed. The air felt weird, though.

Artavian seemed to sense my wariness. "This cell is warded and sound-proofed. The Prince has decided to ah, forego the pleasure of hearing you sing until the Solstice." His lips twitched in a conspiratorial smile. "You will have longer chains for more movement so you'll be able to look out the window this time." He frowned at the last.

"Why did he decide to upgrade me?" I asked as he fastened a long chain to my leg shackles. "Especially after making me slave away on his tower in an effort to 'humble' me." I made quotes in the air.

He cocked his head to the side at my gesture, but he seemed to understand the gist. "I don't think he intends to send you back there tomorrow. This cell is warded and soundproofed," he repeated in emphasis, eyes pleading me to grasp some significance in the words. "Now I must treat your wounds."

After he finished cleaning my blisters and broken skin from the whiplashes, Artavian left to get food.

I slumped on the cot, my aching muscles crying out in relief to be in a normal sitting position. The grime I was covered with messed up the blanket, but I was too tired to give a shit.

My orange cat friend leapt between the bars of the window and scampered up on my lap. *Your mate is here. I smelled him when he arrived.*

My heart slammed into my ribcage. Zareth was here?

I clutched the cat tight to my chest. *Are you certain?*

Yes. He has your scent all over him. He rubbed his cheek against my chin. *They put him in your old cell. I tried to tell him about you, but he doesn't speak my language.* His ears laid back. *And then the evil one came.*

It took a moment to form a response over my thudding pulse. *Did he hurt him?*

I do not know. You told me not to let the Evil One see me. I will look in on him for you when he leaves. His ears twitched as he sniffed me. *Where were you? You smell of blood and pain.*

As I explained my day of toiling on the tower, I realized why I was sent there in the first place. Stefan wanted me out of the way when Zareth came. And now he was in my old cell. That explained the upgrade to my accommodations.

Artavian's repeated words now made sense. *"This cell is warded and soundproof."*

Stefan didn't want us to be able to hear or sense each other. A triumphant smile curved my lips. Thanks to my friends, his efforts were futile. The smile died as I realized that didn't change the facts. We still couldn't communicate. What did Stefan not want me to hear?

What was he doing to Zareth?

***

Zareth

The cell was ice cold, as Stefan doubtless had intended. Even colder was the absence of Zareth's magic. However, his brother could not take it all. With his faelin senses and mating bond, he could feel that Xochitl had been in this cell. He could even smell a trace of her essence.

Fury roared through him as he caught the scent of her blood and the thought of her being chained to this cold hard stone. Zareth strained in his chains, shackled facing the wall. What had Stefan done to her?

And where was she now?

Seething with impotence, he longed to tear himself free and go find her, to bring her out of this accursed place.

But that wasn't the plan.

Although every fiber of his being railed against the thought of surrendering to Stefan, this was the only option that he had. If he had not heeded his sibling's demand, Stefan would have sent his armies to Raijin to capture him and kill and rape his people in the process. He also could hurt Xochitl in retaliation, and Zareth could not let that happen, under any circumstances.

Even then, when he'd surrendered it took all of his willpower to hold back the urge to slap the triumphant sneer off of his brother's face.

Stefan wasn't going to win, he reminded himself.

The cell door opened with a screech.

"Hello, Brother." Stefan's dreaded voice echoed on the stone.

Zareth turned his head to see his brother approach him, wielding a whip.

Stefan bared his teeth in a snarling grin. "I may not be able to kill you yet, but I can use you to feed my hydra."

He withdrew a blade from his robes and Zareth felt a twinge of fear. Was Stefan mad enough to disrupt the Prophecy? They were supposed to face each other on the Solstice. Xochitl was supposed to crown the victor.

The knife slashed downward, tearing at his robes until they were in tatters. Zareth gritted his teeth. He knew the game now. His half-brother thrived on humiliating and inflicting pain on others.

He hissed as the knife grazed his back, drawing blood.

Stefan laughed. "Oh yes, and now I can make you pay for every time you thwarted my plans and took what was mine. I am meant to be king, you should have known that." The crack of the whip echoed harshly against the stone walls before it struck Zareth's flesh. "How dare you take my bride and try to steal my throne!"

Zareth gritted his teeth, unwilling to give his brother a response. To cry out, plead, or argue would only feed him more.

"I wish I could beat you to death now," Stefan growled. "Then I could destroy your mating bond and properly claim my bride."

He must have made some sound, because Stefan halted and leaned against the wall, trying to meet his gaze. "Oh, you don't like that, do you? Well, I didn't like discovering that what was supposed to be my virgin bride is spoiled goods. Although she still has very delectable breasts and her little cunt is oh so tight."

Zareth's stoicism vanished in a red haze of fury. With a growl, he thrashed in his chains, much to Stefan's delight. It was all the incentive he needed. The whip crashed against his back over and over again, lashing him with relentless speed.

His anger was drowned in an ocean of pain before, mercifully, everything went black and his agony bled away.

When he awoke, a hand pressed something cool and gelatinous against his ravaged back.

"Please hold still, my lord," a voice whispered. "I'm almost finished."

Mind grasping for consciousness Zareth could voice one thought. "Xochitl. He violated her. It shouldn't be possible."

"No, he did not." the voice said firmly. "Though he tried. But the second he touched the Lioness, his flesh withered." The voice held a tinge of deprecation. "Not that it was any less unpleasant for her. He beat her most severely."

The loathing in the man's voice brought Zareth further clarity. It was hardly the tone of a loyal servant. But he had a Wurrak accent, and the Wurraks were known allies of Stefan. "Who are you and how do you know these things?"

"I am Artavian Calla, son of Aylmer, Lord of Wurrakia, and the Winter Prince's unwilling apprentice." A blue-robed mage came into view.

Zareth frowned, puzzled. "Why unwilling? Most mages would give their eyeteeth to apprentice with a High Sorcerer. Especially one who could be king."

Artavian nodded. "Making me an apprentice was my father's condition for their alliance. However, I want to be a healer, and though male healers are rare in Wurrakia, I'd hope that a high sorcerer would be accepted. But the Winter Prince does not heal, for one thing. For another—"

"He harms," Zareth finished. "I am beginning to see your quandary." Tasting the air and listening to the vibrations in the mage's voice determined the young man was telling the truth.

"Yes. His cruelty sickens me." Artavian's mouth twisted in revulsion. "Furthermore, he has taught me very little. He mostly uses me as an errand boy and a glorified gaoler."

Gaoler. "Have you seen Xochitl?"

"Yes. She was in this cell until today. Now she's been moved to one that is more comfortable, though more secure.

Stefan can now hear every sound she makes, so I cannot deliver a message." His pale gray eyes swam with remorse. "If it were possible for me to help either of you escape, I would."

Zareth studied the young mage. It seemed he had an unexpected ally. "You have been very proficient in healing my back, at least. The pain is gone."

"My mother taught me her arts. Now I may lower your chains so you can be more comfortable. I would have sooner, but I had to wait for the salve to absorb."

True to his word, Artavian went to a hand crank on the wall and lowered him to the floor. He then extended the chain's slack even further so Zareth could sit.

"Thank you," Zareth gasped as his muscles screamed from being locked in the same position for so long. "Tell me more of Xochitl."

Artavian delayed a moment by fetching a tray that held a crust of bread and a cup of broth. As he set the meager victuals before Zareth, he began. "I've been doing what I can to keep her warm and fed. And Stefan hasn't attacked her since his first attempt..."

As the mage spoke, Zareth was at first relieved to hear that his love had not been raped. He even managed a smile when Artavian spoke of Xochitl disturbing Stefan with vengeful songs.

But when he told him about the construction on Stefan's tower and the involvement of enslaved captives and blood magic, Zareth choked on his broth. "So that's what became of all the missing people. No wonder Stefan had so many." He made a silent vow to liberate them all as soon as the Prophecy was fulfilled. *But how many would still be alive then?* "And he made Xochitl go out there and work with them?"

"Yes, but only for this night," Artavian clarified. "He wanted her far away so she couldn't sense your arrival... and of course another opportunity to make her suffer."

"How much was she hurt?" Zareth wasn't naïve enough to think she would have emerged from that unscathed.

"Blisters on her hands, a chill from the cold, and four lashes on her back, which I cleaned and healed." Artavian's shoulders slumped in blatant despair. "Her mind and heart were injured far worse."

Zareth clenched his jaw until it ached as images of Xochitl enslaved, whipped and bearing witness to untold suffering flashed before his eyes. He'd do anything to hold her. But he'd never be able to tell her that it was all right. Because it wasn't and would never be.

Artavian stood. "I must go before Stefan grows suspicious. I'll tell him you refused to eat to explain the delay."

Zareth nodded. "Thank you for caring for her."

The mage shrugged. "She is the savior of our world and she does not deserve the treatment she's received here. No one does. I'm doing what I can to mitigate her pain."

After Artavian left, Zareth finished his meager meal and hoped Xochitl was getting better sustenance.

A muffled pattering sound came from the wall across from him. Zareth looked up to see an orange cat leap in through window. The feline mewled at him and gave him an unusually intent look.

"Did you come from Xochitl?" he asked.

The cat regarded him with a piercing green gaze before blinking and thumping its tail on the stone. Was that a yes? He wished he could communicate with them as Xochitl could.

But when the cat bounded onto his lap, he had his answer. Her scent was embedded in the cat's fur. A muffled groan of pure yearning escaped from his throat as pressed his face to the cat's side and inhaled. The cat nuzzled him back and purred. Three more joined him until he was surrounded by masses of purring warmth that carried his mate's scent.

A lump formed in his throat. She knew he was here and he had no doubt that she had sent her feline friends to him for reassurance and comfort.

"I don't know if you can understand me," he said as he stroked their fur and scratched their ears. "But if you can, tell Xochitl not to worry about me. Tell her I have a plan. Tell her to trust me."

Gold and silver light shone in from the window. The moons were growing fuller. The Solstice was almost here. And all of this would come to an end.

Chapter Thirty

Xochitl

Even though it hurt to watch, I couldn't tear myself from the window. Stefan's grotesque tower rose higher by the hour as snow flowed down from the sky. With the treacherous cold and ice, I'd seen five people fall from their deaths in as many moon-sets. And even though I couldn't hear the crack of the whips and the screams of the dying, my imagination filled in the blanks.

Which was probably what Stefan intended when he put me in this cell with such a horrible view.

At least I was able to see something optimistic. The moons both grew fuller. Being locked in a cell coupled with the eternal night time, they were all that conveyed a passage of hours. The only sign that my time in this hell would come to an end.

One way or another.

Artavian hadn't said anything directly about Zareth, but he gave enough cryptic statements for me to know he was alive. From how the sorcerer spoke less freely, I gathered that one of the wards in this cell involved some way for Stefan to listen in on me.

I gained even more comfort from my cats, who returned carrying his scent, so I knew they spent time comforting him and hopefully reassuring him that I was alive. They said he tried to talk to them but they couldn't understand him.

They also told me what Artavian couldn't. Stefan had beaten my love unconscious the night he surrendered. My own back ached in commiseration at the news as fury coursed through my veins.

I would kill Stefan. Somehow.

The door opened and four of Stefan's dead-eyed serving women filed in, carrying a brass bathtub. One unchained me from the wall as the others filled the tub with steaming water. My skin itched with longing. The closest thing to a bath I'd gotten was when Artavian had given me a washcloth after my forced labor stint.

"You must undress, my lady," the one who unchained me said.

I looked out the window at the two full moons. "Is it time?"

All nodded and bowed to me. And for once their eyes weren't empty. Their gazes gleamed with hope.

Doubt and worry washed over me in crippling waves. If I was capable of fear, I would have been frozen in panic. I allowed the women to lead me to the tub. As they scrubbed me, my mind raced with unease. What if I failed? I'd been so worried about Zareth, my friends, and the suffering of others, that I'd barely thought of how I was supposed to bring back the sun.

I didn't even know what song I was going to sing.

By the time the maids finished washing my hair, the water had gone cold. They wrapped me in a thick towel and to my surprise, led me out of the cell. For a moment I considered knocking them all out with roundhouse kicks, but dismissed the idea. I still had no magic, so I wouldn't be able to subdue the countless guards even with my fighting skills. And even if I ran, Stefan still held Zareth.

A thought made my muscles lock up. If my magic was gone, what if I couldn't bring back the sun?

Stefan waited in a bedchamber, dressed in a pale blue robe embroidered with snowflakes. The maids stripped the towel from me so I stood naked before him. Oh shit. What if it wasn't the Solstice? What if he wanted to attack me again?

As much as I tried to maintain my dignity, memories of his violence and attempted rape washed over me and I shuddered in disgust.

Stefan sneered. "As appealing as your delectable body is right now, I don't have time to ravage you. We need to ready you for the presentation and my coronation." He tossed me a dress made of shimmering white silk. "Now put this on. Disobey me and," he raised his staff menacingly. "I will take your resistance as an invitation for a quick tryst."

Gagging, I put on the gown as quick as possible. When I was dressed, my captor proceeded to fasten chains of gold around my wrists and neck that connected to a gilded leash that he held in his manicured hand. My feet were left unshackled, though, and I couldn't help but be grateful for that small bit of relief.

Maybe I'd have a chance to kick him.

A small army of servants were then summoned to attend me. They brushed my long midnight and purple hair until it shone, anointed me with perfume, and carefully applied makeup while he watched.

As the women worked, a strange sensation trickled over me. An aura of calm and peace seeped into my bones. Resignation, and a sense that the time was drawing near and I would do what I was born to do. The fact that I didn't really know what that was no longer seemed to matter.

The servants pulled me to my feet, turning me to a mirror. The sight of my reflection, all pure in white and gold, distracted me from the feeling. *This so isn't me!*

"Don't you look lovely?" A maid exclaimed as she set a thin gold circlet on my head.

"Just like an Earth realm bride." Another said dreamily.

Bride? I grimaced. *More like a virgin who is about to be sacrificed!*

"Are you ready, my Princess?" Stefan inquired with a sardonic smirk.

"Do I have a fucking choice, prick?"

He tugged on the leash so hard that I choked and nearly fell on my ass. "You'd better keep a more careful watch on your tongue or somebody will die, and it won't be you."

Striking an arrogant pose, he snapped his fingers in command and two gigantic hulking guards arrived, dragging a slumping black-clad figure into the hall. The figure's dark head lifted and my heart froze as I recognized his face.

"Zareth!" My cry emerged, laden with agony. I'd wished over and over again to see him.

But not like this.

He who had once stood tall and strong in elegantly tailored robes now stooped in weakness, his face covered in a myriad of bruises and stubble from a few day's growth of beard, his eyes blackened where Stefan had struck him. His robes were tattered and grimy, his glorious hair a dirty mess.

"Xochitl..." His voice was a cracked, barely audible whisper.

The sight of the all-powerful High Sorcerer, now so weak he could hardly stand, made my knees shake.

"Now you see that I mean business." Stefan said.

How could he have given himself up? Guilt flooded me for the trouble I'd caused in my fit of temper. I strengthened my resolve to avenge Zareth and all the other captives for all that Stefan had done.

I gazed at Zareth with naked love. "Forgive me." I mouthed.

He gave me a stoic nod and my heart ached anew at the sight of the man I loved brought so low.

Stefan gripped my chin. "If you don't cooperate with me in every way, and I mean *every* way," he squeezed my breast painfully in emphasis, "the love of your life will die. I promise you his death will be agonizing."

Each of his words was another harsh blow to my already aching heart.

I met his gaze and conveyed all of my hatred. "I won't sing if you kill him."

Stefan smirked. "Very well."

We both knew that I had no control over what happened after.

My one consolation was that at least I would be able to save my love's world before we died.

My leash was tugged as my captor pulled me forward and led me down the corridor. Zareth was also dragged in that direction by hulking guards. His labored breathing tempted me to lash out, but I held myself in check. We reached the end of the hallway and Stefan opened the door to lead me onto an enormous stone platform.

The cold slapped me in the face, making my knees buckle.

Stefan jerked my leash. "Artavian! Warm her."

The blue robed mage chanted something in a guttural language, making blessed heat surround me. My muscles relaxed their iron grip and I was able to walk further on the platform.

I didn't have to wonder at its purpose for very long, because as we drew forward I saw the gallows, the block and the guillotine looming ahead, covered in snow.

This used to be an execution site. A bitter laugh trickled from my throat.

Stefan pushed me forward and I soon realized the reason why he had chosen this platform as the ideal spot to present me to the people. This location was visible for miles about the kingdom. I gasped in awe at the sea of millions of spectators before me as snowflakes fell on us all. Humans, faelin, and leprechauns, blurred into one gigantic mass in my vision. From all around I could hear their whispers.

"The Lioness…"

"Look! She's here at last!"

"Why is she in chains?"

"The Lord of Storm and Shadow is chained too."

"Something is wrong…."

My gaze surveyed the crowd, silently pleading them to storm the stage and tear Stefan from limb to limb. But as I looked closer, I knew that was a hopeless cause. Half the crowd was clad in armor and held weapons. Flags with sigils fluttered in the snowy wind. And over half of them composed of Stefan's allies.

If any of them moved now, it would be a bloodbath.

As if reading my thoughts, Stefan grinned in triumph as he strutted over to Zareth. "Behold my moment of glory, dear Brother. The Lioness will fulfill The Prophecy by my side and then I shall be the ruler of Aisthanesthai. Your precious Xochitl will be my bride and I shall enjoy taking her sweet body again and again. Perhaps I will allow you to live to see me wed her and bed her before I kill you."

The fury that burned in Zareth's eyes made Stefan falter for a moment, but then he turned away and gestured for a servant to come forward. The servant was holding a red velvet pillow. On it rested a crown wrought of gold, the points shaped like tongues of flame, and studded with sapphires. I'd seen it before in a book. It was the crown of King Taranis, which had vanished when he'd died.

I wasn't the only one to notice. A gasp echoed from the crowd at this visible proof that the Winter Prince had murdered his father.

Some spat and threw down their flags.

I looked to Stefan's allies, but three quarters of them still waved The Winter Prince's battle standard resolutely. What had he promised them for such loyalty?

"Ladies and Gentlemen!" the murderer's voice rang out, silencing the spectators. "I present to you all—"

He stopped as a glowing white ball launched from the audience right at him.

Yes, I thought. *Vaporize him!*

But Stefan rolled to the side and the incandescent ball whizzed past his shoulders.

It struck Zareth square in the chest.

Heart in my throat, I lunged for him. The chain around my neck stopped me short, strangling me. I fell to my knees and closed my eyes, unable to see my love die.

Stefan's laughter echoed in my ears.

Chapter Thirty-one

Xochitl

My eyes opened at the snap of breaking chains. The smile slipped from Stefan's face.

Instead of being burnt to a crisp, Zareth stood tall and straight, looking regal and powerful once more, despite his tattered robes. Thunder rumbled in the sky as lightning crackled in his eyes. He had his powers back.

Whatever had hit him had healed and restored him, rather than killing him. My gaze whipped to the crowd, but I saw no sign of our benevolent rescuer.

A deadly roar echoed for miles as Zareth threw the guards that held him off the platform and started toward Stefan.

My despair dissolved into joy.

He was going to wipe the floor with Stefan's ass.

The Winter Prince regained his arrogant smirk. "Let the battle commence."

With his own evil smile, a ball of orange flame formed in Zareth's palm. He hurled it straight at Stefan.

Recovering from the surprise, Stefan raised his staff and used it to disintegrate the fireball before he counter-attacked with missiles of ice. Zareth melted them with a wall of fire.

"Guards," Stefan shrieked, "Seize him!"

Stefan's henchmen looked at Zareth and stepped further back. The Winter Prince's eyes blazed as he shot another burst of ice. Bolts of lightning crashed down at him, but he darted away just in time, singeing his robe.

On and on their battle raged. Electricity clashed with ice, balls of fire sizzled and steamed in the air. Witnesses had to duck to avoid being struck by stray blasts.

Shields flared and wavered. My heart rejoiced whenever Zareth struck a hit and plummeted when one of Stefan's attacks hurt my love.

Writhing in helplessness, I watched it all, wishing I could interfere. But every time I tried to move, the odd feeling that came over me earlier returned, and held me back. This was not my part to play in the Prophecy, after all. So I had to wait, immobile and shivering in the winter cold, until the end of the battle for the outcome.

The armies appeared to be under the same condition. They remained still, not a blade drawn.

I turned my concentration back to the fight, noticing that the Zareth and Stefan were no longer using particular elements against each other, now throwing balls of pure magical energy.

My gaze rested on Zareth with growing worry as he stumbled and barely rolled away from an attack. It looked like he was tired and weakening. After all, he wasn't as well-nourished during his imprisonment as I'd been. He slumped against the hanging post for a moment, panting for breath.

But when Stefan closed in for the kill, Zareth knocked Stefan's staff from his grasp. It clattered on the ground below and the pale blue crystal that crowned it went dark. Stefan shrieked and dove after it, but a turquoise dragon swooped down and bit it in two. Xandizion looked at me and winked before flying away.

I wondered why the dragon didn't just swoop down and eat Stefan. But then I realized he was bound by the same prophetic restraint as I was. He may have been able to take the staff, but he couldn't harm the combatants.

Face masked with wrath, Zareth strode to his brother.

"This is for touching her!" He roared and sent a blinding burst of energy at him.

The missile struck Stefan hard in the chest.

"This is for the people!"

Another burst struck him.

"This is for our father."

The next burst was so large and hot that those at the front of the crowd had to step back not to get singed. It hit Stefan so hard that he went flying far up into the air before crashing down on the solid stone platform near the chopping block. Blood poured from the corner of his mouth and he struggled back to his feet. His hair was burnt and his pale blue robed were torn and charred.

My heart raced, waiting for Zareth to finish off the evil bastard.

"And this—"

A flash of blinding light made him falter as Delgarias appeared between the warring brothers. "Stop! The time is too close to risk any interference."

Zareth mumbled a curse before he collapsed in exhaustion right where he stood.

I wasn't anywhere near as subdued. With my leash dragging behind me, I ran to Delgarias and pummeled his chest with my bound wrists. "Damn you, he was winning!"

To my surprise he pulled me into his arms. "Hush. It wasn't time yet. Now I will guard you from both of them and after you sing your song, you may crown your king."

He then bent down and snapped my chains. His lips pressed against my forehead in a gentle kiss and a jolt of pure power spread through my body like wildfire.

I gaped at him, tears running down my cheeks. He'd returned my magic.

"Uncle Del," I murmured. "Thank you."

Just then, I felt a nudge on my shoulder and turned to see Artavian next to me. He handed me the Fender Stratocaster, which was all hooked up and ready to go.

Delgarias gave me a warm smile before he addressed the crowd. "People of Aisthanesthai, I present to you, the Lioness of Light!"

The crowd cheered for a minute, but then they all went silent, eyes locked on me.

I stared back at the divided armies. If I crowned Zareth, they were certain to attack. Though the same would happen if I crowned Stefan.

I needed to show them all that Stefan was evil.

I needed to unite them.

A feeling of Purpose poured into me like a fount. It is time. My mother's words echoed so loud in my mind that it seemed like she was standing next to me. *Fulfill your destiny.*

I gazed up at the two moons, silver and gold, now full against the bright night sky. The words of the Prophecy echoed through my mind.

When the twin moons are full in the sky, Storm and Shadow will clash with Winter's Ice.

And with the Lioness's triumphant roar the people will free themselves from darkness and despair.

The Queen shall crown the King under the new dawn.

I still didn't know what I was supposed to sing and what difference it would make, but I didn't care. I approached the microphone.

Striking a G chord on my guitar, I opened my mouth.

And froze as a swirl of black dizziness engulfed me.

Suddenly, I was transported into a dark candlelit room where two women sat: a beautiful redhead who I recognized as Razvan's new girlfriend. *What was she doing there?* I wondered for a second before my focus shifted to a pale, emaciated crone with a balding scalp covered with bleeding wounds interspersed with wisps of orange hair.

"No!" the creepy one shrieked.

"Do it!" the other shouted. Her voice slammed into my skull, throwing me back to awareness.

My gaze traveled back to the enormous crowd watching me, expectant. My mouth was dry and the pull from that dark vision suffocated me so tightly that I could barely draw breath. The silence of the crowd threatened to engulf me.

I'm losing! My mind flapped like a trapped bird.

The vision sucked me under again. The crone hissed. The pretty red-head fixed me with firm jade-green eyes. *"Do it. Do it now!"*

Then I was thrown back into my body.

My ears pricked and goose bumps covered my body when I heard the drums. I knew that beat... and I knew who played it like that.

The center of the crowd parted as what I'd thought was some rich lord's tent was wheeled forward. The fabric fell away to reveal a crudely erected stage.

My eyes widened in surprise as I saw Aurora, Sylvis and Beau mounted on the stage with their amps and gear. They all looked up at me and smiled. Warmth flowed through me with the realization that my best friends didn't hate me and they were here to help.

Overcome with shock, I looked back at Zareth. *He'd planned this!* He smiled conspiratorially and my heart turned over.

Aurora played the opening drum beat again and arched a brow as if scolding me for missing my first cue.

Grinning at her, I strummed the first melody and Sylvis followed on her guitar with Beau on the bass. Then I lifted my voice to sing the first words of the song that had meant so much to us all; the song that was the greatest of challenges and the greatest of triumphs of our short career: "Stargazer" by *Rainbow*.

> *"High noon, oh I'd sell my soul for water*
> *Four years' worth of breaking my back*
> *There's no sun in the shadow of the wizard*
> *See how he glides, why he's lighter than air?*

I pointed at Stefan, delivering the lyrics with all the scorn in my being. After all these years of listening to and singing this song, I didn't realize until now that it was about him this whole time. Perhaps that was part of the Prophecy as well.

And now I held the key to exposing his evil.

> *Oh I see his face!*
> *Where is your star?*
> *Is it far, is it far, is it far?*
> *When do we leave?*
> *I believe, yes, I believe!"*

As Beau played a bass riff, I turned and threw my magic at the mist obscuring the filthy secret of Stefan's tower. Even over the drums and guitars, I heard the gasps and horrified cries of the audience.

I continued singing, replacing the desert-related lyrics with words to match this winter nightmare.

Facing the captives at the tower, I sang to them directly. This was all for them.

"In the cold and the rain
With whips and chains
To see him fly
So many die
We build a tower of stone
With our flesh and bone
Just to see him fly
But don't know why
Now where do we go?"

One by one the ragged captives threw down their buckets, stones, and wheelbarrows and began shambling away from the construction site to come to me. The overseers and the rogue mages who'd wrought the blood magic did nothing to stop their exodus. They stood frozen, watching me with fearful eyes.

With a wicked smile, I continued the next verse.

"Cold wind, moving fast across the deathscape
We feel that our time has arrived
The world spins, while we put his dream together
A tower of stone to take him straight to the sky."

As I repeated the chorus, my gaze once more covered the ragged captives as they circled the gallows. They swayed with my words.

Sylvis then played out the first exquisite guitar solo. The people of Aisthanesthai watched the performance in awe. The overseers threw down their whips and they and the dark mages began climbing the tower in tandem with the solo. The guitar sang out high and proud before fading away to silence.

The drums and bass resumed as I pointed at the dark mages on the tower.

"All eyes see the figure of the wizard
As he climbs to the top of the world
No sound, as he falls instead of rising

Time standing still, then there's blood on the snow!"

As if my words commanded them, the overseers and mages threw themselves from the tower. And indeed, their blood stained the snow.

I turned back to Stefan, gratified at his fearful pallor as I repeated the chorus a third time, voice rife with accusation.

"Oh I see his face!
Where was your star?
Was it far, was it far?
When did we leave?
We believed, we believed, we believed!"

I then turned back to all the lords, ladies, and their armies, willing them to grasp Stefan's atrocities for the full horror they were.

"In cold and rain
With the whips and chains
To see him fly
So many died
We built a tower of stone
With our flesh and bone
To see him fly."

My intensity increased with the final verse.

"But why, in all the rain,
With all the chains
Did so many die?
Just to see him fly."
"Look at my flesh and bone…"

My hand left my fret board to point at my heart before I turned back and pointed at Stefan's tower, the monstrosity wrought of blood and pain.

"Now, look, look, look, look,
Look at his tower of stone!"

Unfathomable power emanated from my voice as my hand rose to encompass the sky. When I sang the next words, they poured from me in an explosion of heat.

"I see a rainbow rising… look there on the horizon!"

The people took their eyes off of me for the first time since the song had begun, and looked up in wonder. Gasps and choked cries drowned out the music as the sky began to grow pinkish.

Even though I wanted to gawk with them, I continued to sing.

"And I'm coming home, I'm coming home, I'm coming home..."

I struggled to maintain my focus as the guitar's melody spiraled higher and higher with the coming dawn. Just as I began the song's closing chorus, rays of bright light exploded in the sky as the sun appeared on the horizon.

As my voice soared higher, so did the sun.

The people sang the final refrain with me until the music faded, ending the spell of the song. A long moment of tangible silence hovered over everyone as we all gazed in wonder at the majestic beauty of a dawn that none had seen in so long. Then somebody cheered and soon the land was reverberating in applause as they all rejoiced the miracle.

I could only stand there, dumbstruck at what I accomplished.

Delgarias met my gaze. Sometime during the song, he'd covered his head with his hood. His eyes glowed with a blue so pale they looked white.

Then that double-vision thing happened again, and I saw that familiar redheaded woman in the candlelit room superimposed over Delgarias. They both spoke in tandem.

Delgarias's voice roared in my ears while the woman's echoed in my head.

"And the Queen shall seek seven night walkers with seven brides to lead their brethren to battle the unholy father!"

The vision of the woman dissolved and I was left staring at the faelin sorcerer. His face was bright red, like he had a fever, and his features contorted in pain. Still, he gave me a warm smile before he vanished from the stage.

A few tendrils of smoke rose from where he'd been standing.

I blinked and shook my head. Not even a hug goodbye?

Loud cheers brought my attention back to the current situation. The people squinted and pointed at the sun. I don't know how well they could see it, since I was half blind myself.

I did it! A small voice in my head exclaimed. *Holy Shit! I fucking did it!*

With a grin, I bowed at the applauding audience, and sought out my friends, gesturing for them to join me. I couldn't wait to hear how they got here. *And Zareth!* I needed to make sure he was okay.

Just then, the applause died down and Sylvis screamed, pointing. "Look out!"

I turned around to see Stefan standing behind Zareth. His jaw was broken by Zareth's attack, one eye almost swollen shut and he bled from numerous cuts all over his head and body, some parts of him were blackened from being burned.

A triumphant gleam twinkled in his good eye, for in his hand he held a sword, ready to thrust it through his back. My eyes darted to Zareth who, though conscious, was so weakened from the battle that he would most likely be unable to stand, much less fight.

Stefan staggered closer and closer; time slowed to a terrible crawl as I ran to them. I was so far away that there was no way for me to get there in time.

No way to stop him.

Raising the sword over his head, Stefan met my gaze and snarled. "Crown me now, or he dies."

I looked back at Zareth. Visions of him haunting my dreams, meeting him in reality, his kindness, and the love we shared flooded through me like a tidal wave. I couldn't let him die. I couldn't live without him.

"Hurry up," Stefan barked.

Someone handed me the old king's crown.

"No," the former captives wailed.

Rage at this man for daring to harm the one I loved filled my being, boiling and bubbling.

Rage at him for violating me, for trying to use me to fulfill his twisted ambitions, spilled over.

Rage for his destruction of so many lives, and his intent to destroy so many more in the future poured over me like scalding water.

I looked into his icy eyes all I saw was pure and unadulterated evil.

I held the crown and I knew exactly what to do. "Bow your head."

Even though it made my back throb, I embraced my fury until it grew into a white-hot blast that threatened to explode from within me, ripping my body into millions of pieces if I didn't release it.

So I did.

Light burst out from my body as my fury poured forth with an inhuman scream. My back exploded in a burst of agony. The crown melted in my hands until it was a twisted lump of gold.

"Here's your crown." I threw it at Stefan, knocking the sword from his grasp.

Anger and power carried me high up into the air. I glimpsed something in the corner of my eyes.

Something I'd seen before in a dream.

I now had wings, black wings with silver trimmed feathers. With a wicked gleam in my eyes, I floated toward my enemy.

Stefan's eyes widened in mute horror as black wings blotted out the sunlight, throwing a shadow over him. He tried to scream but all that he could get out was a few inarticulate chokes and gurgles.

I smiled sweetly as I cupped my hands and a ball of white, blinding light formed between my palms. The light grew brighter and larger, eclipsing the dawn, and he stared at it, transfixed.

Until I hurled it at him.

Stefan's agonized shriek echoed off the castle walls until the light blasted him in the chest and spread outward. His skin glowed before crackling like paper. His eyeballs melted as the glow brightened until he was completely vaporized.

His death slammed into my chest like a cannonball.

I collapsed to the ground, sighing in relief that the threat to my love was gone. My muscles turned into jelly as all the strength fled from me.

"Xochitl…" Zareth whispered as he staggered over to me. "You saved my life."

"Zareth." Tears spilled down my cheeks as he took me in his arms. I'd been so afraid he'd never hold me again. My heart clenched. Perhaps I could feel fear after all. "I'm sorry I left you. I'm sorry I ruined your father's crown."

"Never mind all that. It's all over." He squeezed me tight. "I love you."

"I love you too." My voice cracked as weariness weighed me down, despite my overwhelming joy. "I thought I'd never get to kiss you again..."

His lips covered mine in a passionate kiss that sent a flare of heat from my head to my toes.

"I'll never let you go again," he vowed. With a trembling hand, he reached out to caress one of my new wings. "You are my angel."

Though my eyes felt like lead, I looked up at Aistanesthai's first morning sky in years.

"It's so beautiful," I whispered, pointing at the pinkish light glittering from fluffy white clouds. "I did it, Zareth. I brought back the sun. Are you proud of me?"

He stroked my hair and held me tight. "Yes, Xochitl, I'm proud of you."

"Good," I breathed and pulled the gold circlet from my head and placed it on his. "There. I crowned you."

The circlet was tiny and looked funny on his head.

I managed a weak laugh before blackness engulfed me.

Chapter Thirty-two

Zareth

Zareth looked up from where he knelt at Xochitl's bedside as Sylvis entered the room, carrying a steaming cup of broth.

"Has there been any change?" she asked softly.

He shook his head. "Aside from her wings disappearing, no."

"But that was a week ago." Sylvis closed her eyes in abject sorrow.

They both looked down at Xochitl's unconscious form, which grew smaller and thinner in the large bed. Isis refused to leave her and was getting thin as well.

After trying every healing skill he knew and consulting every book in his library, he was still unable to revive her.

He'd even brought in a Wurrak healer, for they were famed to be the best. This one had not only studied luminites, she had also treated a few on a sojourn to Medicia.

She'd examined Xochitl, lingering on her comatose body for hours, only to shake her head. "In all of my travels and studies, I've never heard of a luminite falling into a coma." Her lips turned down in a perplexed frown. "But then I've also never heard of one killing a living being before and not falling dead instantly. I'd like to think that the fact that she is still alive is a sign of hope for recovery."

Zareth tried to feel the same optimism, but his hope died every day. He refused to leave Xochitl's side in case he missed it when she awoke, or if— he couldn't finish the thought.

Aurora, Sylvis, and Beau didn't pressure him to take them back to Earth for the same reason, despite the fact that their families had probably reported them missing by now.

The four of them kept a constant vigil, talking to Xochitl as she slept, telling her how the people were recovering after she'd saved the world.

Even though Zareth was bombarded with missives, he sent his new apprentice and seneschal, Artavian, out to meet with envoys.

For now his people were patient with him, focusing on planting crops and rebuilding their magic. Though soon he knew they would expect him to take residence in his father's castle and assume the responsibilities of kingship. The Conclave had sent a crew of competent mages to level Stefan's tower and break the binding spells in its mortar. A group of faelin sorceresses intended to plant a tree on the empty site once it was consecrated.

The dark mages and overseers who hadn't thrown themselves from the tower during Xochitl's song had been captured and executed.

The entire world prayed for the recovery of their new queen, but after two weeks of her remaining comatose, their concentration strayed to recovering all they'd lost in the despair.

But Zareth refused to give up on the woman he loved.

Sylvis held Xochitl up while he spooned broth into her mouth, willing her to swallow.

If his love didn't pull through this, he didn't want to live, much less rule.

Just as he set the bowl on the bed, he heard rapid footsteps thumping up the stairs. Aurora burst through the door, face pale and eyes wide.

"What's the matter?" he asked.

"She's here," Aurora stammered. "She died, but she's *here!*"

He raised a brow. Aside the fact that no one could return from the dead, no one should be here without him opening a portal.

"Who's here?"

Instead of answering, Aurora burst into tears and ran out of the room. Zareth chased her down the stairs.

He froze in the foyer when he saw Beau embracing an ethereally beautiful blonde woman. Sylvis cried out behind him.

Beau's shoulders shook with wracking sobs as the woman held him and stroked his hair, murmuring soothing words in a lilting voice.

The woman looked up and as Zareth's gaze searched her glittering emerald eyes, he knew who she was, even though they'd never met. "By the Fates!"

"Where is she?" the woman asked.

Zareth's knees turned to water as he led her up the stairs.

Chapter Thirty-three

Xochitl

White and gold light pierced through my closed eyelids. I groaned and scrunched them together, but still the brightness persisted. My arms and legs tingled like they'd been numb for ages.

The light flashed brighter as a jolt of energy ricocheted through my body, making me twitch. I opened my eyes and squinted at the light. Someone stood over me, but all I could tell was that it wasn't Zareth. I blinked and waited for my eyes to adjust. The outline filled in until I could discern the figure of a woman.

Her wings came into view first, pearlescent white outlined in gold. My heart thudded in my chest.

—And stopped as I saw her face.

"Mommy?" I croaked pitifully.

A gentle hand that I never thought I'd feel again stroked my forehead. "Yes, I'm finally here."

Was I dead? Was that what all the bright light was all about? Tears filled my eyes as her beloved features filled my vision.

"Is this another dream?" I whispered, half hoping, half dreading. Isis meowed and rubbed up against me, purring.

"No, Sweetie."

I swallowed. "Did I die?"

All those year I'd wished her back and here she was. Yet my heart ached with the realization that if I was dead, I'd never see Zareth or my friends again.

"No. I healed you. You'd fallen into a coma after killing that evil man. Our kind aren't supposed to be able to kill." She brushed aside my tears. "But it was a good thing you did."

Blinking again, I struggled to sit up. The world spun before straightening. A measure of my disorientation eased as I saw that I was in Zareth's bed. Movement from the corner of my eye made me turn to see him and my friends at my bedside.

I looked back at Mom. "But you died."

"Only my body. Our kind transcends back to our home realm of Luminista and gains another one." Tears swam in her eyes. "Leaving you was the hardest thing I've ever done."

My jaw dropped at the revelation that she'd been alive all these years. "Then why didn't you come back?"

Her wings folded behind her as she sat on the edge of the bed. "I couldn't come back to Earth after my body died. There would have been too many questions."

"But what about when I came here?" My conscience railed at me for interrogating her, but I needed to know what happened.

Her finger rose to fiddle with her lower lip, a familiar gesture that made my chest tight. She'd always done that before giving me bad news. "I was imprisoned."

Zareth nodded as if he suddenly understood a thousand mysteries I'd never been aware of. "Ah. I had wondered."

"By who?" My fists clenched at my sides, ready to beat the crap out of anyone who dared keep my mom from me.

Her knuckle scraped her lip. "Your great-grandmother."

My brows drew together. "But why?"

"It is a complicated story. Someday soon I will tell you everything, like I was never able to before." She smiled and brushed a lock of hair behind my ear. "But I escaped, and right now I just want to enjoy being with you. And from now on, nothing will keep me from you again."

That was enough explaining for me. I threw my arms around her and cried. "I missed you so much. Every song I wrote, every time I sang," I rambled. "I hoped you could see me, that you were proud of me."

"I *did* see you," she squeezed me tight. "And I *am* proud of you. Every day."

We clung to each other for a blissful eternity before she wiped away my tears and kissed my forehead. "I'm going to step aside and let you see everyone else who missed you. We have plenty of time to catch up."

Before I could say anything, Zareth pulled me into his arms. His embrace felt like home and the moment his lips claimed mine, I forgot everything else. Magic sparked between us, bubbling in our blood beneath the surface.

"I love you," he whispered, kissing me again. "I love you. I couldn't bear it if I lost you."

"I love you too." Memories of Stefan imprisoning Zareth, beating him, and trying to kill him flashed behind my eyes, making me shudder. "I can't lose you, either. If Stefan had—"

"He didn't. You killed him." He held me tighter. "You saved our world from a great evil." He kissed my fingers. "But I hope you won't be forced to kill again. When you collapsed, I—" he broke off as a tear fell on my forehead.

I pulled his head down for another kiss. Savoring his taste until someone cleared their throat behind us.

"If you don't mind, could you finish your reunion later?" Aurora said drily. "He's not the only one who missed you."

I climbed out of the bed and shambled over to my friends, tears falling down my cheeks as I hugged them one by one. "I was so afraid you all hated me."

"We were pretty pissed, but I don't think we could ever hate you. Not with what we'd been through," Aurora sighed. "And once Zareth told us the truth about what's been going on with you these past couple months, we understood. Though now we're pissed at you for not telling us the truth... and at Sylvis who knew the whole time."

Sylvis pulled me away from Aurora and gave me another big hug. "I kept my promise."

"Aurora, sweetie..." Mom spoke up. "It's my fault Xochitl couldn't tell you anything. I drilled that into her head ever since she could talk. Although I eventually allowed her to tell Sylvis. And I was going to give her permission to tell you and Beau, but then I got sick, and well, died."

My friends looked over at her and visibly melted under her entreating gaze. Beau spoke first. "I'm so glad you're back, Kerainne. You were like a second mom to me and when you died, I cried for days."

Sylvis nodded. "Us too."

"I am sorry for causing you pain. I didn't want to leave any of you."

Aurora, shook her head. "Honestly, we're too happy to see you and Xochitl alive to be mad." She crossed her arms over her chest. "But you might be able to make it up to us by clearing something up."

"I'll be happy to if I can. I'm done with secrets, for the most part."

"Delgarias says Beau and Sylvis and I all have luminite blood. Do you know anything about that?"

My eyes widened. "Whoa, really?"

Mom smiled. "Aside from the fact that yes, I could sense your ancestry the whole time, I'm afraid I don't know anything else, not even which families your ancestors came from, though only five ever dwelled on Earth before the magic died."

Zareth looked at her with a frown. "All the books say that humans cannot mate with luminites."

"It's a very rare occurrence," Mom explained. "The most common was when faelin or some other magical being mated with the luminites and their offspring bred with humans."

I cuddled closer to Zareth, I couldn't wait for his magical touch, for his body to claim mine once more.

"I'm sorry I don't know more," Mom told Aurora before a sudden chiming sound made us all jump.

Zareth stood and smiled at me. "It's Delgarias."

Raising his staff, he opened a portal and the faelin sorcerer stepped through, carrying a covered bowl.

His eyes widened as he saw me conscious and standing. "I sensed when you awoke. You must be hungry. I brought you a stew."

"Thanks, I'm starving." My stomach growled in agreement.

I reached for the stew, but Delgarias froze and dropped it. Zareth caught the bowl while Uncle Del stammered. Meat, potatoes, and broth slopped over on the floor.

"K-Kerraine? Is it really you?" Delgarias's voice was broken in a half sob.

Mom smiled at him. "Yes, Del."

"Your sister?" Painful hope gleamed in his eyes.

She shook her head. "She was not in Luminista, so must still be out there somewhere."

I watched the exchange with wide eyes. My aunt might be alive?

Mom put her arm around me and looked up at Uncle Del. "I've just reunited with my daughter. If you don't mind, may we have this discussion another time? I will tell you all I know, as well as something that would best be shared in private."

Zareth nodded. "And I still need you to tell me about what you said the night of the Solstice. It was another Prophecy."

For a moment it looked like he would argue, then Delgarias bowed. "Of course."

Zareth opened the portal again. "Come back tomorrow?"

The Keeper of the Prophecy nodded before he vanished.

Mom turned back to me. "I understand you got married."

"Yeah!" Sylvis interjected. "I can't believe you didn't invite us. I was supposed to be your maid of honor."

"And 'Ror and I were supposed to be bridesmaids," Beau added.

Mom smiled at them and met my eyes. "Are you happy with him?"

"Yes." The firm truth in the word surprised me. But in such a short time, I knew that Zareth and I were meant to be together. That he would love me forever and never hurt me.

"Then we'll just have to have a second wedding," Mom said cheerfully.

Zareth and I looked at each other and laughed. "Second wedding? Try the fifth!"

"What?" My mom and friends chorused with perplexed frowns.

"Dude, it's a crazy story."

As I cuddled between my mom and my husband, I had a feeling our story had just begun.

Thank you for reading Conjuring Destiny! If you liked this story, keep reading for a preview of Book 4: UNLEASHING DESIRE, coming Fall of 2016!

Preview of Unleashing Desire

Brides of Prophecy, Book 4

Lillian cursed as she stumbled on her way up the hill. The heels of her boots dug into the damp earth in effort to keep her footing. When she reached the top, she paused to take in the view. Dawn's glory shed its light upon the Romanian countryside, gleaming on emerald grass and dew covered wildflowers.

It was a lovely morning for vengeance.

She gripped a finely carved oak stake and approached the ruins of Castle Nicolae.

Even amidst the pinkish glow of the cresting sun and the cheery melody of birdsong, the pile of gray rubble looked ominous. Lillian gulped a deep breath of morning air and suppressed a shiver as she pulled the castle schematic out of her pack. According to the diagram, the chasm leading inside was right in front of her.

Her target lay below, in the bowels of the ancient fortress.

Shoving the schematic back in her pocket, she pulled out her phone and texted the AIU headquarters. "I'm going in."

Her phone vibrated a reply: "Invalid number."

Huh? Double checking to make certain she texted the correct number, she tried again and received the same error message.

Mouth dry, Lillian eyed the castle. Was *he* somehow doing it? She shook her head. That would be ridiculous. It was probably the rural location. He couldn't mess with her if he was asleep.

By all reports, the vampire had been comatose for centuries, only waking once a year to feed. Two months ago, he'd killed the wrong person.

Thumb stroking the stake, Lillian hissed through clenched teeth, "Your death will not go unpunished, father. I will kill Radu Nicolae."

With grim determination, her feet propelled her forward. She groped along the cracked stone until she found the entrance, a narrow fissure in the rock.

Shadows closed over her as if encasing her body in ice. She pulled out her Mag Light, illuminating the treacherous tunnel with a bluish LED glow.

Though she tried to walk as quietly as possible, rocks and debris underfoot marked her progress with skitters and crunches. Darkness chased away the meager rays of sunlight as she descended further into the heart of the ruins.

After contorting her way down through the twisting passage, crumbled rock gave way to smooth stone steps coated in a fine layer of charcoal. There had been a fire here long ago.

Heart pounding in her throat, Lillian made her way down the stairs and found a clean chamber.

No ashy residue or cobwebs remained. A row of backpacks, ranging from new to old, lined one wall. An ancient prison cell dominated the other. She swallowed at the sight of the rusted iron bars. This must have been the castle dungeon. There was even a fireplace with a stack of firewood beside it. A closer look revealed that most of the firewood was made up of sharp stakes.

Lillian shuddered, palm sweating around her own stake. How many people had tried to kill him, only to die in this place? What did he do with the bodies?

At last, Radu Nicolae's slumbering form came into view. Lillian's lip curled with scorn. *This was the big scary monster?* The creature seemed already dead. It lay still, pale, and emaciated. Its cheekbones gleamed in sharp relief above a dark scraggly beard.

Her fingers trembled as she shone the light on the vampire's face. A gasp caught in her throat as she saw his hair. A shade of darkest chocolate, it lay like a silken waterfall in rich waves on the stone slab. Unbidden, she reached out to touch those tresses, to see if they were soft as they appeared.

The sight of the stake in her fist made her snatch her hand back. Her stomach churned in revulsion at her insane impulse.

What was she thinking?

This monster killed her father. She was here to destroy it, not pet it.

Gritting her teeth, Lillian set the flashlight on the slab so the beam pointed over the vampire's supine form. She removed the mallet from her pack and positioned the stake above his heart.

Shoulders vibrating with tension, she raised the mallet and paused to savor her vengeance.

As she brought the mallet down, she had a split second to think, *Wow, he has really long eyelashes.*

Instead crunching bone, a scream rent the air as those lashes lifted to reveal glowing black eyes.

Fangs gleamed in the darkness and Lillian was yanked into the monster's embrace. The stake and mallet fell from numb fingers.

The flashlight clattered to the floor, casting her and the monster in blackness. A feral growl rumbled inches from her ear, sending shivers down her spine.

Fangs pierced her throat, sharp pain exploding from her flesh. The sound of swallowing roared through Lillian's consciousness, heightening her terror.

He's killing me! Oh God, I failed, Father. I'm so sorry...

Then the pain abated and strange sensations crept in. His rhythmic sucking at her neck bled away her panic and tightened things low in her body. The vampire relaxed his grip on her, one hand stroked her back while the other caressed her hair. She could feel his rock hard erection against her body. Her core throbbed. Moisture seeped between her thighs. Of their own volition, her hands gripped his shoulders, pulling him closer.

A low moan escaped Lillian's lips even as her mind screamed, *"No, I can't be enjoying this!"*

Then all was blackness.

***

Radu Nicolae removed his fangs from the huntress's neck with a curse. Something was very wrong here and he would keep this woman alive until he got to the bottom of it.

355

As he gathered her into his arms, he mentally ticked off all that he'd seen in her mind.

The first alarm bell went off at her employers claiming he'd killed the woman's father. Radu remembered all the men he'd killed for the last century. This Joe Holmes had not been one of them. And even if he had killed the man, why did this company of hunters send an inexperienced female to kill him? For centuries, the most skilled hunters had tracked him to his lair, only to die under his bite. This Lillian Holmes was not a hunter at all. She was a scientist, as had been her father. From what he pulled from her mind, they had been studying his kind, with no intention of killing them.

So, why, after her father disappeared, did her superiors pull her aside and lie to her? Why did they send her to hunt him, thus assuring her death? His fingers clenched her arms. They wanted her to die, that much was obvious. And they presumed to use him as a pawn for that end. A growl of fury escaped his throat at the presumption of this AIU...this Abnormal Investigation Unit. Lillian whimpered and Radu loosened his grip slightly.

They would pay. That much was certain. Nobody used him. It seemed he would emerge from his rest sooner than planned...

About The Author

Formerly an auto-mechanic, Brooklyn Ann thrives on writing romance featuring unconventional heroines and heroes who adore them. She's delved into historical paranormal romance in her critically acclaimed "Scandals with Bite" series, urban fantasy in her "Brides of Prophecy" novels and heavy metal romance in her "Hearts of Metal" novellas.

She lives in Coeur d'Alene, Idaho with her son, her cat, and a 1980 Datsun 210.

Follow her found online at http://brooklynann.blogspot.com, as well as on twitter and Facebook.

Keep in touch for the latest news, exclusive excerpts, and giveaways!

Books by Brooklyn Ann

BRIDES OF PROPHECY series

BOOK 1: <u>WRENCHING FATE </u>(February 2014)

She's haunted by her past.

Akasha Hope trusts no one. Her parents were shot down by uniformed men, which forced her to spend most of her life on the run.

She's so close to getting out on her own, making her own dreams come true when he shows up and disrupts everything. Her new legal guardian.

His kindness makes suspicious, while his heart-stopping good looks arouse desires she'd kept suppressed.

He promises her a future.

Silas McNaught, Lord Vampire of Coeur d'Alene, has been searching for Akasha for centuries.

He's perplexed to discover that the woman who has haunted his visions is anything but sweet and fragile. Her foul mouth and superhuman strength covers a tenderness he's determined to reach.

While government agents pursue Akasha and vindictive vampires seek to destroy Silas, they discover the strength in their love.

Can they survive the double threat?

BOOK 2: IRONIC SACRIFICE (October 2014)

Jayden Leigh wants to commit suicide.

Her clairvoyant powers have become so intense that she lost her job and home. Death is the only way to make them stop. Opportunity presents itself when she comes across a sinfully handsome vampire ready to make a kill. Jayden begs him to take her instead. A blissful death in his arms, or the visions ravaging her mind? She'd gladly take the vampire.

Razvan Nicolae is captivated with the beautiful seeress who sacrifices herself for a stranger. Killing such a pleasing asset doesn't interest him. If he could get her powers under control, she could be the key to finding his missing twin.

Controlling her visions and working for a seductive vampire? Razvan's offer is like a dream come true. But her dream turns into a nightmare when a mad vampire cult leader seeks to exploit Jayden's powers to stop an ancient prophecy.

As Jayden finds herself at the center of a vampire war, she realizes that the biggest threat isn't losing her life, it's losing her heart.

BOOK 3: CONJURING DESTINY (October 2015)

BOOK 4: UNLEASHING DESIRE (Fall 2016)

SCANDALS WITH BITE series

BOOK 1: <u>BITE ME, YOUR GRACE</u> (April 2013)

Dr. John Polidori's tale, "The Vampyre," burst upon the Regency scene along with Mary Shelley's Frankenstein after that notorious weekend spent writing ghost stories with Lord Byron. A vampire craze broke out instantly in the haut ton.

Now Ian Ashton, the Lord Vampire of London, has to attend tedious balls, linger in front of mirrors, and eat lots of garlic in an attempt to quell the gossip. If that weren't annoying enough, his neighbor, Angelica Winthrop, has literary aspirations of her own and is sneaking into his house at night just to see what she can find.

Hungry, tired, and fed up, Ian is in no mood to humor his beautiful intruder...

BOOK 2: <u>ONE BITE PER NIGHT</u> (August 2014)

He wanted her off his hands... Now he'll do anything to hold on to her ...Forever.

Vincent Tremayne, the reclusive "Devil Earl," has been manipulated into taking rambunctious Lydia Price as his ward. As Lord Vampire of Cornwall, Vincent has better things to do than bring out an unruly debutante.

American-born Lydia Price doesn't care for the stuffy strictures of the ton, and is unimpressed with her foppish suitors. She dreams of studying with the talented but scandalous British portrait painter, Sir Thomas Lawrence. But just when it seems her dreams will come true, Lydia is plunged into Vincent's dark world and finds herself caught between the life she's known and a future she never could have imagined.

BOOK 3: BITE AT FIRST SIGHT (April 2015)

When Rafael Villar, Lord Vampire of London, stumbles upon a woman in the cemetery, he believes he's found a vampire hunter—not the beautiful, intelligent stranger she proves to be. Cassandra Burton is enthralled by the scarred, disfigured vampire who took her prisoner. The aspiring physician was robbing graves to pursue her studies—and he might turn out to be her greatest subject yet. So they form a bargain: one kiss for every experiment.

As their passion grows and Rafe begins to heal, only one question remains: can Cassandra see the man beyond the monster?

BOOK 4: Spring 2016

HEARTS OF METAL (Heavy Metal Romance)

Book 1: KISSING VICIOUS (August 2015)

Aspiring guitarist Kinley Black is about to get her first big break—as a roadie for Viciöus, her favorite heavy metal band, and for the rock god she always dreamt might make her a woman.

The Roadie

At 15, aspiring guitarist Kinley Black wished she were a boy. At 16, after hearing Quinn Mayne sing, she wanted him to make her a woman. Now, at 22, her dreams have come true. Quinn's band Viciöus needs someone to lug their amps around the country, to strive and sweat with the guys. She just has to act like one of them.

And the rock god

Quinn had to admit the new chick could pull her weight, but that didn't mean his road manager made the right choice. Taking a hottie on a heavy metal music tour was like dangling meat in front of a pack of feral hounds—and Quinn could be part dog himself. But more surprising than her beautiful body are Kinley's sweet licks, so that no man could help but demand a jam session. Quinn will soon do anything to possess her, and to put Kinley in the spotlight where she belongs. And to keep her safe and sound from the wolves.

Book 2: WITH VENGEANCE (Early 2016)

Made in the USA
Lexington, KY
27 February 2017